Also by Jodi Picoult

Songs of the Humpback Whale
Harvesting the Heart
Mercy
The Pact
Keeping Faith
Plain Truth
Salem Falls
Perfect Match
Second Glance
My Sister's Keeper
Vanishing Acts
The Tenth Circle
Nineteen Minutes
Change of Heart
Handle With Care
House Rules
Sing You Home
Lone Wolf
The Storyteller

Jodi Picoult & Samantha van Leer
Between the Lines

Jodi Picoult grew up in Nesconset, New York. She received an A.B. in creative writing from Princeton and a master's degree in education from Harvard. Her novels include *The Storyteller*, *Lone Wolf*, *Sing You Home* and *House Rules*. She lives in New Hampshire with her husband and three children.

Jodi's UK website is www.jodipicoult.co.uk and she can be found on Facebook and Twitter at facebook.com/JodiPicoultUK and twitter.com/jodipicoult. She also has a YouTube channel www.youtube.com/user/JodiPicoultOfficial.

JODI PICOULT

Picture Perfect

HODDER

First published in America in 1995 by Berkley Publishing Group
A division of Penguin Group USA
First published in Great Britain in 2009 by Hodder & Stoughton
An Hachette UK company

This paperback edition published 2013

3

A CIP catalogue record for this title is available from the British Library

ISBN 978 1 444 75439 1

Typeset in Berkeley Book by Palimpsest Book Production Limited,
Falkirk, Stirlingshire

Printed and bound by CPI Group (UK) Ltd, Croydon CR0 4YY

Hodder & Stoughton policy is to use papers that are natural,
renewable and recyclable products and made from wood grown
in sustainable forests. The logging and manufacturing processes
are expected to conform to the environmental
regulations of the country of origin.

Hodder & Stoughton Ltd
338 Euston Road
London NW1 3BH

www.hodder.co.uk

For my mother – my biggest fan, my first reader,
my sounding board, my friend

ACKNOWLEDGMENTS

M any people made the research of this book possible: Arlene Stevens, CSW, and Executive Director of the *Response* hotline of Suffolk County, New York; Brenda Franklin of Yorktown Productions; Doug Ornstein, former AD at Warner Brothers; Keith Willis; Sally Smith; Ina Gravitz; Dr James Umlas; Dr Richard Stone; and Victor A. Douville, Chair of Lakota Studies at Sinte Gleska University. For a variety of services rendered, my gratitude also goes to Tim van Leer, Jon Picoult, Jane and Myron Picoult, Kathleen Desmond, Cindy Lao Gitter, Mary Morris, Laura Gross, and Laura Yorke. And finally, a very special thanks to Jean Arnett.

1993

L ong ago on the shores of the Atlantic there lived a great Indian
warrior called Strong Wind. He had a magical power – he could
make himself invisible – which enabled him to walk around in the
camps of his enemies and steal their secrets. His home was a tent that
stood beside the sea in a calm, calling breeze, and he lived there with
his sister.

His skill as a fighter carried his reputation far, and many maidens
wanted to marry him. But Strong Wind would have none of their silly,
simpering smiles, their false boasts of being the perfect match. He said
that he would marry the first maiden who could see him coming home
at night.

It was a test he'd conceived to reveal a maiden's truthfulness. Many
came to walk down the beach with his sister as the sun hissed into the
sea, wishing to capture his heart. Strong Wind's sister could always see
him, even when he was invisible to the rest of the world. So when her
brother approached, she would turn to the current girl who peered over
the horizon. 'Do you see him?' And every waiting maiden would quickly
lie: Yes, yes, there he was. Strong Wind's sister would ask, 'With what
does he draw his sled?' The answers were many: With the hide of a
caribou. With a long, knotted stick. With a length of strong hemp. His
sister would know the lies for what they were, simple guesses, and she
knew that Strong Wind would not choose this girl whose footsteps
mirrored hers in the wet sand.

In the village lived a mighty chief, a widower with three daughters.
One was years younger than the others. Her face was as lovely as the

first rain of summer; her heart could hold gently the pain of the world. Her older sisters, gnarled with their own jealousy, took advantage of her nature. They tried to detract from her beauty by leaving her clothes in rags, cutting off her shining black hair, burning the smooth skin of her cheeks and throat with glowing coals. They told their father the girl had done these things to herself.

Like the other maidens in the village, the two older sisters tried to see Strong Wind coming through the twilight. They stood on the beach with his sister, feeling the water run over their legs, and waited. As always, Strong Wind's sister asked if they saw him, and, lying, they said yes. She asked how he drew his sled, and, lying, they guessed rawhide. When they entered his tent, the flaps shuddered in the wind. They hoped to see Strong Wind bent over his dinner, but they saw nothing at all. Strong Wind, knowing their deception, remained invisible.

The day the chief's youngest daughter went to seek Strong Wind, she rubbed her burned face with earth to cover her scars and patched her skirt with bark from the trees. She passed other maidens on the way to the beach, who laughed to see her go and labeled her a fool.

But Strong Wind's sister was waiting, and when the sun slipped heavy in the sky she took the girl to the beach. As Strong Wind drew his sled closer, his sister asked, 'Do you see him?' The girl replied, 'No,' and Strong Wind's sister shivered at the sound of the truth. 'Do you see him now?' she asked again.

At first the girl did not speak, but her face was turned to the sky and her eyes were as bright as fire. 'Oh yes,' she finally breathed, 'and he is wonderful. He dances on the clouds and he walks with the moon on his shoulder.'

Strong Wind's sister turned toward her. 'With what does he draw his sled?' she asked.

'With the rainbow.'

She too stared at the sky. 'And what is his bowstring made of?'

The girl smiled, and the night washed over her face. 'Of the Milky Way,' she said. 'And his arrows are tipped with the brightest of stars.'

Strong Wind's sister knew that because the girl had admitted she hadn't seen him at first, her brother had shown himself to her. She took the girl home and bathed her, running her palms over the pitted skin until all the scars disappeared from her body. She sang while the girl's hair grew thick and black down her back. She gave her her own rich clothes to wear and showed her into Strong Wind's tent.

The next day Strong Wind married her, and she walked with him across the sky and looked down on her People. The girl's two sisters were livid and shook their fists at the spirits, demanding to know what had transpired. Strong Wind resolved to punish them for the hurt they had caused his bride. He changed them into aspen trees and dug their roots deep into the earth. Since that day, the leaves of the aspen tremble in fear of the coming of Strong Wind. No matter how quietly he approaches, they shiver, because they cannot put out of their minds his great power, and his rage.

– Algonquin Indian legend

Chapter One

The first thing the groundskeeper saw when he went to tend to the small cemetery behind St Sebastian's was the body that someone had forgotten to bury.

She was lying on top of a grave, her head pressed close to the headstone, her arms crossed over her stomach. She was almost as white as the seven faded granite markers that surrounded her. The groundskeeper took a deep breath, dropped his trowel, and crossed himself. He inched toward the body and leaned over, casting a shadow.

Somewhere overhead a gull screamed, and as the woman's eyes flew open, the groundskeeper turned and ran through the iron gate into the dizzying streets of Los Angeles.

The woman looked into the sky. She did not know where she was, but it was quiet; and since her head was pounding, she was grateful. She tried to remember how she had gotten there in the first place.

Sitting up, she touched the gravestone and squinted as the letters dipped and blurred before her eyes. She pulled herself to her feet and balanced against the stone for support. Then she leaned over and retched, clutching her stomach and blinking back tears at the pain shooting through her temples.

'A church,' she said aloud, jumping at the pitch of her own voice. 'This is a church.'

She walked to the gate and stared at the cars and buses going by. She had taken three steps away from the church before she realized she did not know where she was supposed to go. 'Think,' she commanded herself. She put a hand to her forehead and felt the slip of her own blood.

'Jesus,' she said. Her hand was trembling. She felt for a tissue in the pocket of her jacket, a worn bomber jacket she couldn't remember buying, and came up instead with a tube of Blistex and $2.24 in change. She stepped back toward the graveyard and looked behind the headstones for a pocketbook, a knapsack, a clue.

'I was mugged,' she said, wiping her brow with her sleeve. 'I must have been mugged.' She ran to the door of the rectory and banged, but it was locked. She moved to the gate again, planning to go to the closest police station and tell them what had happened. She would give her address and she would call . . .

Who *would* she call?

She stared at a bus sighing at the corner stop. She didn't know where she was. She didn't know the closest police station.

She didn't even know her own name.

Chewing on a fingernail, she stepped back inside the gate, where she felt safer. She knelt beside the grave she'd been lying upon and rested her forehead against the cool headstone. Maybe the priest would be back soon, she thought. Maybe someone would come by and offer to help her. Maybe she'd just stay right there.

Her head began to throb, a drumbeat that threatened to split her in two. She sank to the ground and lay back against the gravestone again, pulling her jacket close to ward off the chill of the earth.

She would wait.

She opened her eyes, hoping for answers, but all she could see were clouds that covered the sky like a bruise.

There wasn't enough land in California.

He could *feel* it, beating like a hammer at the base of his throat, this claustrophobia born of the hissing asphalt under his tires and the condos pressed so close they left no room to breathe. So he kept driving west to find the ocean, hopefully before it got dark. He had never seen it. There had only been pictures, and accounts from his mother and his father.

He remembered stories his father had told him, stories he hadn't believed at the time, of Indians jailed in the 1800s who died overnight because they couldn't stand the confinement.

He thought of the statistics from the Bureau of Indian Affairs, which said that sixty-six percent of Indians who left the reservations returned, unable to live in the cities. Of course, he was not entirely Sioux. But he was not entirely white, either.

He smelled it before he saw it. The wind carried him the salt from the waves. He parked the rusted secondhand pickup on the shoulder of the road and ran down the sloping dune. He did not stop running until his sneakers were submerged, until water stained the thighs of his jeans like tears.

A gull screamed.

William Flying Horse stood with his arms outstretched, his eyes fixed on the Pacific Ocean but seeing, instead, the brindled plains and rolling Dakota hills that he would not call home.

On the Pine Ridge Reservation in South Dakota, Route 18 took you into town, and if you wanted to get anywhere else you navigated by natural landmarks or long-abandoned vehicles, since there weren't many other roads. But it had been three days since he'd moved to Los Angeles and Will had yet to get his bearings.

He was renting a little row house in Reseda, which was close enough to the LAPD to eliminate the need for a long commute, and far enough away for him to feel like he wasn't attached to his job. He didn't have to report to work until tomorrow – the paperwork for the position had been done through the mail – and he had planned to use this time to find his way around LA.

Will slammed his fist onto the steering wheel. Where the hell was he? He groped along the front seat, looking for the map he'd tossed away minutes before. He squinted at the tiny red roads, but the overhead light in the pickup had been one of the first things to go, so he pulled to the curb underneath a streetlight. He peered at the map in the soft glow. 'Shit,' he said. 'Beverly Hills. I was here an hour ago.'

For the first time in decades, he wished he was more of an Indian.

He blamed his faulty sense of direction on his *wasicun* blood. All his life he'd heard stories of his grandfather's father, who tracked the goddamned buffalo by the slightest rising of the wind. And when the woman his father loved had left without a word, hadn't he ridden for miles using only his intuition to find her? Compared to that, how difficult could it be to find the San Diego Freeway?

Once, when Will was little, he'd followed his grandmother into the woods to collect roots and leaves for her medicines. He'd picked the ones she pointed to, cedar and sweet flag and wild licorice. He'd turned his back only for a moment, and his grandmother had disappeared. For a while Will had wandered in circles, trying to remember his father's lessons about footprints left on broken leaves, snapped branches, the sense of movement in the heavy air. It was hours before his grandmother found him again, cold and curled beneath the burl of an oak. Wordlessly she pulled him by the hand in the direction of home. When the small log house came into view, she turned and cupped Will's chin in her hand. 'You,' she sighed. 'So white.'

He had only been ten, but that was the moment he knew he would never be like his grandparents. To them, to everyone who lived around him, he would always be *iyeska*, a mixed-blood. He had spent the next twenty-five years acting as white as he could, figuring if he could not be like his father's people, he would be like his mother's. He threw himself into his schoolwork so that he'd be able to go to college. He spoke only English, even at his grandparents' home where Lakota was the primary language. He nodded when his white bosses described the Sioux as lazy alcoholics and when the words ran cold through his blood; he wrapped his indifference around him like a cloak.

Well, he was white now. He was off the reservation and he was planning to stay, and as for finding his way out of Beverly Hills, he'd do what every other white man would do: he'd find a gas station and get directions.

Shifting gears, Will eased the truck away from the curb and started down the street again. The opulence of Beverly Hills amazed him – the wrought-iron gates and the pink marble fountains, the lights that winked from great Palladian windows. There was a party going on at one of the houses. Will slowed down to glimpse the silent ballet of waiters and guests and it took a moment for him to notice the flashing lights of the police cruiser pulling up behind him.

Co-workers, he thought, as he stepped out of the pickup to ask directions. There were two officers. One was blond, and that was all Will had time to notice before the man slammed his head against the cab of his truck, pinning his arm behind him.

'Look what we got here, Joe,' he said. 'Another fucking spic.'

'*Listen*,' Will heard himself rasp, and the cop brought his free hand down between Will's shoulder blades.

'Don't talk back to me, Pedro,' he said. 'We've been following you for ten minutes. What the hell business do you have in a neighborhood like this?'

'I'm a cop.' Will's words fell heavy to the pavement.

The man released his wrist, and Will pushed away from the truck and faced him. 'Let's see your badge.'

Will swallowed and looked him in the eye. 'I don't have it yet. I don't have my piece, either. I just got here; I start work tomorrow.'

The officer's eyes narrowed. 'Yeah, well, if I don't see no badge, I don't see no cop.' He nodded to his partner, who started to walk back to the cruiser. 'Get the fuck out of here.'

Will clenched and unclenched his fists as he watched the cop's retreating back. 'I'm one of you,' he shouted, and behind the thick plate glass of the police cruiser's windshield, he saw the officer laugh. Walking back to his truck, he stared at the people at the party on the hill, laughing and drinking like nothing at all had happened.

The moon slid behind a cloud as if it were embarrassed, and at that moment two truths struck Will: He did not like LA. And he was not white.

When she awakened the sun had set. She sat up and leaned against the familiar gravestone. Somewhere to the east, a searchlight was cutting across the sky, and she wondered if some awards show was scheduled for that night – they were a dime a dozen in LA.

She pulled herself to her feet and began to walk toward the gate. With each footstep, she spoke aloud a different female name, hoping that one might jar her memory. 'Alice,' she said. 'Barbara. Cicely.' She had gotten to Marta by the time she reached the street – Sunset Boulevard, she knew it right away and she realized she was making progress, since she hadn't remembered that earlier. She sat at the curb, in front of the sign that listed the name of St Sebastian's priest and the hours of confession and masses.

She knew she wasn't a member of the congregation – that she wasn't even Catholic – but she felt she'd been there before. She felt she'd *hidden* there, really, or taken refuge. What would she possibly have been running from?

Shrugging, she dismissed the thought and peered into the distance. Across the street and down the block was a billboard for a movie. '*Taboo*,' she read aloud, wondering if she'd seen it, since the title seemed so familiar. The poster showed a man half in silhouette, but even with the shaded features it was easy to tell that the actor was Alex Rivers, America's sweetheart. He'd successfully starred in everything from action thrillers to Shakespeare, and she remembered reading somewhere that his Q-rating for recognition ranked above the President's. He was smiling at her. 'At theaters everywhere,' she read, hearing the catch in her own voice.

Later on, when Will thought back to the moment, he realized it was the owl's fault. If he hadn't braked at the sound of that screech owl, he never would have stopped; and if he had never stopped, he wouldn't have made all the wrong decisions.

By some stroke of luck he'd found Sunset Boulevard, and although he knew Sunset Boulevard ran into the freeway, he wasn't sure if he was going in the right direction. The two gas stations he'd passed had been closed, and by now his right eye had nearly swollen shut and all he wanted to do was crawl into his bed and try to forget what had made him move to California in the first place.

He had just passed a McDonald's when he heard the call, sharp and piercing, like the cry of a child. Will had certainly heard owls before, but not since he'd left South Dakota. His grandparents, like many people on the reservation, believed strongly in the omens of birds. Since birds took flight, they were closer to the spirit world than man was, so ignoring a message from a bird might mean missing some warning or promise from powers greater than oneself. Will, in keeping with his rejection of the Sioux culture, had shrugged off the significance of hawks and eagles and ravens, although he couldn't bring himself to completely disregard owls, which his grandmother said were signs of death.

'Maybe it's the car,' he said aloud, and almost simultaneously he heard it again, a shrill scream that pulled at his insides.

He braked. Behind him, a van swerved, its driver cursing through the open window. Will pulled over in front of a Catholic church and parked in a towaway zone.

He got out of the truck and stepped onto the sidewalk, lifting his face to the sky. 'Okay,' he said sarcastically. 'Now what?'

The woman who came through the gate at the side of the church was faintly outlined in white, like a ghost. She saw Will and started to walk a little faster, a smile breaking across her face. Stunned, Will stared at her. She reached just as high as his shoulder and she had dried blood at the edge of her scalp. She came closer, until she stood just inches away, looking at the bruise above his eye. She reached out, this woman Will did not know, and brushed her fingers over the skin. He had never felt anything like it: a touch more quiet than a breath. 'Not you too,' she whispered, and then her eyes rolled back and she started to fall to the ground.

Will caught her and settled her in the passenger seat of his truck. When she started to stir, he sat as far back against the driver's-side door as he could, certain she'd scream when she found herself in a stranger's car. But her eyes blinked open and she smiled so easily that Will found himself smiling back.

'Are you okay?' he asked.

She swallowed and ran her hand over her hair, smoothing it away from her face. 'I think so,' she said. 'Have you been waiting long?'

She spoke as if she had known him all her life, which made Will grin. 'No,' he said. 'I just happened to be passing by.' He stared at her for a moment. 'Listen,' he said, 'if you're waiting for someone, I can wait with you until they get here.'

The woman froze. 'You don't know me?' Will shook his head. 'Oh God.' She rubbed her eyes. 'God.' She looked up at him through tears. 'Well, that makes two of us.'

Will wondered what he had gotten himself into, sitting in his own truck with a woman who was crazy, or so high she couldn't think clearly. He smiled hesitantly, waiting for her to fall back to reality. 'You mean you don't know me either.'

'I mean I don't know *me*,' the woman whispered.

Will looked carefully at her clear eyes, at the clotted cut on her temple. *Amnesia*, he thought. 'You don't know your name?' He switched automatically into the questioning he'd learned as a tribal police officer in South Dakota. 'Do you remember what happened to you? What brought you to the church?'

The woman glanced away. 'I don't remember any of that,' she said flatly. 'I suppose I should turn myself in to the police.'

The way she said it, like she'd committed a capital crime, made Will smile. He thought of driving her downtown to the Academy, the headquarters of the LAPD. Even if he wasn't officially on the roster, he surely could pull some strings and check the APBs, see if in fact anyone had been looking for her. He shifted slightly, wincing at the pain that shot over his eye. He remembered the blond cop in Beverly Hills, and he wondered if they all would be like that come Monday.

'*I'm* the police,' he said quietly, and even as the words were forming Will knew he would not take this woman to the LAPD, not after what had happened to him, not right away.

Her eyes narrowed. 'Do you have a badge?'

Will shook his head slowly. 'I just moved here. I live in Reseda. I start work tomorrow.' He caught her eye. 'I'll take care of you,' he said. 'Do you trust me?'

She looked at the sharp angles of his face, at the light shifting over his black hair. Nobody else had come. Yet when he had appeared, she'd run to him without any hesitation. Surely for someone who was not thinking with reason, but only with gut instinct, that had to count for something. She nodded.

He held out his hand. 'I'm William Flying Horse. Will.'

She smiled. 'Jane Doe.' She placed her fingertips against his palm, and with her touch this strange city fell into place. Will thought about the song of the owl, and this gift that had literally dropped into his arms, and as he glanced at her he knew that in some way she was now his.

Chapter Two

She kept skipping October. She was supposed to be reciting the names of the months in reverse order, as per instructions of the emergency room doctor, but she kept jumping from November to September. Her face flushed, and she looked up at the man who had been examining her. 'I'm sorry,' she said. 'Let me try that again.'

From across the room where he'd been watching for ten minutes, Will exploded. 'Jesus,' he said, moving closer. 'I'm perfectly fine, and I wouldn't be able to do that without messing up.' He glared at the doctor. He'd brought the woman to the emergency room because it was correct police procedure, at least in South Dakota, but now he was having second thoughts. As far as Will could tell, these stupid exercises had done nothing but make her more frazzled.

'She's lost consciousness at least twice in the past few hours,' the doctor said dispassionately. He held up a pen, inches from her face. 'What is this?'

She rolled her eyes. Already she'd answered questions about where she was, what day it was, who the President was. She'd counted forward and backward by threes and memorized a short list of fruits and vegetables. 'It's a pen.'

'And this?'

'A pen cap.' She glanced at Will and grinned. 'Or is it a cow?' As the doctor's eyes snapped up to hers, she laughed. 'I'm *kidding*,' she said. 'Just a little joke.'

'See?' Will said. 'She can make jokes. She's fine.' He crossed his arms, uneasy. Hospitals made him nervous; they had ever since he was nine years old and had watched his father die in one. Three days after the car accident, his mother already buried, Will had sat with his grandfather waiting for his father to regain consciousness. He had stared for hours at his father's lax brown hand contrasting against the white sheets, the white lights, and the white walls, and he knew it was only a matter of time before his father left to go somewhere he belonged.

'All right.' At the sound of the doctor's voice, both Jane and Will stood straighter. 'You appear to have a mild concussion, but you seem to be on the mend. Chances are you'll recover your more distant memories before you recover the recent ones. There may be a few minutes surrounding the actual blow to the head that you never recall.' He turned to Will. 'And you are . . . ?'

'Officer William Flying Horse, LAPD.'

The doctor nodded. 'Tell whoever comes to get her that she should be observed overnight. They need to wake her every few hours and just check her level of alertness; you know, ask her who she is, and how she's feeling, things like that.'

'Wait,' Jane said. 'How long until I remember who I am?'

The doctor smiled for the first time in the hour he'd been with her. 'I can't say. It could be hours; it could be weeks. But I'm sure your husband will be waiting for you downtown.' He slipped his pen into his jacket pocket and patted her shoulder. 'He'll be filling you in on the details in no time.'

The doctor swung open the door of the examination room and left, his white coat flying behind him.

'Husband?' she said. She stared down at her left hand, watching the diamonds on the simple band catch the fluorescent light. She glanced up at Will. 'How could I have missed this?'

Will shrugged. He had not noticed it himself. 'Can you remember him?'

Jane closed her eyes and tried to conjure a face, a gesture, even the pitch of a voice. She shook her head. 'I don't *feel* married.'

Will laughed. 'Well, then half the wives in America would probably kill for your kind of blow to the head.' He walked to the door and held it open for her. 'Come on.'

He could feel her one step behind him the entire way to the parking lot. When they reached the truck, he unlocked her door first and helped her into the seat. He turned the ignition and fastened his seat belt before he spoke. 'Look,' he said. 'If your husband's looking for you, he can't file a missing persons report until twenty-four hours go by. We can go down to the station now if you want, or we can go first thing in the morning.'

She stared at him. 'Why don't you want to take me there?'

'What are you talking about?'

'You're hedging,' Jane said. 'I can hear it in your voice.'

Will faced straight ahead and put the truck into reverse. 'Well, then you're not listening too well.' A muscle jumped along the side of his jaw. 'It's up to you.'

She stared at his profile, a chiseled silhouette. She wondered what she had said to make him so angry. For right now, at least, he was her only friend. 'Maybe if I get some rest,' she said carefully, 'I'll remember everything when I wake up. Maybe everything will look different.'

Will turned to her, taking in the tremor of her voice and the hope she was holding out to him. This woman he knew nothing about, this woman who knew nothing about *him*, was putting herself in his hands. It was the most he'd ever been given. 'Maybe,' he said.

Jane was asleep by the time they reached the house in Reseda. Will carried her back to the bedroom, settling her on the naked mattress and covering her with the only blanket he'd unpacked. He took off her shoes, but that was as far as he'd go. She was another man's wife.

At Oglala Community College, in some culture class he'd been forced to take to graduate, Will had learned the punishment the Sioux meted out for a woman's adultery in the days of the buffalo. It had completely shocked him: If his wife had run away with another man, the husband had the right to cut off the tip of her nose, so she'd be marked for life. To Will, it seemed to contradict everything else he knew about the Sioux. After all, they did not understand ownership of the land. They believed in giving away money, food, and clothing to friends down on their luck, even if it meant that they'd become poor as well. Yet they branded a wife as property, a husband as an owner.

He watched Jane sleep. In a way, he envied her. She'd managed to discard her past so easily, when Will had to work so hard to put his own history out of his mind.

Will touched the edge of Jane's collar where blood had dried. He would get some cold water and soak that. He brushed her hair away from her forehead and looked over her features. She had ordinary brown hair, a small nose, a stubborn chin. Freckles. She was not the blond bombshell of his adolescent dreams, but she was pretty in a simple way. Someone must have been frantic to find her missing.

He lifted his palm from her neck, planning to get a washcloth, but was stopped when her hand shot up from her side, her fingers closing around his wrist with lightning speed. *Jesus*, he thought, *the reflexes of a cougar*. Her eyes opened, and she glanced around wildly as if she'd been trapped. 'Shh,' Will soothed, and as he gently tugged to free himself, Jane let go, frowning as if she wasn't really sure why she'd grabbed him at all.

'Who *are* you?' she asked.

Will walked to the door and turned off the light. He looked away so that she would not be able to see his face.

'You don't want to know,' he said.

*   *   *

Will's first memory involved bailing his father out from jail.

He was three, and he remembered the way his mother looked standing in front of the sheriff. She was tall and proud and even in the dim lighting she looked very, very pale. 'There's been a mistake,' she said. 'Mr Flying Horse is one of my employees.'

Will did not understand why his mother would say his father worked for her, when she knew that he worked for Mr Lundt on the ranch. He did not understand the word 'assault' although he thought 'battery' had something to do with making Christmas toys work. The sheriff, a man with a florid cauliflower face, stared closely at Will and then spat not an inch away from his foot. 'Ain't no mistake, ma'am,' the sheriff said. 'You know these goddamned Indians.'

His mother's face had pinched closed, and she pulled out her wallet to pay the fines his father had been charged. 'Release him,' she hissed, and the sheriff turned to walk down a corridor. Will watched him grow smaller and smaller, the pistol at his hip winking each time he passed a window.

Will's mother knelt down beside him. 'Don't you believe a word he says,' she told him. 'Your father was trying to help.'

What he learned, years later, was that Zachary Flying Horse had been in a bar when there was an incident. A woman was being hassled by two rednecks, and when he'd stepped in to intervene, a fight had broken out. The woman had run out of the bar, so when the police came it was Zack's word against that of two white locals.

Zachary stepped out of the corridor in the jail behind the sheriff. He did not touch his wife. 'Missus,' he said solemnly. 'Will.' He lifted his boy up onto his shoulders and carried him into the hot Dakota sun.

They walked halfway down the block before Will's father swung him off his shoulders and caught his wife up in a tight embrace. 'Oh, Anne,' he sighed against her hair. 'I'm sorry to put you through that.'

Will pulled on the edge of his father's plaid shirt. 'What did you *do*, Pa?'

Zack grabbed Will's hand and started down the street again. 'I was born,' he said.

It would have been impossible for her to miss the note Will had left her, sitting as it was on the toilet lid with a fresh towel, toothpaste, a twenty-dollar bill, and a key. *Jane*, Will had written, *I've gone to work. I'll ask around about your husband, and I'll try to call later today with some answers. I don't have anything in the refrigerator so if you get hungry, go down to the market (3 blocks east). Hope you're feeling better. Will.*

She brushed her teeth with her finger and looked at the note again. He hadn't said anything about what she should do if she awakened with a perfect understanding of her name and address – not that it really mattered, since she still couldn't remember. At least she was lucky. Her chances of running into a drug addict or a pimp on Sunset Boulevard had been much greater than running into someone from out of town, someone who'd leave a perfect stranger his house key and twenty dollars without asking any questions or expecting something in return.

A light came into her eyes. She *could* do something in return; she could unpack for him. Her taste in decorating might not be like his – in fact, she had no idea what her own taste was like – but surely having the pots and pans in the cabinets and the towels in the linen closet would be a nice thing to come home to.

Jane threw herself into the task of putting Will's house in order. She organized the kitchen and the bathroom and the broom closet, but she didn't really have to get creative until she got to the living room. There, in two boxes, carefully layered in newspaper, was a series of Native American relics. She unwrapped beautiful quilled moccasins and a long tanned hide painted with the image of a hunt. There was an intricate quilt and a fan made of feathers and a circular beaded medallion. At the bottom of the box was a small leather pouch trimmed with beads and bright feathers, on which was drawn a running horse. It was closed tight with a sinew thong, and although she tried, she could not open the bag to see its contents.

She did not know what most of these objects were but she handled them as gently as she could, and she began to piece together more about Will. She looked around the bare walls and thought, *If I were in a strange place, I'd want something that reminds me of home*.

No one had come by the Academy looking for a missing woman. Will spent the day being introduced by the captain to other people in the LAPD, getting his badge and his assignment. When he registered for his gun, the officer who took down the information asked if he'd rather have a tomahawk; his new partner got a great kick out of calling him Crazy Horse. But these were things he'd faced before. He did not see the officer who'd blackened his eye; however, Beverly Hills was a separate precinct. When giggling secretaries asked about the bruise, he shrugged and said someone had gotten in his way.

It was after four o'clock before he got up the nerve to knock on his new captain's door and tell him about Jane. 'Come over here,' Watkins said, waving Will inside. 'You think you got the hang of things yet?'

Will shook his head. 'It's different.'

Watkins grinned. 'South Dakota it's not,' he said. 'A couple of celebrity traffic violations, a drug bust, and it'll be old hat.'

Will shifted in his seat. 'I wanted to speak to you about a missing persons case,' he said. 'Actually, I want to know if—' He stopped, and smoothed his palms against his thighs to gain his composure. There was no right way to go about saying he'd skirted procedure; Jane should have been brought into the precinct and photographed by now. 'I found a woman last night who's got amnesia. We went to the hospital, but since it was late, I didn't bring her in right away.' Will looked up at the captain. 'Have you heard anything?'

The older man shook his head slowly. 'Since you weren't on duty yet,' he said, 'I'm not going to count this against you. But she needs to be brought in for questioning.' Watkins looked up at Will, and at that moment Will knew that in spite of the captain's absolution, he would start out with a strike against him. 'Could be her memory loss is related to a crime.' Watkins fixed Will with a sharp glance. 'I assume you still know her whereabouts. I'd suggest you bring her down as soon as possible,' he said.

Will nodded, and started toward the door. 'And Officer,' Watkins called after him, 'from here on, you play by the rules.'

Will pulled on the collar of his uniform the whole drive back to Reseda. The goddamn shirt was choking him. He wouldn't last a week wearing it. He turned the corner of his block wondering if Jane had remembered her name. He wondered if she'd still be there.

She met him at the door wearing one of his good white shirts, knotted at the waist, and a pair of his running shorts. 'Is someone looking for me?' she asked.

Will shook his head and stepped over the threshold of his house. He stood perfectly still in the entrance, surveying the neatly stacked, empty boxes and the proof of his history hanging over the walls where anyone could see.

The fury came so quickly he forgot to hide it away. 'Who the hell gave you the right to go through my things?' he yelled, stomping across the carpet into the middle of the living room. He whirled to pin his gaze on Jane and found her crouched against the wall, her hands overhead as if to ward off a blow.

The anger ran out of him. He stood quietly, waiting for the rage to clear out of his vision. He did not say anything.

Jane lowered her arms and stiffly got to her feet, but she wouldn't look Will in the eye. 'I thought I'd be helping you,' she said.

'I wanted to thank you for everything, and this seemed to be the best way.' Her eyes raked the wall where the little leather pouch hung beside the painted hunting scene. 'I could always change things if you don't like them hanging this way.'

'I don't like them hanging at all,' Will said, lifting the moccasins from their spot on the fireplace mantel. He grabbed an empty carton and began tossing the items back inside.

Jane knelt beside the box and tried to organize the fragile pieces so they wouldn't be crushed. She had to do it carefully; she had to make it right. She ran her fingers over the feathers of the small leather pouch. 'What is this?'

Will barely glanced at what she was holding. 'A medicine bundle,' he said.

'What's in it?'

Will shrugged. 'The only people who know are my great-great-grandfather and his shaman, and both of them are dead.'

'It's beautiful,' Jane said.

'It's worthless,' Will tossed back. 'It's supposed to keep you safe, but my great-great-grandfather was gored by a buffalo.' He turned to see Jane fingering the bundle, and his face softened as she looked up at him. 'I'm sorry,' he said. 'I didn't mean to go off like that. I just don't like these things hanging where I can see them all the time.'

'I thought you'd want something to remind you of where you came from,' Jane said.

Will sank to the floor. 'That's exactly what I ran *away* from,' he said. He sighed and ran a hand through his hair, looking to change the subject. 'How're you feeling?'

She blinked at him, noticing for the first time that he was wearing the blue shirt of a police officer, the LAPD patch over his upper arm. 'You're wearing a uniform,' she blurted out.

Will smirked. 'You were expecting a headdress?'

Jane stood up and offered her hand to Will, pulling him to his feet. 'I remembered how to cook,' she said. 'You want dinner?'

She had fried chicken, steamed beans, and baked potatoes. Will carried the platter to the center of the living room floor and chose a breast for each of them, placing the meat onto two plates. He told her about his first day of work, and she told him how she'd gotten lost on her way to the market. The sun bled through the windows and cast Jane and Will into silhouette as they fell into an easy silence.

Will picked at the pieces of the chicken, sucked the meat from the bones. Suddenly, he felt Jane's hand close over his. 'Oh, let's do this,' she said, her eyes bright, and he realized he was holding the wishbone.

He pulled and she pulled, the white bones slipping through their greasy fingers, and finally he came away with the bigger piece. Disappointed, Jane leaned back against a stack of boxes. 'What did you wish for?'

He had wished for her memory, but he wouldn't tell her. 'If you say it, it won't come true,' he said, surprising himself. He smiled at Jane. 'My mother used to say that. In fact, she was the last person who pulled a wishbone with me.'

Jane hugged her knees to her chest. 'Does she live in South Dakota?'

He almost didn't hear her question, as he was thinking about the fine curve of his mother's jaw and the spark of her copper hair. He pictured her hand and his own curled over the edges of the forked chicken bone, and he wondered if her wishes had ever come true. Will looked up. 'My mother died when I was nine, in a car accident with my father.'

'Oh, how awful,' Jane said, and Will was amazed that her voice could hold so much pain for a stranger.

'She was white,' he heard himself saying. 'After the accident, I lived with my father's parents on the rez.'

As he started to speak, Jane reached onto the platter and pulled out a pile of bones Will had left. She settled them onto her plate and moved them around with her hands, seemingly unaware of what she was doing. She glanced up at him and smiled. 'Go on,' she said. 'Tell me how they met.'

Will had told this story many times before, because it tended to wrap itself around a woman's heart so neatly she'd tumble into his bed. 'My mother was a schoolteacher in Pine Ridge town, and my father saw her one day when he was getting some feed for his boss at the ranch. And her being white, and him being Lakota, he didn't really understand his attraction, much less what he was going to do about it.' Mesmerized, he watched Jane's hands wrap a strip of sinew from one bone around a second one. 'Anyway, they went out a couple of times, and then it came to summer vacation and she decided things were moving along too fast, so she just up and left without telling my father where she was going.'

Jane neatly laid five bones in parallel lines against the edge of her plate. 'I'm listening,' she said.

'Well, it sounds stupid, but my father said he was riding fence and he just *knew*. So he left in the middle of the day, on this borrowed horse, and he set out sort of north-northwest without any idea where he was headed.'

Jane looked up, her hands stilling. 'Did he find her?'

Will nodded. 'About thirty-five miles away at a diner, where she was waiting for a friend to pick her up and drive her home to Seattle. My father pulled her in front of him on the horse and wrapped an extra saddle blanket around them.'

Will had listened to this story so many times as a child that even now, he imagined the words in his mother's voice instead of his own. *'Years ago, this is how my people fell in love,' your father told me, and he wrapped that blanket so close we were sharing one heartbeat. 'I would have come to you at night, and we would sit outside in this cocoon, and with all the stars as witnesses I would tell you that I loved you.'*

'My God,' Jane sighed. 'That is the most *romantic* thing I've ever heard.' She pulled a new handful of bones from the tray between them. 'Did your mother go back with him?'

Will laughed. 'No, she went to Seattle. But she wrote him letters all summer and they got married a year later.'

Jane smiled and wiped her hands on a napkin. 'How come people don't do things like that nowadays? You grope around in the back of a sedan in high school and you think you're in love. Nobody gets swept off their feet anymore.' Shaking her head, she stood up to clear the plates. She picked up the near-empty serving platter and then dropped it, hearing its ring and the splatter of grease.

On her plate she'd re-created the skeleton of the chicken.

The bones were carefully structured, in some cases even bound together at the joints. The wings were folded neatly against the rib cage; the powerful legs were bent as if running.

She put her hand to her forehead as a wealth of terms and images flooded her mind: the slender arm bone of a ramapithecus, a string of molars and cranial fragments, green tents in Ethiopia that covered tables laden with hundreds of catalogued bones. Physical anthropology. She'd spent entire months in Kenya and Budapest and Greece on excavations, tracking the history of man. It had been such a tremendous part of her life, she was shocked even a blow to the head could make her forget it.

She lightly touched the femur of the reconstructed chicken. 'Will,' she said, and when she lifted her face her eyes were shining. 'I know what I do.'

Chapter Three

Will liked Jane better before she remembered she was an anthropologist. She kept trying to explain her science to him. Anthropology, she said, was the study of how people fit into their world. That much he understood, but most of the other things she said sounded like a foreign language. On the drive to the police station Monday evening, she'd outlined the best methods for skeletal excavation. When Watkins questioned her for a notice he'd insert in the *Times*, she'd told him that until someone came to claim her, she'd be happy to help in forensics. And now, the following morning, while Will was working his way through a bowl of Cheerios, she was trying to explain the evolution of man.

She was drawing lines across her napkin, labeling each branch with names. Will was beginning to see why her husband hadn't shown up. 'I can't follow this,' he said. 'I can't even do math this early.'

Jane ignored him. When she finished, she sighed and leaned back in her chair. 'God, it feels so good to *know* something.'

Will thought there were probably other things more worth knowing, but he didn't say this. He pointed to a spot on the napkin. 'Why'd they become extinct?'

Jane frowned. 'They weren't able to adapt to the world,' she said.

Will snorted. 'Yeah, well, half the time neither can I,' he said. He picked up his hat, getting ready to leave.

Jane's eyes brightened as she turned to him. 'I wonder if I've discovered something really important, like the Lucy skeleton, or that Stone Age man in the Tyrolean Alps.'

Will smiled. He thought of her crouched over a site in the red sand of a desert, doing what made her happy. 'Feel free to dig in the backyard,' he said.

That Tuesday morning, the LAPD ran Jane's picture in the *LA Times* with a small blurb requesting information about her, and Jane remembered discovering the hand.

After Will had left, Jane took herself to the local public library. It was a small branch library, but it did have a neat little section of textbooks on anthropology and archaeology. She found the most recent book, hunched over the polished table, and began to read.

Familiar words jarred images in her mind. She saw herself in the British countryside, kneeling beside an open pit in which lay the tangled remains of an ancient Iron Age battle. She could remember brushing earth from the bones; feeling for the pits on a sternum made by lances and arrowheads, or the cleanly severed vertebrae that cried decapitation. She had been someone's assistant then, she remembered, labeling specimens with India ink, carrying trays of bones to dry in the sun.

Jane flipped the page and that's when she saw the hand. It was exactly as it had been when she'd found it in Tanzania, fossilized into a stratum of sedimentary rock, tightly grasping a chisel made of stone. Hundreds of anthropologists had combed Tanzania looking for evidence of the stone-tool industry they thought primitive man had the level of intellect to conceive. Following the lead of her colleagues, she had gone down one year to reopen a forgotten excavation site.

She hadn't been looking when she found the hand. She'd just sort of turned around, and there it was, shoulder level, as if it had been reaching for her. It was an extraordinary find; delicate bones were rarely preserved. For fossilization to occur, skeletons had to remain undisturbed by animals and swirling waters and shifts of the earth, and if any pieces of a skeleton were lost, they tended to be the extremities.

Even as she was working, she had known this would be her break into the field. She had found what everyone had been searching for. She had carefully labeled the chisel, the hundreds of digits of bone, had cleaned them and preserved them with a synthetic resin.

Jane turned back to the book and read the caption beside the photograph of the hand. *Dated to over 2.8 million years, this hominid hand and chisel are the oldest known proof of stone-tool industry {Barrett et al., 1990}.*

Barrett. Was that her last name? Or had she only been someone's assistant, someone who had taken the credit for her own discovery? She skimmed through the index of the book, but there was no other reference to Barrett. None of the other books even carried a picture of the hand; it was too recent a find.

Shaking slightly, she walked to the reference desk and waited for the librarian to look up from her computer. 'Hello,' she said, flashing her most winning smile. 'I was wondering if you could help me.'

She found Will bent over a desk that seemed too small for him, sorting through paperwork. 'Police reports,' he said. 'I hate this shit.' He swept them to the side of the desk with his arm and gestured to a chair nearby. 'You see your picture yet?' Will held up the newspaper.

Jane grabbed the paper out of his hands and scanned the copy. 'God,' she muttered. 'They make me sound like a foundling.' She threw the newspaper back onto Will's desk. 'And have you been swamped with calls?'

Will shook his head. 'Be patient,' he said. 'It's not even lunchtime yet.' He wheeled his chair back and crossed his ankles on his desk. 'Besides,' he added, 'I'm getting used to having you as a housekeeper.'

'Well, you'd better start looking for a replacement.' She tossed him the Xerox copy of the page in the book she'd read that morning. 'That's my hand.'

Will peered at the blurry picture and whistled. 'You look damn good for your age.'

Jane snatched the paper back and smoothed it on the edge of the desk. 'I discovered that hand in Africa,' she said. 'I might very well be "Barrett".'

Will raised his eyebrows. '*You* discovered *this*?' He shook his head in disbelief. 'Barrett, huh?'

She shrugged. 'I'm not really sure, yet. That could just be the lead scientist who was excavating the site.' She pointed to the reference. 'I could be "et al". I bullied a librarian into getting me more information,' she said, beaming. 'I should know who I am by tomorrow afternoon.'

Will smiled at her. He wondered what he would do when she left him to go back to her life. He wondered how empty his house would feel with just one person in it, whether she'd call him from time to time. 'Well,' he said, 'I guess I should start calling you Barrett.'

She stopped and turned her face up to his. 'To tell you the truth,' she said, 'I've gotten used to Jane.'

An early riser, Herb Silver had taken his breakfast poolside at six a.m.: tomato juice, grapefruit, and a Cuban cigar. Squinting up at the sun, he had opened the Tuesday *Times* and stared at the picture of the woman on page 3 until his cigar fell, unnoticed, from the corner of his mouth into the shallow end. 'Holy shit,' he said, reaching for the cellular phone in his bathrobe pocket. 'Holy fucking shit.'

They wouldn't have stopped filming for any of the other actors on the film, but he was one of the executive producers as well as the leading man, and any money wasted would come out of his own pocket. He wiped his arm across his forehead, grimacing as a streak of makeup came off on the sleeve of the velvet doublet. It was twenty fucking degrees in Scotland, but the set designer had ordered a hundred torches to line the great hall of the castle where they were filming *Macbeth*. Consequently, he couldn't make it through a single take before his own sweat blinded him.

Jennifer, his mousy little assistant, was standing with the portable phone next to a spare suit of armor. Taking the phone, he walked a discreet distance away from her and the *People* reporter who was covering the filming. 'Herb,' he said, still in accent, 'this better be damn good.'

He knew his agent wouldn't call him on location unless it was a dire emergency, an Academy Award nomination, or a part that would boost his career even higher. But he'd already received an Oscar nomination this year and he'd been choosing his own roles for ages. His fingers gripped the receiver a little tighter, waiting for the transatlantic static to clear.

'—newspaper this morning, and there she—' he heard.

'What?' he shouted, forgetting the cast and crew around him. 'I can't hear a thing you're saying!'

Herb's voice came clearly into his ear. 'Your wife's picture was on page three of the *LA Times*. She was picked up by the police and she doesn't remember her name.'

'Oh Jesus,' he said, his pulse racing. 'What happened to her? Is she all right?'

'I just read this two minutes ago,' Herb said. 'She looks okay in the picture. I called you right away.'

He sighed into the telephone. 'Don't do anything. I'll be home by' – he checked his watch – 'six tomorrow morning, your time.' When he spoke again his voice broke. 'I've got to be the first one she sees,' he said.

He hung up on his agent without saying goodbye and started barking instructions to Jennifer. He called over her shoulder to his co-producer. 'Joe, we've got to stop filming for at least a week.'

'But—'

'Fuck the budget.' He started toward his trailer, but then turned and touched Jennifer's shoulder. She was already bent over the telephone making plane reservations, her hair falling around her like a curtain. When she looked up he held her gaze, and she saw something in his striking eyes that very few people ever had: a quiet desperation. 'Please,' he murmured. 'If you have to, move heaven and earth.'

It took Jennifer a moment to shake herself back to reality, and even after he'd been gone for several seconds she could still feel the heat where his hand had held her shoulder; the weight of his plea. She picked up the phone again and began to dial. What Alex Rivers needed, Alex Rivers would get.

At seven a.m. on Wednesday, the telephone began to ring. Will ran from the bathroom into the kitchen, wrapping a towel around his waist. 'Yeah?'

'It's Watkins. I just got a call from the station. Three guesses who's showed up.'

Will sank down to the kitchen floor and let the bottom drop out of his world. 'We'll be there in a half hour,' he said.

'Will?' He heard Watkins's voice as if from a long distance. 'You really know how to pick 'em.'

He knew he had to wake Jane and tell her that her husband had come to claim her; he knew he had to say the reassuring things that she'd expect him to say during the ride to the Academy, but he didn't think he could do it. The feelings Jane brought out in him went deeper than a matter of a fateful coincidence. He liked knowing that she tried to cover her freckles with baby powder. He liked the way she had of talking with her hands. He loved seeing her in his bed. He told himself that he would simply put on the mask of indifference he'd worn for the past twenty years, and that within a week his life would be back to normal. He told himself that this was what was meant to be all along. And at the same time, he saw Jane running from the cemetery gate beneath the owl's cry, and he knew that even when she was gone she would be his responsibility.

She was sleeping on her side, her arm curled over her stomach. 'Jane,' he said, touching her shoulder. He leaned closer and shook her lightly, shocked to notice that the pillow and blanket no longer smelled like him, but like her. 'Jane, get up.'

She blinked at him and rolled over. 'Is it time?' she asked, and he nodded.

He made coffee while she was showering, in case she wanted something in her stomach before they left, but she wanted to go right away. He sat beside her in the pickup and drove in silence, letting all the words he should have been saying clutter the space around him. *I'll miss you*, he had planned to tell her. *Call if you get a chance. If anything happens, well, you know where I am.*

Jane stared glassy-eyed at the freeway, her hands clenched in her lap. She did not speak until they turned into the parking lot of the police station. At first, her voice was so quiet that Will thought he had heard her incorrectly. 'Do you think he'll like me?'

Will had expected her to wonder aloud about whether she'd remember her husband the minute she laid eyes on him, or to speculate about where her home was. He had not expected this.

He didn't have a chance to answer. A flock of reporters pushed their way toward the truck, snapping flash cameras and calling out questions that tangled with each other in a knot of noise. Jane shrank back against the seat. 'Come on,' Will said, sliding his arm around her shoulders. He pulled her toward the driver's-side door. 'Just stick close to me.'

Who the hell was she? Even if she was this Barrett person, this anthropologist, and even if she'd discovered that hand, this kind of press coverage seemed to be a little overboard. Will guided

Jane up the steps and into the main lobby of the station, feeling her warm breath make a circle against his collarbone.

Standing beside Captain Watkins was Alex Rivers.

Will dropped his arm from Jane's shoulders. Alex *goddamn* Rivers. All these reporters, all these cameras had nothing to do with Jane at all.

The corner of Will's mouth tipped up. Jane was married to the number-one movie star in America. And she'd completely forgotten.

The first thing she noticed was that Will had stepped away from her. For a moment she was certain she wouldn't be able to stand on her own. She was afraid to look up and face all those people, but something was keeping her on her feet and she needed to see what it was.

She lifted her head and was bound by Alex Rivers's eyes.

Taboo.

'Cassie?' He took a step forward, and then another one, and she unconsciously stepped closer to Will. 'Do you know who I am?'

Of course she knew him; *everyone* knew him, he was *Alex Rivers*, for God's sake. She nodded, and that's when she noticed how faulty her perception had become. Alex Rivers's face kept shimmering in and out, the way the heat rising off asphalt in the summer sometimes makes you see double. One moment, Cassie saw him glossy and larger than life; in the next, he seemed to be nothing more than a man.

An instant before he reached for her, all of Cassie's senses seemed to converge upon one another. She could feel the warmth coming from his skin, see the light reflecting off his hair, hear the whispers that wrapped them closer together. She smelled the clean sandalwood of his shaving cream and the light starch of his shirt. Tentatively, she stretched her arms around him, knowing exactly where her fingers would meet the muscles of his back.

Anthropology, she thought, *the study of how people fit into their world.*
She closed her eyes and fell into the familiar.

'God, Cassie, I didn't know what happened. Herb called me
in Scotland.' His breath fell just over her ear. 'I love you,
pichouette.'

It was that word that made her pull away. She looked up
at him, at this man every woman in America dreamed about,
and she took a step back. 'Do you have a picture?' she asked
softly. 'Something that shows, you know, you and me, somewhere?'

She did not question why, days ago, when she wasn't thinking
clearly, she had so easily trusted Will; yet here she was asking for
proof before she'd let Alex Rivers take her away. Alex frowned
for a moment, and then pulled his wallet out of his back pocket.
He handed her a laminated picture, a wedding photo.

It was certainly him, and it was certainly her, and she looked
happy and cherished and sure. She gave it back to Alex. He put
away his wallet and held out his hand.

She stared at it.

Somewhere behind her, she heard a desk clerk snicker. 'Shit,'
the woman said, 'if she got her doubts, I'll go with him.'

She laced her fingers through Alex's and watched as his expression completely changed. The vertical line of worry between his
brows smoothed, the thin line of his lips softened into a smile,
and his eyes began to shine. He lit up the room, and Cassie felt
her breath catch. *Me*, she thought, *he wants me.*

Alex Rivers let go of her hand and put his arm around her
waist. 'If you don't get your memory back,' he whispered, 'I'll just
make you fall in love with me all over again. I'll take you back
to Tanzania and I'll mix up all your bone samples and you can
throw a shovel at me—'

'I'm an anthropologist?' she cried.

Alex nodded. 'It's how we met,' he said.

She bubbled at the thought of that. Her hand. It was her hand, after all; and through some miracle of God Alex Rivers seemed to be in love with her, and—

Will. She turned to see him standing a few feet away and shrugged out of the circle of Alex's arm. 'I *am* an anthropologist,' she said, smiling.

'I heard,' he said. 'So did most of LA.'

She grinned at him. 'Well. Thank you.' She raised her eyebrows. 'I wasn't really expecting it to end this way.' She stuck out her hand, and then impulsively threw her arms around his neck. Over her shoulder, Will did not miss the flicker that iced Alex Rivers's eyes for a fraction of a second.

He loosened Jane's – Cassie's – arms and held them down at her sides, furtively slipping into her palm the piece of paper he'd marked with his address and phone numbers. He leaned forward to kiss her cheek. 'If you ever need anything,' he whispered, and then he stepped back.

Cassie stuffed the paper into the pocket of her jacket and thanked him again. She apparently led a storybook life. What would she possibly need?

Alex was waiting patiently at the door of the station. He framed Cassie's face in his palms. 'You don't know—' he said, his voice faltering. 'You don't know what it was like to lose you.'

Cassie stared at him, absorbing the fear in his tone. She was frightened too, but that seemed secondary all of a sudden. Acting on instinct, she smiled up at Alex. 'It wasn't for very long,' she said softly, reassuringly. 'And I wasn't very far away.'

Cassie watched Alex's shoulders relax. Amazing – when he seemed to be calmer, she felt better too.

Alex glanced out at the swarming media. 'This isn't going to be pleasant,' he said apologetically, as he anchored her close to his side and opened the heavy front door.

He held one hand in front of his eyes and pushed a path for them through the growing throng of paparazzi and cameramen. Cassie looked up, dazed, only to see a looming face and then the explosion of a flashbulb. The early air closed in around her throat and, blinded, she had no choice but to turn her face into Alex's chest. She felt him squeeze her arm, felt his heartbeat against her shoulder, and she willingly sacrificed herself to the strength of this strange husband.

Chapter Four

T he Malibu apartment was known for its natural spotlights. It
    had been built with ninety-two plate-glass windows, strategic-
ally located for eastern, western, and overhead exposure so that no
matter where you were, the sun placed you center stage. Alex stood
in front of a wall of glass, beautifully backlit, running his thumb
over the edge of an oval inlaid maple box. 'You got this in Lyons,
I think,' he said to Cassie. She was sitting in a love seat the color
of a blush, and when he sank to the floor in front of her, grasping
her hand, she couldn't help but gasp. It was like having the character spring off the movie screen, suddenly flesh and blood.

It was an odd feeling, seeing a stranger a few feet in front of
you and knowing that you had shared his bowl of cereal, warmed
your feet against his calves, traded him your whispers in a soft,
mussed bed. Cassie wished she could throw herself into the
charade, but she could not. Alex was the actor, not her, and she
was painfully aware of the shifting zone that moved with her,
blue and magnetic, forcing a distance between them even when
they touched.

Alex sighed. 'You're not going to start acting like I'm larger
than life, are you?' he said. 'You never did before.'

Cassie gave him a half-smile. She had been quiet on purpose,
figuring the less she said, the less of a fool she'd make of herself.
'This takes a little getting used to,' she said. She glanced at the
white alençon curtains, the pickled-wood coffee table, the pink
marble sink of the wet bar.

Alex leaned close to brush a kiss against her forehead, and she couldn't help it, she stiffened. Since Alex had claimed her at the station, he hadn't hesitated to touch her. It was ridiculous, really, to feel as skittish as she would on a blind date, since Alex had said they'd been married for three whole years. Still, she couldn't seem to see herself in the day-to-day routine of a marriage. Instead her mind kept flashing through images she knew she'd been fed by the media: Alex Rivers at a black-tie benefit for AIDS research, Alex Rivers accepting a Golden Globe award, Alex Rivers juggling coconuts during a break on the set of *Robinson Crusoe*.

Suddenly he stood up, bathed in sunlight, and Cassie lost track of her thoughts. She did not remember Alex, she did not feel comfortable around him, but she was fascinated by him. The silver shine of his eyes, the proud line of his jaw, the muscles corded in his neck, all called to her. She studied him as she would Michelangelo's David: fluid, beautiful, but far too steeped in his own perfection to be singled out for her.

'It's a good thing we came here,' Alex said. 'If you're overwhelmed by the apartment, I can't imagine what you'd think of the house.'

On the way to the Malibu Colony, Alex had tried to jar Cassie's memory with descriptions of their three homes: the house in Bel-Air, the apartment in Malibu, and the ranch just outside of Aspen, Colorado. He said that they spent most of their time at the house, but that Cassie had always preferred the apartment because when they were married she'd redecorated it.

'What's it like?' she had pressed, eager for some detail that would shake free her past.

Alex had just shrugged. 'It's little,' he said.

But when the Range Rover pulled up to the towering whitewashed building, Cassie had stared at the rounded edges, the princess's turrets, the tiers and tiers. The last thing it was was *little*. 'It looks like a castle,' she had breathed, and Alex had thrown his arms around her. 'That's what you said the first time you saw it,' he'd said.

'Cassie?' She jumped now at the sound of her name. She hadn't even heard the telephone ring, but Alex was holding the receiver, mouthpiece covered. 'Herb says he won't sleep until he sees that you're all right.' He took a step closer to her and laid his palm against her cheek, his eyes darkening. 'Well, I don't give a damn,' he said. 'You've got to rest.'

He lifted the telephone to his ear. 'No, Herb,' he said. 'Five minutes is too long. No—'

Cassie stood up and put her hand on his arm. It was the first time she had actually reached out to touch Alex, instead of him touching her. He turned to her, the telephone forgotten, his eyes locked onto her own. 'It's okay,' she said quietly. 'Tell him to come over. I'll be fine. I don't want to rest.'

He murmured something into the telephone and she watched the way his lips formed the words. She waited for him to hang up, but he didn't. He cupped his hand over the receiver again and moved closer, until they were separated by the space of a breath.

Cassie did not close her eyes as Alex kissed her. Her hand fell away from his arm to hang at her side, and she tasted faint traces of coffee and vanilla. When he pulled away, she was still leaning toward him, her eyes wide and waiting for the flood of memories she was certain would come.

But before that could happen, Alex gestured helplessly at the phone. 'I have to talk to him. I left *Macbeth* mid-scene, you know, to get you. Poor Herb has to clean up the mess I made.' He ran his hand over her hair. 'Why don't you poke around a little? I promise, no more than five minutes.'

As Alex turned away and started rattling questions into the telephone, Cassie moved downstairs to the middle level of the apartment. She wondered if she should change her clothes before Herb arrived. She wondered who Herb was.

She started toward the master bedroom, where Alex had showed her, earlier, a closet full of silks and rainbow cottons that belonged to her. She reached the arched hallway Alex had pulled her through before. This time, she stopped to look at the pictures that hung against the stark white walls. There was one of Alex on the beach outside the apartment, buried up to his chest in sand. Of Cassie herself, grinning, her arm thrown casually around the shoulders of a skeleton. There was a picture of a dog she did not recognize, and one of Alex on a rearing horse. Finally came a photo of Cassie in bed, white sheets pulled just up to her breasts, a lazy smile across her flushed face.

She thought of the pressure of Alex's kiss. She tried to imagine his hands tracing their way down her spine.

She looked at the picture again, and she wondered if Alex had taken it.

Herb Silver was five feet tall, bald, with a handlebar mustache and pointed ears that made Cassie think of a Munchkin. He met Alex at the door of the apartment and shoved a greasy brown paper bag into his arms. 'So, I figure it's lunch and what's a *goy* like you going to have in his kitchen?' His eyes darted behind Alex's substantial height, searching for Cassie, pushing Alex aside as he began to rummage in the bag. 'There's pastrami on rye with sauerkraut for you, and three knishes and for God's sake, don't eat all the *forshpeis* by yourself this time. Ah!' He held out his arms to Cassie. 'You were trying to give me my third heart attack?'

Herb Silver was Alex's agent at CAA. He had moved to LA over twenty years earlier, but he told everyone that even though you could take Herb Silver out of Brooklyn, you couldn't take Brooklyn out of Herb Silver. Cassie reached out and hugged him, his head coming under her chin.

Herb kissed her on the mouth. He ran his hands lightly down her arms as if he were checking for broken bones. 'So, you're fine?'

Cassie nodded, and Alex stepped forward, offering her half of a paper-wrapped knish. 'She's perfect,' he said with a full mouth.

Herb raised an eyebrow. 'Does the girl have a voice of her own?'

'I'm fine,' Cassie said. 'Really.' She looked from Alex to Herb and then back at Alex again, silently thanking the little man for forcing his entry this afternoon. With Herb added to the mix of her mind, Alex couldn't help but seem more familiar.

Alex clapped an arm around Herb's shoulders and led him upstairs to the dining room. 'Cassie – can you get the plates? All right, Herb, tell me what Joe's doing in Scotland.'

Cassie wandered into the kitchen, grateful for something to do. Somehow the ordinary things, like finding plates, or cooking, or watching the shower steam up the bathroom, made her feel at home. Alex had seemed so much less threatening that morning when they were doing things together – him pouring juice and her finding the ice, standing side by side and chopping peppers for an omelette, picking up a stack of papers the wind had scattered to the floor. There was an intimacy to simple tasks, things everyone knew and everyone did, that formed a floor of false comfort and security beneath even two strangers.

Herb and Alex were talking in the dining room, a running river of syllables she caught from time to time. Cassie looked from one cabinet door to the next, wondering where the dishes were. She opened the door closest to her. Tablecloths, and a breadbasket. The door beside it revealed wineglasses.

'Joe's filmed the six lousy scenes that don't revolve around you – the witches, and something or other with Banquo. He says Melanie did a tour de force with the hand-washing bit.' Herb watched Cassie open a third and fourth cabinet, bite her lip, and then check beneath the sink. 'What's with her head?' he whispered to Alex. 'She's still a little *meshugge*?'

Alex shrugged. 'The doctor told her it's going to take some time for her to remember who she is, and what the hell knocked her out.' His eyes followed Cassie as she finally opened the cabinet that held the dishes. 'In the meantime, I figure I'll just keep her near me. Safe.' He grinned at his agent. 'Shit. If *I* can't bring back her memory, I don't know what *can.*'

Cassie brought back three plates and a stack of paper napkins. She hovered at the edge of the table, the outsider. 'I could only find wineglasses,' she said.

Herb waved toward her chair. 'Just sit. We can drink out of the bottles.' He unwrapped a sandwich with a colossal amount of meat jammed between the slices of bread, and Cassie watched his mouth contort to seal around the bulk of it. 'I hope you've thanked your lovely wife, Alex, for the free PR.' Herb pinched Cassie's cheek. 'Nationwide coverage of the heartbroken Alex Rivers shielding his wife is *exactly* the kind of pre-Oscar coverage we need.' He held his sandwich inches from his mouth. 'It can't hurt all your buddies at AMPAS to see you being a family man before they cast their Best Actor and Best Director votes. You know, I'm going to call Michaela this afternoon and see if we can't milk this on *Oprah*. You can plug *Taboo*, maybe we can get Cassie on for the last five minutes—'

'No.' At that last word, Cassie jumped. Alex hadn't spoken particularly loudly, but he'd slammed his fist on the table so force-fully that he had cracked one of the hand-painted tiles that made up its surface. Cassie watched a tiny line of blood trickle down Alex's wrist, but he did not bother to wipe it away. His eyes narrowed, and he leaned across the table toward Herb, upsetting a bottle of soda. 'You will not exploit my wife on television to stack my odds for the Oscars.'

Herb blotted his mouth with a napkin, as if he were used to this kind of outburst every day. 'Okay, okay,' he said.

Stunned, Cassie sat motionless, watching the clear stream of Sprite puddle onto the carpet. She looked up at Alex. 'I don't mind,' she said. 'If you think it will help you—'

'I said *no*,' Alex bellowed. His fingers, clenched white around the edge of the table, suddenly relaxed. 'Cassie,' he said more softly. 'The *soda*.'

Cassie pushed back her chair and flew into the kitchen. A dishcloth. She spun around, intuitively opening the cabinet that housed a stack of simple folded cloths. She efficiently mopped up the tiles on the table and then, kneeling between Herb and Alex, she pressed the cloth to the carpet. She scrubbed for a full minute. In fact, she was so intent on cleaning the mess, she didn't notice the breaking weight of the silence that settled on her shoulders, forcing her to bow her head, preventing her from looking up at Alex.

'There,' Cassie said to herself, breathless. She rocked back to her heels.

Alex pulled her up to sit on his lap. 'Sorry, Herb,' he said sheepishly. 'You know how I get about her.'

'Who wouldn't?' Herb picked up the second half of his sandwich and began methodically sifting through the corned beef, eliminating every other slice. 'Goddamn cholesterol.'

Cassie watched him pile the meat on the side of his plate. She shifted uncomfortably, feeling Alex's thighs beneath hers. She realized she was shaking, and almost as quickly, Alex banded his arms around her. 'Cold?' he whispered against the curve of her ear, and before she could answer, he tightened his embrace.

'I'm going to fly back to Scotland on Friday,' he said. 'I'm taking Cassie with me.'

'You are?' Cassie said, turning in his arms to stare at him.

Herb nodded. 'UCLA's giving her a sabbatical?'

UCLA? Cassie struggled off Alex's lap. 'What does UCLA have to do with it?'

Herb smiled indulgently. 'Alex probably didn't get around to telling you yet. You teach there.'

'I thought I was an anthropologist.'

'You are,' Alex said. 'You teach anthropology there.' He grinned at her. 'Let me see if I've got it right this semester – you're teaching

Archaeological Field Training, The Australopithecines, and you're heading a tutorial for Golden's course on biology, society, and culture.'

Cassie rounded on him, furious, her anger eating away at the distance between them and making her forget her quiet role as an observer. How could he have neglected to mention this? She'd told him about the hand she'd found in the library the day before, the first clue to her identity. And at the police station, when he'd confirmed her profession, she'd practically crowed. For someone so concerned with his own career, Alex should have understood. 'Why didn't you tell me this before? I've got to call someone there. I might have missed a class. They might have seen the paper—'

'Cassie,' Alex said, 'calm down. I had Jennifer call to let them know you're all right and to tell them you'd be taking off sick for a couple of weeks.'

'And who the hell is *Jennifer*?' Cassie yelled.

'My *assistant*,' Alex said. His voice, low and soothing, ran over her shoulders and her back. He came to stand in front of her, grasping her upper arms and forcing her to look into his eyes. 'Take it easy,' he said. 'I only want you to get better.'

'I'm *fine*,' Cassie exploded. 'I'm perfectly *fine*. I may not be able to remember who I am, Alex, but that doesn't make me an invalid. I'd probably remember a lot more if you weren't so intent on making all my decisions for me and—' Suddenly, her words dropped off. Alex's voice had been soft as rain, and his arms were offered for comfort, but his fingers bit into her skin. Cassie looked down to a spot where a small smear of blood from the side of his injured hand had marked her shirt.

He was staring at her so intently he didn't even know he was hurting her. Cassie felt her cheeks burn. She was accusing him, although she only knew half the facts. She had yelled at him, when all he'd done was try to help. She turned away from Alex, mortified that she had screamed like a banshee in front of him, in front of his agent. What had she been thinking? Of course she'd go to Scotland. She had the rest of her life to teach at UCLA.

Alex brushed her hair back from her forehead. He seemed to be waiting for her to come to her senses. 'I'm sorry,' Cassie murmured. 'I just wish you'd said something.' She pulled away from him, letting that uneasy shadow fall back into place between them. She smiled through her embarrassment at Herb, then walked onto the patio that led to the beach.

'Whew,' Herb said, standing and stretching his arms overhead. 'I don't think I've ever seen Cassie act like that.'

Alex watched his wife walk over the bright sand, the wind covering her footsteps almost as quickly as she made them. He saw her pick up a stone and throw it as far as she could, aiming to shatter the sun. 'No,' he said quietly. 'Neither have I.'

It was the summer of 1975 and she and Connor lay on their backs on the floating dock, rubbing their toes against the rough wood, challenging each other to see who could stare longest at the burning sun. 'You're cheating,' she said. 'I can see you squinting when you think I'm not looking.'

'Am not,' Connor said indignantly. 'You just can't think of any other way to win.'

She was twelve and she was with her best friend, and it was one of those absolutely perfect days on Moosehead Lake, one that moved so slowly you were sure you were stuck in a photograph until, wham, just like that, it was over too soon. 'God,' she said. 'I'm totally blind.'

'Me too,' said Connor. 'All I see is black.'

'Truce?'

'Truce.' Cassie sat up, groping along the dock past her fishing pole and Connor's to find the skinny bones of his wrist. She pulled until she knew he was sitting up too.

She had known Connor for as long as she could remember. He lived next door and his father worked at the bait and tackle shop in town. They had stolen still-hot elephant-ear cookies from her parents' bakery; they had been in the same class since second grade; they had learned to sail together on a battered old Sunfish bought with their pooled paper route money. They had both forsworn marriage, each thinking that with the exception of the other, the opposite sex was a miserable lot; they talked constantly of running away to the Canadian border, just to see if they could actually do it. Their parents said they were each other's flip side, inseparable, two halves of a whole. Cassie liked that idea a lot. It made her think of a picture in their biology textbook of a hermit crab that lived with a sea anemone on its back. The sea anemone, carried by the crab, had a better chance of finding food, and the crab was better protected by the sea anemone's sting and camouflage. Separate, they had to take their chances. Together, they had a whole new chance at survival.

Connor jumped to his feet. 'Want to fish?'

'Again?' said Cassie. 'No.'

'Want to race back?' He gestured toward the sliver of shore.

'What about our poles?'

Connor dropped to a crouch. 'I could teach you to do a backward dive.'

For a second Cassie's eyes gleamed – Connor could do anything when it came to diving. He'd tried to show her once or twice, but she hadn't been a very good student. Still, a *back* dive.

'Okay,' she said. 'What do I do?'

Connor positioned her beside him on the floating dock so that they stood with their backs to the water, their toes balanced right on the edge. Then he bent at the knees and executed a perfect dive, slicing the water with his hands before his body followed like the silver slip of a knife. He surfaced beside the dock and wiped mucus from his nose. 'You do it.'

Cassie sucked in her breath. She bent a little, hopped, and slipped on the wet dock. The only thing she remembered for a long while after that was the horrible sound her skull made as it cracked against something hard and unforgiving.

Connor was already in the water when she blacked out, and he slung an arm across her chest and scissor-kicked his way back to the shore. He dragged her across the sand, Cassie's heels cutting dark wet furrows in their wake.

When her eyes blinked open, something was blocking her view of the sun, something black and looming. *Cassie*. She rubbed her hand against the back of her head.

Connor was staring at her as if she'd come back from the dead, instead of just passed out for a minute or two. 'You okay?' he said. 'You know who I am?'

Cassie snorted; she couldn't help it. As if she could ever forget Connor. 'Yeah,' she said. 'You're my other half.'

Connor stared down at her, his face so white she knew she had given him a good scare. For a moment neither of them said a word. Connor found his voice first. 'Come on,' he said. 'Let's get some ice for you.'

They swung open the screen door of Cassie's house, leaving damp footprints and a shadow of sand on their way into the kitchen. 'It would have been a perfect dive,' Cassie tossed over her shoulder. 'Next time, I think—' She stopped at the doorway so abruptly Connor slammed against her back, and unconsciously, she leaned toward him. Her mother was slumped across the kitchen floor, soaked in a pile of her own vomit.

Setting her lips in a tight line, Cassie knelt beside her mother with a wet dishrag, wiping her cheek and her mouth and the collar of her shirt. From the corner of her eye, she saw Connor silently retrieve the bottle of gin that had rolled underneath the radiator. Her mother was supposed to be at the bakery, since it was only three o'clock. There must have been another fight. Which meant she didn't know when, or whether, to expect her father home.

'Ma?' Cassie whispered. 'Ma, come on. Get up.' She looped her mother's arm around her neck and hefted the dead weight in a dragging fireman's carry. With Connor watching from the doorway, she draped her mother across the living room couch and covered her with a light quilt.

'Cass?' Her mother's voice was soft and breathy, a dead ringer for Marilyn Monroe's. She reached blindly to find her daughter's hand. 'My good girl.'

Cassie tucked her mother's hand under the quilt and wandered back into the kitchen, wondering what she could scrounge up for dinner. If she had a meal set when – if – her father got home, then he wouldn't get angry, and if he didn't get angry her mother would be less likely to drink herself out cold again. She could make everything okay.

Connor stood in the kitchen packing ice into a plastic baggie. 'Get over here,' he said. 'The last thing *you* need is for your head to swell some more.'

She sat down on a chair and let Connor hold the pack to the curve of her neck. It wasn't like Connor hadn't seen this before – he knew *everything* about her – but even the first time, he had just offered his help and kept quiet. He hadn't looked at her with those moon eyes that she knew meant pity.

Ice water ran down the hollow between Cassie's shoulder blades, and in spite of Connor's first aid, a headache was beginning to kick through her. She stared out the window at the floating dock, which looked so far away she could hardly believe she had been there minutes before. Cassie sighed. The problem with absolutely perfect summer days was that they were bright bull's-eye targets for something to go outright wrong.

She woke up to the cool sting of aloe being rubbed along her calves. 'You're going to pay for this later,' Alex said. 'You're so red it hurts me to look at you.'

Cassie jerked her leg away and tried to roll over, feeling uncomfortable with the intimate slip of Alex's palms over her own skin. She winced at the pain when she tried to bend her knee. 'I didn't mean to fall asleep.'

Alex glanced at his watch. 'I didn't mean to let you sleep for six hours, either,' he said. 'After Herb left, I sort of got tied up on the phone.'

Cassie sat up and shifted degrees away from Alex. She watched the sun cut a ribbon across the ocean. An older woman came strolling down the beach with two weimaraners. 'Alex!' she called, waving. 'Cassie! Are you feeling all right?'

Alex smiled at her. 'She's fine,' he yelled. 'Have a nice walk, Ella.'

'Ella?' Cassie murmured. 'Ella Whittaker?' Her eyes widened, trying to catch a glimpse of the statuesque woman who, fifty years back, had been a pinup girl and a screen legend. 'The Ella Whittaker who starred in—'

'The Ella Whittaker who lives two doors down,' Alex said, grinning. 'God, you've got to get your memory back soon, or you're going to scour the Colony asking for autographs.'

For several minutes he did not speak, and Cassie could feel the quiet settle around them. She wanted to say something to Alex, anything, but she didn't know what sorts of things they talked about.

As she turned toward the violet line of the horizon, Alex's voice curled over her, light as silk. 'I *was* going to tell you about UCLA. God, I never would have *met* you if you weren't working there, so I owe them a lot. I really didn't do it deliberately. I just forgot.' He reached for her hand and brought it to his lips. His eyes were the sloe-black of smoke. 'Forgive me?'

He's acting. The thought rushed through Cassie's mind so violently she pulled her hand free and turned away, shaking. *How do I know when he's acting?*

'Cassie?'

She blinked at him, held in his gaze, and by bits and degrees she softened. She couldn't think about UCLA, about who was wrong and who was right, not just now. He was hypnotizing her; she knew this as well as she knew that she had been made for him, as well as she knew that any doubts she had about Alex would mirror her own faulty judgment.

Cassie began to hear and feel the unexpected: a tangle of sweet Mexican violins, a wet wind from an everglade, the song of one hundred hearts beating. She thought to run, some instinct telling her this was the beginning of the end, but she could no sooner move than turn back time. The world as she knew it was falling away, and the only place left for her to go was toward Alex.

'Forgive me?' he repeated.

Cassie heard the sound of her own voice, heard the words she couldn't remember thinking. 'Of course,' she said. 'Don't I always?'

A wave rolled over Cassie's ankles, frigid and authentic. The magic broke, and then it was just the two of them, she and Alex, and that was starting to seem all right. 'I came prepared with a bribe,' Alex said. 'I made it myself.' He was smiling at her, and she smiled back hesitantly, thinking, *He understands. He knows he has me in the palm of his hand.* He pulled up the front of his shirt to reveal a neatly wrapped square package tucked into the waist of his jeans. 'Here.'

Cassie reached for the tinfoil, trying not to look at the smooth, sculptured muscles of his chest. She unwrapped it. 'You made me Rice Krispies Marshmallow Treats? Are they my favorite?'

'No,' Alex laughed. 'In fact, you hate marshmallows, but it's the only thing I know how to cook and I thought for *sure* you'd remember that and take pity on me.' He tugged it out of her hand and took a bite. 'I grew up on these,' he said, his mouth full.

Cassie turned to him, her eyes gleaming. 'Alex,' she said. 'Where did I grow up?' *Maine.* She knew even before he spoke the word what the answer would be. 'And who was Connor?'

Alex's eyes widened, so she could see the ring of gold around the edge of his irises. 'Your best friend. How do you – did you remember all this?'

She grinned, excited. 'I was dreaming the whole time I was asleep,' she said. 'I remembered a lot of things. Moosehead Lake, and Connor, and . . . and my mother. Do we ever go there? Do I talk to my parents a lot?'

Alex swallowed. 'Your mom's dead, and, well, when I first met you, you told me the reason you went to college in California was to get as far away from Maine as you possibly could.'

Cassie nodded, as if she had expected this. She wondered how much Alex knew about her parents. She wondered if she'd ever been brave enough to tell him. 'Where are your parents?'

Alex rolled away from her, turning to face the ocean. She watched his profile set, and she had a sudden memory – this was the way he looked minutes before he filmed a scene, when his own personality drained away and was replaced by the character he was playing. 'They're in New Orleans,' Alex said. 'We don't see much of them, either.' He rubbed his palm against the back of his neck and closed his eyes. Cassie wondered what he was seeing, what made him curl into himself. To her surprise, a sharp ache stung her chest, and she knew right away she had felt it so that he wouldn't have to. When Alex looked up at her, old ghosts still shifted in his eyes. 'You really don't remember me, do you?' he said quietly.

He was inches away but she could feel the line of heat between them as if they were touching. Cassie put her arms around him, shivering as she took in more of his pain. 'No,' she said. 'I don't.'

They made popcorn in the microwave for dinner and watched a Monty Python rerun on TV. They played War with a deck of cards they found buried in the broom closet. With a pillowcase draped on his head for a wimple, Alex performed Lady Macbeth's 'Out, damned spot!' speech, curtsying low when Cassie laughed and clapped. Her eyes were shining when he jumped down from the cleared coffee table he'd used as a stage. She did not know Alex, but she liked him. Surely that was more than most marriages survived on.

Alex pulled her to her feet. 'Tired?'

Cassie nodded, letting him slip his arm around her waist. As they walked down the stairs to the bedroom, she wondered what the sleeping arrangements would be. They were married, so he could sleep anywhere he pleased; but she'd really only had one day to get reacquainted with him, and she supposed he might chivalrously offer to stay in a guest bedroom for the night. She wondered if she wanted him to.

At the door to the master bedroom, Alex stopped walking. Cassie stepped away from him, her arms pressed to her sides. She could not bring herself to look at Alex, whose questions, even in the silence, seemed to fill the hallway.

He tipped her chin up and kissed her gently. 'Good night,' he said, and then he turned toward a guest room a few doors down.

Cassie watched him for a moment, then walked into the bedroom and closed the door. She pulled her shirt over her head and stepped out of her shorts, tossing them on the four-poster bed en route to the bathroom. Stripping off her underwear, she stood in front of the mirrors that lined an entire wall beside the sink. She cupped her hands over her breasts and frowned at the small swell of her stomach. She couldn't imagine what had attracted Alex Rivers.

She picked up the bottles and jars that dotted the countertop – facial creams and exfoliating scrubs and clear astringents that seemed to belong in equal proportion to Alex and herself. She had already brushed her hair and washed her face when she realized there was no toothpaste. There were two toothbrushes – one green, one blue – and she didn't know which one was hers, either.

She checked in the cabinets that were recessed into the walls, but all she could find were pale peach towels and two thick terry cloth bathrobes. She wrapped one around herself, rubbing her hands down the heavy brushed cotton. Maybe Alex had tooth-paste in *his* bathroom, and surely he'd want his toothbrush.

She didn't know which room he had gone into, and she was about to knock on random doors when she heard him speaking a little farther down the hall. 'Life's but a walking shadow.' The door was ajar, and in the reflection of the bathroom mirror she saw Alex standing over the sink, his eyes hollow. 'A poor player that struts and frets his hour upon the stage,' he murmured, his voice no louder than a whisper. 'And then is heard no more.'

Stunned, Cassie clutched the toothbrushes in her hand and leaned against the doorframe to see a little better. This was not Alex. He had transformed himself into a man beaten, a man who saw his life for what it would become – a flash in someone else's memory, then something forgotten.

Cassie fought back the urge to push the door open and wrap her own hope tight around him. She did not know this new stranger, she knew him even less than she knew Alex, but she understood that she had come to help.

She thought about what Alex had said at the police station, the terror in his voice: *You don't know what it was like to lose you.* And she began to see that the famous Alex Rivers came undone just as easily as the next person.

Cassie took one step forward and Alex opened his eyes, seeing her reflection. He was Alex again, and smiling, but in the darker gradients of his eyes she could see the terror and the numbness of Macbeth. She wondered if he had always been like that, if every character became a tiny part of him. She knew that actors, in some part, had to draw and embellish on their own experi-ence, and the thought of so much despair buried somewhere in Alex wrenched her. 'Where do you get it? All that pain?'

He stared at her, shaken by her second sight. 'From myself.'

She moved first, or maybe he did, but then he was holding her and opening the tie of the robe, running his hands up and down her sides. The toothbrushes fell to the floor and Cassie wound her fingers in his hair, burying her face in the hollow of his shoulder. She inched her hands down his back as if she were feeding a seam, bunching the fabric of his shirt until her hands burned the skin at his waist.

He kissed hungrily, bumping them against walls and door-frames as he pushed his way back toward the master bedroom. Cassie fell against the bed, and he pulled apart the sides of her heavy robe, pinning her arms while the moon danced over her skin. His tongue traced the bend of her jaw, the curves below her breasts, the white lines of her thighs.

Cassie opened her eyes, dazed by the image of his body over hers. Alex pressed his lips to her stomach. 'Beautiful,' he said.

He's acting.

As it had earlier that day, the thought came out of nowhere, and when it took root in her mind she began to struggle. But Alex's weight was on her, pressing. He cradled her face in his hands and kissed her so honestly she thought she would shatter. And then she remembered the spell he had woven between them that afternoon; the emptiness that had opened like a raw wound in her own stomach when she heard him speak as Macbeth.

The moment they came together, Cassie understood why they belonged to each other. He filled her, and she took away his scars. Cassie wrapped her arms around Alex's neck, surprised by the tears that leaked from the edges of her eyes. She turned her face to the open window, breathing in the sweet mix of herself and Alex and endless ocean.

She was drifting off to sleep when Alex's voice slipped over her. 'You don't have to get your memory back, Cass. I know who you are.'

'Oh?' she said, smiling. She drew Alex's arm around her. 'Who am I?'

She felt Alex's peace curl against her like a benediction. He pulled her back against his front, into the place where she just fit. 'You're my other half,' he said.

Chapter Five

I n another time and place, Will Flying Horse would have been a Dreamer.

He was eleven when his eyes opened in the middle of the night, seeing and not seeing at the same time. It was summertime, and outside the cicadas sang in the quiet of the half moon. But Will's head screamed with the thunder, and when his grandparents rushed to the side of his bed, they could see violent blue bolts of lightning reflected in his pupils. Cyrus Flying Horse reached across the glowing blanket of his grandson's bed to grasp his wife's hand. 'Wakan,' he murmured. 'Sacred.'

Although many things had changed for the Sioux over the years, certain habits died hard. Cyrus was a man who had been born on a reservation, who had seen the development of television and automobiles, and who, a month later, would watch a man walk on the moon. But he also remembered the things his father had told him about the Sioux who had visions. To dream of the thunder was powerful. If the dream was ignored, one could be struck dead by lightning.

Which was why, one morning in 1969, Will Flying Horse's grandfather took him to see the shaman, Joseph Stands in Sun, about becoming a Dreamer.

Joseph Stands in Sun was older than the earth, or so it was rumored. He sat outside with Cyrus and Will on a long, low bench that ran the entire length of his log cabin. As he spoke, he whittled, and Will watched the wood as it first took the shape of a dog, then an eagle, then a beautiful girl, changing with every brush of the shaman's hands. 'In the days of my grandfather,' Joseph said, 'a boy like you would search for a vision when he was ready to be treated like a man. And if he dreamed of the thunder, he would become a *Heyoka*.' Joseph peered down at Will, and for the first time Will noticed that the man's eyes were different from any other eyes he'd ever seen. There were no irises at all. Just black, fathomless pupils. 'Do you know this, boy?'

Will nodded; it was all his grandfather had talked about on the walk over to the shaman's cabin. A hundred years earlier, the Heyokas had been tribal clowns, men who were expected to behave strangely. Some moved only backward, some spoke in a different tongue. They dressed in rags and slept without blankets in the winter, wrapped themselves in thick buffalo skins in the summer. They would dip their hands in boiling water and pull them out unscarred, proving they were more powerful than other men. Sometimes they received a vision from the spirits, warning of danger or another's death. As Heyokas, they had the power to prevent it; but because they were Heyokas, they'd receive nothing for themselves in return for their efforts. Will had listened patiently to his grandfather, and the whole time he kept thinking he was damned glad it was 1969.

'Well,' said Joseph Stands in Sun, 'you cannot be a Heyoka; this is the twentieth century. But you will have your thunder dream.'

Three nights later, Will sat naked in a sweat lodge across from Joseph Stands in Sun. He had seen the lodges before; sometimes teenagers built them and smoked peyote in the cramped, curved quarters, getting high enough to run bareassed through the fields and dive into freezing streams. But Will himself had never been inside one. From time to time Joseph poked at the glowing stones that were used to create heat. Mostly he sang and chanted, syllables that swelled and burst like bottle rockets inches before Will's eyes.

As dawn was sneaking across the plain, Joseph took Will to the top of a flat butte. Will would rather have been anywhere else than on a rock ledge, naked, but he knew better than to disgrace his grandfather or Joseph Stands in Sun. Respect your elders: it was the way he'd been taught. Shaking, Will did as he had been told. He faced the sun with his arms outstretched, keeping perfectly still and trying to ignore the grass that whispered around Joseph's legs as he walked away. He stood for hours until the sun began to sink again, and then his legs gave out beneath him. He curled onto his side and began to cry. He felt the butte tremble, the sky melt.

On the second day, an eagle flew over his head from the east. Will watched it circle, moving so slowly that for entire minutes it seemed to be suspended just an arm's length away. 'Help me,' he whispered, and the eagle flew through him. 'You have chosen a life that is difficult,' it cried, and then it disappeared.

It might have been hours that passed; it might have been days. Will was so hungry and faint he had to force air in and out of his lungs. In the moments his mind was clear, he cursed his grandfather for believing in this kind of crap; he cursed himself for being so easily led. He thought of school baseball tryouts that past spring, of the *Playboy* he had hidden under his mattress, of the tingling smell of his mother's Pond's cold cream. He thought of anything that seemed leagues apart from the Sioux way of life.

We are coming, we are coming. The words whistled over the plain, wrapping themselves around Will's neck and drawing him to his feet. Directly overhead was a dark, roiling cloud. Exhausted, starving, delirious, he threw back his head and opened his arms, willing a sacrifice.

When the thunder began in his head, he realized he was no longer on the ground. High above, and peering down, Will saw the girl. She was small and thin and she was running in a snowstorm. From time to time the blizzard winds would sweep around her, blocking her from Will's view. He thought she was running away from someone or something, but then he saw her stop. She stood at the heart of the storm, arms outstretched. All the time, she had been trying to find the center.

'Help her,' Will said, and he heard the words echoed a hundred times around him. He was standing on the ground again. He knew he would remember none of this. He knew that even as a man, this would be the nightmare that tugged at his consciousness in the heavy minutes after waking.

When the sky shattered and the rain came, Will screamed into the wind. Eyes wide, he watched lightning crack the night in two, splitting his world into equal halves that rocked, broken shells, at his feet.

Even the sun loved Alex. Cassie touched her fingers to his jaw, mesmerized by the fact that the one sliver of morning light in the bedroom had managed to fall directly over his sleeping form. His skin was dark, shadowed by beard, marked just below his chin with a tiny curved scar. Cassie tried to remember how he had hurt himself. She watched his eyes shift beneath his lids and wondered if he was dreaming of her.

She curled herself out of the bed, careful not to wake him. Smiling, she hugged her arms around herself, thinking that she was quite rightfully the envy of every woman in America. If she had had any doubts about the validity of her marriage to Alex, they were gone now. Two people could not make love like that without a history. Cassie laughed. If her heart stopped beating that very second, she could say she'd lived a fine life.

It is a good day to die. The words stopped her, and a shiver ran down her body before she realized they had not been spoken out loud. Recovering, she padded into the bathroom and stared into the mirror, touching her fingers to her swollen lower lip.

A lecture. It had been the opening line to a lecture she'd heard by a colleague at UCLA. Cassie let her hands drop to the marble sink basin, sighing with relief as she realized she was not facing an omen, but a genuine memory. It was a course on Native American culture, and that phrase was part of the ritual prayer spoken by tribal warriors of the plains before riding off to do battle. Cassie remembered telling the professor he sure knew how to draw a crowd.

She wondered what Will was doing now. It was Thursday morning; he'd probably be on his way to work. He had left her his phone numbers. Maybe later she'd call him at the station, tell him she lived in a castle in Malibu, mention she was flying to Scotland.

Cassie brushed her teeth and dragged a comb through her hair, careful to place each item back on the counter quietly so that Alex wouldn't stir. She tiptoed back into the bedroom and sat on a chair in the corner.

Alex was snoring lightly. She watched his chest rise and fall a few times, then stood up and walked to the closet across the room that held all of his clothes. She pulled open the door and drew in her breath.

Alex's closet was twenty times neater than her own. On the floor, on little shoe trees, were lines of sneakers and Italian loafers and black patent leather formal dress shoes. A hanging closet organizer proudly displayed folded sweaters, Shetland and Norwegian on one side and cotton on the other. His shirts stood stiffly on cedar hangers. A lingerie chest tucked into the corner of the walk-in closet was lined with neatly folded silk boxers and socks – arranged in separate drawers by their uses.

'My God,' Cassie whispered. She ran a fingertip over the line of shirts, listening to the music of the hangers batting each other. Neatness was to be expected, especially if one had a good house-keeper. Something, though, something else made this closet cross the line between fastidious and obsessive.

The sweaters. Not only were they segregated by material and folded neatly, they were arranged in color order. Like a rainbow. Even the patterned sweaters seemed to have been placed by predominant color.

She should have laughed. After all, this was odd to the point of being funny. This was something to joke about.

But instead Cassie felt tears squeeze from the corners of her eyes. She knelt before the rows of shoes, crying in near silence, pulling a sweater from its appropriate spot and holding it to her mouth to muffle the sounds she made. She bent over, her stomach knotting, and she told herself she was losing her mind.

It was the stress of the last few days, she thought as she wiped her cheeks. Cassie walked back to the bathroom and closed the door. She ran the water until it was so cold it numbed her wrists, and then she splashed some onto her face, hoping to start over.

For days, they had been talking about the blizzard. It was going to hit sometime after three on Friday. It was going to be the storm of the century. Fill your bathtubs with water, the weatherman said. Buy batteries and firewood. Find your flashlights.

The only thing that could have been better, Cassie decided, would be if the blizzard hit on Sunday, so school would be canceled the next day.

Cassie walked into the kitchen. She had been at Connor's all afternoon but had promised her mother she'd return before the first flakes fell. Cassie's mother was terrified of snow. She had grown up in Georgia and had never seen snow until she moved to Maine when she got married. Rather than being efficient about a winter storm – like Connor's mother, who had taken out candles and bought extra gallons of milk to store in the drifts – Aurora Barrett sat at the kitchen table with wide eyes, listening to the weather reports on her transistor radio and waiting to be buried alive.

The one thing Aurora did like about nor'easters was that they provided a chance to accuse her husband of everything that had gone wrong in her life. Cassie had grown up understanding that her mother hated Maine, that she hadn't wanted to move there, that she didn't want to be a baker's wife. She still dreamed of a house with lawns that rolled down to the river, of a latticed bench veiled by cherry trees, of the melting southern sun. While Cassie watched, tucked in the shadows, her mother would rail at Ben and ask just how temporary ten long years in the same godforsaken place could be.

Most of the time her father would just stand there, letting Aurora's anger blow over him. Technically, it *was* his fault: he'd promised Aurora that as soon as it paid to sell the bakery with a tidy profit, they'd move back to her neck of the woods. But the bakery lost money every year, and the truth was, deep down, her father had no intention of leaving New England. Ben had given only one piece of advice to Cassie as she was growing up. *Before you decide what you want to be*, he said, *know where you want to be.*

It did not snow that night until Cassie went to sleep, and when she woke in the morning the world had changed. Outside, a white lawn rolled right up to her bedroom window, and hills and drifts had smoothed the landscape so completely she almost lost her sense of direction. She grabbed an apple and stuffed it in her pocket; then she sat at the kitchen table to pull her boots on.

She heard the argument clearly, although it came from her parents' room upstairs. 'Sell the bakery,' her mother threatened. 'Or I can't tell you what I'll be driven to do.'

Cassie's father snorted. 'What could you possibly be driven to that you don't do already?' Cassie jumped as a blast of wind whitened the window before her. 'Why don't you just go home?'

Go home. Cassie's eyes widened. For a long while there was silence, save the shrieks and moans of the storm. Then she heard her mother's exit line. 'I'm not feeling well now. Not well at all.' And after that came the unmistakable ting of the bourbon decanter Aurora kept on her vanity being opened. The more she drank, the less Cassie's father could tolerate her. It was a vicious cycle.

'Jesus Christ,' Cassie's father said tightly, and then he thundered down the stairs. He was dressed as she was, ready to brave the blizzard. He glanced at Cassie and touched her cheek, almost an apology. 'Take care of her, will you, Cass?' he said, but before she could answer, he left.

Cassie finished lacing up her boots and cooked an egg, soft-boiled, just the way her mother liked. She carried it up on a plate with a piece of toast, figuring if her mother had something else in her stomach, it might not be so bad today.

When Cassie cracked the door open, Aurora was lying across the bed, her arm flung over her eyes. 'Oh, Cassie,' she whispered. 'Honey, please. The *light*.'

Cassie obediently stepped inside, shutting the door behind her. She smelled the cloying sweetness of the bourbon hovering at the edges of the room, mingling with traces of her father's rage.

Aurora took one look at the breakfast tray Cassie had set down and started to cry. 'Did he tell you where he went? He's out there, in this, this *blizzard*—' She jerked her arm toward the window to prove her point. Then she rested her forehead against her hand, rubbing the bridge of her nose. 'I don't know why this happens. I just don't know why.'

Cassie took one look at her mother's eyes, red-rimmed and raw, and she planted her hands on her hips. 'Get up.'

Aurora turned toward her daughter and blinked. 'Pardon me?'

'I said get up.' She was only ten, but she had grown old long ago. Cassie pulled her mother off the bed and started handing her clothes: a turtleneck, a sweater, bulky socks. After a moment of disbelief, Aurora began to follow her, silently accepting what she offered.

When Cassie opened the front door, Aurora took a step back. The chill of winter followed her inside. 'Go,' Cassie commanded. She jumped into the snow, grinning for a moment as the drifts hollowed up to her thighs. She turned to her mother. 'I mean it.'

It took fifteen minutes to get Aurora more than five feet away from the front porch. She was shivering and her lips were nearly violet, unaccustomed as she was to being outside in a storm.

The wind ripped Cassie's hat off and sent it dancing over the snow. She saw her mother bend down, like a child, and touch the drifts.

Cassie scooped a mittenful of snow and rounded it into a neat ball. 'Mom,' she yelled, a minute's warning, and then she threw it as hard as she could.

It hit Aurora in the shoulder. She stood perfectly still, blinking, unsure what she'd done to deserve that.

Cassie leaned down and made a pile of snowballs. She tossed one after another at her mother, leaving her mark on Aurora's shoulder and breast and thigh.

Cassie had never seen anything like it. It was as if her mother had no idea what was expected of her. As if she had no idea what to do. Cassie clenched her hands at her sides. 'Fight back!' she yelled, her words freezing in the cold. 'Goddammit! Fight back!'

She leaned down again, more slowly this time, waiting for her mother to copy her movements. Aurora was sluggish with alcohol, and she stumbled as she straightened, but in her palm she held a snowball. Cassie watched as her mother wound her arm back and sent the snow flying.

It hit her square in the face. Cassie sputtered and wiped the ice from her eyelashes. Her mother was already building a small arsenal. In the blinding white, Aurora's eyes didn't look nearly as red; in the frigid cold, her body was starting to move with a little more rhythm.

Cassie strained her ears to catch a sound over the howl of the wind. It was clear and fine, her mother's laugh, and it got louder and lighter as it broke free from where it had been locked. Smiling, Cassie whirled in the snow, arms outstretched, and offered herself up to the soft, sweet blows.

Whenever Will woke up with the blankets knotted at his hips and his chest soaked with sweat, he knew he'd been having the thunder dream. But he did not dwell on the details; in fact, over the years, even though the number of dreams increased, he found it easier and easier to dismiss them. He'd get up and shower, sloughing off with the sweat the memories that bound him to the Sioux.

Having been scheduled for the evening shift on Thursday, Will slept in and dreamed of the thunder until the phone jolted him awake. 'This is Frances Bean at the library,' a voice said. 'We have the materials you requested.'

'I didn't request any materials,' Will started to mumble, stretching to place the receiver back in its cradle.

'. . . anthropology.'

The word was all he heard, faint and fading, and he pulled the phone back to his ear.

The library was small and dark and quiet as a tomb on a Thursday morning. After identifying himself at the front desk, Will was handed a sheaf of papers secured with a rubber band. 'Thanks,' Will said to the librarian, moving to a spot where he could read Cassie's articles.

Two were from technical journals. The third was from *National Geographic*, and it was composed of dozens of photographs of the illustrious Dr Cassandra Barrett at the Tanzania site that had yielded the hand. Will quickly read the anthropological significance of the hand and its stone tool, but found nothing Cassie hadn't mentioned. He skimmed ahead to the paragraphs that mentioned Cassie herself.

'Dr Barrett, young enough to look more like one of the UCLA students she often brings on excavations than the head scientist, admits she's more comfortable on a muddy site than on the lecture circuit.' Will mouthed the words silently, staring at a photograph on the facing page of Cassie bent over the ground, dusting off half of a long, yellow bone. Will skipped to the final line of the copy: 'In a field dominated by men, Dr Barrett seems to emerge as a leader, *hands* down.'

'Patronizing bastard,' he murmured. He scanned the page, looking for another picture of Cassie. Seeing none, he flipped back to the beginning of the article. On page 36 of the magazine was a photo of the hand itself; and spread beneath it for comparison was Cassie's hand. Another picture of her took up the rest of the page. She was caught in shadow, with the sun behind her the way all those *National Geographic* photographers liked, and her chin was tilted up just the slightest bit. Will touched his thumb to her throat. The photo was too dark to show her eyes. He would have given anything to see her eyes.

He wondered how a woman perfectly at home in the African grasslands could also be happy being hounded by paparazzi at premieres. He wondered how you could go from writing a piece for a scholarly journal to scanning the *Enquirer* for stories that defamed your husband's character. He wondered how the hell Alex Rivers had met Cassandra Barrett; what they did on Sunday mornings; what they talked about at night, wrapped around each other, when no one else was there to listen.

Will left the articles on the table, everything but that one page with the picture of Cassie in silhouette. He folded the picture when the librarian's head was bowed to her computer screen, and then tucked it into the pocket of his jeans. He thought about walking home with it there, knowing it would get soft and faded at the edges until he could barely see Cassie's face at all.

Chapter Six

C assie opened the front door of the apartment, and there stood the most beautiful woman in the world. At first, she could do nothing but stare at the woman's long, shining hair; her spring-green eyes. She wore a silk shirt the color of the inside of a casaba melon, a cashmere beret, a tremendous scarf wrapped twice around to serve as a skirt. 'Can you believe this, Cass?' she said in a thin, reedy voice that didn't match anything else about her. She pushed past Cassie, holding her right arm with her left, as if it were something she'd rather be rid of.

The woman's arm was encased from wrist to elbow in a black plaster cast. 'Tell me,' the woman whined. 'What am I supposed to do about Clorox?'

'Clorox?' Cassie murmured, stumbling up the stairs behind her and watching this stranger pour a glass of orange juice from her own refrigerator.

The woman smirked. 'What's the matter? Alex have you up half the night talking about himself again?'

Cassie's hands clenched defensively at her sides. She did not know who this woman was, but Alex had been incredibly considerate. Yesterday while Cassie slept on the beach, he'd had John, his driver, bring over every photo album and slide carousel that could be found at the house. When she'd awakened, Alex had sat beside her in the dark, quiet library in the apartment. He had connected names with unfamiliar faces, sketched a past for Cassie in simple lines. He had added long descriptions of the minutes that had mattered, and Cassie had leaned against the easy comfort of Alex's shoulder, closed her eyes, and watched her life explode with shape and color.

The woman drained her glass of orange juice, sat down on a tall maple stool, and wrapped her legs around it. Cassie narrowed her eyes, trying to recall a picture Alex had showed her yesterday from an album she'd put together in college. 'Didn't you used to be blond?' she said.

The woman wrinkled her nose. 'Like a zillion years ago. Jesus,' she said. '*What* has gotten into you?'

Alex crept up so quietly behind Cassie that the only indication she had of his approach was the darkening of the woman's eyes. He was wearing only a towel knotted around his waist. 'Ophelia,' he said coolly, tossing an arm around Cassie. 'Nothing quite like seeing you first thing in the morning.'

'Yeah,' Ophelia snorted. 'The pleasure is mine.'

Fascinated, Cassie watched them, glancing at Ophelia again. No wonder she hadn't felt threatened. The most beautiful woman Cassie had ever seen had shown up on her doorstep, but she paid as much attention to Alex as she did to her orange juice, and Alex only wanted to leave.

Alex pointed to her black cast. 'Tendinitis? Overexertion? Some other occupational hazard?'

'Fuck you,' Ophelia said lightly. 'I slipped on a sidewalk.'

Alex shrugged. 'Could have been worse.'

'Worse? I'm supposed to be shooting a commercial next week, a *national* commercial for Clorox, my right arm pouring bleach into a damn measuring cup—'

'You're an actress too?'

Cassie's quiet question stopped Ophelia's tirade. She flicked her eyes toward Alex. 'What the hell did you do to her?'

Alex smiled at Cassie, reassuring her. 'You ever read the papers, Opie, or is that past your level of education?'

'Reading gives you crow's feet. I watch the news on TV.'

Alex leaned against the marble island in the center of the kitchen, his arms crossed over his chest. 'Cassie got into some kind of accident last Sunday and hit her head. She was found by a cop in a graveyard, and she didn't remember her name. She's still just getting her memory back, in bits and pieces.'

Ophelia's eyes widened until Cassie could see a ring of white around the green. Then she turned to Alex. 'How convenient for you,' she said. 'No doubt you've painted yourself as a saint.'

Alex ignored Ophelia's comment, leaned over, and kissed Cassie's forehead. 'Her name's Ophelia Fox, and it's not her real one – but then there isn't too much of her that's real anymore. She's a hand model; she was your best friend in college and your roommate when we first met, and as far as I can tell, she's the only character flaw I've ever found in you.' He tightened the towel around his waist and headed toward the stairs. 'And Ophelia,' he said, grinning, 'if you're real nice to me, I'll autograph your cast.'

Cassie wondered how an anthropology major would have ever met anyone like Ophelia Fox, but before she could even put the question into words, Ophelia came toward her. She ran her long, tapered fingers over the fading cut at Cassie's temple. 'Thank God,' she said. 'I don't think you'll scar.'

Cassie burst out laughing. That had been the least of her worries. She stepped back from Ophelia, scrutinizing her face, this time for recognition. 'You're beautiful,' she said honestly.

Ophelia waved her hand in the air, dismissing the compliment. 'My eyes are too close together and my nose twists a half-centimeter to the right.' She held out her good hand, pale, nearly hairless, capped by five sculptured nails with white moon tips. 'Now *these* are beautiful. Each time, they use a little bit more of me. The last ad got up to my shoulder, so I figure it's only a matter of time.'

Even Alex, who Cassie figured was as big a star as they came, wasn't as wrapped up in himself as Ophelia. But she looked so serious, holding her hand out and flexing it just so, that Cassie could only smile. 'Can I get you something else?' she said, pointing to the empty juice glass.

Ophelia walked toward a cabinet and stuck her hand inside, rummaging and coming up with an English muffin. 'I'll get it. I know my way around.'

'Good,' Cassie said. 'Maybe you can give me a tour.'

Ophelia turned away from the toaster, anxiety drawing her features tight. 'God, Cass, how long is it going to take? It must be awful.'

Cassie shrugged. 'I've got Alex here.'

'Fat lot of help *he'll* be,' Ophelia muttered.

Cassie faced the counter and began to cut a strawberry into eight tiny slices. She cut methodically, listening for the click of the blade against the marble with each slice. 'Why do you hate each other?' she asked.

Cassie couldn't be sure if Ophelia didn't want to answer the question, or if she hadn't heard it. 'Butter?' Ophelia said. She closed her eyes as if divining its location, and then opened a compartment of the refrigerator. 'Ah,' she said. She tried to hold the muffin with her bad arm while she spread the butter with the other hand, but the muffin kept slipping out of her grasp.

'Here,' Cassie said. 'Let me do it.'

She handed half to Ophelia, who was staring at her forearm as if it were a foreign object. 'I can't put any pressure on it yet. It's driving me up the wall. And it itches like hell.'

'How did you get hurt?'

She shrugged. 'It was the end of a perfectly horrible day. I was at this photo shoot for *Parents* magazine, and I'd spent the afternoon holding a series of naked three-month-olds in the air—' She reached her arms in front of her as a demonstration. 'Anyway, they were zeroing in on the baby's ass and my hands under its armpits. So this one kid – a boy – starts peeing on me. And I'm wearing that washed silk shirt I got at Versace last month – remember? I showed it to you – and I just *know* the stain isn't going to come out.' She paused, taking a bite of her muffin. 'And then they tell me before I leave that they'll let me know if – if – they decide to use the picture for the next issue. So I step outside and it's raining cats and dogs and I have no umbrella, and next thing I know, I'm lying on the ground in the middle of a mudslide, and my arm is caught underneath me and I'm dying from the pain.' She grinned. 'I did, however, make a date with the doctor in the emergency room.' She turned to Cassie. 'Did you know that they don't just make white casts anymore? You have a choice of anything – pink, green, even fuchsia. I thought I'd go with black, you know, because it matches most of my night outfits.'

Cassie leaned against the counter, exhausted from Ophelia's explanation. 'Enough about me,' Ophelia said. She smiled, and Cassie could see what she meant – her nose was a little bit off center. 'How are your bones holding up?'

'Bones?'

'God, Cass, all you've been talking about is your field class this semester. I figured it was lodged so deep in your mind that a coma couldn't make you forget. You're going to . . . let me think . . . Kenya, I believe, in May, with the seniors.'

'I haven't been to UCLA yet. Alex has to get back to *Macbeth*, so we decided I'd take a leave of absence and go with him.'

'We decided?' Ophelia shook her head. 'You mean *he* decided. You *never* go on location with Alex. Not during the school year, anyway. You must have knocked out more than your memory, because the Cassie I know couldn't stand to miss two lectures in a row without having apoplexy.' Ophelia smiled. 'Maybe I should take you to the university today. Lock you in your dusty old office for an hour or two with your research, and then let Alex drag you kicking and screaming to Scotland.'

Cassie felt her hand tighten around the knife she was holding. She had no more reason to believe Alex than she had to believe Ophelia, but she did. Cassie swallowed and placed the knife on the kitchen counter beside the cut strawberry. She ran her finger over a red puddle of juice and seeds; the heart of the fruit, the blood. 'Why do you and Alex hate each other?' she asked again.

Ophelia sighed. 'Because Alex and I are too similar to get along. We're at different levels, but we're in the same business. We're both obsessed with work. And we both want you to ourselves.'

Cassie laughed, but the sound seemed to shatter the air around her. 'That's ludicrous,' she said. 'You're my friend. He's my husband. There's plenty of room in my life for both of you.'

Ophelia leaned back against the center island, lifting her face to the skylight overhead. 'Tell that to Alex,' she said. 'From day one, he's been trying to swallow you whole.'

As if he had been eavesdropping, Alex came back from an errand later that morning with a box full of bones. He pretended to stagger under its weight, walking toward Cassie. She sat at the kitchen table, leafing through photo albums, her eyes riveted to a faded picture of a blond boy. He was lean and sinewy, just at the edge of growing up, and his arm was looped over Cassie's neck. She was thirteen, but there was none of that awkward teenage break between boys and girls distancing them. In fact, from the way the picture had been taken, it was difficult to tell where one of them stopped and the other began.

Cassie did not look up, did not notice the wooden box with its scientific packing labels. 'Alex,' she said, 'where does Connor live now? Why don't I keep in touch with him?'

'I don't know. He's the only thing you've ever refused to talk about.'

Cassie touched her finger to a fine line of flyaway hair coming off Connor's cheek. 'It must have been a fight. One of those stupid kids' fights that you feel rotten about for years, but are still too embarrassed about to make right.'

Alex pried open the box. 'I doubt that. You're a fanatic for picking up the pieces.' He tossed several small bone chips into the air, heavy and yellowed, and Cassie caught them like a practiced juggler. 'And here,' he said, 'are some pieces for you to pick up.'

Alex spilled the contents of the box onto the dining room table, obliterating the facing pages of the open photo album. 'Don't say I never bring you anything,' he said, grinning.

Cassie brushed away the soft cotton wool and newspaper used for transport, running her fingertips over the fifty or so fragments of bone. Each was labeled with India ink, left-sloping European handwriting marking the grave, the site, the date of discovery. 'Oh, Alex,' she murmured. 'Where did you get this?'

'Cambridge, England,' he said. 'By way of Cornwall, according to the laboratory I bought it from.'

'You *bought* me a skull?'

Alex ran a hand through his hair. 'You don't know what I had to go through to get them to let me take it home. I had to tell this Dr Bother—'

'Dr *Botner*?'

'Whoever – I had to make a huge "contribution", tell him who you were, and convince him that I was certain you'd wind up sending it back as a museum exhibit, instead of keeping it as a conversation piece in some actor's home.' He absently picked up a piece of cotton wool and strung it apart like taffy. 'And to keep it a *secret*, I had to negotiate this over the telephone in the six minutes you weren't at my side.'

Cassie stared at him. 'You did this yesterday?'

Alex shrugged. 'I bought it when I was in Scotland. But I rushed the shipment yesterday. I didn't know how long it would take you to feel like yourself again, and I wanted it to seem like home.'

Cassie smiled, and as always, he wondered why photographers always rushed to capture his image rather than hers. If his features reflected anything, it was the light given off by Cassie. 'Of course,' she pointed out, 'any other woman would have been satisfied with roses.'

Alex watched Cassie's hands automatically begin to sort the pieces of the skull in size order. 'I wouldn't trade you for the world,' he said.

Cassie had been unwrapping the mandible. She paused, staring down at her hands. Then she stood and leaned forward to kiss Alex. 'I must be the luckiest person in California,' she said.

Alex let himself fall into her, grasping at her words and the electric feel of her skin against his. He did not know what to say to her; he never knew what to say; he was used to speaking what others had written. He wished he'd learned long ago how to put into words the feeling that if she was gone, if she ever left, he would cease to exist. But he couldn't tell her, so he did what he always did: he slipped into character, the first one that came, willing to do anything other than face the limits of himself.

He broke away and changed the mood: light comedy, now a clown. Glancing down at the scatter of bones, Alex raised his eyebrows. 'You're luckier than *he* was,' he said.

He left Cassie separating her bones into five lines, plus the mandible, and went downstairs to get the second half of her present: the Durofix and pillars of plasticine, the sandbox she'd use to support pieces of the skull while putting it together. He'd taken all this from her laboratory at the house.

By the time he returned, Cassie had already laid out several pieces of bone, end to end, and Alex could see how they would easily fit together. 'The packing label says he's from the Dark Ages,' Cassie said. 'I've named him Lancelot.' She reached into the box Alex held, pulling out the Durofix and laying a thin line of the glue along one edge of bone. Setting it sideways in the sandbox, she affixed the second piece, then built up a buttress of sand to hold the pieces until the fixative dried. 'I'm going to put the vault together, and then do the face separately if I can. While they're drying I can set the condyles of the mandible into the glenoid cavities to see if the teeth occlude correctly before I permanently set the face.'

Alex shook his head. 'And they say people can't understand *Shakespeare*.'

Cassie smiled, but did not look up from her work. 'Well, no one has to understand what I'm saying. He's my audience' – she ran a finger along Lancelot's jawbone – 'and his hearing is completely shot to hell.'

She worked for an hour, fitting pieces together in a three-dimensional jigsaw puzzle. Alex sat across from her, absolutely stunned.

Cassie peered at him. 'Haven't you ever watched me do this before?' When Alex shook his head, she grinned. 'Do you want to help?'

For a second his eyes gleamed, but then he gently picked up a minute piece of the ancient face and ran his thumb over the spiked edge. 'I wouldn't have any idea what to do,' he said. 'I'd be more of a pain in the ass than anything else.'

'It's easy.' Cassie's small hands guided his to a second piece, and she fitted the edges together in a way that made perfect sense. 'You can glue these two for me.' He stared at the image of her fingers wrapped over his, her palms holding his own, then at the chips of bone. No one would ever think of connecting him with Cassie when they were apart, but once they'd been brought together, they, too, appeared to be an ideal match.

Cassie mistook his silence for confusion. 'Give it a try,' she said. 'It's like a model. You must have done models as a kid.'

As a kid, Alex had spent most of his time alone, daydreaming and exploring his way around the rural outskirts of New Orleans. He preferred to stay hidden, and for hours at a time he'd climb cherry trees to read books he'd pinched from the public library: *Huckleberry Finn*, *The Red Badge of Courage*, *The Joy of Sex*.

Alex's parents hated each other but cared too much about what other people thought to get a divorce. His mother turned away from him because he looked too much like his father; his father turned away from him because Alex was not the sort of son

Andrew Riveaux had dreamed of: one who willingly waded the bayou with him, hunting grouse; one who could shoot a perfect round of trap and hold his whiskey afterward with the boys.

On Alex's twelfth birthday, Andrew Riveaux bought his son a complicated wooden model of a Conestoga wagon, the kind that had crossed the Oregon Trail Alex was learning about in school. 'I'll help you with that, boy,' his father said, and Alex believed that this promise of time spent together was even better than the present.

Alex opened the box and carefully laid out the smooth wooden parts, the metal rings that would brace the covering of the wagon. 'Not so fast,' his father said, slapping away his hands. 'You got to earn the parts.'

The wagon was built in accordance with the number of times Alex acted, in his father's eyes, like a man. He shot his first goose, carrying it home by its quivering feet and stopping twice to throw up his breakfast, and in return his father helped him structure the box of the wagon. He sailed a pirogue through the black vines of the bayou after dark, using his sense of smell for direction, and found the shack of the old witch woman his father bought rotgut whiskey from, which won him the model's front seat and the hitch for the horses. He fell out of a tree and broke his leg clear through the skin and did not shed one tear, and that same night his father sat on the edge of his bed to help his trembling fingers stick spokes into four wagon wheels.

Sometime when he was thirteen, he finished the model. It was delicate and perfect, inch for inch a miniature of history. Alex finally glued the muslin wagon cover in place and one hour later took the model out to the woods behind his house and smashed it to pieces with a fallen branch.

'Alex. *Alex.*' He jumped at the sound of Cassie's voice. Her eyes were wide, and she was waving a paper towel in front of him. 'Here,' she said. 'You're bleeding all over yourself.'

He looked down at his lap, seeing the fragments of crushed

bone and the cut running down the side of his thumb. 'Jesus,' he said. 'I'm sorry.'

Cassie shrugged, holding the damp towel to his hand, applying pressure. 'They're fragile. I should have told you that.' She smiled hesitantly. 'Guess you aren't aware of your own strength.'

Alex turned away. Cassie had completed the face; it stared up at him through empty eyes from a bed of sand. He sat silently while Cassie put together the back of the skull. Almost all of the pieces were there, and he watched her neatly placing four fragments around the spot where the bone he had broken would have fit.

He stood up, mumbling something even he did not understand. All he knew was that he had to get out of that room before Cassie finished. He wouldn't be able to see the skull anymore as a sum of all those parts; instead his eyes would be drawn to what was missing, to what he had ruined.

'We're going to rob a graveyard,' Cassie had announced, 'on Halloween.' It was two weeks away, and it was the perfect dare, and Connor never turned those down. She had been trying to find something to get Connor's mind off his worries – his father had lost his job and had taken to spending his days in the garage with a fifth of scotch, and it was becoming increasingly clear that Connor wouldn't be able to afford college, although he was desperate to become a veterinarian. Cassie had seen the spark in his eyes, and she knew she'd hooked him.

So now, Halloween night, they were sneaking out at midnight. They had done their research: seniors at school told them that the police sat up every year at St Joseph's but the pet cemetery off Mayfair Place was unguarded.

They stole down the street like cats, keeping to the shadows and holding their knapsacks away from their bodies so that the trowels and picks didn't bang together. They walked past evidence of the night that had already ended: trees strung with toilet paper, rural mailboxes dripping with eggs. Cassie walked ahead, and Connor watched her footsteps in the moonlight, careful to step exactly where she had.

The pet cemetery was a small gated area bordered by silvery pines. Everyone in town had buried something here – a cat, a guinea pig, a goldfish – although many of the graves were unmarked. By silent agreement, Connor and Cassie moved toward one of the few headstones in the cemetery. It heralded the resting place of Rufus, an unpopular mastiff that had been the only crea- ture to escape the sharp side of old lady Monahan's tongue. Rufus had been dead for six years, and Mrs Monahan for three, so Cassie didn't really think they'd be offending anyone by digging up the dog's bones.

'You ready?' Connor was looking around nervously, but he already had his pick in hand. Cassie nodded. She pulled out her tools and waited for Connor to strike the first blow.

The dog was buried so deep that Cassie wondered if there'd been a coffin. The Monahans had been the richest family on the lake, after all, and Rufus was their only child. She scraped at the soft earth with her hands, shoveling out what Connor loosed.

He was standing four feet into the pit, his legs braced on the sides of the dug walls for fear of stepping right on Rufus when he least expected it. He leaned over and chipped the edge of his trowel against something unforgiving. 'Holy shit,' he said.

Cassie wiped the sweat out of her eyes. 'You find it?'

Connor swallowed. He had turned a shade of gray. Cassie reached out a hand to pull him up, and when he was on level ground again, he fell to his knees to vomit. He wiped his hand across his mouth.

Cassie stood with her hands on her hips. 'For God's sake, Connor,' she said. 'How're you ever going to sew a dog's intes- tines back together if you can't even handle seeing them already dead?' Shaking her head, she leaped into the pit, wincing a little when her sneaker struck bone. She leaned over and started pulling the thin white curves up, one by one, tossing them inches from Connor's feet. In a way she was surprised. She'd been thinking of the skeleton as one big piece, like in the cartoons, not something that time could break into fragments.

Finally, she reached through the dirt and pulled out the dog's skull. Bits of hair still covered the crown. 'Awesome,' she breathed, rolling it out of the pit toward Connor.

He was sitting with his back to the grave, his eyes shut tightly. 'You ready to go?' he said, his voice scratchy and rough.

Cassie felt a grin split her face. 'Jeez, Connor,' she said. 'If I didn't know you better I'd think you were scared shitless.'

Connor stood up in one fluid motion, turning and grasping Cassie's arms with a strength just beneath the point of pain. He shook her so hard her head snapped back. 'I am *not* scared,' he said.

Cassie narrowed her eyes. Connor never treated her like this. He never hurt her. He was the only one who didn't. Angry tears burned under her lids. 'Coward,' she whispered, saying anything that would strike his heart and make him sting as badly as she did.

They stayed like that until time stopped, and all Cassie could feel was the cut of Connor's fingernails in her skin and the heat of his gaze as it swept her face. A tear streaked out of the corner of her eye, and Connor let go of one of her shoulders to wipe it away.

He had never touched her like that, either. So softly that she wondered if she had imagined it, or if it had been the night air. 'I'm not a coward,' he whispered, coming so close the words fell onto her own lips.

Neither of them knew how to kiss. They both turned in one direction, then the other, and finally they came together in a quiet sigh. Heat funneled up through Cassie, burning her fingertips where she touched Connor's shoulders. She was certain she would leave her marks.

She opened her mouth to him, and when his tongue touched hers, all she had the power of mind to think was, *He tastes the same as me*.

Years later, when Cassie thought about her profession, she tried to understand what exactly had made her choose anthropology. Unconsciously, she had made her decision at age fourteen, that night at the pet cemetery. But she never knew if it was because of the marvel the bones themselves held for her, or because of a first kiss under moonlight, or simply in tribute, since it was the last time she saw Connor alive.

They stood in the cemetery for an hour, learning each other all over again. The moon turned them white, two ghosts lost in a kiss, glowing bones at their feet. Then they walked slowly back to Cassie's house, joined at the hand, this time with Connor leading.

Chapter Seven

To celebrate the resurrection of Lancelot of the Dark Ages, Alex told Cassie he'd take her out to dinner. 'Le Dôme,' he said, dialing a number he'd memorized. He glanced at Cassie. 'You might want to straighten up a little.'

Of course she had planned to, she'd been buried in sand and plasticine all day; but it still hurt to know that Alex had found something wrong with her.

'Louis? Alex Rivers. Yes, tonight; nine o'clock. Just my wife and I. In the back, please.' He gently placed the phone into the receiver and lifted the skull from the dining room table, bending the jaw back and forth in mock conversation like a deadly parody of Señor Wences. ''S all right?' he mimicked.

Cassie smiled, she couldn't help it. ''S all right.' She wrapped her arms around herself, wondering what she would find in her closet to wear.

But to her surprise, Alex followed her into the bedroom and opened her closet. He found a three-piece gray silk suit, cut in simple lines, and tossed it onto the bed. 'There you go,' he said, as if he did this all the time.

Cassie leaned against the doorframe of the bathroom and folded her arms. 'Do I get to pick for you, too?' she asked dryly.

Alex glanced up, confused, as if he was only just realizing what his actions must look like. 'You *always* ask me to pick,' he said. 'You say I know what people are wearing these days.' He began to put the ensemble back into the closet.

Cassie bit her lip. 'No,' she said, stepping forward. 'I like it. I mean, I didn't know. It's fine.'

She scrubbed herself in the shower until her skin was iridescent and her hair was laced with the scent of lilies. She sang 'Hey Jude' at the top of her lungs and wrote her name in the steamed glass. When she opened the door, Alex was standing there, looking ethereal in the hot mist and smoky mirrors. He was naked, and this only embarrassed her more. She crossed her arms over her breasts and turned away. 'I didn't know you were in here,' she said.

'I could have heard you singing in San Diego,' Alex said. He smiled and caught her wrists, pulling her hands free. 'I've seen it all before,' he said gently. He wrapped a towel around her hips, pulling her near.

'I thought we were going to dinner,' Cassie said.

'I'm working up an appetite,' Alex said. He traced the edge of her nipple with his tongue. 'I'm a growing boy.'

He could do this to her, start a fever raging and make her blood ache. Cassie reached between them and guided him inside her, scratching at his shoulders in an effort to get closer. At some point the fogged mirrors cleared, and over Alex's bent head she watched them in triplicate, a chimera with tangled arms and legs, heaving and swelled with its own power. Her face was flushed, her damp hair strung around her neck. She reached out toward her reflection. *My God*, she thought. *Is this me?*

An hour later they were at Le Dôme, making their way to a quiet table in the back in between handshakes and promises for lunch and called greetings. For a Thursday night, the restaurant was crowded. Cassie stood nervously behind Alex, her hand curled into his, while he conducted business over other people's dinners. She watched him speak to a studio executive, and it took her several minutes to realize that Alex was carrying on a conversation about the weather in Scotland while the other man was discussing the advantages of syndication. Hollywood did not talk to each other, but rather at each other. Cassie couldn't help but think of three-year-olds who hadn't yet learned to share.

While Alex ordered wine, Cassie screened herself with her menu. She already knew what she was going to have, but she liked being hidden. It seemed as though every table seated either a celebrity trying to look supremely bored or an ordinary person craning his neck to see what Alex Rivers was having for dinner.

Alex pulled the top of her menu down with one finger. He was smiling at her. 'This,' he said, 'is why we don't get out much.'

They had just toasted Lancelot when a woman slinked toward the table sighing Alex's name. Cassie leaned forward, breathless. She had believed Ophelia was beautiful, but nothing could have prepared her for the sight of this woman. Dressed in a floor-length sheer black sheath that wrapped her from her neck to her wrists, she threw her arms around Alex's neck. A slit ran the length of her leg and Cassie noticed she wore no underwear, just thigh-high stockings. 'Where,' she gushed, 'have you been hiding yourself?'

'Miranda,' Alex said, nearly pushing the woman from his lap, 'you remember my wife. Cassie, Miranda Adams.'

Miranda Adams leaned toward her, close enough for Cassie to smell the cloud of alcohol that hovered about her. She straightened, and Cassie was shocked to realize she could see right through the woman's dress. Miranda's nipples were dusky and triangular, and over her left breast was a series of birthmarks, or maybe a tattoo, in the pattern of the constellation Orion.

She assumed Alex and Miranda had worked together, although it was difficult to picture. The only films Cassie could remember starring Miranda Adams had featured her as a bouncy, wholesome virgin.

'We're eating,' Alex said pointedly, and Miranda executed a little pout. She kissed him full on the mouth, leaving a ring of red lipstick that Alex wiped away before she even left the table.

Cassie wondered if Alex had made love to her before coming to Le Dôme just because of scenes like this. He had wanted to, yes, but it seemed that he had also needed her to know that he was hers, no matter what. Even now she could feel patches of her skin that were warmer than others, still glowing with Alex's imprint. 'Is she the one who was in your trailer naked?' Cassie asked.

Alex's jaw dropped. 'Where the hell did you hear that?'

She wasn't sure; she thought she'd read it in a tabloid headline at Trancas Market: ANGEL SETS OUT TO HAVE A DEVIL OF A TIME. She smiled, just to let Alex know it didn't bother her.

'Yes,' he said, 'she was in my trailer, naked, but my assistant Jennifer was the one who found her there.' He leaned toward Cassie and kissed her softly, and they both turned in the direction of a bright camera flash.

'Goddammit,' Alex murmured, clenching his fists around the pristine tablecloth. Cassie thought of the shattered tile in their dining room table, the blood that had run down the side of Alex's hand; she found herself praying that he would not stand up and make a scene just right now. Alex pushed back his chair.

He stopped as Louis, the maître d', walked toward the table where the picture had been snapped and physically hoisted the diner to his feet. It was no one Cassie knew, but she realized that didn't mean much these days. The man had a half-filled plate in front of him, and a camera bag strapped to the back of his seat. Louis escorted him in the direction of the door, and then came to Alex's table, bowing. 'My apologies, Mr Rivers,' he said. He pulled a roll of film from his pocket, unraveling it into a long shiny arc and laying it on the table. 'And with our compliments, another appetizer.'

She ate half of Alex's rack of lamb, and he ate half of her crab. For the most part nobody else bothered them, with the exception of Gabriel McPhee and Ann Hill Swinton, a rare pair of happily married young actors who swung by the table on their way out. Gabriel held their little girl in his arms, shifting her weight from side to side as he said hello to Alex. They talked for a few minutes, until the child started to scream and kick and people began to stare.

As they left, Alex shook his head, as if he needed to become re-accustomed to the quiet. He picked up a spoon and studied his reflection, distorted long and upside down.

'We don't have any children,' Cassie said.

Alex glanced up at her. 'Did you think I was hiding them from you?'

Cassie laughed. 'I was just wondering. I mean, we've been married for three years, and, I don't know, you said I'm thirty—'

'Oh my God,' Alex said. 'Not only do you have amnesia, you've also broken your biological clock.' He grinned at her. 'We might have kids, maybe down the road, but three years isn't that long to get to know each other. Plus, you head down to Africa for a month every summer, which wouldn't be easy with a kid. We decided to wait while our careers settled around us.'

Cassie wanted to ask him why they could afford three residences, but not a nanny. She wanted to ask him what would happen *if*. She thought about Ophelia, earlier that morning, smirking: *You mean* he *decided*.

She lifted her eyes, preparing an argument, but was stopped by the look on Alex's face. His jaw was tight and his skin was unnaturally pale. 'You've been taking your Pill, haven't you? I mean, I never even thought to show you where they are.'

There was no way that Cassie could know he was thinking of his own father, and that damn model wagon, and of the fact that he had sworn off children because he did not want to turn into someone like Andrew Riveaux. Still, in that way she had of sensing his pain, she reached across the table for his hand. 'Of course,' she said, although she had not seen any birth control pills since she'd arrived home. 'We decided.'

Alex took a deep breath. 'Thank God,' he said. He pushed

back his chair and stretched his legs. 'I'm going to go to the bathroom. I don't think anyone will bother you when I'm gone.'

Cassie rolled her eyes. 'I think I can take care of myself.'

Alex stood. 'Sure. Last time I let you out of my sight, you wound up at the LAPD.' He walked through the rows of tables, turning heads. Cassie watched the easy movement of his body and the confidence that clung to him as closely as a shadow.

She was so busy watching Alex that she did not see the man sit down at the table. He was good-looking, though nowhere near Alex's caliber, and slightly shorter and lighter of frame. Cassie smiled shyly. 'Can I help you?'

The man leaned forward and grasped her hand, whispering his lips along the edge of her wrist. 'I've been waiting all night,' he said, and Cassie pulled away.

'I'm afraid I can't remember your name.' Cassie sat as stiffly as possible in the chair, her eyes darting left for Alex's approach. She wanted this man gone by the time Alex got back. She wanted to get rid of him herself.

'I'm devastated. Nicholas. Nick LaRue.' He spoke with a strange accent she could not place, something that was neither Continental nor eastern.

Cassie flashed him her brightest smile. 'Nick, then. I'm afraid Alex and I are on our way out. I'll be happy to tell him you said hello.'

He reached for her wrist, pressing her hand to the table so that pulling away again would attract attention. His other hand began to dance the length of her arm. 'Who said I came to see Alex?' he said.

'Get your fucking hands off my wife.' Alex stood behind her, and Cassie closed her eyes, instinctively sinking toward his heat. Suddenly she sat erect. Nick LaRue. He had been in that movie with Alex, the new one, *Taboo*. Their characters were best friends, partners in a jewelry heist. But she could remember Alex coming home from the set, stalking the house like a panther, anger seething

from his skin. 'He thinks his trailer should be closer to the sound-
stage than mine.' 'He's holding out for top billing.' And what had
she done? She'd poured Alex a drink every night, promised him
that in ten weeks, or eight weeks, or six, he'd never have to work
with Nick LaRue again, and then she'd given him herself to help
him forget.

Alex had taken off his jacket and Cassie felt it draped over
her lap, warmer than his own skin. Nick stood opposite him,
and Cassie stared into his eyes only to see twin images of Alex,
drawn in rage. The diners at the other tables started to file out
of the room like sand in an hour-glass, and sure enough, when
the last one had disappeared the two men each took one step
closer.

In the front of Le Dôme, Louis called the police. He would
certainly not be the one to interfere, and even if he had been a
foot taller and thirty pounds more muscular, he wouldn't have
been able to choose a side. Both Alex Rivers and Nick LaRue were
A-level clients.

Cassie shrank back against the wall. She did not think anyone
had ever fought over her before, and she wasn't sure if she should
be flattered or sickened. She saw Alex's fist swinging forward and
she closed her eyes, knowing anywhere the unmistakable sound
of bone striking bone.

Will liked having the beat on Sunset. He and his partner – a
Hispanic named Ramón Pérez, and this irony did not escape him
– drove for hours at a time down Sunset and back, anticipating
a summons. From time to time there was a drug bust, a construc-
tion detail, an occasional robbery, but more often Will just stared
out the window and waited for action. Yesterday he'd gone into
Cassie's church and lit a candle for her. He sat in a pew in the
back, whispering a one-way conversation to her God that basically
hoped she was doing all right.

'Hey, Crazy,' Ramón said. 'Wake the fuck up.'

Ramón still insisted on calling him Crazy Horse, which Will did not find funny and which he'd warned him against several times, to no avail. 'I wasn't sleeping,' Will said.

'Yeah, well, then tell me where we were just dispatched.'

Will turned his face to stare out the window.

'Le Dôme,' Ramón said. 'Le Goddamn Dôme. Two hot-shit movie stars having a fight.'

Will sat up and pulled his regulation hat low on his head while Ramón read him the off-the-book code on celebrity disturbances. *You don't rough them up. You call them Mr So-and-so. You never bring them down to the station. You don't borrow trouble.*

Le Dôme was a simple little place, but fifty people milled in front of its doors, some spilling into the valet parking lot. Ramón pushed past the crowd into the restaurant, nodding to a small, nervous man in a tuxedo. 'I'm Officer Pérez,' he said. 'What seems to be the problem?'

Will shook his head. Any asshole could follow the sounds of breaking glass and landed punches toward the back of the restaurant. Will walked past the maître d' through the main area of the restaurant until he saw Alex Rivers beating the shit out of his most recent co-star.

He pulled Alex Rivers off Nick LaRue just as Ramón came into the room. 'Get that one,' Will said. He pushed Rivers out of LaRue's line of sight, and then he noticed Cassie. She was pressed against the wall as if she'd been hoping it might swallow her. She looked beautiful, her hair down over her shoulders, her husband's blood spotting her expensive silk blazer.

As she saw Will, she seemed to come to life. She stepped toward them, setting her shoulders beneath Alex's arm to take his weight. She had the grace to blush.

Will smiled at her. 'What are the chances of this happening?' he said, hating himself the minute he spoke, the minute Alex Rivers's eyes slid to Cassie, thinned with suspicion.

'Excuse us,' Cassie murmured, leading Alex toward a chair.

She shrugged out of her jacket and held a white cloth napkin to a gash under Alex's lip. Will watched the slender muscles of her arms.

'You let him sit with you,' Alex sneered. 'You let that piece of shit sit with you.'

Cassie laid her hand on his shoulder, trying to estimate the price of peace. 'Shh,' she said. 'We can talk about it later.' She glanced around the room until she found a waiter. 'Ice,' she commanded.

Alex ran his eyes up and down the length of her body. 'Asking for it,' he said. 'Dressed like a fucking whore.' He tugged her short skirt down where it had ridden up during the confusion, tossed her jacket back to her.

Slowly, she lowered her hands to her sides. She folded the napkin and placed it on the table, slipping her jacket on again and shrinking into the chair beside him.

You don't rough them up.

Ramón walked over to Alex Rivers, addressing him by name and complimenting him on *Taboo*, as if he were just meeting him backstage. He helped Rivers stand and led him over to Nick LaRue, who Will figured either had agreed to apologize or was the biggest fool in California.

Will sat in the chair vacated by Alex Rivers. It was still warm. When Cassie kept looking straight ahead, her brow furrowed like she was working through a puzzle only she could see, Will touched her knee. 'Hey,' he whispered. 'Things are okay?'

Cassie nodded and swallowed hard. 'He was fighting for me,' she said.

Will didn't know what to say to that. He thought of the Xerox of Cassie he had in his wallet, of the day he'd given her back to Alex Rivers. He supposed he would have fought for her too.

Will smiled at her, letting silence soak the space between them. 'I saw pictures of the hand,' he said finally.

Cassie turned her palm over in her lap so it lay facing up.

She flexed the fingers, making a fist, and then stretched them open and stared, as if she was trying to read her own future.

The Riverses' driver barreled into the room, protectively drawing Cassie to her feet and letting her burrow against his side. 'I was getting a pack of Camels over at Nicky Blair's,' he said. 'If I'da known, missus, I woulda been here.'

Alex Rivers turned toward them. John looked from his employer's face to Nick LaRue's. 'Looks like you won, Mr Rivers,' he said.

Alex walked over and grinned. As he bent his forehead to Cassie's, the driver discreetly moved away.

Will didn't. He figured it was still police business, so what the hell. 'I'm sorry,' Alex said to her. 'I didn't mean to jump at you. This was in no way your fault.' He cleared his throat, starting to say something else, but then just shook his head and repeated his first words. 'I'm sorry.'

He kissed her very lightly. When they moved apart Cassie was staring up at Alex like he'd invented the sun.

Cassie glanced at Will as Alex steered her out of the restaurant, but she didn't risk a smile. Will understood. He followed them out the front door, watching as a path parted magically through the crowd. He listened to Alex call out goodbyes to people he knew as if nothing had happened.

You don't borrow trouble.

Cassie was watching him out the rear side window as their Range Rover pulled away; Will was sure of that. He had let her go a second time, but he knew there would be another chance. His grandmother had taught him there was no such thing as coincidence. *There are millions of people in the world*, she had told him, *and the spirits will see that most of them, you never have to meet. But there are one or two you are tied to, and the spirits will cross you back and forth, threading so many knots until they catch and you finally get it right.*

Ramón came outside to stand beside him. 'Unbelievable,' he

said. 'Some poor asshole does that, and he's booked and held on bail. Alex Rivers gets pissed and the whole fucking world stops for him.'

Will turned to his partner. 'What time is it?'

'Almost eleven.'

He had an hour before he went off duty. 'Cover for me,' Will said, and without offering an explanation he started to jog down Sunset. He ran for miles until he came to St Sebastian's. The heavy doors were locked, but he stepped behind the church into the familiar cemetery. This time he did not pray to the Christian God, who had been too slow to act, but to his grandmother's spirits. In the distance he heard thunder. 'Please,' he whispered. 'Help her.'

Chapter Eight

'How could you do this to me?'

The woman's voice shrieked through the receiver, startling Cassie. She let the phone drop between her pillow and Alex's, muffling the scream somewhat, but not enough to keep Cassie from wondering what exactly she *had* done.

Her eyes felt like sand had been ground into them. She rubbed her lids, but that only made it worse. Although Alex had apologized at Le Dôme, when they came home to the apartment last night, he hadn't been speaking to Cassie. He made it patently clear, removing his clothes in silence, locking himself in the bathroom to shower. By the time he'd slipped into bed, Cassie had shut the lights and curled on her side, wanting to cry. But sometime in the middle of the night, Alex had reached for her, his unconscious carrying through what his conscious mind refused to do. He held her tight against him, an embrace that ran the ragged edge of pain.

'Michaela.' Alex's hand groped over Cassie's shoulder in an effort to find the telephone. 'Michaela, shut up.'

Cassie rolled over to face Alex, who was coming awake by degrees. He held the receiver to his ear, and his mouth was drawn in a tight line, bisected by a thin red cut that ran to the cleft of his chin. Near his right eye was a bruise shaped like a tiny penguin, and covering his ribs was a string of black-and-blue welts. Amazingly, he smiled. 'To tell you the truth,' he said into the phone, 'that was the *last* thing on my mind.'

He turned onto his side, closed his eyes, and shook his head. 'Of course,' he murmured. 'Don't I always do what you want?' With a wicked grin, he let the receiver fall back against the pillow and reached his hand toward Cassie. His palm skimmed her breast. Cassie stared at the telephone. She could hear the woman chattering in high rippling notes that reminded her of a xylophone, or maybe parakeets.

Alex had put last night aside as easily as he might have closed the cover of a well-read book. The fight at Le Dôme, the accusations afterward, the dismissal in the quiet of their own bedroom – all this he'd either forgotten or classified as trivial enough to pass over. This, Cassie marveled, was a talent. Imagine: A world without grudges. A world free of guilt. A world where you weren't condemned for the consequences of your actions.

She had spent half the night trying to pinpoint what exactly had made Alex angry at her, so she was more than willing to start with a clean slate. She reached for Alex, trailing her hand down his side and over his hip.

Suddenly he rolled away from her, grabbing the phone and motioning for Cassie to find him a pen. She rummaged in her nightstand and found a grubby pencil and a receipt for something that cost $22.49. Alex flipped the receipt over and began to scribble across it. 'Mmm. Yes. I'll be there. Yeah, you too.'

He threw the pencil across the room and sighed, making the little piece of paper flutter to the edge of the bed. Cassie sat up and reached for it. 'LA County Hospital?' she read. 'Twelve-fifteen, seventh floor?'

Alex covered his eyes and ran his hand down his face. 'Seems that Liz Smith's column starts off with a mention of my . . . disagreement last night with Nick LaRue.' He sat up and walked naked to the window, cantilevering the shade so that the first pink sunlight sliced across his back in parallel lines. 'Michaela's having a fit, because you *don't* attract bad press a month before the Oscars. She's trying to counter-balance the public's impression by throwing some good PR my way. God only knows how she did it at six in the morning, but she's arranged some photo opportunity that involves me and the leukemia patients in the pediatric ward of the hospital.'

Alex walked around the perimeter of the bed to sit beside Cassie. She reached up, touching the bruise on his face. 'Does it hurt?'

He shook his head. 'Not as much as leaving you alone for lunch will.' He looked down, drawing a series of circles on the sheet that covered her thigh. 'Cassie,' he said, 'I want to apologize again. I don't mean to – you know I'm not—' He balled his hand into a fist. 'Hell, sometimes I just explode.'

Cassie held his face between her palms and kissed him gently on the mouth, so that she wouldn't hurt him. 'I know,' she said. She felt something thick swelling up inside of her that caught at the back of her throat, and it took several seconds to realize it was not love but simply relief.

When there was a knock at the door, Alex pulled on a pair of boxer shorts. He opened it to reveal a small, stout woman who looked very familiar to Cassie, although that might have just been her features, because she looked like everyone's grandmother. She had thin brown hair pulled into a knot, eyes the color of old wood, a smile as sad as the rain.

'I heard the telephone ring, Mr Rivers, so I figure maybe this is an early day for you, *sí*?' She deftly moved the lamp to the far side of Alex's nightstand and set down the tray she had been carrying. The *LA Times*, coffee, apple muffins, and something rolled in powdered sugar that smelled like heaven.

Mrs Alvarez. The name echoed through Cassie's head, until she whispered it aloud. 'Mrs Alvarez?' She sat up so quickly the sheet fell away to her waist. This was the Mrs Alvarez who kept the apartment when they were living at the house. Who had more pictures of Jesus in her room than of her own three sons. Who had taught Cassie to make flan and who once, when Alex was away on location, had held Cassie in the dark in this very bed while a nightmare slipped out the window. 'Mrs Alvarez,' she repeated breathlessly, immensely proud of herself.

Alex laughed and sat down beside Cassie, wrapping the sheet around her again. 'Congratulations,' Alex said to Mrs Alvarez. 'With one funnel cake, you managed to do what two days of living with me couldn't.'

Mrs Alvarez blushed, the color spreading from her high collar like a stain. '*No es verdad*,' she said. 'Mrs Rivers, you want I help you pack today?'

Cassie turned toward Alex. She wondered how Mrs Alvarez had known to come back this morning. She herself had forgotten about Scotland. 'It's up to you,' Alex said. 'Although I think you're going to want to take heavier clothes than what you've got here. I'll have John swing by to pick you up around three, and we'll go over to the house. The flight doesn't leave till nine tonight; it's a redeye.'

Mrs Alvarez wrinkled her forehead as she spread a napkin over Cassie's lap, so white she couldn't see its edges against the bedsheet. The housekeeper poured two cups of coffee and added cream to one, handing it to Alex. 'Well,' she said, 'you yell if you change your mind.' Smiling at Cassie, she backed her way out of the room.

Alex fed Cassie a piece of muffin and kissed her hard on the lips. 'So,' he said. 'The prodigal memory returns.'

'In fits and starts,' Cassie admitted. 'Who knows? By the time we get to the house, I may even be able to find my own way to the bedroom.'

Alex skimmed the front page of the Friday paper and then handed it to her. 'I'm going to take a run down the beach,' he said, reaching under the covers to find her leg. 'Feel free to stay in bed until I get back.'

She pretended to read the national news while Alex was stretching his hamstrings, but the minute he closed the door behind him, she flipped to Liz Smith's column. TA-BOO-BOO, the subheading announced. *Alex Rivers and Nick LaRue, who play, in this recent release, inseparable buddies, proved to the patrons of Le Dôme last night that what you see on screen is only an act. According to a reliable source, these two came to blows over Rivers's wife, Cassandra. When it comes Oscar night, will everyone be thinking of Rivers's nominated performance in* The Story of His Life, *or of his celebrated right hook?*

Shaking, Cassie turned the page. She closed her eyes but could not clear from her mind the anger that had seared through Alex last night.

Nothing Nick LaRue said had caused the fight. Cassie knew that as well as she knew Alex, she supposed. Anyone else would have had an argument, or issued a tight, quiet threat, but Alex had been pushed over the edge. There had been something running hot in his system that had fanned the tiniest spark into a conflagration. It wasn't Cassie herself – he'd said so, and he seemed to be happy with her that morning. Maybe it had to do with the pressure of the Academy Awards. Maybe it was being away from *Macbeth*.

She glanced down at the newspaper and noticed that she had folded the paper to the Friday movie listings section. She scanned the ads for *Taboo*, teasers that matched the billboard she'd seen on the night Will found her. She saw that the Westwood Community Center was offering a one-day Alex Rivers film festival as part of their tribute to the Academy Award nominees.

Smiling, Cassie ran her finger over the listings. A trio of Alex's movies, starting at nine o'clock in the morning. They'd be showing *Antony and Cleopatra*, the Shakespeare film that had proved his range, and one of the first movies he'd made after they were married. *Desperado*, a revisionist Western that had been his first film. And also *The Story of His Life*, the family drama for which Alex had received three Oscar nominations.

Cassie glanced at her watch. She had two hours to get to

Westwood. She jumped out of bed and took a quick shower, pulled on jeans and the sweatshirt Alex had worn yesterday. She found John in the kitchen with Mrs Alvarez and asked if he'd be able to drive her, and they practically collided with Alex on their way out the door. 'Where are you off to?' he panted, sweat running down the sides of his neck.

'I'll see you at three,' Cassie said, throwing him her widest smile and slipping past him before he had a chance to ask more.

She settled into the back seat of the Range Rover, giddy as a teenager. Closing her eyes, she buried her face into the overlong arms of Alex's sweatshirt, breathing Malibu, sandalwood, him.

The Westwood Community Center was nothing more than a recreation hall for senior citizens, who made up the lion's share of the early-morning audience for the Alex Rivers Film Festival. Cloaked in the anonymity of an outsider, Cassie moved through the knots of elderly women in the lobby. 'Like Gary Cooper,' one woman said. 'He can do anything on screen.'

She smiled, realizing she had experienced something no one else in the room had. She wanted to stand spread-eagled on the black and white linoleum tiles and scream, *I am Alex Rivers's wife. I live with him. I eat breakfast with him. He's real to me.*

When they started to let people into the amphitheater, Cassie held back and counted the number of fans Alex had here in Westwood. She imagined herself laughing with him later, telling him about the lady with the muffin-shaped hair who carried an autographed eight-by-ten of him and stuck it to the seat beside her, and about the old man who had yelled at the admissions booth, 'Alex *who*?'

She sat in the back row, where she could watch and listen to everyone else. *Desperado*, the Western that everyone in Hollywood had predicted would be a dismal failure, was the first movie to be shown. Cassie hadn't known Alex when he made the film, and actually, it hadn't been Alex's movie. The lead actress had top

billing – Ava Milan. She played a woman who'd been taken pris-
oner as a child by a group of renegade Indians, and who had
grown up with the nomadic tribe, found a husband and a decent
life. Alex was her brother, who had seen his entire family shot
and grew up swearing vengeance. The whole movie spiraled to
a climax in which Alex found his sister in the Indian camp and
went on a rash of senseless shooting, killing most of the village
and Ava's character's husband in the process. After a chilling solil-
oquy where she told her brother the life he'd just taken from her
was better than anything she could have hoped for as a white
woman in 1890, she slit her own throat in front of him.

The critics had gone wild. Westerns were not in at the time,
but Native Americans were. *Desperado* was the first movie to
portray them as individuals, not as a faceless enemy. Alex Rivers,
twenty-four, moved ahead of a pack of current young actors to
become a standout, and his character, Abraham Burrows, became
the first in a long line of complex, flawed heroes.

Cassie slipped low in her seat as the screened names rolled
over the red dust of the Western set. ALEX RIVERS. A chill ran
from her collarbone to her fingertips. The first moment Alex
stepped onto the screen, she drew in her breath. He looked so
young, and his eyes were lighter than they seemed now. He stood
with his feet apart, his hands fisted at his sides, and he let out a
yell that shook the red-curtained walls. Not even a word, just a
syllable that made his presence undeniable.

It struck her how much her perception of Alex had changed
in just a few days. When he had come for her at the police station,
she had seen him as he was on screen: ten feet tall and un-
approachable. But she knew better now. Cassie smiled. She'd have
a hell of a time convincing even one other person in this theater
of the truth, but Alex Rivers was just like anyone else.

Will was waiting for a furniture delivery. He'd had it with using
his mattress as a dining room, living room, and general all-purpose

recreation area. He had bought stuff at the first place he'd seen, a little store with decent prices that let him pay on monthly installments.

The furniture van came just when they said it would, at ten o'clock. Two big men brought each piece to the door and said, 'Where's it go?' When they got to the living room, Will kicked the extra boxes out of the way. He disconnected his brand-new television and VCR and waited for the movers to bring in the teakwood entertainment center. He'd bought that just because of its name: entertainment center. Kind of sounded like you were having a party in your house, even when you were alone.

The VCR was an impulse buy. He just didn't see how he could live in the movie capital of the world and not have one. He didn't know how to set the clock and he'd be damned if he was going to thumb through the manual to figure it out, so it had been flashing 12:00 for twenty-four hours now. It was his day off, Friday, and when these guys finished bringing in the furniture he was going to do the following things in this order: eat a bowl of cereal at his new kitchen table, flop down belly-first on his new bed, sprawl across his couch and flip on the TV with the remote, and then watch a movie.

It was past noon by the time he walked down to the convenience store to rent something. He wasn't looking for anything in particular. The Korean proprietor told him his first two choices were out, and then held up a beaten red box. 'You try this,' he said. 'You like it.'

Desperado. Will couldn't help but laugh. It was a film from the early eighties, and it co-starred Alex Rivers. 'Shit,' he said, pulling a five from his pocket. 'I'll try it.' If Rivers was as young as he figured from the dates on the box, he probably wasn't very good, and after last night, Will felt like getting a laugh at his expense.

Will bought a bag of natural popcorn and walked home. He sat down on the new couch and started the movie with his remote, fast-forwarding through the warnings and the previews.

When Alex Rivers first came onto the screen and let out a howl like a Sioux war cry, Will snorted and tossed a handful of popcorn at the TV.

He did not know what the movie was about, but he remembered all the controversy that had surrounded it. It was written up in a lot of tribal papers, opinions that had split down the middle: complaints for its inaccuracies, praise for its portrayal of Native American family life and the hiring of Indian actors. Will watched it long enough to see the actress who played Alex Rivers's sister marry some strapping Mandan brave. She was small and blond, and her face was very close to the one Will had seen at night as an adolescent, when he tossed under sheets in his grandfather's house.

'Fuck this,' Will said. He hit the little red button on his remote, getting great satisfaction out of seeing Alex Rivers's image wiggle and black out as the tape ejected from his VCR. He sat up, spilling the popcorn into the cushions of the couch. 'They don't know a thing,' he muttered. 'They make these shitty movies and they don't have a clue.'

Will switched off the TV, too, staring at the screen for a moment until the snow stopped dancing in front of his eyes. He looked at the video box lying on the floor on its side. Then he walked to the two boxes he'd moved out of the way for the delivery. Prying open the top one, he rummaged through the newspaper Cassie had tried to pack between the artifacts he'd so carelessly thrown inside.

He pulled out the medicine bundle that had belonged to his great-great-grandfather, who – like his grandfather – had dreamed of the elk, and that's what the pouch was made of. Will fingered the fringes; the skin of the bag itself. Elk Dreamers had been highly revered among the Sioux. People turned to them when they were looking for the person they should love.

Will had known a guy in the reservation's police department who had married a white woman, moved to Pine Ridge town, coached his kid's Little League team. Like all cops, he carried a piece, but he also carried a medicine bundle. In 1993, believe it or not, he wore the thing every day looped right around his holster. He said it brought him luck, and the one day his daughter borrowed it for show-and-tell he'd been shot in the arm by a drug addict.

There were other people on the reservation, people his own age, who still had bundles. Nobody batted an eye. Will had to admit, there were stranger things.

He walked into the kitchen and found a hammer and a picture hook. For a moment he sat with the medicine bundle, rubbing it against his cheek and feeling the soft chamois of history. It wasn't his medicine bundle, so it wasn't going to do him any good, but it wasn't going to do any damage, either.

Will tried to remember where Cassie had hung it that day, and he set the bag between his teeth to stand on the couch. He held his palms up to the smooth white wall, hoping to feel some of the heat her gifted hands had left behind.

Like everyone else in the Westwood Community Center, Cassie cried at the end of *The Story of His Life*. It was easy to see why Alex had been awarded his first nomination for a Best Director Oscar, although the nomination for Best Actor had raised some controversy about why Alex and not Jack Green, the veteran actor who portrayed his father, had gotten the nod. Jack had been nominated for Best Supporting Actor; it could have gone either way. LA bookies were saying Alex was a favorite in his two categories, Jack a dead lock for *his*, and the film would win Best Picture.

Many of the senior citizens shuffled out after the film, having come primarily to see the movie that all the speculation centered on. But Cassie couldn't have been dragged from that theater. She realized the reason she had come to the festival in the first place was to see *Antony and Cleopatra*, the epic movie that Alex had made shortly after their marriage.

The credits started scrolling over the screen, accompanied by the sad notes of a sitar. Cassie pulled her hair out of its ponytail and fanned it over the back of the seat. She closed her eyes just before Alex spoke Antony's first words, and she willed herself to remember.

It was the first indication she had that Alex was not the man she had married. He came home from Herb Silver's office clutching a script. She had been in her laboratory at the house, scanning her itinerary for the upcoming trip to Tanzania, when Alex burst through the door and planted himself in front of her. 'This,' he said, 'is the part I was made for.'

Later, Cassie had thought about what he said; it would have made more sense to say, *This part was made for me*, instead of the other way around. But like Antony, from the minute he first touched that script Alex had become a megalomaniac.

The lines came easily to him, falling from his lips as if he'd never had to study them, and although Cassie knew Alex had a photographic memory, she had never even seen him crack open the script. 'I am Antony,' he told her simply, and she had no choice but to believe him.

He was not the favored actor for the role. He hadn't even been considered until he'd asked Herb to submit his name. Cassie knew he was nervous about it. So on the morning he was to meet with the casting director, she waved the cook away from the kitchen and made him an omelette herself. She put in peppers and ham and Vidalia onions, cheddar cheese and Colby and a dash of paprika. 'Your favorite,' she said with a flourish. She laid the plate in front of him at the table. 'For good luck.'

Alex would have looked up at her, maybe grabbed her by the hips and swung her onto his lap for a kiss. He would have offered her half and hand-fed it to her from his own fork. But that morning his eyes darkened, as if he had devoured something whole that was now burning its way out. He swept the plate off the table with his arm, not even glancing as it shattered against the pale veined-marble floor. 'Bring grapes,' he whispered, already in accent. 'Plums and sweetmeats. Ambrosia.' He turned away from Cassie, who stood frozen at his side. He stared over the length of the table at something she could not see. 'Bring a feast for a god,' he said.

Cassie ran from the table. From the bedroom, she called in sick to the university, truly believing she was on the verge of throwing up. She heard John come in to get Alex, and when the door closed behind them, she curled up on the mattress and tried to make herself as small as humanly possible.

Alex did not come home until after dinner. She was still in the bedroom, sitting at the window and watching the horizon swallow the sun. She kept her back to Alex when he opened the door, waiting rigidly for his apology.

He did not speak. He knelt behind her and ran his fingers from her jaw to her neck, stroking lightly. He let his lips run the path of his hands, and when he tipped her chin back to kiss her, she gave herself up to him.

He made love as he never had before. He was rough with her until she cried out, then so gentle she had to press his hands against her, craving more. It was not an act of passion but possession, and every time Cassie tried to pull herself an inch away from Alex's fever he drew her tighter. He held himself back until he felt her closing around him, and as he pushed her down into the bed he whispered into the shell of her ear. 'You did know,' he said, 'how much you were my conqueror.'

When he was breathing steadily, asleep, Cassie slipped from the bed and picked up the script he'd dropped by the window. She walked into the bathroom and sat on the toilet lid for hours skimming the play she had last read in high school. She cried when Antony, in love with Cleopatra, married Octavia for peace. She whispered aloud the scene where Antony, realizing Cleopatra had not betrayed him after all, begged a serving soldier to run him through with his own sword. She closed her eyes and saw Antony dying in Cleopatra's arms; Cleopatra poisoning herself with the asp. In Act III, she found it: the line Alex had murmured to her in the quiet after. But she had not made love with Alex. It had been Antony touching her, obsessed with her, filling her.

A woman to Cassie's left began to cough violently, and Cassie opened her eyes only to realize she had missed the bulk of the movie. Alex wasn't even on the screen anymore. The actress who had played opposite him, a very beautiful woman who had gone on to do nothing else of great merit, was singing Antony's praises. Cassie whispered the words with her: 'His legs bestrid the ocean; his reared arm crested the world; his voice was propertied as all the tuned spheres.' It had been the role of a lifetime for Alex, the one that opened Hollywood's eyes enough to realize here was an actor who could do anything at all, who could sell gold to Midas himself. And was it any wonder? *A man who ruled the world. Unparalleled ambition.* There were so many similarities between Antony and Alex, it was difficult to know if he had had to act at all.

She wanted to see him. Not as he was on screen, filled to the skin with a character's thoughts and deeds, but as himself. She wanted to talk to the man who told her he had threatened kidnapping as an alternative to marrying him, the one whose dimples her children would have, the one who bought her ancient skulls and plasticine. She wanted to stand on the moors of Scotland with him, his arms around her, their pulses slowing to match.

Not waiting for the end of the movie, she pulled Alex's sweatshirt closer around her and started up the aisle of the amphitheater. She would meet him after his engagement at the hospital, and they'd ride together to Bel-Air, and she'd tell him about the forty-two senior citizens who had come to see him that morning. He would kiss the warm spot the sun crowned on her hair and she would lean against him, letting the whole back seat fill up with the wonder of them, together.

Cleopatra's words trailed behind her like a bridal train as she stepped into the humid afternoon. *Think you there was, or might be, such a man as this I dreamed of?*

Chapter Nine

Michaela Snow, Alex Rivers's publicist, met him in the parking lot of the hospital. 'Alex, Alex, Alex,' she said, her heavy arms seeming to move of their own accord to wrap around his neck. 'If I didn't love you, I'd kill you.'

Alex kissed her cheek and embraced her as best he could – she weighed much more than he did, so his arms didn't make it the whole way around her middle. 'You only love me because I make you so much money,' he said.

'You've got me there,' she said. She snapped, and a small, thin man tumbled out of the back of her van. He held three brushes threaded between the fingers of one hand, and a sponge dabbed in pancake in the other. 'This is Flaubert Halloran,' Michaela said. 'Freelance makeup.'

'Flaubert,' the man repeated, in a voice that reminded Alex of the glide of a cat. 'Like the writer.' He stuck the wooden ends of the brushes in his mouth like a seamstress's pins and began to cover the bruise at the corner of Alex's eye. 'Nasty, nasty,' he said.

Michaela kept checking her watch. 'Okay, Flo, that's all.' She pulled Alex's wrist, dragging him behind her toward the hospital. 'I've got three major networks, *People*, *Vanity Fair*, and the *Times* expected to show. The story is that this is a charitable kind of thing you do every year, and only a leak to the press – thank you very much – has led to this coverage. Make something up about a long-lost cousin who died of leukemia.'

Alex grinned at her. 'Or an illegitimate son?'

Michaela steered him through the glass doors of the hospital. 'I'd murder you,' she said. She handed Alex a sheaf of publicity photos from *Taboo* and a gaggle of balloons in blue and gold, then shepherded him into an elevator. Michaela reached in to push the button to the seventh floor. 'Remember, act shocked to see all the cameras, but recover quickly, and feed them a sob story that will win you another Oscar nomination.' She winked at him and waved, her tiny red nails blinking in the flesh of her palm. '*Ciao*,' she mouthed.

Act? he thought, his smile fading as the elevator doors closed before him. He was already acting. It had taken nearly every imaginative skill he had to meet Michaela in the parking lot and pretend that this was just like any other PR engagement. For years Alex had studiously avoided hospitals, for years he'd buried his memories of a New Orleans pediatric ward. As he moved through the halls, the familiar ammonia stench and the spartan white walls began to close in around him. He tensed the muscles of his arms, expecting to feel the prick of a needle, the drain of an IV.

He had been born with a hole in his heart, a condition that consigned him to a childhood on the sidelines. The backwoods GP who'd heard the murmur had referred Alex's mother to Charity in the city, where a specialist could check the severity of the defect, but when she forgot the appointment – more than once – he told her her son would have to play it safe, rather than sorry. *Don't run*, Alex had been told. *Don't exert yourself*. He could remember watching other kindergartners race across the damp playground. He could remember closing his eyes and picturing his heart – a punctured, red, child's valentine.

When he was five and still couldn't play outside, he listened to soap operas in the afternoons with his mother, who did not seem to notice or care that he was there. Once on the TV a lady with the bright hair of a fairy had pressed her cheek to a man's bare chest and murmured, *I love you with all my heart*. After that, when Alex pictured his heart, he did not just imagine the hole.

He also saw the extent of the damage: all the love he'd gathered for and from other people draining out, an unstoppable sieve.

No wonder, Alex had realized, blaming himself for his parents' indifference in that way young children have of twisting outcomes and events. That was the first time Alex decided to be someone else. Rather than face the flaws in himself, he'd pretend he was a swashbuckling pirate, a mountain climber, the President. He pretended he lived in a normal family, that during dinner his parents asked him, *How was your day?* instead of hissing in angry Cajun French. And at age eight, when he was pronounced cured, he brought those fantasies to life, preferring someone strong and bright to the frightened boy he had been.

He convinced himself that he was impervious to pain, mettled of superheroic proportions. He could remember holding his palm over a burning candle, feeling the skin welt and take fire, telling himself that anyone who could survive such trying feats would not be affected by his mother's disinterest, his father's taunting. He got very good at believing what he forced himself to believe. In fact, thirty years later, Alex had had so much practice at dissembling, he was hard-pressed to remember what would remain if all his careful masks fell away.

With the self-control for which he had become famous, Alex shook free of his memories and steeled himself to the situation at hand. This was a hospital, true, but it had nothing to do with him; it meant nothing at all to him. He'd do his job, he'd pretend he liked being there, and he'd get the hell out.

It didn't surprise Alex that to reach the kids he first had to struggle through a knot of doctors and nurses. He smiled politely, covertly glancing over their bobbing heads to find the quickest route to the patient wards, so that he'd look like he'd been there many times before. They tugged at his coat, telling him how much they had loved this movie or that. They all called him Alex, as if sitting in a darkened theater with his image for two hours at a time made them think they'd known him all their lives.

'Thanks,' he murmured. 'Yes, thank you.' He managed to make it down the hallway to the pediatric cancer ward, when the cameras rounded the corner. He looked up long enough to register faint disapproval, maybe a trace of surprise, but he recovered and smiled politely and said some children were expecting him.

Michaela hadn't prepared him for the sight of the kids. One goddamned glance and he was five years old again, shivering in a thin johnny while he waited for the doctors to read him his future. Had he looked like this?

The children peppered the floor in their pajamas, some trailing open robes. Their eyes were too large for their heads. They were carbon copies of each other: thin, haunted, bald; evoking images of concentration camps. He could not even tell the boys from the girls until they spoke. 'Mr Rivers,' one little girl lisped. She couldn't have been more than four, but he was no good at judging these things, and he knelt down so that she could climb onto his back. She smelled of medicine and urine and surrender. 'Here,' she said, dropping a wet cracker into the pocket of his tweed jacket. 'I saved this one for you.'

He would have thought they were too young to see his films, but nearly every kid there had seen *Speed*, the one about the test pilot. The boys wanted to know if he'd really gotten to fly that F-14, and one even asked if the actress who played his girlfriend had tasted as good as she looked.

He gave balloons to the smaller children and autographed photos to anyone who asked. When a thirteen-year-old named Sally came closer for hers, he leaned toward her conspiratorially. 'You know, the best way to remember the places you've been is to kiss a pretty girl wherever you go,' he said, just loud enough for the tape recorders to pick up his words. 'Think you can help me?'

She blushed furiously and offered her cheek, but at the moment Alex went to kiss her she turned and landed her lips right on his mouth. 'Wow,' she breathed, holding her fingers over her lips. 'I gotta call my ma.'

It had struck Alex at the moment the flashbulbs went off that not only had he given Sally her first kiss, but probably her last. He felt himself starting to sweat as the room swam around him, and he had to take several deep breaths to steady his nerves. Physically, he had gotten better; physically, he had been lucky. But there were all kinds of hidden dangers in childhood, things that reared up and stole your innocence before you were old enough to fight back. He wondered which was worse – a child whose spirit could not outlive a broken body; or, like himself, a man whose apparent health hid a soul that had died years before.

'Jesus Christ, John,' Alex said, stretching his arms out over the back seat of the Range Rover. 'Unless she was running off to meet some other guy, what's the big secret?'

John looked at him in the rearview mirror. 'I don't know, Mr Rivers,' he said. 'I promised the missus and all.'

Alex leaned forward and grinned. 'Ten bucks more a week for you if you give me the town where you dropped her off. Twenty bucks if you come completely clean.'

John chewed his upper lip. 'You won't tell her I said nothing?'

Alex crossed his fingers over his chest. 'And hope to die,' he said.

'She went to the movies.'

'That's the big secret?'

John smiled at him. 'She went to *your* movies. Some festival in Westwood.'

Alex started to laugh. She could have watched anything he'd made – from the rushes to the uncut versions to the screen copies themselves – in the privacy of her own home. But then again, maybe that's why she didn't want him to know. Maybe the real show was seeing other people's reactions to Alex on camera.

'You have a copy of today's paper, John?' Alex reached for the *Times* as John handed it through the partition in the Plexiglas. He skimmed through the entertainment section until he reached the movie listings. *Desperado, Antony and Cleopatra*, and of course, *The Story of His Life*. He smiled. If Cassie wanted to see him at work, he could make it that much easier.

He asked John to turn off the radio and he closed his eyes, tuning out the world and in to his senses. Before the film rolled, he always found a quiet corner where he could slip into character. It was a matter of breathing; of concentrating so hard on the pattern and then altering it just slightly to match the way his character would.

Where breathing started, life followed. Antony drank in the air, as if taking in the entire world with one single breath. When he opened his eyes he saw a world of green and gold that had been spread at his feet. He murmured the names of the exits on the highway in a precise British accent. He did not deign to look at John; he would not do so with his servants. He rolled down his window and let the wind gust over his face, blowing his hair back and scalding his eyes. He touched the smooth leather seats and thought of the curves of his queen.

At the apartment, when Alex made no move to get out of the car, John shrugged and ran up the walk to collect Mrs Rivers. He was used to this sort of thing from his employer. It wasn't his nature to talk, but sometimes he'd pick up Mr Rivers and drop off a completely different man.

Cassie was laughing as she stepped into the car. 'Move,' she said. 'You're hogging the back seat.' Alex was sitting in the center, and he stared at her but made no effort to shift to one side or the other. Assuming this was some game, she flopped down beside him, landing half on his thigh.

She felt his hand on the back of her neck, gentle and tense at the same time, as if even a caress could serve to remind her how easily he could overpower her. She narrowed her eyes and turned to him. 'What in God's name did they do to you at that hospital?'

His fingers tightened almost to the point of pain, and she cried out softly before she could stop herself. He was looking directly at her but she had the sense he was seeing someone else. Panicked, she clawed at Alex's wrist. 'Cut it out,' she whispered, and before she could ask him again what was the matter, his body pinned her to the seat and his mouth seared over hers in a kiss that was not like Alex at all.

He's acting.

She dug her nails into his arms and bit down on his lip until she had enough force to push him away. 'Stop it,' she ordered. 'Just stop it now.'

For a moment he froze, his eyes paling to the gray of Arctic ice and then slowly draining of life until all that sat across from Cassie was a shell. And then something shuddered its way up his body, moving like a blush, bringing color to his skin and settling as a spark in his eyes. He was Alex again, and he shrugged. 'You didn't have to bite me,' he said. 'I just figured you'd like a first-hand performance, too.'

Still cautious, Cassie curled up at the far side of the back seat. 'Who told you where I went?' she accused, her eyes sliding to John in the front.

Alex reached for her hand and laced his fingers with hers. 'I know everything about you,' he said, smiling.

She was beginning to think that he did. He was back to being the Alex she'd grown accustomed to in the past few days, funny and gentle and comfortable as a worn armchair. Cassie wondered if this was just another character he'd played along the line, one he kept himself wrapped in most of the time.

She shook her head to clear it. What was she thinking? She had seen Alex with his guard down – when he talked about his parents, when he tried to teach her karate on the shallows of the beach, when he reached for her in his sleep and whispered her name. It was impossible to act all the time; it was ridiculous to think that what she saw was not real. She squeezed his hand. 'Sorry,' she said. 'I don't usually bite.' He turned slightly, patting his side, and she willingly slid closer to him. 'But what made you pick *Antony*, for God's sake?'

Alex smiled. 'You used to love Antony when we were first married,' he said.

Cassie opened her mouth to object, but changed her mind. Alex was right. He did know everything about her, and at the present moment she still knew next to nothing, and the only choice she had was to believe him.

They drove for fifteen minutes in silence, and then Cassie felt Alex kiss the top of her head. 'You're probably just nervous about meeting the staff all over again,' he said.

Cassie stared out the window. She knew she was passing trees and roads and flowering bushes, but the car was moving so quickly that the world was just puddled in colors; she could pick nothing out individually. 'Yes,' she said. 'That must be it.'

The house stood at the end of a mile-long driveway up a winding hill in Bel-Air, a white mansion with wrought-iron grillwork and a slate roof. The front porch supported a second-story veranda where floor-length lace curtains blew through open French doors. Roses climbed up a trellis on the left side of the house; heliotrope wound its way up the right. In the distance Cassie could see formal gardens and two smaller houses, little white replicas of the main house. It looked for all the world like a Louisiana plantation.

'My God,' she whispered, hearing the gravel crunch beneath her sneaker as she stepped out of the car. 'I can't possibly live here.'

Alex took her by the elbow and guided her up the porch steps. John opened the front door, a magnificent oak panel carved with the head of a lion.

The parlor was an overwhelming room with a cathedral ceiling, a double curved staircase, and rose marble floors. Cassie stared down at her feet, which rested in the reflected pool of light from a multicolored cathedral-style window over the door. Alex's initials spread like a stain over her left shoe and her ankle.

'Cassie,' he said, and her head snapped up. 'John has told everybody about your . . . little problem, and they'll go out of their way to help you today before we go to Scotland.'

Cassie ran her eyes over the line of figures that stood at the bottom of the left-hand staircase like a row of toy soldiers. There was John, of course, who was not only the driver and bodyguard, apparently, but a majordomo of sorts. There was a man with a pastry apron wrapped around his large frame, a young girl in a simple black and white maid's uniform. Another man stood off to the side, as if he was unwilling to be associated with the household staff. He stepped forward and offered his hand. 'Jack Arbuster,' he said, smiling. 'Your husband's secretary.'

She wondered what in the world Alex needed a secretary for when he already had an agent, a publicist, and a personal assistant. She thought maybe he was in charge of answering fan mail, or paying the utility bills.

'I need to catch up on a few things before you fly out,' Jack said to Alex. He winked at Cassie apologetically.

Alex put his arm around her waist. 'Give me an hour,' he said to Jack. 'I'll meet you in the library.' As Jack walked off, Cassie followed him with her eyes, trying to see what was around the corner. Tugging her sideways, Alex pulled Cassie past the maid, the cook, and John. 'Come on,' he said. 'I'll show you as much as I can, and if worse comes to worst I'll leave you with the blueprints till you can find your way around.'

He took her to a library paneled in cherry and filled with first editions of hundreds of British and American classics, pointing out one entire shelf filled with copies of scholarly journals and magazines that featured articles Cassie herself had written. He led her through a dining room whose table could seat thirty, a projection room with a pristine screen and ten overstuffed couches. In the kitchen, she stuck her head in the stainless steel refrigerator and counted the copper pots that were racked above the marble island, and was given a bite-size apple turnover by the cook as a parting gift.

There were six bathrooms and ten bedrooms, each decorated with pale silk wallpaper and French lace curtains. There were three sitting rooms and a recreation center with pinball machines, a bowling lane, a pool table, and a big-screen TV. There was a whole wing she hadn't even seen when Alex brought her upstairs to the master bedroom. He opened the double doors to a suite, comfortably furnished with breezy striped sofas and thick Persian rugs. A stereo was recessed into the wall, in addition to a television and a VCR. Flowers were arranged in bowls on several tables, beautiful blooms that brought out the lavender and blue accents of the room and that, Cassie knew, were not native to California.

'We must spend a lot of time up here,' Cassie said, stepping behind Alex through an adjoining door that revealed a tremendous bird's-eye maple sleigh bed.

Alex smiled at her. 'Well,' he said, 'we try.'

Cassie stepped up to the bed and traced the whorls in the patterns of wood. 'This is bigger than a king-size, isn't it?'

Alex flopped onto the mattress belly-first. 'I had it made up special. I have this theory about beds – they're like goldfish bowls. You know how if you keep goldfish in a bowl, they stay the size of your thumb? Well, when you move them into a pond, like we have out back, they grow ten times that size. So I figure the bigger the bed, the less I'll be stunting my growth.'

Cassie laughed. 'I think you've passed puberty.'

Alex grabbed her wrist and pulled her down beside him. 'You've noticed?'

She rolled toward him, staring at the light beard that already broke the smooth line of his jaw. 'Where's my lab?'

'Out back. The little white building – the second one you come to. The first one is where John lives.'

Cassie frowned. 'He doesn't stay in the house like Mrs Alvarez?'

Alex sat up. 'We like having the place to ourselves at night,' he said simply.

Cassie walked to the gaping fireplace that stood opposite the bed, then fingered the empty brandy decanter on the mantel. *Aurora*, she thought, and she felt Alex's hands on her shoulders. 'It's only for show,' he whispered, as if he could read her mind.

Cassie spun around. 'Go earn your keep,' she said, smiling. 'If I'm not back in an hour, send out the National Guard.'

When Alex left, Cassie stood at the open French doors, looking out over the suburbs of LA and the blue swells of mountains. A gardener she hadn't met was rooting through a bed of fragile lilies, and in the driveway John was polishing the rear fender of the Range Rover. She located her laboratory, just to the left of a profusion of flowers planted in the shape of a fleur-de-lis. Beyond the garden was a white limestone path that led down a sloping hill toward something she could not see.

She flew down the opposite staircase, the one she hadn't walked up, just to see if it felt any different. She walked out the door and tested a rocking chair and the hanging porch swing before running down the limestone path like a child. When she was far enough away from the house to be certain nobody was looking, she spread her arms to the sun and whirled around, laughing and smiling and skipping to beat the band.

There was a landscaped pool with a man-made waterfall that Alex had forgotten to tell Cassie about, and a genuine maze made of thick boxwood hedges. She wandered inside, wondering if she knew her way to the center and out again. The sharp corners of the maze came up quickly as she ran through the narrow aisles, scratching her arms on fresh-cut branches. Dizzy, she let herself sink to the cool grass. She lay on her back, overwhelmed by Alex's house and Alex's grounds.

If a bug hadn't crawled up the inside of her arm, she never would have noticed the stone. She rolled over, which brought her eye-level to the cuttings from the boxwood. Neatly hidden inside the hedge was a small pink slab of rock.

It was not oval, not really; it was too rough-hewn and lopsided for that. Cassie reached under the brambles, feeling the branches tangle around her wrists like bracelets. It was rose quartz, and she had brought it with her all the way from the East Coast. Chiseled crudely on its flattest side were the letters *CCM* and the year *1976*.

She could not remember why she had hidden it under the boxwood in the middle of Alex's maze. She could not remember if she'd ever told Alex it was there. But she realized it was the first piece of evidence she truly believed; the first thing she'd seen since losing her memory that convinced her she had once belonged here.

Cassie rolled onto her back and held the rock on her chest. She stared into the sun until this beautiful world Alex had offered her went black, and then she whispered Connor's name.

On November 1, 1976, a little after seven in the morning, Connor's father walked into the kitchen where he and his mother were eating cream of wheat and killed them both with a 12-gauge shotgun. Between the time it took Cassie to call the police about the shots and to run through the path in the woods to Connor's house, Mr Murtaugh had managed to turn the gun on himself.

Connor's father had blown himself clear into the living room, but Mrs Murtaugh lay on the floor. The back of her head was gone. Connor had fallen nearly on top of her, and there was a tremendous hole where his chest had been.

With a calm born of shock, Cassie sat down beside Connor and pulled him into her lap. She touched her fingers to his lips, still warm. She thought about kissing him, like she had the night before at the graveyard, but could not bring herself to do it.

The police and the paramedics dragged Cassie away from Connor's body. She sat in a corner of the kitchen with a rough wool blanket wrapped around her shoulders, answering the same questions over and over. No, she had not been present at the scene of the crime. No, she hadn't seen Mr Murtaugh this morning. No, no, no.

Everyone knew how close Cassie and Connor had been, and she was excused from school until after the funeral, but that didn't keep her from hearing the whispers. *They said he pulled the trigger on himself with his own toe. Couldn't get himself a job, and turned to the bottle. Killed an innocent boy like that, in the prime of his life.* At least the problems in her own house she could see coming. Connor's family had been rotting beneath its candy surface, festering where no one could see.

The day of the funeral it snowed. Connor didn't have a will, so his body was disposed of the way his parents' bodies had been; he was cremated. The ashes were blown over Moosehead Lake. Cassie watched as the urn holding Mrs Murtaugh was opened, then the one holding her husband. When they spread Connor's ashes, Cassie started to scream. No one could stop her; not even when her father clamped a gloved hand over her mouth did the sound diminish in intensity. It wasn't right that for the rest of forever Connor and his father would be mixed together. She wanted them to do it over. She wanted them to give Connor to her.

She felt snow freeze her eyes wide open when what was left of Connor was given to the wind. A breath of gray, insubstantial and shifting like smoke, screened the sky and disappeared just as quickly. It was as if Connor had been a figment of Cassie's imagination. As if he had never existed at all.

She slipped away from the other people paying their respects and, still wearing her good dress and her snow boots, started to run around Moosehead Lake. It was tremendous, and she knew she wouldn't be able to get very far, but by the time she sank to her knees in the snow, gasping, she was a mile away from the site of the funeral. She let the snow melt through the thin fabric of her skirt, cold enough to paralyze. She dug with her fingers into the frozen ground until her nails were cracked and bleeding.

She realized that although she had tried for years to ease her mother's pain, she would never be able to ease Connor's. So she would do the next best thing: she would hurt for him. She carried the piece of rose quartz home with her and sat in the garage near her father's tool chest, using a hammer and an awl to make the headstone Connor hadn't been given. She worked until her hands cramped. Then she curled her arms around her knees and rocked herself back and forth, wondering why, since both their hearts had been ripped out, she wasn't dying too.

Friday evening, Will Flying Horse was sitting on his new green couch watching a game show and eating a partially cooked TV dinner when the electricity went out. 'Shit,' he said, watching the blinking clock on his VCR fade into nothing. He set his plate beside him on the couch and tried to remember where the fuse box was.

It wasn't as bad as it could have been; it was dinnertime, so there was enough light outside to see his way into the basement. The strange thing was that none of the breakers had been tripped. He walked back upstairs and stepped onto the front porch of his house. In the windows next door and across the street he could see a kitchen light burning steady; a mute dog jogging across a TV. It was just him.

He called the electric company, but could only record his address and problem on a voice-mail system. God only knew how long it would take for workers to get the message. So he started pulling candles out of his kitchen cabinets, ugly red egg-shaped ones that a former girlfriend had bought him one year for his birthday. He carried four of them into the living room and lit them with a book of matches he had in his pocket.

As the sun went down, a shadow crept across him. The fringes of the medicine bundle above his head stirred, restless in the quiet. Will listened to the rhythm of his own pulse. There was nothing to do but wait.

Elizabeth, the maid, carried into the bedroom a suitcase that was bigger than she was. 'Will you need a hanging bag, too?'

Cassie didn't know. 'I guess I will,' she said, and the maid immediately turned to leave. 'Wait,' she called. She furrowed her brow. 'I can't find the closets.'

Elizabeth smiled. She walked through the suite and the bedroom into the short hallway that led to the green marble bathroom. When she leaned her shoulder against the wall, Cassie was amazed to see the wallpaper spring open to reveal a hidden closet. 'Yours,' Elizabeth said, and then she did the same thing on the other side. 'Mr Rivers's.'

She walked out of the room, leaving Cassie to stare at the rows of sweaters and blouses and furs that belonged to her. The closet was bigger than the housekeeper's quarters at the apartment. Cassie had never seen so many clothes in one place.

She began to pull things she thought she should pack from the drawers – comfortable turtlenecks and cotton cardigans, underwear and extra bras and a small quilted bag for her makeup. She wanted to take a pair of loafers from the bottom of the stack of shoe boxes, but she thought she might be able to get to them without removing the boxes on top. She slid the box out halfway, trying to wedge the loafers under the lid, but the support gave out and the contents of her closet came tumbling down.

Surrounded by a mess of lingerie and high heels and bush jackets, she almost missed finding the tiny compartment. She'd pushed against it and its latch sprang free. It was another hidey-hole that worked on the same principle as her closet. It was tiny, no bigger than a breadbox. Cassie wondered if that was where she kept her jewelry.

Inside was a stack of paperback romances, the glitzy kind that showed a half-dressed woman bent under a pirate on the front cover, the kind an anthropologist would never be caught dead reading. Cassie laughed out loud. Was this her big secret? What did Alex keep in his compartment? *Hustler?*

She picked up a handful and leafed through the titles. *Save Me Again. The Fire and the Flower. Love's Burning Flames.* Maybe Alex made her hide them. It wouldn't do for the public to find out that the wife of America's leading man read these things in her spare time.

A box was trapped in the corner behind the stack of books. Cassie identified it by sight, its pink cover open, one of its two foil-wrapped tests still cradled inside. First Response. For use the first day of your missed period.

She glanced outside the closet, into the stunning green bathroom. She could clearly see herself bent over the vanity of the sink, waiting the requisite three minutes. She recalled the way the small pink circle had crept its way upward from the swab of the test kit. *Pink, Pregnant. White, Not Pregnant.* She had cried into the sink, her hands on the fourteen-karat fixtures, surprised by how cold real gold could be.

Cassie sank down onto the pile of fallen clothes, clothes Alex had bought her, clothes that matched all the trappings of a life like this. She pressed the heels of her hands against her eyes, trying to push away the image of the graveyard at St Sebastian's, and what had driven her there.

It was the night Alex was scheduled to fly to Scotland for on-location shooting, and he was in one of his moods. She had learned to gauge him by his eyes: the darker they turned, the further away she stayed. It had been months since the last time. She should have known.

At dinner, Alex kept drumming his knife along the edge of the table. It made a dull, thudding noise against the tablecloth and Cassie's heart took up its rhythm. 'How did it go today?' she asked.

Alex clattered the knife against the edge of his plate. 'It is over budget; it is being directed by a moron; it is barely a week into production.'

He ran his hands through his hair. 'Thank you so much for bringing it up.'

Cassie sat back in her seat and concentrated on keeping her mouth shut and eating with the minimal amount of noise. She had found out today about the baby and she wanted to tell Alex before he left, but maybe this wasn't the time. She had to catch him at the right moment. She had to be able to make him see that it wasn't lousy timing; it was going to change their lives. It was going to give them a second chance.

Alex pushed back his chair. 'I have to pack. I've got less than an hour.'

Cassie glanced at his plate, full of food he'd pushed around but barely eaten. 'I'll make a sandwich for you to take on the road,' she said, but Alex had already left the room.

In the three years since it had begun, Cassie had become very good at staying out of Alex's way. After all, it was a big house, and with the staff gone for the night no one would think it strange if she went down to her lab at three in the morning, or decided to finish a book in the library until the sun came up. But her instincts weren't sharp that night; she had spent too much time during the day drawing rosy images of a little boy with Alex's silver eyes. She walked to the bedroom and sat in the middle of the bed, where she could watch Alex pack. Looking at him would be like getting a glimpse of her baby. 'Do you want me to get together your shaving kit?' Alex shook his head. She reached for a sweater he'd tossed into the bedroom. 'I'll fold for you,' she offered, and she started, arm over arm, but Alex's hand caught her wrist.

'I said I'd do it,' he muttered.

Something was eating away at Alex from the inside, something that had been part of him long before she'd ever met him. It was what made him the consummate actor, although nobody else in the world knew it. They saw the pain, but after Alex had cloaked it in another character's actions. Only Cassie had looked at him when his open eyes went blind; only Cassie had pressed her hands to his chest and felt the skin stretched over a heart swollen with rage.

She loved him more than anything in the world. Even more than herself – hadn't she proved that? She knew that even if she couldn't heal him this time, the next time he hurt she would be able to. That's why Alex had come to her. She was the only person who could make it better.

But it was a double bind. She was the only one close enough to Alex to help, but that also brought her underfoot. It wasn't his fault that she got in the way. When it happened, she could only blame herself, forgive him.

Alex sank down beside her on the bed. 'I don't want to go to fucking Scotland,' he said, his voice rough. 'I want to take some time off. I want this goddamn Oscar broadcast to be over and I want to drop off the face of the earth.'

'So do it,' Cassie urged, rubbing the muscles in his shoulders. 'Put Macbeth *on hold, and come with me to Kenya.'*

Alex snorted. 'And what the hell will I do while you play in your sandbox?'

Cassie flinched. 'Read screenplays,' she suggested. 'Get a tan.'

Alex began throwing clothes in the suitcases that he'd laid open on the floor. 'Today I found out about the pre-Oscar interview we taped with Barbara Walters.' He sighed. 'She's putting me on with some comedian and Noah Fallon.' Cassie stared at him blankly. 'For Christ's sake, Noah Fallon. He's up for Best Actor too.' Alex sat on the floor, his knees drawn up to his chest. 'She's airing me second. Fucking second. Fallon's going last.'

Cassie smiled at him. 'At least you're in the broadcast,' she said.

Alex turned away from her. 'In the past three years, when Barbara Walters's Oscar special features a nominee in the third slot, that nominee has won. It's like a goddamn barometer of how the Academy's votes will go.'

Unsure of what to say, Cassie slipped off the bed and wrapped her arms around him. 'I'm not going to win,' Alex said, his words falling softly onto her shoulder.

'You'll win,' she whispered fiercely. 'You're going to win.'

In the way that it usually happened, Alex changed in the space of a heartbeat. He stood, grabbing Cassie by her wrists and shaking her so hard her hair fell down around her face and her neck snapped back. 'How do you know?' he demanded, his breath hot against her cheek. 'How do you know?'

Words caught in Cassie's throat, the ones she always wanted to defend herself with that never slipped past her clenched jaw. Alex shook her again, and then pushed her to the floor so she was at his feet.

She tripped over the luggage as she fell, and struck her head against the closet door, feeling a wound open that did not hurt nearly as much as the shame that ran through her. She had just enough time to see Alex's foot coming at her, and instead of curling into a ball as she usually did, she rolled so he caught her square on her back, the pain running up her spine but sparing her stomach.

'My baby,' she breathed, and then her hands flew to her mouth and she prayed that Alex hadn't heard. But he was already facing away from her, his head in his hands. He knelt down at her side, cradling her the way he always did when the anger had subsided, his hands running over her with the tenderness that was a Siamese twin to his rage. 'I'm sorry,' he whispered. 'I didn't mean to.'

'It's not your fault,' she said, because she knew her lines, but for the first time she didn't believe her own words. Anger started to seep from a crack deep inside her that had been patched over too often to hold fast. Goddamn you, she thought.

She knew Alex needed her, but she also realized she could not stay. She couldn't risk the safety of this child made by her and Alex. She would do for her baby what in three years she had not done for herself.

When John buzzed in over the intercom, Alex left Cassie's side and threw all his clothes, suits included, into the suitcases. He dragged the luggage outside the door and then leaned over to kiss her. 'I love you,' he said, the words swollen. He laid his hand over hers where it rested on her stomach.

She waited until she heard the car crunch out of the driveway and then she grabbed her jacket and walked out of Alex's house. The world swam, and she had to concentrate with every footstep to convince herself she was doing what had to be done. She told herself that if she went away now while Alex was out of town, maybe it wouldn't hurt him quite as much.

She walked down the street with no destination in mind. She would have gone to Ophelia's but that was the first place Alex would look when he found her missing; and there was nobody else she could turn to. It was Cassie's word against Alex's gold-plated media image, and like her Greek prophetess namesake, no one would believe her when she spoke the truth.

She had been so close. Cassie's fists were balled into her lap, she was crying, and she realized that she had betrayed herself by losing her memory. Otherwise, she would have been able to stay one step ahead of Alex.

He had been supportive and considerate, probably because she hadn't started shrieking accusations to the press the minute she'd laid eyes on him at the police station. Not that she ever would do such a thing; Alex should have understood that much. She didn't mean to hurt him – she had *never* wanted to – she only wanted to protect herself. She'd never thought that the two were mutually exclusive.

However, Alex did, so he had found her. But the life he had spread before her like a winning hand was not what it had seemed. She'd live in Alex's magnificent castles, smile into his smoky eyes while the cameras flashed, spend the hollow parts of the night blossoming under his touch, and still, it could happen again.

In the past, even Alex's promises hadn't prevented a reoccurrence. She didn't have a choice. She wished he could see that as clearly as she did.

He would be coming into the bedroom any minute to pack for the Friday night red-eye flight, but she was not going to Scotland. Cassie stood up, grabbing an old canvas tote bag with the name of a public television station written across it. She threw as many pieces of clothing as she could inside and then grabbed a handful of underwear and shoved it into the gaps. She pulled a baseball cap scrawled with the name of Alex's production company low on her head and she walked out the door of the bedroom.

It was not a prison, at least not in the usual sense of the word, so the people Cassie passed on the way out did not think of stopping her and asking where she was going. She walked by the pool and the maze and the flower gardens. She went out a back gate of the scrolled iron fence and cut across a neighbor's lush yard, trespassing until she came to a street.

She walked faster and faster, wary of being followed. After a while, she started to run. Her footsteps grew heavier, but she forced herself to keep going. And hours later, when she thought she was safe, she sank to her knees, and she made herself remember.

1989–1993

*P*etrels, hearty Arctic birds, live on the highest parts of the cliffs. From their proud perches they can swoop down on the birds that are not nearly as overweening, calling out songs of their magnificence which carry over the freezing seas.

Once, there lived a petrel who was so arrogant he could not find a mate among his flock. He decided that he would marry a human, and conjured a spell to give himself the form of a man. He sewed together the thickest sealskins to make a stunning parka, and he preened until he was remarkably handsome. Of course, his eyes were still the eyes of a petrel, so he made himself dark glasses to finish his disguise, and looking like this, he set his kayak into the water to find a wife.

At the same time, a widower lived on a quiet shore with his daughter Sedna, a girl so beautiful that word of her form and features spread far beyond the tribe. Many men came to woo her, but Sedna would not marry. None of their pleas could break through her pride to reach her heart.

One day a handsome man arrived in a splendid sealskin parka. He did not drag his kayak onto the beach, but hovered at the edge of the breaking waves and called to Sedna. He started to sing to her. 'Come, love,' he chanted, 'to the land of the birds, where you will never be hungry, where you will rest on soft bear skins, where you will have feathers to clothe you and ivory necklaces, where your lamps will always be full of oil and your pot full of meat.'

The song wrapped itself around Sedna's soul and drew her closer to the kayak. She sailed with the stranger over the sea, away from her home and her father.

For a while she was happy. The petrel made their home on a rocky cliff and caught fish for her daily, and Sedna was so enchanted with her husband that she never thought to truly look around her. But one day the petrel's glasses slipped off his nose and Sedna looked into his eyes. She glanced away and saw a home built not of thick pelts but of rotting fish skins. She slept not on a bear skin but on the tough hide of a walrus. She felt the icy needles of the ocean spray and knew she had married a man who was not what she had thought he was.

Sedna cried with grief, and although the petrel loved her, he could not stop her tears.

A year passed, and Sedna's father came to visit. When he reached the cliff where she lived, the petrel was out hunting for fish, and Sedna begged her father to take her back home. They ran back down to his kayak and set out into the sea.

They had not been paddling long when the petrel came back to his nest. He shouted for Sedna, but his cry of pain was swallowed by the howl of wind and sea. Other petrels found him and told him where Sedna was. He spread his arms, his wingspan blotting out the sun, and flew toward the boat that held Sedna and her father.

As he watched them paddle even more furiously, the petrel grew angry. He beat his wings into the wind, creating currents, forcing a surge of icy waves. A storm raged up at his cries, and the sea became so frenzied the boat rocked from side to side. Sedna's father realized the bird was so powerful that even the ocean was furious at the loss of the petrel's wife. He knew that to save himself, he had to sacrifice his daughter.

He threw Sedna into the frigid water. She sputtered and splashed, her skin blue with the cold. She managed to grab at the side of the boat tightly with her fingers, but her father, terrified by the thunderous beating of the petrel's wings above his head, hit at her hands with the kayak paddle. Sedna's fingertips broke off and fell into the sea, where they turned into whales and dove away. Resurfacing, Sedna caught hold of the gunwhale again, but her father struck out a second time. The middle digits of her fingers shattered like ice and fell into the water to become the seals. One more time she managed to reach the boat, but her father batted at her hands until the third joints broke off and became walruses, and Sedna sank heavy to the bottom of the sea.

Sedna became a mighty spirit who controls the sea creatures that were born of her fingers. Sometimes she whips together storms and crashes kayaks against the rocks. Sometimes she causes famines by luring the seals away from the hunters. Never does she break the surface of the water, where she might again encounter the petrel.

— Eskimo Indian legend

Chapter Ten

I'm going to tell you the truth.

But the story starts long before I'd ever met you, long before anyone had ever heard of Alex Rivers. It begins on the day that Connor Murtaugh moved into the house next door – the same day I went home to dinner and told my mother that when I grew up, I planned to be a boy.

I was five years old, a prim and proper little girl in training to be a southern lady. The fact that we lived in Maine hadn't kept my mother from schooling me to become the finest Georgia peach. I could read a little, and out of necessity I could even cook simple things like soup and grilled cheese and, of course, strong black coffee. I had mastered the art of tossing my hair over my shoulder and lowering my lashes to get what I wanted. I smiled without showing my teeth. Most adults found me charming, but I had no friends my own age. Bringing them home to play was unthinkable, you see, which made most of the kids in school think I was strange or stuck-up. And then Connor's family moved from an apartment across the lake to the house beside mine.

I spent that first day helping him carry boxes and lamps, answering his questions about my birth date, my most hated food, and where you could find fat worms for bait. He overwhelmed me, and for the first time I began to see there was more to living than keeping your knees pressed together when you sat on a chair, and brushing your hair one hundred strokes each night. So I traded my Mary Janes for an old pair of Connor's sneakers that fit when I jammed rolled-up socks into the toes. I learned the fine arts of sprinkling salt on slugs to dry them out and skidding belly-first across mud puddles.

I credit Connor for many reasons in my decision to become an anthropologist, but especially because he was the first person to show me how wonderful the earth feels when you squeeze it through your fingers. These days my hands are almost always dirty, and although Connor has been dead for seventeen years, he's still on my mind.

I don't believe in UFOs, or reincarnation, or ghosts, but I do believe in Connor. All I can say is that from time to time, I feel him. He shows up whenever things are going wrong. I think it is probably my fault that he never got to fly off to heaven, or wherever old souls go, since he spent his childhood taking care of me and apparently still feels compelled to do so.

So, you see, I was expecting him that hot Monday in August when I was pacing the halls of the anthropology department, waiting to hear about tenure. I had been an assistant professor at UCLA for two years now, after having received my BS, MA, and PhD there. I wanted tenure. People who had been there less time than I had made associate prof. I had finally threatened Archibald Custer, the head of the department, with a bald-faced lie about alternative options at an eastern college.

I wasn't really expecting to receive tenure, because at twenty-seven I was still younger than even the adjunct profs and the lecturers. But it wasn't my fault it had taken them longer to get to the same place I was. I was proud of the fact that I had decided thirteen years earlier what I was going to do with my life, and then stuck fast to my original plan.

I was leaning against the water cooler that stood outside the departmental secretary's office when I felt the light pressure on my spine that I knew meant Connor was watching. If he was here, I reasoned, the news couldn't be good. 'They're going to pass me over,' I whispered. There – I had said it, and as I admitted to my lack of success, the words fell to the floor in front of me, heavy and sluggish like failure always is.

'I hate being affiliated with a university,' I said quietly, running my hand down the wall.

It was not the truth. I hated the political bullshit, but I fully embraced the money and the grants. I loved the way the red tape magically disappeared when I tried to open an excavation in another country. And I knew that in a week I'd forgive Custer, and all the people who received promotions. I'd forgive the whole board that voted me down. This year, I'd have to figure out what it was that I was doing wrong, and work a little harder.

'You know what I wish,' I said, 'I wish the good things in life weren't all clustered together when you were little.'

They weren't, for most people. When was the last time I'd walked across the campus barefoot? Or missed a class because I had overslept? When was the last time I had gotten dead drunk or awakened in a stranger's bed or come up short of cash at the supermarket?

Never. I didn't let myself live on the edge, although I didn't really think I was missing anything. Spontaneity made me uncomfortable. My single-mindedness was what was going to get me a promotion.

Someday.

But I had this sense that if Connor could come back to life, he would be disgusted with me. He'd want me to do the things we used to talk about: live on Tahiti for a couple of months, take up bonsai or rock climbing.

I tried to push Connor out of my mind in preparation for my meeting with Archibald Custer. He was standing in the open doorway of his office, monolithic, as if he expected to conjure whomever he wanted to see by the sheer force of his position. He was argumentative, pigheaded, and sexist. I didn't much like him, but I knew how to play by his rules.

'Ah, Miss Barrett,' he said. He spoke by holding a transmitter to a box built into his throat, his own vocal cords having been severed due to throat cancer a few years back. The undergraduates thought he was creepy, and I had to agree. Except for his height, he always reminded me a little of the sketches done of *Homo habilis*, and I had to applaud him for choosing such a form-fitting profession.

He didn't like me either, not only because I happened to be female and young, but also because I was a physical anthropologist. He was a cultural anthropologist – made his name by squatting right down with the Yąnomamö years ago. There had always been a friendly rivalry between the two camps of anthropology, but I couldn't forgive him for what he'd done after I'd defended my dissertation. I had written a piece about whether violence was innate or learned, an age-old debate between physical and cultural anthropologists. The popular belief tended toward a cultural approach, saying that although aggression was innate, planned aggression – such as war – was brought about by the pressure of living in societies, not by our evolutionary history. I argued back, saying that this might be true, but society itself wouldn't have come about unless the territorial nature bred into our genes required man to make rules.

All in all, it was a decent rebuttal to the cultural anthropologists, and this had Custer fuming. My first year as a lecturer he'd assigned me to courses that all ranked under cultural anthropology, and when I complained and asked to go on a field site, he had simply raised his eyebrows and said he thought it might do me some good to become more well-rounded.

Now he waved me into his office and motioned me toward the chair that faced his tremendous desk. He was grinning, goddamn him, as he started to speak. 'I'm sorry to tell you—'

I jumped up from the chair, unable to hear any more. 'Then don't tell me at all,' I said, smiling tightly. 'I assume I've been passed over, thank you very much, and I'll just save you the trouble.' I took a step toward the door.

'*Miss Barrett.*'

I stopped with my hand on the doorknob and turned.

'Sit down.'

I slipped into the chair again, wondering how many points this had set me back in Custer's mind.

'You'll be on an unusual assignment this first quarter,' he continued. 'Indeed, you're always pining away about going on location.'

I leaned forward in the chair. Were they starting some new field class during the fall semester? My mind raced through the possible sites: Kenya, Sudan, the Isles of Scilly. Would I be heading the group, or working with someone else?

'Now, I'm afraid the associate professorship isn't going to be a possibility this term,' Custer said. 'Instead, we've recommended you for a sabbatical.'

I tightened my fingers around the armrests of the chair. I hadn't *applied* for a sabbatical. 'If you'll excuse me, Archibald, I have to say in my own defense that for the past three years—'

'You've been exemplary. Yes, I know. We all do. But sometimes' – he winced here – 'sometimes that just isn't enough.'

Tell me about it, I thought.

'We've chosen you to reopen the old UCLA site at Olduvai Gorge. Get it ready for a freshman field expedition,' Custer said, sitting back in his chair.

I set my jaw. They wanted me to be a gofer – to set up for a class I wasn't worthy enough to teach. It was a job any graduate student could do. It was not what I had worked so hard for, what I had written my dissertation for. It was not what I had planned as a step up on the steady climb of my career. 'Surely I'm not the best-trained person for this job,' I hedged.

Custer shrugged. 'You're the only faculty member who hasn't been . . . scheduled . . . for classes next semester,' he said.

I listened to the words he spoke, but clearly heard the truth. He was telling me I was the only one who was expendable.

*   *   *

Less than thirty-six hours later, I was in Tanzania, sitting under the cool linen shade of a makeshift awning on the tiny piece of Olduvai Gorge that UCLA had requisitioned for its field classes. I was still angry at being banished, but I hadn't argued with Custer. It would have been a mistake. After all, I'd have to come back in ten weeks and beg for a teaching assignment.

I'd tried to convince myself that this little sojourn would be better than I expected. After all, Olduvai Gorge had been Louis Leakey's first site in East Africa. Maybe I'd hit it big too: discover the missing link, or something else that would set my colleagues on their collective ears and change the current outlook on human evolution. The odds were against it, but I was still young and there were millions of years of history left to unearth.

However, the scouting I'd done in the morning had convinced me that like the other anthropologists who scoured the site for decades after Leakey's discoveries, I wasn't going to turn up anything new. I had no idea how I was going to keep myself busy for ten weeks. Setting up the site for the field class meant pinpointing the spots where an excavation would be likely to yield fossils, but it seemed the class could dig in the basement of Fowler Hall and have just as much luck as they would here.

As the sun climbed higher, I walked casually across the site, rummaging in my big straw bag for the book I'd begun to read on the plane. I glanced up, making sure that I was alone before I pulled it out.

Ridiculous. My heart was pounding, as if I were about to be discovered with a gram of cocaine. It was only a dime-store romance novel, my one vice. I didn't smoke, I rarely drank, I'd never done drugs, but I was completely addicted to those stupid books on whose covers an overripe woman lounged in the arms of a drifter. I was so embarrassed that I wrapped them in brown parcel paper, like I used to do with textbooks in elementary school. I would read them on public buses and on the benches outside at UCLA, pretending they were anthropological treatises or Pulitzer Prize-winning fiction.

I couldn't help myself. I knew the psychological explanation for this had something to do with what was lacking in my own life, but I told myself it didn't matter. I had started a few years ago after my roommate, Ophelia, had posed for a book cover in the arms of some glorious man. I had read that first paperback, and then I couldn't stop. There was solace in knowing that never in any tribe or any ancient race had people existed like this. It made me feel, well, more normal.

But that didn't keep me from hoping, I suppose. Still, if a romance novel was going to spring to life, it would be with someone like Ophelia in its title role. She was beautiful and statuesque and sexy – not simple and practical, like me. It would have been nice to be the kind of woman for whom wars were started, but I was not holding my breath. To date, no knight was wearing my colors, no adventurers had come to find me across time and distance. Then again, I lived by choice in LA, where beautiful women were the norm, not the exception. On the other hand, in these books there was no plastic surgery, no concealing cosmetics, no step aerobics classes. I thought of Helen of Troy, of Petrarch's Laura, and I wondered if they really had looked so different from me.

'Excuse me,' a voice said. 'Your tent is in my viewfinder.'

I started at the unfamiliar sound and instinctively buried the paperback in the soft red sand. My head snapped up to see two men, their faces silhouetted against the high sun. 'Pardon me?' I said, coming to my feet.

The men were clearly not natives; their foreheads were sunburnt and peeling and they hadn't the good sense to be wearing hats. 'My viewfinder,' the taller man said. 'You're going to have to move.'

I bristled. 'I'm afraid you're wrong,' I said. 'This site belongs to the University of California.'

The man threw up his hands, disgusted, and turned his back on me.

The second man held out his hand. 'I'm George Farley,' he said. 'I'm an AD.' He gestured over his shoulder. 'Edward here is our DP.'

I smiled at him warily. *AD, DP.* 'Cassandra Barrett,' I said, hoping this was the appropriate response.

George waved an arm toward the sweep of the gorge. 'We're filming a movie here, and when Edward was doing long-range pans today, he kept getting your tent. You see, we were under the impression we'd be the only ones here this time of year.'

A movie? How they had gotten permission to film in Tanzania was mind-boggling, but I could see that the already excavated sites on the edge of the Serengeti plain would save the production costs of bulldozing their own. 'Well,' I said, 'I'm sorry to disappoint you. But I'm working here too.'

'Tell her to take the tent down, then.'

The cinematographer – the *DP* – had not even bothered to turn around when he spoke, and my hands clenched at my sides. 'I'm afraid I can't,' I said, biting off each word. 'It's too hot to work without an awning.'

'Work?' The cinematographer pivoted, and slowly smiled. George Farley's eyes burned like a man who's discovered gold. 'You're an anthropologist?'

Against my better judgment, I nodded.

'Ah,' Edward sighed. 'There is a God.'

George led me back beneath my linen awning. 'You're a UCLA anthropologist? You're here on an excavation?'

'Believe me,' I said, 'this isn't exactly an excavation site.' I explained the program at the university; the various field sites used around Africa to teach excavation hands-on.

'So you're not really working,' George pressed. 'You might have some . . . free time.'

'I might,' I said.

'Three hundred dollars a day,' George said. 'Yours, if you'll agree to be a technical advisor on the movie.'

It was more than I made at UCLA; it was certainly enticing. Without knowing a thing about the movie, I thought of how tempting it would be to actually *profit* from Custer's enforced sabbatical. I thought of the satisfaction I would get from screwing Custer in a way that didn't jeopardize my future at the university.

When I did not say anything, George jumped forward to fill the silence. 'It's a film about an anthropologist, and the star, Alex Rivers, insists that we get him the real McCoy so he can learn about excavation firsthand.'

'Insists?' Edward interrupted, smirking. '*Demands*.'

I raised an eyebrow. 'Don't you have one already?' I said. 'Seems to me you'd have thought of that before you came all the way out here.'

George cleared his throat. 'You're right, and we did, but he had to leave unexpectedly about a week ago.'

'In the middle of the night,' Edward added, under his breath. 'Probably by force.'

George gave him a dark look. 'Alex isn't as bad as all that,' he said, turning back to me. 'We wired the States but it would take time we don't have to find someone and you . . . well, you—'

'I've dropped into your viewfinder,' I said lightly.

'Three hundred and fifty,' George said. 'And a room at the lodge in town.'

It wasn't ethical; it wasn't something Archibald Custer would condone. It would mean spending all my free time babysitting a spoiled movie star who'd already fired someone, instead of poking through the site for my own research. I opened my mouth, prepared to decline their offer graciously, when I thought of Connor. *Don't you ever wonder what you're missing?*

'Well,' I said, smiling brilliantly, 'when do we start?'

George had left me with an improvised contract scribbled on the rear flap of the romance novel I'd been reading, and almost immediately I'd taken down my awning and driven into town to call Ophelia. Me, on a movie set with Alex Rivers. Personally, I wasn't expecting much from a celebrity – living in LA had shown me how shallow and egocentric their worlds were – but I knew Ophelia would consider this a tremendous stroke of good fortune. She devoured the trade journals, always knowing what producer had hooked up with what director and what star; she stared like a groupie when we walked past movies that were being shot on the streets of LA. I could imagine what her reaction would be – she'd die, or at least she'd say she was going to, because that was her answer for most things, from winning a part as an extra on a TV commercial to running out of lettuce when making a salad.

Ophelia Fox had been my roommate since we'd been thrown together by a computer our freshman year at UCLA. Back then, she'd had the unfortunate name of Olivera Frug, and she'd still been a B-cup and a blonde. I sort of anchored Ophelia to the real world, and in return, well, I suppose she made me laugh.

I also knew more about Ophelia than anyone else did. When I stayed at UCLA during my first Christmas break because there was nothing for me in Maine, I was surprised to see Ophelia was staying too. In her usual flip manner, she told everyone it was a way to work on her tan. But on Christmas Eve we got drunk on a bottle of Glenfiddich, and when Ophelia thought I had fallen asleep she began to talk. She spoke of the stepfather who had been feeling her up since she was twelve. She spoke of the smell of his aftershave. She spoke of the insomnia she cultivated so that she would be able to hear the slightest breach of her bedroom door. When the sun came up we did not unwrap presents, but instead shyly treasured this gift of each other.

We were unlikely friends, but we were inseparable. When Ophelia began to remake herself in a different image, I stood by her. After all, I understood what she was trying so hard to disguise. She bought herself breast implants as a graduation gift and legally changed her name; and while I started work on my master's, she threw herself into the task of finding us an apartment close enough to the studios for her and to UCLA for me. It was a small place, but the rent was low, and we'd been there now for almost seven years.

'Go ahead,' the operator said.

'Ophelia?'

I heard her let her breath out in a rush. 'Thank God you called,' she said, as if I were a half-mile away. 'I'm having a crisis.'

I grinned. 'You're always having a crisis,' I pointed out. 'What's the problem today?'

'I'm supposed to meet my therapist at four o'clock, you know?' Ophelia had been seeing someone to enhance her self-assertiveness ever since she had decided the sessions with the psychic weren't working. 'Right now I'm seeing him twice a week, and I'd really like to cut back to once, but I don't know how to tell him that.'

I didn't want to laugh, I didn't mean to, but the sound leaked out. I covered it with a cough.

'Maybe I just won't go,' she sighed. 'I'll tell him Thursday.' She was quiet for a moment, and then seemed to remember where I was. 'And how's Africa?' she dutifully asked.

Ophelia did not understand my attraction to anthropology – to her it was a glorified way of getting filthy – but she knew how much it meant to me. 'It's much more interesting than I expected,' I said. 'I'm moonlighting.'

'As a safari guide?'

'As a technical advisor on Alex Rivers's new movie.'

I heard a crash in the background. 'Ohmigod, ohmigod, ohmigod,' Ophelia said. '*How* did this happen?'

Relating the entire story to Ophelia brought back my original doubts. 'I know I'm going to regret this,' I said. 'If it wasn't for the money – and for a chance to screw UCLA – I wouldn't be doing it.' I grimaced. 'I bet he won't even want to get his hands dirty.' I let my breath out slowly, mulling over the consequences of a hasty decision. I didn't like Custer, but I could avoid him when I was at the university. I wasn't going to like Alex Rivers, but I had committed myself to being his shadow for ten hours a day.

'I'm sending you clothes,' Ophelia announced. 'My black sleeveless dress and the pink satin bra and—'

'Ophelia,' I interrupted, 'I'm his technical advisor, not his mistress.'

'Still,' Ophelia countered, 'you never know. Just sign for the damn package and you can stuff it into your bag and forget about it.' She took a shaky breath. 'I can't believe this. I just can't believe this. I *knew* I should have majored in anthropology.' Her voice tumbled over her words, racing with excitement. 'God, Cass,' she said. '*Alex Rivers!*'

I smiled. If I even wore that bra within twenty yards of Alex Rivers, Ophelia would probably frame it when I got home. 'He's just a person,' I reminded her.

'Yeah,' Ophelia said. 'A person who makes four million per film and has the entire female population casting him in their fantasies at night.'

I thought about this: Alex Rivers had not been in any of my fantasies, but then again most of my dreams had to do with chipping away at piles of dirt and finding men who'd lived millions of years ago. I tried to remember which of his films I had seen. I must have gone to them with Ophelia, because she was really the only person I spent my free time with, and she usually forced me to see the latest box office hit. Vaguely I remembered *Desperado*, some Western made when we were in college, and *Light and Shadows*, which had been one of the token Vietnam coming-of-age pictures of 1987. There were a few action films whose titles I couldn't remember, and then the last one I'd seen, about six months ago, that love story. *Applewild*. I'd forgotten about that one. It had surprised me, because I'd never seen Alex Rivers cast as a romantic hero, and he had made me believe in him.

The film's message had stayed with me the whole drive home: Better to have loved and lost than never to have loved at all. I wondered if it was really true. Love, to my knowledge, was nothing more than a planned seduction. In college, I had lost my virginity to a fraternity boy, just because I wanted to know what it was like. There hadn't been any great ache around my heart, or a connection of the spirits. There was the speeding of my blood, the mix of our hot breath, and the simplicity of sex.

There had not been many others, but I didn't think I was missing much. Most of the time I was too busy to notice. I would have liked kids, one day, but I would only create a child with someone I really cared about, and to this date the only person I had ever even imagined falling in love with was Connor.

'I have to go,' I said. 'This is costing a fortune.'

'Call me Thursday after you meet him.'

'Ophelia—'

'Thursday.'

I closed my eyes. 'We'll see,' I said. 'No promises.'

I had never seen so many people who were paid to do nothing. People sat on the ground, on folding canvas chairs, on boulders. There were cranes set up with tremendous cameras, and wires leading everywhere. A man wearing headphones sat in front of a portable sound system colored with knobs and levers. Everyone was talking, George and Edward were nowhere to be found, and no one seemed to be in charge.

I was used to being sent to desolate locations without knowing a soul, but here I was out of my element. It seemed everywhere I placed my foot I got it tangled in some cord, and I had run right into a man carrying a profusion of wigs and tweed caps, knocking him to the ground. 'Oh my God,' I said, 'let me help you.' But he had just given me a dirty look, gathered his things, and rushed away.

I walked up to a woman who sat on a high canvas chair labeled SCRIPT. 'Excuse me,' I said. 'I'm looking for the director.'

She sighed, but she didn't look up from the open loose-leaf binder she held in her lap. 'You and me both, babe,' she said. She scribbled a note with a red pencil, and then yelled out someone's name, waving him over with her hand.

I bobbed and weaved past people with walkie-talkies looped into their belts. Lying across a table was a pile of scripts. '"In His Image",' I read aloud, running my fingers over the Warner Brothers insignia at the bottom.

'Can I help you?' A harried-looking man stood in front of me, tapping his foot. He snatched the script out of my hand.

'I'm looking for Bernie Roth,' I said. 'The director.'

The man sneered at me. 'Like I don't know who he is?' He snapped his fingers as two brawny men walked by carrying a heavy black rope. 'Hey – hey, where are you going with that? I told you it was supposed to go *behind* the tent.'

'Wait,' I said as he scurried after the rope, 'Bernie Roth?'

'In a minute,' he stalled. He yelled after the two men carrying the rope. '*Behind* the tent!'

I slung my knapsack onto the table and pulled a khaki baseball cap onto my head. If Mohammed can't get to the mountain, I figured, I'd just wait for the mountain to come to Mohammed. Sooner or later, someone was going to try to locate me. I sat down with my back against a tall tree, and hugged my knees to my chest.

I tried to think about Alex Rivers. I knew what he looked like, of course – he was on the cover of a magazine every month, or so it seemed. He was, in a word, stunning. His brown hair was shot with gold; his jaw was square and marked by the cleft of his chin. He had a full, generous mouth that always looked as if he was holding back a secret. And his eyes, his claim to fame, were remarkable. They were the split-silver of an empty mirror, and like a mirror, when you looked into them even in a publicity photo, you could swear you were seeing your soul.

I supposed it wouldn't be a hardship to face him every day.

I was surprised at the quiet. No cameras were rolling, no one was waving frantically and calling 'Action', no one was even saying anything that resembled a line. A fine red dust covered all the photographic equipment, as if it hadn't been used recently at all. No wonder it took twelve weeks to make a two-hour film.

The set, from what I could see, was in three parts. The first section was the actual excavation site of Olduvai Gorge, looking not much different from the UCLA site a half-mile away. The second area was a series of tents, and in front of one of them was an actress I had seen before but couldn't name. She was wearing khaki shorts and a Kalahari bush jacket, and I decided that my first piece of technical advice would be to tell the costume designer that the *National Geographic* look was nowhere near as realistic as a comfortable old T-shirt.

The third set was on a raised platform, designed to look like the inside of a tent. There was a cot and a collection of artfully arranged empty cartons, a low trestle table. On a shelf was a patterned china bowl and pitcher, and I couldn't help laughing out loud. China?

After a few minutes a girl came to sit beside me. 'Shit, it's hot,' she said. She smiled, the first real smile I'd seen since I arrived. 'Who are you here with?'

'Just me,' I said, taken aback by the question, as if I were supposed to bring a date. 'I'm the technical advisor on anthropology.'

'Wow,' the girl breathed. 'You mean you do this for a *living*?'

I smiled at her. 'I thought it was supposed to be the other way around. You know, me being impressed because you're in the movies.'

'Oh, I'm not really in them,' she said. 'I'm Janet's assistant.' She pointed to the woman in the Kalahari bush jacket who was scanning a script. 'My name's LeAnne.'

I introduced myself and shook her hand, and then gestured toward the milling crowd. 'How come no one's doing anything?' I asked.

LeAnne laughed, getting to her feet. 'It's the business,' she said. 'A lot of hurry up and wait. Come on, I'll bet you don't know where the oasis is.'

When she started to walk away I followed her. Inside a long, low tent was a feast. My eyes ran from one end of the table to the other, taking in sweating pitchers of mango juice and lemonade, piles of bananas and kiwis, finger sandwiches filled with chicken salad and something that looked like sliced egg, covered platters of coleslaw and sesame noodles. 'Is this lunch?' I asked.

LeAnne shook her head. 'Mr Rivers likes knowing there's something to eat between takes. He arranges the whole thing, or actually, Jennifer does. She does for him what I do for Janet. If you think this is something, wait till you see the layout at lunch. Yesterday we had king crab. Can you believe that? King crab, in *Africa*.'

I hesitantly took a banana, peeling it back and walking out of the tent into the hot sun. I lifted up my face, shielding my eyes. 'What is this movie about?'

LeAnne was shocked that no one had told me. It was a sort of science fiction film; Alex Rivers was playing an anthropologist who unearths a partial skeleton that seems, at first sight, to predate anything ever found before. But when he gets the bones carbondated, he finds they come from the 1960s. Then he notices that the chemical makeup of the bones isn't quite what it should be, even if it had been an ancestral skeleton. Turns out it's an alien, and that of course makes him wonder about the origins of man in the first place.

I nodded politely when LeAnne finished. Not something I would go see, but it would probably sell tickets.

I followed her back to a small knot of people, all of whom I was introduced to and whose names I promptly forgot. Most of the crew were sitting on the ground now. LeAnne started talking to another woman about the condition of the bathroom facilities on location, and I leaned back against a tall canvas chair.

It was just like the one the script woman had been sitting on, only this one said ALEX RIVERS across its back. Still, it was empty, and Alex Rivers didn't appear to be around, so I climbed into it.

LeAnne gasped and grabbed my wrist. 'Get off that,' she said.

Startled, I jumped down, forming a cloud of dust that had everyone on the ground coughing. 'It's just a chair,' I said. 'No one was sitting there.'

'It's Mr Rivers's chair.' I stared at her, waiting for the explanation. 'No one sits in Mr Rivers's chair.'

For God's sake. This was going to be worse than I had anticipated. I tried to convince myself that three hundred and fifty dollars per day was more than enough compensation for explaining the rudiments of collecting bone fragments to a man who thought china pitchers belonged in an off-site camp and who was so full of himself that only his own precious bottom could touch his canvas chair.

I knew something was about to happen by the shiver that ran through the air almost as quickly as the whispers spread. The crew started to stand, brushing off their shorts and returning to their respective positions on the set. Three men climbed up the dolly to the camera; the sound technician pressed his hand to one headphoned ear and rewound a portion of tape.

The man who had run after the rope called out for a woman named Suki. 'Female stand-in,' he yelled. 'Suki, we need you for lighting.' A woman who was not Janet the actress wandered toward the tents, and immediately a series of lights were set up around her and shifted into position.

I stared directly into one bright white beam, which was why I didn't see him until he almost walked on top of me. Alex Rivers threw his jacket onto the chair I had dared to sit upon, not noticing me any more than he seemed to notice the air around him. He was talking quietly with someone I assumed was Bernie Roth, since he looked nearly as important and wasn't paying attention to anyone either.

Alex Rivers was saying something about the black rope that I'd seen earlier. He brushed my arm as he moved past me, and I jumped backward.

It wasn't that he'd collided with me; it was the heat of his skin. I rubbed my own shoulder, certain there would be a red blister or a welt, some proof of what I'd felt. I watched him walk away from me, amazed when my sense of perspective did not kick in. Instead of Alex Rivers getting smaller and smaller, he seemed to fill my entire field of vision.

Without realizing what I was doing, I walked behind the tents, keeping several feet away from where he stood, but close enough to listen. He and Bernie Roth and a tall, muscular man were fingering the black rope that had been brought in earlier. A fourth man was bent back under the force of Alex Rivers's anger. 'Listen to me,' he said, cutting off whatever the man had been saying. 'Just listen to me. Sven can jump with this rope, but this rope isn't white like I told you. You have two choices. You can go into town and try to find a rope that is white that he can jump with, or you can use this black rope and have me pissed off at you for the next eleven weeks.' He ran his hand over his face as if he was very tired. 'This is about safety. The key criterion is whether or not Sven can use the rope for the stunt. Secondary is what the hell color it shows up against a background.'

The muscular man and the terrified set dresser walked off to the left, leaving me with a direct view of Alex Rivers. I stared at his profile, the muscles at the base of his jaw, the wind lifting light strands of his hair.

What a sanctimonious asshole! I knew nothing about making movies, but I had seen my share of bureaucracy at UCLA, and

Alex Rivers was no better than Archibald Custer. He milked the advantage of his position, and of the astonishment that everyone couldn't help but feel around him. Well, if I'd learned anything in the anthropology department, it was that you couldn't let the people who made decisions walk all over you. You had to put yourself in their league if you wanted them to believe you really belonged there.

I swallowed, then took a step forward. I'd introduce myself to him and Roth, mention the bush jacket and the ludicrous china pitcher, and then I'd give Rivers a piece of my mind.

But as soon as I stepped into Alex Rivers's line of vision, I froze. He held me spellbound, and I truly couldn't have said if I was in the Serengeti or Belgium or circling Mars. It had nothing to do with his features, although they were certainly arresting. It had to do with his power. There was something about his stare that made me unable to turn away.

His eyes gleamed, catching the light like the surface of a still pond. Then he looked away, as if he was searching for something. When he caught my eye again, he was smiling. *Resplendent*. The word caught in my throat, and I wondered how I could spend hours working steadfastly beneath the high African sun, but become dazed by the image of a single man.

'Hon,' Alex Rivers said, 'can you get me something to drink?'

I blinked at him, but he was already moving away with the director at his heels. Who the hell did he think he was? Who the hell did he think I was?

His assistant. Or rather, he had been looking for his assistant and couldn't find her, and decided that obviously I'd been placed on this earth to serve at his beck and call. Like everyone else. I watched him settle into his high canvas chair, the soft seat and back molding around him, already cast in his form.

There was nothing I liked about him. I thought about what I would say when I called Ophelia. *Guess what*, I would begin. *Alex Rivers is a pompous bastard who orders people around. He's so wrapped up in himself he can't see two feet away from where he's standing*. And even as I was thinking this, I was walking toward the tent with the movable feast.

I hated him for making me forget what I had been about to say; I hated him for getting me to come here in the first place; I especially hated him for making my pulse catch at odd intervals, pounding like the drums of the natives I sometimes heard over the wind when I was digging on site. I picked a red plastic cup from a stack on a table and filled it to the brim with ice, knowing that it would take only minutes to melt. Then I added juice – papaya, I guessed – and I stirred it with a disposable knife, waiting until the cup began to sweat and the liquid had taken the temperature of the ice.

Alex Rivers was still sitting on his royal throne, leaning toward a woman who was dusting his face with a light powder. When he noticed me, he reached out his hand for his drink and awarded me a second smile. 'Ah,' he said. 'I was beginning to think I'd never see you again.'

I smiled at him and dumped the juice and the ice, even the cup, into his lap. For a moment, I watched the stain spread over his trousers. 'No such luck,' I said, and then I turned and walked away.

Chapter Eleven

I expected Alex Rivers to curse under his breath, demand my name, order me to be fired. As for me, I kept walking, with every intention of leaving the set, even leaving Tanzania. But Alex Rivers did the one thing that could make me turn around: he laughed. He had a deep, rich laugh, the kind that rained down warm. He caught my eye the moment I looked back. 'So,' he said, smiling. 'I assume you felt my temper needed to be cooled off?'

I probably could have withstood his wrath, but his understanding was my undoing. My knees began to shake and I grabbed onto a piece of lighting equipment just to stay upright. I was struck by the full force of what, exactly, I'd just done. I had not spilled a freezing drink on some assistant, some costume designer. I had deliberately antagonized the man I was supposed to be working with. The man who was paying me three hundred and fifty dollars a day just to be helpful.

He stood up and walked toward me, holding out his hand as if he knew very well I was seconds away from falling down. 'Alex Rivers,' he said. 'I don't think we've met.'

From the corner of my eye, I noticed the crew pretending very hard to look busy while they watched the scene unfolding before them. 'Cassandra Barrett,' I said. 'From UCLA.'

His eyes brightened to a shade of silver I had never seen before. 'My anthropologist,' he said. 'It's good to meet you.'

I glanced down at the crotch of his wet khaki pants, soaked

in a stain the shape of a butterfly. I smiled right at him. 'The pleasure was all mine,' I said.

He laughed again, and I found myself hoarding the sound so that I would be able to remember it later when I was in my bedroom at the lodge, the old yellow ceiling fan spinning over my head. He took my arm. 'Call me Alex,' he said. 'And I'll get you a script so you know what's going on. Bernie!' he called out. 'Come over here and meet our technical advisor.'

The director of the film, who looked for all the world like a shadow ready to jump at Alex's commands, shook my hand politely and excused himself to find someone in the cast. It was easy to see that this was Alex Rivers's show. He started talking to me before I registered the importance of his words. 'You want me to dig something up?' I said. 'Now?'

Alex nodded. 'The scene we're shooting this afternoon involves my character's initial discovery of the skeleton. I mean, I could sort of go on instinct, but I know I wouldn't be right. There has to be a method, doesn't there? You don't just reach into the sand and pull up a leg bone?'

I winced. 'No,' I said. 'You certainly do not.'

He had taken my arm and was pulling me toward the gaping hole where most of the finds from Olduvai Gorge had been unearthed. 'I just want to watch you for a little while,' he said. 'I want to see your movements, and your concentration, those kinds of things. That's what I need.'

'What you need is a tarp,' I said. 'If you were really going to find something of value, you'd have set up a black tarpaulin over the site so that whatever bones you do locate don't get bleached out by the sun.'

Alex grinned at me. 'That's *exactly* why I wanted you here,' he said. He motioned to two men who were standing off to the side, fixing the leg of a tent. 'Joe, Ken, can you guys find some kind of tarpaulin to stretch across this thing? It has to be—' He glanced at me. 'Does it *have* to be black?'

I shrugged. 'Mine usually are.'

'Black, then.' As the men turned to go, Alex called back the one named Ken. 'Congratulations on the little girl,' he said. 'I heard you got the news last night. If she looks like Janine, she'll be a beauty.'

Ken broke into a big smile, and ran off after the other prop man. I stared at Alex. 'Is he a good friend?'

'Not particularly,' Alex said. 'But he's a member of the crew. It's my business to know something about everyone on the crew.'

I squatted down at the edge of the site and sifted through the chalky dirt. If he was trying to impress me, he wasn't going to get very far. 'That's impossible,' I said. 'I mean, there have to be at least a hundred people around.'

Alex stared at me so forcefully I felt myself looking up at him before I even wanted to. His voice was tight and controlled. 'I know everyone's name and everyone's wife's name. Back when I was bartending I learned that if people think you're paying attention to them, they're more likely to hang around. It's easy for me to remember, it makes them feel important, and things get done twice as fast because of it.'

He spoke as if he was defending himself, as if I had challenged him, when that wasn't my intention at all. The truth was, I was shocked. It was hard to reconcile the man who had thrown a tantrum over a length of rope with the man who made it a point to know the names of everyone working for him. 'You didn't know my name,' I pointed out.

'No,' he said, and then he relaxed. He offered me a brilliant smile. 'But you made sure I'll never forget it.'

We settled down to the task at hand, kneeling in the excavated pit. I showed Alex the different tools used to dig, the gentle brushes used to clear the excess earth. I tried to explain the markings on the plain that would indicate the presence of fossils, but this was difficult to understand unless you had been trained.

'There,' I said, sitting back on my heels. 'That's pretty much all I can show you.'

'But you haven't shown me anything at all,' Alex complained. 'I need to watch you excavate a skull or something.'

I laughed at him. 'Not from this site,' I said. 'Everything's been stripped dry.'

'Pretend,' Alex urged. He grinned. 'It's easy. I've built a career on it.'

I sighed and bent into the pit again, trying my best to imagine a bone fragment that was not there. I was starting to see why my predecessor had left. Maybe pretending was easy for Alex Rivers, but – as he'd said – this was his career. *Mine* was based on hard evidence and physical proof, not an overactive imagination. Feeling like an idiot, I swept away a top layer of red dust and ran my fingers over the bumpy ground. I took a small pick and began to dig in a circle around this nonexistent skull. I brushed the earth with my fingers and wiped away perspiration on my forehead with my shoulder.

I closed my eyes and tried to imagine how big this invisible skull might be. I could not picture it at all; I felt ridiculous trying. I had been trained too fully in the literal to even consider the figurative. 'Look,' I said, planning to tell Alex this wasn't my cup of tea.

But before I could finish my sentence, Alex Rivers crouched down behind me. He reached his arms around my shoulders, almost like an embrace, and covered my hands with his own. 'No, *you* look,' he said, and he nodded toward the site I had been digging. I blinked, and what was only earth now looked like bone. A trick of the light, I thought, an illusion. Or maybe the sheer power of Alex Rivers's imagination.

He was unlike anyone I'd ever met. He did know everyone's name; that was apparent as soon as the set was being readied for filming. He politely left me sitting next to his assistant, Jennifer. As he went to crouch behind the camera and talk with Bernie Roth about the best way to approach a particular shot, he joked with the male stand-in who had to sweat in the hot sun while the lights and reflective panels were set up around him.

He was a hundred places at once; I got tired just trying to find him here and there. But every time I glanced down at the script in my lap or wandered to the low table stacked with storyboards, I'd feel his eyes on me. I would turn around and sure enough, there was Alex Rivers, fifty feet away, staring at me as if I were the only other person for miles around.

The scene they were filming was exactly what Alex had said it would be: his character, a Dr Rob Paley, finding the bones of what he thinks is a fossilized hominid. Bernie had climbed onto the crane that held the Panavision camera, and was walking Alex through the scene. 'I want you to come in . . . that's right, a little slower . . . and crouch down, good, like that. Now what are you doing with your hands? Try to remember, you haven't had any luck for a good three weeks now, and suddenly you strike gold.' Alex stood up and shouted a question at Bernie, but the wind carried it away before I could make out the words.

When they were ready to film, all the people holding walkie-talkies stood in a spread line, shouting 'Quiet!' one after the other, a human echo. The cameraman murmured, 'Rolling,' and the sound technician, bent low over his electronic oasis, said, 'Speed.'

In the seconds before Bernie called for action, I watched Alex slip into his role. All the light drained out of his eyes, and his body relaxed so dramatically it seemed as if he'd been sucked dry. And then, within seconds, the energy snaked back through his body, straightening his spine and flashing in his eyes. But he didn't have the same face. In fact, if I had passed him on the street, I would have taken him for someone else.

He moved differently. He walked differently. He even *breathed* differently. Like a tired old man, he made his way across the yellow strip of plain, carefully lowering himself into the excavated pit.

He pulled a pick and brush from his pocket and began to dig. I smiled, watching my own idiosyncrasies being played before the camera: the habit I had of picking left to right, the methodical sweep of the brush like an umpire at home plate. But then came the moment when his character discovers the skeleton, skull first. Alex's hands swept over the spot he'd cleared, and he paused. Moving faster now, he began to chisel away at the earth. A fragment of bone appeared, planted minutes before by a set dresser. It was yellowed and cracked, and I found myself leaning forward in my seat to get a better look.

Alex Rivers lifted his face and looked directly at me, and in his eyes I saw myself. His expression was the same one I'd worn at that dazzling moment when he held his arms around me and, out of nowhere, I'd seen a skull. I recognized my own surprise, my dedication, and my wonder.

I began to feel hot. I pulled at my loose cotton collar and lifted my hair off the back of my neck. I took off my baseball cap and fanned myself with it, wishing he would turn away.

He threw back his head and turned his face to the sun. 'My God,' he whispered. He looked like any scientist who knew, in his heart, he had made the discovery of his life. He looked like he'd been doing this for ages. He looked, well, like me.

I had spent years working toward the anthropological discovery that would raise my status among colleagues. I had fashioned the moment over and over in my mind the way most women picture their weddings: how the sun would feel on my back, how my hands would spread through the earth, how the bone would flow smooth beneath my palms. I had envisioned my face turned to the sky, my prayers offered up in exchange for this gift. Although I'd certainly never discussed it with anyone, least of all Alex Rivers, he had played the scene exactly the way I had imagined mine.

He'd robbed me of the most important moment of my life, one that hadn't even happened yet. It was this injustice that made me spring from my canvas chair the moment the director called 'Cut.'

I could barely hear the claps and whistles of the crew over the pounding within my own head. *How dare he*, I thought. He said he'd only wanted to watch me dig. He didn't say anything about mimicking my expressions and my instincts. It was as if he'd climbed inside of me and sifted through my mind.

I ran to the hospitality tent, complete with cots and electric fans and pitchers of ice water. Dipping a paper towel into a bowl, I dripped water down my neck. I felt it run in the valley between my breasts, down my stomach, into the waist of my shorts. I leaned closer to the bowl and splashed some onto my face.

He knew me so well. He knew me better than I know myself.

In the distance I heard Bernie Roth make the decision to use that single take, since Alex couldn't possibly be any better. I snorted and threw myself down on a cot. I had made a contractual commitment; I would see it through. I would show Alex Rivers whatever technical moves he wanted; I would let him know what props he'd need and what was inaccurate in the script. But I wouldn't let him get close, and I would never show him my heart. I'd already done that once because he'd taken me by surprise, but it wasn't going to happen again.

I fell asleep for a little while, and when I woke up a fine sheen of sweat covered my body. Sitting up, I reached for the paper towel I'd used before. I wet it again and set it across the back of my neck.

The flap of the tent that served as a door whipped open to reveal a young man with a ponytail of bright red hair. His name was Charlie; I'd talked with him earlier. 'Miss Barrett,' he said, 'I've been looking all over for you.'

I gave him my nicest smile. 'And here I thought no one cared.'

His fair skin flushed and he looked away. He was a gaffer – something to do with lighting. He'd told me that earlier and I had whispered the word several times to myself, just liking the way it lay on my tongue. 'I have a message for you,' he said, but he wouldn't meet my eye.

To put him out of his misery I took the note he was holding. It was a simple piece of brown paper, the kind the rolls of back-grounds were wrapped in for transport. *Please join me for dinner. Alex.*

His handwriting was very neat, as if he'd spent hours getting it just right. I wondered if he signed his autographs as precisely. I crumpled the paper in my hand and looked at Charlie, who was obviously waiting for an answer. 'What if I say no?' I asked.

Charlie shrugged, already starting to leave. 'Alex'll find you,' he said, 'and he'll make you change your mind.'

He could make miracles. I stood in the doorway of what had been a set only hours ago – the interior of his character's tent – and surveyed the fine white linen tablecloth, the tall bayberry candles in ivory holders, the champagne chilling in a silver bucket. Alex was standing at the opposite end of the tent, wearing a dinner jacket, black trousers, white bow tie.

I blinked. This was *Africa*, for God's sake. We weren't even staying at a motel, only a camping lodge twenty miles from Olduvai Gorge. How had he managed this?

'That's all, John,' Alex said, smiling at the man who had driven me back to the set in a jeep. He was a friendly man, big as a sequoia.

'He's very nice,' I said politely, watching John's retreating figure in the red glow of the standing torches outside the tent. 'He told me he works for you.'

Alex nodded, but did not take a step toward me. 'He'd give up his life for me,' he said seriously, and I found myself wondering how many others would as well.

I was wearing the black sleeveless dress that had arrived cour-tesy of Ophelia that afternoon, and low black flats that had at least a pound of sand in them. I had spent the past three hours showering and drying my hair and rubbing myself with a lemon after-bath lotion, all the while trying out different conversations

where I took Alex Rivers to task for his performance that afternoon.

But I hadn't expected him in evening wear. I couldn't tear my
eyes from him. 'You look wonderful,' I said quietly, angry at myself
even as I spoke the words.

Alex laughed. 'I think that's my line,' he said. 'But thanks. And
now that you've seen the effect, can I get out of this before I
melt?' Without waiting for me to answer, he stripped off the jacket,
unlaced the bow tie, and rolled up his sleeves past his elbows.

He pulled out a chair for me and lifted a silver dome from a
plate of crudités. 'So,' he said, 'what did you think of your first
day on a movie set?'

My eyes narrowed, recognizing my opportunity. 'I think that
I've never seen so much time wasted in my life,' I said simply.
'And I think that it's shameless to steal someone else's emotions
for your own performance.'

Alex's jaw dropped, but he recovered himself just as quickly.
He lifted the china platter. 'Carrot?' he said calmly.

I stared at him. 'Don't you have anything to say?'

'Yes,' he said thoughtfully. 'Why do we keep getting off on the
wrong foot? Do you just hate me, or is it all actors?'

'I don't hate anyone,' I said. I glanced at the crisp napkins and
delicate crystal, thinking of all the trouble he'd gone to. This was
obviously his attempt at an apology. 'I just felt used.'

Alex looked up. 'I didn't mean to hurt you,' he said. 'I was
trying to – well, hell, it doesn't matter what I was trying to do.'

'It matters to me,' I blurted out.

Alex did not say anything. He stared over my shoulder and
then shook his head. When he spoke, it was so quietly I had to
lean forward to catch his words. 'The problem,' he said, 'with
being one of the best is that you still have to get better. But you're
competing with yourself.' He looked at me. 'Do you know what
it's like to do a scene, to have everyone slap you on the back and
tell you how great you are, but to realize that you've got to be

just as good the next time, and the next?' His eyes glowed in the candlelight. 'What if I can't? What if the next time is the time it doesn't work?'

I knotted my hands in my lap, not knowing what I was supposed to say. It was obvious that I had touched a raw nerve – Alex Rivers was not bragging; in fact, he seemed truly terrified that he might not be able to live up to the very image he'd created.

'I steal people's reactions – you're absolutely right. It keeps me from having to dig deeper into myself. I guess I'm afraid that if I stick to my *own* experiences, one day I'll be looking for something to draw upon and I'll find out instead that I've run dry.' He smiled faintly. 'The truth is, I can't afford to let that happen. Acting is the only thing I'm good at. I don't know what else I could do.' He stared at me. 'For what it's worth,' he said, 'I'm sorry it had to be you.'

I lifted my hand as if I were going to touch him, but changed my mind. A faint flush covered Alex's cheeks as he realized what he had admitted to me. I looked away, wondering why if *he* had been the one to expose himself, *I* felt so vulnerable.

The going story about Alex Rivers in Hollywood, courtesy of Michaela Snow, was that he had graduated from the drama department at Tulane, had come to LA, and was tending bar at a hot night-spot one evening when a big-time producer proceeded to get shitfaced. Alex had driven the man home, and a day later the producer had screen-tested him. The movie was *Desperado*; he'd won the part and had stolen the film. People in the business believed that everything had come easily to Alex Rivers. That if he hadn't been in the right place at the right time, there would have been a second coincidence, or a third.

It was hard to separate the fact from the fiction, so most of the time Alex did not try. He left his childhood in a puddle on a back lot at Paramount and re-created himself to fit the mythic proportions drawn by the press. The truth was, he became a workaholic – not because of the money or fame, but because he did not like himself as much as the characters he brought to life. He did not let himself believe that there was anything remaining of the vulnerable boy he had once been. The other truth was that the closest Alex had ever come to a stage at Tulane was mopping it as a custodian. His unheralded arrival in LA was as a hitchhiker on a meat truck. And he never would have left Louisiana in the first place if he hadn't believed that he'd killed his own father.

It had been one of those weeks in New Orleans when the humidity grabbed you by the balls and blew its fetid breath into your lungs. Andrew Riveaux had been gambling for three consecutive days and nights in a back room off Bourbon Street, although at first his family did not notice. Alex was too busy working at the university, trying to amass enough money to support his mother and to set himself up in his own place. He barely lived at home as it was; he spent most nights in the narrow dormitory beds at the invitation of rich daddy's girls who found him brooding and intemperate, an adventure from the wrong side of the tracks.

Likewise, Lila Riveaux did not mark her husband's absence. She slept most of the time, incubated and buffered by a Valium haze, so drugged she could not distinguish the days of the week, much less which ones Andrew bothered to put in an appearance. On that afternoon when Alex stopped in at the trailer park to check on her, she was so pale and still that he forced himself to feel for her pulse.

Alex was in the closet kitchen, cutting vegetables to add to a can of broth for dinner, when he heard his father laugh outside. His father had two laughs: one mean one, used for degradation; and one fake one, used for sucking up. This was the second kind, and after the briefest pause, during which Alex nicked his own finger, he went back to his task.

Andrew Riveaux had brought someone home. Alex listened to the heavy footsteps, the rumbling voice. He heard his father open the folding panel door to the only bedroom and yell out his wife's name.

Alex stepped from the kitchen in time to see his father ushering this fat, florid man toward Lila, unconscious on the bed. He noticed that his father's gold chain and crucifix were gone, that his skin was yellowed with alcohol. He watched the stranger stroke his hands over the roll of his belly, and then turn to Andrew. 'She gonna wake up?' he asked, and that was how Alex understood how much his father had lost.

Alex stood like a witness to a raging fire, both mesmerized and immobilized by shock, knowing that he had to move or be heard, and understanding at the same time that these simple acts were beyond his control. His breath came in hoarse, square blocks, and finally the paring knife he was holding dropped to the floor.

Andrew paused in the act of sliding closed the bedroom door. He glanced at Alex. 'She won't know,' he said, as if this made it all right.

His first punch folded his father in the middle. His second broke his father's nose. The bedroom door cracked open, and the stranger stood gaping in his boxers. He looked from Alex to his father and back. Then he pointed a finger at Andrew. 'You owe me, you fucker,' he yelled, and pulling up his pants, he slammed out of the trailer.

Alex's third punch toppled his father into a curio cabinet that had been Lila's pride and joy. Andrew Riveaux struck the back of his head on the corner, opening a flow of blood that seeped between his fingers. He fell unconscious, but not before he'd smiled – *smiled* – at his son. He did not say the words, but that didn't prevent Alex from hearing them: *Well, shit. You* can *fight.*

Through the open bedroom slider, Alex could see his mother. Her shirt was open, her bra pushed up and cutting into her neck, her nipples red and exposed and obscene. She had slept through the whole thing.

He took back the money he'd left on the kitchen table for his mother and stuffed it into his pocket. Then he stared at his father's body until the blood leaking from his skull touched the edge of Alex's shoe. He waited for some emotion to claim him: regret, dismay, relief; but he felt absolutely nothing, as if the man who had committed this deed were in no way connected to himself.

And even after learning that his son-of-a-bitch father had not died that day, Alex did not admit for years that what had stayed with him all this time was not the sound of his father's skull cracking, or the smell of his blood on the wet commercial carpet, but the fact that when Alex had least been trying, he had momentarily turned into exactly the kind of son Andrew Riveaux had wanted him to be.

Alex stood and began to wrestle with the cork in the champagne bottle. As he moved, I could sense him shutting away the part of himself I had just seen, turning once again into a celebrity. 'You know, I've been acting for seven years now, stealing expressions and experiences from my friends and my family and people I meet on the street. If they even notice, they're flattered by it. No one's ever had the nerve to say anything to me like you did.' His voice gentled, and I waited to see where this was all leading. 'You surprise me,' he said quietly. 'Not many people surprise me anymore.'

I looked at him carefully until all the polish and flash fell away, leaving only the man himself. 'Well,' I admitted softly, 'you've surprised me, too.'

The cork flew out of the bottle, exploding into the soft underbelly of the tent and falling to land in my lap. Champagne ran down the sides of Alex's hands, onto his trousers. 'I'm running up quite a dry-cleaning bill for you,' I said.

Alex smiled and poured some into my glass. 'This doesn't stain as badly as papaya,' he said. He lifted his own glass and clinked it against mine. The sound, like the lightest of bells, carried on the wind.

'I guess we should toast to the movie,' I said.

'No.' Alex leaned so close I could smell the spice of his after-shave. 'I think we should definitely toast to you.'

I watched the fluted glass come up to his lips, and then I turned away to stare at the flickering candles. Our entrées were sitting beneath silver domes on the cot across the tent. Perched on a rickety shelf were two individual fruit tarts. 'You're making it very hard for me to stay angry,' I said.

'Well,' Alex said, 'at least I'm finally doing *something* right.'

I blushed, staring down at my plate. I wanted him to serve the food. Sing. Shout. Anything but look at me like that.

I could find my way across a desert by noting the position of the sun. I knew how to put a skull back together when it was split into fifty pieces. I could run complicated computer analyses that explained the significance of a bone's dimensions. But I could not sit at a dinner table across from a man and feel at ease.

I just didn't have much practical experience with it. And any fantasies I'd harbored didn't cover the pitfalls that cropped up in reality: the long moments where there was nothing to say, the horrible echo of a dropped spoon against my plate, the way Alex could stare at me as if he saw right through my skin. I thought about the heroines in those books I had read during the flight to Tanzania. Most of them would have tossed their long, flowing hair over their backs by now and parted their cherry lips and leaned invitingly over the table. All of them knew how to tease and how to flirt. At the very least, they'd be able to make conversation without looking like fools.

But Alex knew nothing about anthropology, and I knew nothing about movies. Talking about the weather in Tanzania was pointless, since it stayed constant for months. He didn't want to hear about my flight over. Without the shield of anger I had worn into the tent as protection, I had very little to say to Alex Rivers. He probably was wondering what had made him invite me to dinner in the first place.

'So tell me, Cassandra Barrett—'

'Cassie,' I said automatically. I looked up at him. 'You can call me Cassie.'

'Cassie, then. Tell me how you wound up chipping away at rocks in the African desert.'

I leaped into the conversation, grateful for the chance to *do* something. 'I was a tomboy,' I said. 'I liked to play in the dirt.'

He walked toward a low wooden crate I hadn't noticed and pulled out two small silver bowls packed in ice. 'Shrimp cocktail?' he said.

I smiled as he set the plate in front of me. 'How did you *do* this?' I said, shaking my head.

Alex lifted a shrimp on the tiny fork. 'If I told you, it wouldn't be magic anymore.'

We ate quietly, and I watched the candles dance shadows on his cheeks and light the edges of his hair. He was golden, that was the word. I'd look at him one moment and see a man asking me about my courses at UCLA, and then I'd take a breath and see Apollo himself.

During the main course, Alex mentioned that he had been born outside of New Orleans. 'My father was a doctor and my *maman*, well, she's just the most beautiful woman I've ever seen.' He smiled. 'I remember watching her in her garden when she thought no one else was around. She'd pull off her straw sunbonnet and turn her face up to the sky and laugh like she was the happiest woman in the world.'

I looked into my plate, thinking of my own mother, who would have traded everything she owned to get back to the South. I thought of how I'd watch her when she thought no one was looking, bent over her tumbler of bourbon, toasting herself. I closed my eyes, trying to picture what it must have been like to grow up as a child in Alex Rivers's family.

'My daddy didn't much care for acting,' Alex said. 'But then he saw me in a play in college – Tulane – and he became my number-one fan. Up till he died a few years back, he kept the promotional posters of every film I was in hanging on the walls of his office.'

'And your mother still lives in New Orleans?' I said.

'Tried getting her to move to LA, but she wouldn't do it. She said her roots have grown too deep to dig up now.'

I tried to conjure the pictures my mother had colored in my mind of the South, a land of grace and blue-leafed willows and iced drinks with crushed mint. It seemed as different from LA as I was to Alex Rivers. 'You must miss New Orleans,' I said. 'Hollywood's got to be a different world.'

Alex shrugged. 'I grew up in one of those old French mansions,' he said. 'Black shutters and climbing roses and scrolled iron benches in the garden. When I came to LA and made it big, I built a house just like it in Bel-Air.' He smirked. 'Of course, if you've been on one of those Star Tours, you've probably even seen the mailbox.'

I smiled at him. 'And just how did you know you'd made it big?'

Alex laughed. 'One day I was at the grocery store. It was just after *Light and Shadows* was released – that was the Vietnam film. Anyway, I was in the produce aisle and I was squeezing cantaloupes, you know, like my mother showed me when I was in college, to test them for ripeness. So I finally chose two and made my way down to the scallions, and I looked back to see a crowd around the melons. All these women were grabbing the cantaloupes I'd picked up but didn't take – the damn *green* ones – and telling each other they'd gotten one Alex Rivers had touched.' He grinned. 'That's the worst part,' he said. 'I can't go anywhere. I can't do anything. I have absolutely no privacy. That day, in 1987, was the last time I went grocery shopping.'

'What do you do for food?' I asked, horrified.

'I hire people. I have someone to buy my food, buy my clothes, make my phone calls, drive me around. Christ, I could probably hire someone to go to the bathroom for me if I wanted to.'

'Ah,' I said, smiling. 'The advantages of being in a position of power.' I stood up and cleared the two plates away – a delicious goose in plum sauce with a candied rice stuffing. 'So what do you *do* all day?'

Alex laughed. 'Come to think of it,' he said, 'very little.'

He refilled the champagne glasses while I carried the dessert to the table. 'Blueberries,' I said. 'That's my favorite.'

I wasn't saying it just to be nice. You couldn't grow up in Maine and *not* like blueberries; they grew wild in the woods between my house and Connor's. These weren't nearly as good – not that I was about to tell Alex – but they reminded me of summer and a life I'd had a hundred years before. I lifted the fork to my mouth and took another bite. 'We used to pick blueberries in Maine,' I said to Alex. 'They grow all over the place, and we'd pluck them right off the bushes to eat.' I smiled. 'The warm ones were the best, because they tasted like the sun and they left purple stains on our fingers.'

Alex reached across the table to take my hand. He turned it over in his, slowly rubbing his fingertips across mine. 'Here,' he said, touching my palm as if he could see the marks. 'And here.' He glanced at me. 'I wish I'd been the one with you.'

I pulled my hand away. I could feel a stream of sweat breaking across my back. 'I think I'd better go,' I said quickly. 'Thank you for a wonderful dinner.' I stood up before I could change my mind; before he could change it for me.

Alex stared at me for a long minute, and then he got to his feet and unrolled his sleeves. He pulled on his dinner jacket and walked me outside the tent. The twin torches flaming at the entrance to the set painted the earth in shades of red that shimmered and started and burned. 'I told John I'd drive you back,' Alex said quietly. 'I hope you don't mind.'

'I don't want to put you out,' I said, but even as I did I knew there was no alternative. I would have been terrified to drive to the lodge myself this late at night; and it wasn't as if I could simply call a taxi.

Alex helped me into the jeep and swung into the driver's side. He lit a cigarette, and that surprised me – I hadn't expected him to be the type to smoke. But he only took a few drags, and then he threw it out the window, so I was left without its glowing crimson tip to make out the lines of his face.

He didn't say a word the entire way back to the lodge. I knew I had offended him, and I tried to rewind the evening in my mind, but other than our original argument, the only thing that might have been misconstrued was pulling my hand away from his. I just didn't want to make a mistake, that's all. I didn't know how to play the kind of casual games someone like Alex Rivers did. *He'll get over it*, I told myself. *He's just not used to someone saying no.*

When he pulled the jeep to a stop in the parking lot of the lodge and opened my door, I tried to think of the most gracious way I could say goodnight without running the moment my feet touched the grass. Then I laughed. He was just a man. An actor. What was I so afraid of?

Myself. I knew the answer even before Alex closed the car door, trapping me in between his arms. I had been afraid of what else he could do to me ever since I'd watched him act out my own dreams on film that afternoon. I took a step backward, pressing up against the side of the jeep. Alex stared at me, but he was standing in the shadows and all I could see was the remarkable silver of his eyes. 'You're beautiful,' he said simply.

I turned away. 'Don't lie,' I said. 'Don't act.' I had heard myself described as intelligent, ambitious – but no one in my entire life had ever told me I was beautiful. I always thought that Connor might have, but he hadn't had the chance.

I was angry all over again, as angry as I had been when the night started, because Alex Rivers had ruined a perfectly good evening. Before he'd opened his mouth, I could have looked back on this and smiled, remembering the time I'd dined by candlelight on the Serengeti. I could have gone to bed that night and closed my eyes and padded my recollections with sparkling conversation and the finest traces of romance, until it played just the way I'd wanted it to. But Alex had crossed the line with a blatant lie, and suddenly the whole night seemed like one big joke at my expense.

Alex grabbed my shoulders. 'I'm not lying,' he said. 'I'm certainly not acting.' He shook me gently. 'What is the matter with saying you're beautiful?'

'Because I'm not,' I said as easily as I could, hoping that might make it hurt a little less. 'Look around you. Look at Janet what's-her-name, or any other actress you've worked with.'

He held my face between his hands. 'You bring a sexy black dress to the middle of nowhere. You listen to me so carefully when I'm talking, you'd think I'm telling you the secrets of the universe. You're not afraid to tell me I'm an asshole when I'm being an asshole. And,' he said, 'you talk about picking blueberries like you were just doing it a few hours ago, so all I can see is that stain on your fingers and your lips. Cassie, if that isn't beauty, I don't know what is.'

He started to lean toward me, and I kept my eyes wide open when he kissed me because I wanted to see if I affected him the way he affected me. I could feel the heavy white moon at my shoulders, pushing me closer to Alex. I heard the steady beat of his heart and the soft whir of the fans in the lodge nearby and I started to believe that this was real.

When he pulled away from me, his fingers were still resting on my throat, and they were shaking. I smiled at him. 'I never said anything about a stain on my lips,' I said.

Alex put his arm around my waist. 'I'm beginning to think this is the best film I'll ever make,' he said. He helped me up the steps outside the lodge and into the main hallway. It was pitch dark, most of the other members of the cast and crew having gone to bed in anticipation of an early makeup call. He walked up the stairs beside me and led me to my door. With every step I could feel him pulling away. By the time he stood in front of my room, I wondered if I had imagined everything.

Alex turned toward me, as if he meant to kiss me again, but instead he started speaking in a fast, furious whisper. 'My father wasn't a doctor,' he said. I noticed his voice was deeper, guttural; that his eyes burned the way they had earlier when he'd spoken of failure and fear. 'The closest he ever came to a doctor's office was when he shot himself in the foot after drinking a fifth of scotch. I was his biggest disappointment because I turned out nothing like the son of a bitch, and he used to beat me up every now and again just to remind me how much better he was. My *maman* couldn't tell the difference between a hothouse flower and a plastic centerpiece. I came into this world bringing her pain and she never let me forget it. I spent my whole childhood hiding from the two of them and losing myself by pretending I was someone else. And the house I built in LA does exist in N'Orleans – but the nearest I ever came to it was spying from a tree in the woods out front, watching the little girls who lived there turning somersaults on the lawn and flipping up their skirts in the process.' He took a deep breath. 'That shit I told you over dinner is the story my PR woman wrote when I told her I needed a history. But I won't lie to you, and I won't act.'

My mouth dropped open. I wanted him to know that I liked this – the black truth – much more than his alter ego.

I wanted to reach out to him, to tell him now about my mother, about my family.

I touched my hands to the soft hair curling at his temples. Twice this night he had trusted me with the truth, and for this, I would help him. I was more qualified than he ever could have imagined. He whispered my name, and I leaned against him, running my hands down his back and marveling at how comfortably we fit together. The last thought I had before his lips touched mine was that Alex Rivers was a much better actor than anyone could guess.

Chapter Twelve

A week after I started to spend all my free time with Alex Rivers, I began to dream about Connor at night. I had the same dream over and over. In it, Connor and I were both adults, but we were lying on our backs on one of the floating docks of Moosehead Lake. Connor kept pointing to the sky, outlining the patterns of the clouds. 'What do you think?' he asked, several times, but to me every formation took the shape of Alex – his profile, his windblown hair, his sculpted jaw. I told this to Connor, going so far as to gesture, my palm pale against the bright summer blue. But no matter how hard I tried, I could not get Connor to see.

I had spent six days watching Alex acting as Rob, unearthing his skeleton and coming to a crisis of faith. He realizes that human evolution is following the same path as the evolution of this alien species he's found: a meteoric rush toward extinction. He decides to bury what he knows, rather than rewriting history.

It surprised me that filming wasn't done in order, although I could certainly see the monetary advantages to shooting all the scenes in a given location at once. 'How do you do it?' I had asked him. 'How can you build up to the emotion you need in that last scene, and then go back and pretend it never happened?' And Alex had just smiled, and told me it was what he was paid to do.

He *did* get emotionally involved; in spite of what he said he couldn't help it. It leaked out at night when he was just being himself. One evening we'd sat at the edge of Olduvai Gorge and Alex told me about the time he was fourteen, when his father had coaxed him back and forth across the living room, swatting at his face and his side in an effort to make Alex land a punch. When Alex finally did, knocking out several of his father's teeth, Andrew Riveaux had smiled through the blood. *Boy*, he'd said, *that's the way a man fights*.

After a long silence, Alex lifted his eyes to mine. 'Sometimes I think that if I held a press conference tomorrow and told the world that Alex Rivers had a deadbeat drunk father and a mother who was off the wall, no one would bother to print it anyway. They've all got this image of me, and they're not about to change it, and the funny thing is, I think the man they've made in their minds is going to outlive me.'

I reached for his hand, because I didn't know what I should say, but he gently pushed me away. 'That's why I liked the script of this movie,' he said. 'It's a moral dilemma: Do you tell the public something they'd find appalling? Or do you let them go on believing what they need to?' He shook his head. 'Makes you wonder about Darwin,' he said.

But no matter how much time I spent with Alex, Connor was the focus of my dreams at night. I had linked the two of them in my mind. I would fall asleep thinking of Alex and wake with Connor's name on my lips, as if Connor, jealous, had started threading his way into my subconscious. One night my dream was so vivid that when I woke up I could still feel Connor's breath on my cheek, and this worried me. Most of the time, Connor left me on my own. But when he thought I was in trouble, he was harder to shake than my own shadow.

We were waltzing around the perimeter of the shallow pond behind the lodge, keeping time to the sounds of an African night. 'I can't keep up with you,' I said, breathless. 'You're going too fast.'

'You're going too slow.' Alex whirled me around a curve, lifting me off the cool, dark ground. As he set me back on my bare feet, my ankle buckled, and I pulled him with me to roll down a gentle slope. With every turn his body braced mine, or mine supported him, a sensuous volley of power. We landed with our fingertips inches from the muddy water, Alex tangled beneath me.

I tentatively rested my head on his chest. With the exception of that first goodnight kiss, this was the most bodily contact Alex and I had had. It was difficult to know what he wanted of me. Alex was friendly, open, but not physical. I wasn't sure if he was taking it slow; if he was taking it *anywhere*. As for me, well, I was hoping for more. In fact, I had braced myself for a one-night stand, and during the past week I had almost convinced myself that this would be all right, but Alex made no moves of seduction. More often than not, I reached out for Alex under all kinds of pretenses, shamelessly trying to prevent him from keeping his distance.

I breathed in the scent of his soap and his sweat. 'Sorry,' I murmured. 'Ballroom dancing was never my forte.'

Alex laughed, a deep rumbling sound against my ear. 'It's an acquired talent,' he said. 'My mother used to make me take classes twice a week. I hated it – those white gloves and overperfumed fat girls who stepped on my feet – but damned if I don't still remember every step we ever learned.'

I smiled into his shirt. 'You must have had an unconscious wish to escort a debutante. Or be Arthur Murray.'

Alex smirked. 'Not likely.' He gently stroked my hair, and I curled into the contact. 'I think my body just liked the exercise.'

He had told me several nights before about being born with a hole in his heart, about not being able to run and play until he was nearly eight. 'Imagine that,' Alex had said dryly. 'A romantic hero with a broken heart.'

I had heard the weariness in his voice, the pain of a little boy who saw himself as defective and did everything in his power to compensate for his weakness. I wondered why he had mentioned this to me. I let myself pretend it was because he thought I'd truly understand.

As I closed my eyes against his chest, remembering, Alex stiffened and sat up. I looked away, ashamed that I had made him uncomfortable by holding him. I shook my head, cataloguing the reasons Alex Rivers did not want – did not need – someone as inexperienced as I was.

Alex turned toward me. 'There have been a lot of women,' he said carefully, 'but I don't let anyone get close. You need to understand that. The truth is, I don't want to be disappointed again. Not by someone else's shortcomings, and especially not by my own. So I act like it's not that important.' He shook his head. 'Cassie,' he said, 'I'm so damn tired of acting.'

Moving on instinct, I leaned toward Alex and slipped my hand under his shirt. He was telling me what I had no right to expect, although I knew it was far too late. I had not been in many relationships, but I had had Connor, so I understood that this was how it all started. You fell in love with someone because of the tilt of his smile, or because he could make you laugh, or in this case, because he made you believe that you were the only one who could save him. When it finally came, it might be a one-night stand for Alex, but not for me. By then I would have given him too much.

I heard Alex's quick draw of breath as my skin skimmed over his and settled, palm placed against his chest. I smiled into his eyes as I held his heart in my hand.

Sunday was the day off for the cast and crew, although leisure time in Tanzania left much to be desired. I was sitting on a swing in the shade, when Alex slid an arm around my waist as if it were the most natural thing in the world.

And it really was beginning to feel like that. I had all but abandoned the UCLA site. After that night on the edge of the pond where Alex had set the terms for a relationship, we were inseparable. In fact, Alex and I had been together so frequently that when he was missing, people on the crew came up to ask me if I knew where he was. I had felt a little uncomfortable at first, the way he'd so easily drape his arm over my shoulder while I was demonstrating how to clean a fragment; or the way, in front of everyone, he'd tell me what time to meet him for dinner. He reminded me of primate studies of territoriality I'd followed: males conspicuously leaving their mark to let others know where they weren't welcome.

But on the other hand, no one had ever been so possessive of me that they'd tried to stake a claim, however temporary. And, well, it felt good. I *liked* knowing that in the morning, I was the first person Alex would seek out. I liked kissing him goodnight and knowing a passerby in the hall had seen us. I was acting like a teenager for the first time in my life.

Alex drew me closer. 'I have a surprise,' he said, whispering the words against my ear. 'We're going on safari.'

Immediately, I pulled away and stared at him. 'We're doing what?'

Alex smiled. 'Safari,' he said. 'You know, lions and tigers and bears, pith helmets and ivory poachers. Things like that.'

'No one poaches ivory anymore,' I said. 'The only thing they'll let you shoot with is a camera.'

Alex stood, pulling me to my feet. 'Well, I for one am sick of cameras. I'm all for taking it in with the eyes.'

I followed him, already picturing the rolling Serengeti, the slow-moving herds stirring breezes. A single black jeep was waiting at the foot of the porch, and a slight native with a brilliant white smile offered his hand to help me climb in. 'Cassie,' Alex said, 'this is Juma.'

Juma drove us for over an hour into the heart of Tanzania, jostling us over brush and gullies that were never intended as roads. He stopped in the shadow of a small grove. 'We wait here,' he announced, and he pulled a blue-checked blanket from the jeep and spread it over the grass for us to sit on.

The plains faded purple at the edge of the horizon, and the sky overhead was the color blue the word had been invented for. I stretched out on my back. Beside me, Alex lay propped up on one elbow so that he could watch me. That was another thing I'd had to get used to in his presence – the focused attention. He would stare at me as if he was taking in every movement, every subtle change. When I told him it made me uncomfortable, he had shrugged.

'Can you honestly tell me you don't notice the way I look?' he had said, and of course, I'd laughed at the idea. 'Well, I can't keep from noticing you, either.'

His eyes started slowly at my hairline and traveled down the bridge of my nose, my cheeks, my neck, and my shoulders. He left a physical warmth in his wake, as if he'd actually touched me. 'Do you ever miss Maine?' he asked.

I blinked into the sun. 'Not so much. I've been at UCLA since I was seventeen.' I paused, thinking of how much of the explanation I had avoided. Although Alex had told me the truth about his family, I had yet to let him in on my own secrets. In the past weeks I had thought a hundred times about telling him, but two things had stopped me. First, the moment was never right. And second, I was still afraid I would scare him away.

The sun filtered through the penny-size leaves of the tree we were sitting beneath, casting a shadow of lace across Alex's legs. If I told him and he ran in the other direction, so be it; I had been convincing myself all along that this fling couldn't amount to anything. After all, what was he going to do when the filming ended? Fly back to LA with someone like me on his arm, and announce to his glittering friends that I was the woman of his dreams?

'Alex . . .' I said hesitantly. 'Do you remember me telling you that my parents owned a bakery?'

It was *all* I had told him, really, when pressed for details about myself. It was the only safe thing I could say. Alex nodded, lifting his face to the sun. 'You helped make meringues,' he said.

I swallowed. 'I also helped pick my mother up off the floor every time she passed out.' I kept my eyes trained on Alex's face so I'd know exactly when the impact of my words had hit. 'She was a drunk,' I said. 'A southern belle to the last, but a drunk.'

He was looking at me now, but I couldn't read his expression. 'What about your father?'

I shrugged. 'He told me to take care of her.'

His hand came toward me very slowly and cupped my cheek, and his skin beside mine was hotter even than my shame. 'Why are you telling me this?' he asked.

'Why did you tell *me*?' I whispered.

Alex gathered me up in his arms and held me so tightly I couldn't separate his heartbeat from my own. 'Because we're two of a kind,' he said. 'You were made to take care of me, and I'm going to take care of you.'

I struggled at the thought of that, but then I sank into the comfort he was offering. It was nice not having to be the one in control, for a little while. It was nice to be the one who was protected, instead of the one who'd been protecting everyone else.

We both sat up quickly at the sound of thunder. But there wasn't a cloud in the sky, and suddenly Juma appeared at our sides with a pair of binoculars. 'Over there,' he said, pointing, and what was a gray cloud on the horizon crystallized into flesh and blood.

Each elephant moved deliberately, one heavy footstep dragging into the next. Their skin seemed older than parchment, their tired eyes blinking in the dust. From time to time one would raise its trunk and trumpet, a high, heralding two-step scale.

Minutes later came a group of giraffes, their ears brushing softly against the low white clouds. I could hear Alex draw in his breath as one broke from the pack to step in our direction, its legs buckling gently at the knees and straightening, stiltlike, long yards away. The giraffe was the color of Caribbean sand, dotted with spots on its back and neck. It reached its face into the tree above us and began to taste the leaves.

Then the elephants began to trumpet fiercely and band together in a vaudeville shuffle; the giraffes marched knock-kneed across the plain. When the only thing I could sense was the whistle of the tall grass, I heard the unmistakable roar of a lion.

He moved with the lazy grace of a victor, and his mane stood away from his face like a ring of fire. Several paces behind him was a lioness, thinner, sleeker, standing in his shadow. She lifted her eyes, a ghostly sea green, and bared her teeth without making a sound. Alex's hand squeezed mine.

The lions stayed only long enough to sniff our scent on the air. They moved silently across the plain, now shoulder to shoulder. I wondered if these animals mated for life. The wind parted for them and they disappeared as quietly as they came. I stared for a moment at the spot where they had stood, trying to envision how a creature so beautiful could, in the space of a moment, draw blood.

'Let's stay here,' Alex said quietly. 'Let's just build a hut on the edge of this plain and watch the lions cut across our backyard.'

I smiled at him. 'Okay,' I said. 'You can accept your Oscar via satellite.'

We picked up our blanket and crawled into the back of the jeep. Alex's leg pressed against mine from hip to ankle. Juma turned on the ignition and began to bump us over the pitted ground toward home.

At the set, John had left us a jeep and a picnic basket with fried chicken and fresh bread. Alex and I sat in companionable silence for half an hour outside the tent with the setting sun melting into the edges of our collars and heating the ground between us. It was early September, and it was beastly hot. 'You know what I miss?' I said. 'About Maine?' Alex shook his head. 'I miss the seasons. I miss the snow.' I closed my eyes, trying, in this broiling heat, to imagine my fingertips blue with the cold, my eyelashes catching the first flakes of winter.

'One of my houses is in Colorado,' Alex said. 'Near Aspen. We'll go this winter. I'll take you to see snow.'

I turned to him. I wondered if I would be with him this winter. My mind flickered back to that lion, striding silently through the bristling grass, his lioness following. 'Yes,' I said. 'I'd like that.'

I knew he was thinking of the lions too, and of those other animals who had shaken the ground with their footsteps. As the sun dropped behind the edge of the distant hills, he leaned over and kissed me.

It was not the way he had kissed me before – not quiet, not gentle, not testing. He bruised my lips and ground his body against mine, wild and primitive, forbidden. His hand unbuttoned the front placket of my shirt and slipped inside. His palm skimmed over my bra, cupping my breast. 'Is it all right?' he whispered.

I had known it was coming to this; I had known from the moment he'd left me at my door at the lodge that first night. And although I didn't have the experience I knew he would expect, or the skill and finesse of other women, I could no more stop him than reverse the flow of my own blood.

I nodded and felt him pull my shirt over my head, but his hands were always on me, running down my back and unhooking my bra and pushing my hair away from my face. He picked me up and half carried, half dragged me inside the tent on the set, laying me down on the narrow cot. Kneeling on the rough wooden floor, he pulled off my sneakers and socks, then wriggled my shorts and my underwear over my hips.

My cheeks were burning, and I reached for the blanket to cover myself, but this was only a movie set and there wasn't any. I tried to cross my hands in front of me, but Alex wrapped them around his neck and kissed me again. 'You're beautiful,' he said. He ran his fingertips gently over my body, the way a sightless person learns another's face, and as I opened to his touch I started to think that maybe I was as beautiful as he believed.

I didn't know how to touch him, or what exactly to do, but Alex didn't seem to mind. He stood up to pull off his own clothes, and I stared at the lines of his body. I realized it was like looking into the sun – you shouldn't do it, because you'd turn your face away and be blind to everything else.

When his mouth came over my breast, I heard the sound of my own voice, or maybe the rise of the wind. Darkness slipped inside the tent with us, covering our bodies by degrees until I could just see a sliver of Alex here and there, illuminated by moonlight, and feel his skin sticking to mine. His hand moved between my legs and his words fell at my temples and I closed my eyes.

I saw the Serengeti, filled with animals as it had been ages ago. They chirruped and whistled and cried in the night; they moved in a measured parade. Overhead was a banner of stars that slipped under my skin, swelling and shining and aching for freedom that came only when Alex sank deep inside.

When I finally stopped quivering, Alex began. He called out my name, collapsing on top of me. He looked at me with the eyes of a lion.

'Is that the first time you've ever – you know?' he whispered.

I turned away, mortified. 'You can tell?'

Alex smiled. 'It's the way you're staring at me. Like I just finished creating the heavens and the earth.'

I tried to push him off me, to put a little space between us. Now that it was over, I wasn't sure it ever should have happened. 'I'm sorry,' I murmured. 'I don't do this with many men.'

Alex rolled us onto our sides. 'I know,' he said. I flushed again, thinking of all the women he must have slept with; of how much more they instinctively knew how to do. He caught my chin, making me look up at him. 'I didn't mean it like that. I meant that I like feeling you're mine.' He kissed me softly. 'So you won't be doing this with many men, after all.'

He smiled as he said it, but he tightened his grip possessively, as if I might actually have plans of leaving. I hesitantly traced my finger around the muscles of his chest and felt him stir inside me. I pushed my hips closer to his and heard him groan. 'Jesus,' he said. 'What you do to me . . .'

I pretended to hold him back. 'How do I know you're not acting?' I said.

Alex grinned. 'Cassie,' he said, 'when I'm acting, I'm never *this* good.'

If Sven, the stunt man, hadn't come down with the flu, Alex and I wouldn't have had a fight. But that Monday morning – the morning after – I arrived at the set, trying to act as casual as possible, only to find out that the scene scheduled for filming had been changed. Instead of Sven leaping from a low cliff with the infamous black rope, Alex and Janet Eggar would be filming the one love scene in the movie.

Janet Eggar was a young actress who, Alex had said, was doing her very first GLS – Gratuitous Love Scene. Bernie had as much as told me that Janet's role was completely insubstantial; that it had been written into the script simply because if she showed her boobs, people would pay to see the movie. I watched her move jerkily from the costume designer to the makeup crew. She stood with her back to me and opened her robe so that base could be applied to her body.

I kept trying to catch Alex's eye. He had arrived on the set long before I had that morning to catch up with the changes in schedule, so I hadn't had the ride over to the set to see what he made of last night. He had driven me back to the lodge and left me at the door of my room with a sweet goodnight kiss that made my insides hum. But thinking of gossip, he'd gone off to his own room and left me to lie awake all night, naked beneath the bedroom ceiling fan, touching myself in the places he had hours before.

As the sun came up, I told myself once again that I was not going to expect anything. For all I knew, he did this with some member of the cast or crew of every movie. I could think whatever I wanted to, but I realized that any promises I made myself were destined to be broken.

Alex was wearing a pair of jeans and no shirt, and he was in a foul mood. He barked orders to the prop people; he yelled at Charlie, the gaffer, for getting in his way. When Jennifer brought him a copy of his script, apologizing for the coffee stain across one page, I thought he would take her head off.

But when he looked at Janet, white-faced and shaking in front of the camera equipment, he seemed to soften. I watched his eyes travel the length of her robe and then return to her face. He walked over to Bernie and murmured something, and the director held up his hands for quiet. 'This is going to be a closed set,' he announced. 'Everyone not immediately involved with the filming of this scene can go back to the lodge and meet here after lunch.'

I watched Bernie lead Janet to the tent, to the cot where Alex and I had made love the night before. He spoke to her and gestured with his hands and she nodded and asked a couple of questions. In the distance I heard the last of the jeeps driving away, and I realized only a handful of people were left.

I wasn't in any way connected with the filming of the scene – any technical expertise I could offer wasn't going to help someone like Janet Eggar. But I saw her reclining on the narrow cot, and then her features changed into my own, and I knew that there was no way I was going to leave.

Bernie walked over to me. 'You're still here?' he said. 'You didn't hear what I said, maybe?'

Before I could open my mouth, Alex was standing beside me, his hand on my shoulder. 'She stays,' he said simply.

Bernie took up his position beside the camera, and he walked Alex and Janet through a fully dressed rehearsal of the scene. If I hadn't been so embarrassed about the location, I probably would have laughed: I couldn't imagine taking direction about which side to turn to when you kissed, where you could and where you couldn't put your hands, how to breathe. Janet and Alex each had a little spray of breath freshener under the pillow, and when Bernie had set up the scene to his satisfaction, they squirted some into their mouths and professionally turned to the cot.

Janet removed her robe under the white sheet with Alex chivalrously shielding her from the view of the cameramen. Then, as if he did it all the time, Alex shucked off his jeans and climbed completely naked onto the cot.

It was a horrible take. Janet's voice cracked in the middle of her line; she kissed Alex as if she were in bed with a corpse. When Alex went to pull the sheet down to her waist, per Bernie's direction, Janet stiffened and sat upright, clutching her arms over her chest. 'I'm sorry,' she said coolly. 'Can we try this again?'

But after two more disasters, Alex rubbed his hand over his face and stood up. He turned around, and everyone on the set could see how aroused he'd become. I looked into my lap and traced the hem of my shorts. He'd said he wasn't acting with me. He should have been acting with her.

'Okay,' Alex announced. 'Everyone, undress.'

Bernie started muttering in Yiddish, but Alex kept talking, drowning out the sound of the director's voice. 'It's only fair that if Janet and I are down to skin, the very least you all could do is strip to your underwear.' He looked over his shoulder, to where Janet was starting to smile.

One of the cameramen was the first to do what Alex had asked, pulling off his T-shirt and pants to reveal a huge belly hanging over Jockey shorts. LeAnne, Janet's assistant, shrugged off her clothes until she stood in her bra and panties. 'It's like a bikini,' she said to no one in particular.

Clothes flew into piles at the edges of the set, and by now Janet Eggar was laughing out loud. Alex sat on the cot, talking to her. With a sigh, Bernie unzipped his shorts to reveal purple silk boxers, and that left only me.

Everyone was staring, wondering why I deserved the special treatment, so without even thinking twice I reached for the bottom of my shirt. Alex caught my eye and shook his head very slightly, but I smiled at him. I pulled the shirt over my head and tugged off my shorts, knowing that the entire time, his eyes were on me.

When filming resumed, Janet seemed much better. I watched her fall back against the cot, her hair spread over the pillow. I watched Alex's breath steal over her skin. I wondered how much of her he was touching; how many times he'd have to shoot this; whether the sheets still smelled like us.

After the sixth take, when Janet and Alex were laughing as if they'd been doing this forever, I saw how my nails had cut into the soft wooden armrests of my chair. In the stifling heat, the scene being played before me kept turning into the one I had lived the night before. My throat became so dry I could not swallow. I watched Alex with another woman, holding her the way he should have been holding me, and that's when I realized I had fallen in love.

I knew he would come after me the moment he finished, but I didn't want to see him. I never wanted to see him again. I had tried – I had really tried – but a casual liaison just wasn't my style.

I had spent all last night preparing myself to face the truth, but that didn't keep me from feeling its pain. Alex hadn't felt a whole world open up at my touch. Alex hadn't lain under the circles of a ceiling fan, praying for time to stop before it all went downhill again. To Alex, I had been nothing more than a rehearsal.

I was halfway to the remaining jeeps, planning to get into one and drive myself as far away from this production as possible, when Alex caught up with me and grabbed my arm. 'Wait,' he said. 'You've got to give me a chance.'

I whirled around and glared at him. 'You've got one minute,' I said.

'I didn't know we were going to film this today, Cassie. It's terrible timing. If I had, I never would have brought you back here last night. I didn't want you to watch that, but I didn't want you to think I was sending you away, either.'

'You *enjoyed* it,' I said. 'I *saw* you.'

'I didn't enjoy it,' he yelled. 'It's my job.'

'Well, what does it matter to you anyway?' I shouted back. 'You've already had me. You've got Janet Eggar foaming at the mouth. Why don't you just go on back and finish what you've started while everyone else goes to lunch?'

Alex took a step back. 'Is that what you think of me?' he said tersely. His fists were clenched at his sides, white with stress. His eyes flashed, and for a moment I thought he would lash out or push me aside as he stormed back to the set.

I did not say anything for a while, stunned silent by the strength of Alex's checked rage. 'I wish I knew what to think of you,' I whispered. 'I kept seeing us. The same tent, Alex. The same cot. The same everything, except this time it wasn't me.' When his face started to swim in front of my eyes, I turned away. 'Please don't make me watch that again,' I said. I pushed past him, running until I couldn't hear his voice over the hammer of my heart. And I told myself over and over I should have known that someone who could love so hard and so well could also hate, and hurt, as deeply.

He was twelve, and he'd been shoplifting for years, so in theory he shouldn't have been stupid enough to get caught. But lately girls had been looking awfully good to him, and the blonde at the checkout with breasts the size of mangoes was giving him the eye, so before he could get the can of Pepsi into his pocket a beefy fist clamped over his wrist and spun him around. Alex found himself staring into the pitted face of the security guard for the second time that week, and when he let his gaze slide sideways he realized that the checkout girl hadn't been looking his way at all.

'Are you just plain stupid,' the guard said, 'or is there some other reason you came back to this store?' Alex opened his mouth to answer, but before he could speak he was tugged out the electronic door and marched to the police station.

The precinct was busy with pimps and dealers and felons, and the booking officer had little patience for a kid being brought up on shop-lifting charges. The sergeant looked from Alex to the security guard. 'I'm not gonna waste a lockup,' he said. Compromising, he handcuffed Alex to a chair in front of the booking desk.

They fingerprinted him and took down his information, but even Alex knew it was all just to scare the shit out of him; he was a minor, and in New Orleans shoplifting only earned you a slap on the wrist. The sergeant cuffed him to the chair again and Alex sat quietly, his knees drawn up to his chest and his free arm clasped around his ankles. He closed his eyes and pretended he was on death row, at the eleventh hour.

Some time later, the sergeant noticed him. 'Shit,' he said. 'Didn't someone come for you yet?'

Alex shook his head. The sergeant asked for his phone number and dialed it, leaning on the desk and staring into an arrest log. He glanced up at Alex. 'Your mama and daddy work?' he asked.

Alex shrugged. 'Someone should be home,' he said.

'Well,' the officer said, 'someone's not.'

An hour later the sergeant tried again. This time he got Andrew Riveaux; Alex knew by the way he held the phone several inches away from his ear, as if whatever ran through his father's veins might be catching. After a minute the sergeant handed the phone to Alex.

The cord stretched to its limit. Alex put the receiver to his ear. He did not know what to say; 'Hello' didn't seem quite right. His father began shouting an orange stream of Cajun curses, and ended by saying he was going to beat Alex's hide. 'I'll be there in fifteen minutes,' he said, and severed the connection.

But Andrew Riveaux did not come in fifteen minutes, or even in an hour. From his position on the chair Alex watched the sun go down and the moon float into the sky like an old ghost's white, wrinkled face. He knew this was part of the punishment – the pity he'd get from the officers as they passed and the secretaries who pretended not to see him. He shifted uncomfortably, needing to pee but unwilling to call attention to himself by asking to be unlocked.

The sergeant noticed him on his way home at the end of the shift. 'Didn't you call home?' he asked, puzzled.

Alex nodded. 'My father's coming,' he said.

The policeman offered to call again, but Alex shook his head. He did not want the sergeant, whom he'd begun to consider an ally, knowing the problem was not that his father could not come to pick him up, but simply that he did not *want* to.

He wondered if his father had deliberately decided to leave Alex hanging, or if he'd found something better to do – haul his crawfish traps, drink, be a fifth in a poker game. His mother might have come – Alex tried to believe that – but if his mother had been sober enough to comprehend that Alex was at the station, she would have been kept in her place by her husband.

Alex put his head on the arm of the chair and closed his eyes.

After three in the morning, he was awakened by the strong smell of perfume. A whore was sitting on the chair beside his. She had cherry hair and skin the color of mahogany and eyelashes as long as his little finger. She wore a string of jet beads that looped over one of her breasts, as if to outline it. She was chewing gum – grape – and she held a fistful of money.

She was the most beautiful woman he'd ever seen.

'Hi,' she said to Alex.

'Hi.'

'I'm picking up my friend,' she said, as if she needed to justify being in front of a booking table. 'How come you're locked onto the chair?'

'I went crazy and strangled my whole family,' Alex said, not batting an eye. 'And they ran out of jail cells.'

The whore laughed. She had big, horsey white teeth. 'You're a cute one,' she said. 'What are you? Ten? Eleven?'

'Fifteen,' Alex lied.

The woman grinned. 'And I'm Pat Nixon,' she said. 'What did you do?'

'Shoplift,' Alex murmured.

'And they're keeping you overnight?' Her eyebrows shot up.

'No,' Alex admitted. 'I'm waiting to get picked up.'

The whore smiled. 'Story of my life, babe,' she said.

He had not told her anything, really; not about his family, or how long he'd been sitting there, or how he'd rather be cuffed to this chair for a year than have to own up to the fact that the man who would walk into the station the next day at noon to claim him was indeed his own father. He knew about whores; knew part of their appeal was the way they accepted any baggage that came with you and made you believe you were more than you actually were. He knew they made a career of pretending to feel things they did not feel. All the same, it seemed natural when she put her arm around Alex and pulled him closer, as if their individual chairs did not stand in the way.

Alex pillowed his cheek on the whore's breasts, thinking of the blonde checkout girl and letting his cuffed arm twitch, handicapped in the dead space between them. It took only fifteen minutes before her friend was sprung from the cells below, hissing and spitting like a cat as she walked with the security matron. But during those minutes, Alex closed his eyes and took in the heavy smells of the whore's hair spray and cheap perfume, letting her sing old Negro spirituals to him until the world fell away, until he could believe that affection was a birthright.

Filming stopped unexpectedly for three days and Alex disappeared. I was too embarrassed to show my face around the rest of the crew, and I hadn't really spent much time with anyone other than Alex, so there was no one to talk to. I stayed in my room at the lodge, coming out only for meals and eating alone. I thought about breaking my contract, and flying home to LA before Alex had a chance to return to the set.

But instead I sat on my bed and read every romance novel I had brought, casting myself as the heroine and Alex as her lover. I heard the dialogue in the pitch and cadence of his voice. I pretended and pretended until I couldn't remember what had really happened and what I had imagined while reading through the dark, cool corners of the night.

One night when the moon was settling, the doorknob to my room turned. There were no locks; the lodge was too old for that. I saw the door swing on its hinges and I got up from the windowsill, remarkably calm about facing a stranger.

Instinctively, I must have known it was Alex. I watched him step into my room and close the door behind him. It was dark, but my eyes had adjusted, so I could easily see the shadows under his eyes and the wrinkles in his clothes, the two-day growth of beard. My blood began to sing with the thought that maybe he had been as miserable as I had.

I didn't notice the jar in his hand until he set it on the bureau across from the bed. 'I brought this for you,' he said simply.

It was an ordinary jelly jar, the kind Connor's mother had used every summer for canning the wild grape jam she boiled down. It was filled halfway with a clear liquid that looked like nothing more exotic than water.

Alex took a step forward and touched the jar. 'It's not cold anymore,' he said. He sat down on the edge of the bed. 'I flew to New York and then got on a puddle jumper to Bangor, but there aren't any mountains in Maine cold enough in September. And I couldn't come back empty-handed, so I took a plane to the only place I could be sure of finding it – I know people who've heli-skied in the Canadian Rockies in August.' He propped his elbows on his knees and rested his face in his hands.

'Alex,' I said quietly. 'What exactly did you bring me?'

He looked up at me. 'Snow,' he said. 'I brought you your snow.'

I reached for the jar and turned it over in my hands, picturing him on the top of a glacial mountain, scooping a handful of snow into a jelly glass to bring back to me, thousands of miles away. I could feel myself smiling from the inside out. 'You traveled halfway around the world to get me a jar of snow?'

'Sort of. I couldn't think of anything else to make you understand the other day. I didn't want – I didn't—' He stopped and took a deep breath, thinking over his words. 'I've never met anyone like you, but I didn't have a chance to tell you that before I had to shoot that damn love scene. I wasn't crazy about leaving the way I did, but you wouldn't have listened to me anyway. So I figured, you know, actions speak louder than words.'

I sat down beside him on the edge of the bed, still holding the jar of water. I leaned over and kissed him on the cheek, wondering what I was supposed to do now. I folded my hands in my lap. 'Thank you,' I said.

Alex turned to me and smiled. 'That's only half your present,' he said. 'I also wanted to get you something that wouldn't melt.' He reached into his pocket and pulled out a gift I could not quite see in the shifting light. But at that moment the sun broke over the horizon, and it caught in its soft pink glow the shine of a diamond solitaire.

Alex reached his hand around to brush the back of my neck. He pulled me forward until our foreheads were touching, bent over this brilliant ring that was even brighter than his eyes. I listened to his words, searching for a hint of my future, but when he spoke, he sounded for all the world like he was grasping at a lifeline. 'God,' he said hoarsely. 'Please say yes.'

Chapter Thirteen

Instead of a wrap party, we had a wedding. After thirteen weeks of filming, Alex stood up on the platform that had held a small set and announced to the cast and crew the secret we'd kept for weeks. Even Bernie, the director, was shocked. He broke the stunned silence by leaping onto the platform and clapping Alex on the back. 'Holy shit,' he bellowed, grinning. 'How come you didn't tell me?' And Alex laughed. 'Because you, Bernie,' he said, 'were the first person I expected to wire the tabloids.'

Everyone had known we were seeing each other; it was obvious in the way that Alex treated me. But I think people were surprised that it had turned out to be more than it seemed. I had to believe that flings between actors and others were commonplace. Marriages, though, were a different story.

I had believed Alex when he told me whatever shortcomings a simple ceremony in Tanzania had would more than cancel out the nightmare of trying to keep unwanted reporters and crazed fans away from a wedding in the States. Besides, the only people I would have invited were Ophelia and a few colleagues and maybe, out of filial duty, my father. I had never spent hours dreaming of myself wrapped in white satin, sweeping down an aisle littered with rose petals. It didn't matter to me, I told Alex, if he wanted a justice of the peace.

But in Africa, you know, it's easier to find missionaries than judges. 'I want you to get married in a church,' Alex had insisted.

'And you're not wearing khaki, either.' *Really*, I tried to tell him. *That isn't me*. But something kept me from pressing my point. I was marrying Hollywood's crown prince, and like everyone else, he expected a transformed Cinderella. And when you got right down to it, what I wanted more than anything was simply to be whatever Alex wanted me to be.

The six weeks between the time when I accepted Alex's proposal and when he announced it were the best six weeks of my life. Part of the magic was the feeling that we were doing something illicit. Alex would meet me in the food tent, sneaking away from the cameras and creating enough of an uproar with his disappearance to guarantee time for a fast, hard kiss. We spent three days of torrential rain locked in my room at the lodge, making love and playing backgammon. We showered together before the sun came up; we spoke of cinematography, of the substance of bones. One cool night, in Bernie's room, as I sat between Alex's spread legs and watched the daily rushes, he wrapped a light blanket around us, and then with everyone just a breath away, slipped his hands under my shirt and beneath the waist of my shorts, stroking me to a fever.

Alex made me feel like someone I had never been, and even the promise of a wedding couldn't keep me from thinking that one morning I would wake up and find that this had never happened. So in much the same way as I catalogued my anthropological samples with India ink, I found myself mentally filing away each memory I made with Alex, until they curled through my mind like a string of rosary beads, waiting to offer comfort.

A flash startled me back to the scene at hand. Joey, the site photographer, had just taken our picture. He handed the Polaroid to Alex, but not before I caught a glimpse of my own white face, slowly gaining color as the chemicals set. Alex's face was taking longer to come into focus. 'A keepsake,' Joey said, and then he leaned forward and kissed me right on the mouth.

I spent the better part of the next hour letting Alex do the talking to all the people offering congratulations. Meanwhile, I watched him. The sun flashed off his hair and outlined the familiar curve of his shoulders. Most of the women narrowed their eyes at me, wondering what I could possibly have to attract Alex that they didn't. People whose names I still couldn't remember made lewd comments about the narrow beds at the lodge and glanced toward my flat stomach when they thought I wasn't looking. But still, they were looking at me – to see what they had missed the first time around. Suddenly, I had status. Alex's power and prestige rubbed off on me simply by association.

'Next Wednesday,' Alex was saying. 'We'll give you all the details.'

I felt a peck at my shoulder, and turned to see Jennifer, Alex's little assistant, hovering beside me. 'I just wanted to tell you,' she said hesitantly, 'if you need anything, you know, like for the wedding or whatever, I'd be happy to help you out.'

I smiled at her as warmly as I could. 'Thanks,' I said. 'I'll let you know.'

She looked away before I'd even finished my sentence, and I turned to see Alex nodding at her. 'Just the person I wanted to find,' he said, and Jennifer scurried to his side. He put his hand on the small of her back and pushed her a few feet away from me. 'Sorry,' he said to me, grinning, 'but if you listen in, you'll spoil the surprise.'

I watched Jennifer whip a notebook out of nowhere and extract a pencil from the folds of her long, dark hair. She scribbled furiously as Alex counted off points I could not hear from this distance. Once, when she asked him a question, Alex glanced at me and ran his eyes over me from head to toe, then turned back. I tried to watch them but people milled between us, pumping my hand up and down and speaking platitudes that could have been a foreign language. I lost my view of Alex in a sea of suntanned faces. I thought I might actually faint, although I'd never done that in my life, and then out of nowhere Alex stood at my side again and I realized that I hadn't been ill at all; it was just that half of me had been missing.

Several nights before the wedding I dreamed that Connor met me on the Serengeti at dusk and told me I was making the biggest mistake of my life.

'It's not like you think,' I told Connor in my dream. 'I'm not just infatuated with him because he's an actor—'

'I *know*,' Connor interrupted. 'That's what's worse. It's like you don't even notice the things the rest of the world does because you're so busy seeing him as a little wounded bird whose broken wing you can fix—'

'*What* are you talking about?' I exploded. 'He's not some charity case.' I concentrated on seeing things as Connor would. I wasn't trying to replace him, but there were enough similarities between my relationship with him as a child and my relationship with Alex now to make me realize that I couldn't help but compare the two. Like Connor, Alex protected me – and he was the only person I let close enough to do it. Like Connor, Alex could finish my sentences before I did. But unlike Connor, for whom I had ultimately come too late, I was just in time to take care of Alex.

In the dream, a run of zebras skirted the edge of the plain, and when they distracted me Connor leaned forward to press his suit. 'You're just the one to make it all better, Cassie, don't you see that? That's what you do best. You took care of your mother and your father and me and Ophelia. You collect other people's problems the way some people collect rare coins.'

At this point in the dream, I tried to wake up. I didn't want to believe Connor; I didn't want to listen.

'There's a problem with wounded birds, Cassie,' Connor said. 'Either they fly away from you one day, or else they never get better. They stay hurt no matter what you do.'

After that, I could feel myself drifting toward consciousness.

I kept my gaze on Connor as he began to fade. I looked him square in the eye. 'I love Alex,' I said.

Connor stepped back as if he'd taken a blow. He stretched out a hand toward me, but as things often are in dreams, he could not quite reach, and I realized that it had been that way between us for a while. 'God help us,' he said.

Three days before our wedding, Alex and I drove to one of the many small lakes dotting the area to camp out overnight. In our jeep we'd packed two sleeping bags, a nylon tent, various pots and pans. I didn't question Alex about how he'd gotten these supplies – I was coming to see that Alex could draw blood from a stone if he wanted to. He unpacked beneath the embrace of a low, flat-leafed tree and began to set up the two-man tent with the grace of a practiced outdoorsman. I sat on the soft ground, shocked. 'You know how to do that?' I said.

Alex smiled at me. 'You forget I grew up on the bayou. I've been running around outdoors all my life.'

I *had* forgotten. But it was easy to forget, when the polished, urbane Alex Rivers was what the world saw most of the time. It was difficult to reconcile the man who brought evening attire to Olduvai Gorge with the man who crouched before me arranging a tripod over a Sterno. 'You're a study in contrasts, Mr Rivers,' I said.

'Good,' Alex murmured. He came up behind me and strummed his fingers down my ribs. 'Then you won't be getting tired of me too soon.'

I smiled at the thought of it. When I turned around to help with the rest of the things in the jeep, Alex gently pushed me down to sit in the shade. 'Rest, *pichouette*,' he said. 'I can do it.'

Alex called me *pichouette*, a word I did not understand, but I liked the way it sounded, rolling from his lips like a trio of smooth pebbles. He spoke his Cajun French sometimes in bed, which I liked. For one thing, it meant he was forgetting himself, since the language came only when he let down his guard. And I liked the rhythm and honey of the words. I'd listen to the whispers against my neck and I would pretend that he was telling me how lovely my skin was, how beautiful my eyes, how he could never let me go.

When Alex finished making camp, I patted the ground beside me. But instead of sitting down, he rummaged through a backpack and extracted a three-piece fishing rod, which he fitted together, threaded, and baited. For another half hour I watched him stand knee-deep in the water, reeling and then casting again, the neon line whizzing through the air like a missile's trajectory. 'Incredible,' I mused. 'You seem so at home here. How do you ever suffer Los Angeles?'

Alex laughed. 'Marginally, *chère*,' he said. 'But I'm not there when I can help it. The ranch in Colorado is three hundred acres of heaven and I can fish and ride and whatever. Hell, I could run around naked if I wanted to, and not come in contact with another soul.' He cursed his bad luck, and threw down the fishing pole. 'Never got the hang of these things,' he said. He turned to me, a slow smile spreading across his face. 'I'm much better with my hands.'

He stepped out of the lake, stalking toward me with his fingers outstretched, but ducked to my side at the last minute to disappear into the woods at the edge of the shore. When he returned he was holding a long, thin branch and a sharp fillet knife. He crouched and laid the branch over one knee, whittling one end to a point. Then he waded back into the water.

Alex stood perfectly still, his shadow rippling on the surface, his arm poised with his makeshift spear. In the time it took for me to draw a breath, he plunged the branch through the water, lifting it to reveal a skewered fish still thrashing on the end. Triumphant, Alex turned to me. 'When in Tanzania,' he said, 'do as the Tanzanians do.'

I was amazed. 'How – how did you know how to do that?'

Alex shrugged. 'It's all patience and reflexes,' he said. 'I'm used to doing it without a stick.' He walked away from me so that I could not see his face, and tossed the fish into a canvas bag. 'You could say my papa taught me.'

We ate several pan-fried fish for dinner and later made love and wrapped up in the blanket, my back pressed to Alex's chest. When he fell asleep I turned toward him, studying his face in the shadow of a silver moon.

A piercing cry made Alex bolt upright, throwing me back onto the ground. He shook himself free of sleep and reached for me, making sure I was all right. 'It's far away,' I told him. 'It just sounds like it's next door.'

Alex lay down again, but his heart was pounding against my shoulder like a jackhammer. 'Don't even think about it,' I soothed, remembering the first times I'd slept outside in the African night. 'Listen to the wind. Count the stars.'

'Do you know,' Alex said quietly, 'how much I hate camping?'

I sat up and blinked at him. 'Then why are we here?'

Alex reached up his hands and pillowed his head upon them. 'I thought you'd like it,' he said. 'I wanted to do it for you.'

I rolled my eyes. 'I spend enough time in makeshift huts to appreciate clean sheets and a sturdy bed,' I said. 'You should have told me.' When I looked down at Alex, his face was turned up to the sky, but his eyes were staring past the moon. I wondered what I had said to upset him. I touched my hand to the smooth white inside of his upper arm. 'For someone who hates camping, you're quite a pro,' I said softly.

Alex snorted. 'I had a lot of unwanted practice,' he said. 'You ever been to Louisiana in the summertime?' I shook my head. 'Well, it's hell on earth,' he said. 'It's so hot the air sweats all over you, and the atmosphere is so heavy you can't breathe right. There are mosquitoes the size of quarters. And it looks like I figure hell looks, too – least down by the bayou. All swamps, dark and muddy, overgrown with cypress and willow, Spanish moss and vines hanging like curtains over the branches. When I was a kid, I'd climb the cottonwoods on the water's edge and listen to the bullfrogs, thinking it was the devil belching up whiskey.'

Alex smiled, although in the limited light it could have been a grimace. 'My papa used to take me out in his pirogue most nights, so it wasn't like I didn't know anything about the bayou. He'd haul up the crawfish traps and take them down to Deveraux's, this restaurant that sits half over the swamp on these huge old cypress stumps. He'd give the catch over to Beau, who owns the place – there isn't anyone who can make crawfish like Beau – and then he'd go in for an hour and drink off his pay.'

'What did you do?'

Alex shrugged. 'I sat outside, mostly, and watched the older kids pulling catfish. You've never seen anything like it – no poles, no lines – they just reach down into the mud and wait and then they haul these twenty-pounders out against their chests.' He sighed and rubbed his hand down his face. 'Anyway, one night instead of stopping off at Beau's, my papa took the boat further up, telling me it was time we did some camping. I was maybe nine or ten, and I asked him why we'd be camping out in the swamp, instead of one of those fancy camp-grounds set up for tourists on Lake Pontchartrain. He told me they were for queers, and then he steered over to the shore. He tossed a tent I hadn't noticed out of the bottom of the boat, and then handed me up too. "I'll be right back," he told me. "You get us some dinner, and I'll take care of the firewood."'

Alex hugged his knees to his chest as the night became several shades cooler. 'Well, needless to say, he didn't come back. Left me with the sun going down to figure out how I was going to eat and where I could pitch a tent without worrying about sleeping with a water moccasin. I got into such a state of panic I was sure my heart would just freeze over, and wouldn't that serve me right after being told it was finally healthy.

'That whole night I waited, too scared to move in case my

father came back and I was gone. I watched that mist and thought every goddamn shadow was him, every stir of Spanish moss was his boat come back. About ten o'clock I was starving, so I took off my sneakers and waded into the swamp and thought about what I'd seen those kids doing all those nights outside of Beau's. I reached down, feeling through the mud. It took me two hours but I got the hang of it, and when the water moved around me and the cold brushed against my leg, I grabbed with all my strength and pulled up a catfish. Smallest thing I ever caught, and the best one I ever tasted.'

I thought of Alex, nine years old, standing in the dark, shaping the shadows with his fear. I thought of him standing with a spear in the middle of an African lake. I remembered the way he'd startled earlier when that animal screamed in the night. 'When did he come back?' I asked.

'The next morning. Found me with the fish skeleton and the ashes of a fire and told me I'd made him proud. I started to cry.'

My eyes widened. 'What did he do?'

Alex smiled. 'Took me to Beau's at seven a.m. and bought me my first whiskey,' he said. 'And he kept leaving me off in the bayou, about once every other month, until I could look him in the eye the next morning and act like I'd loved every minute.' He took a deep breath, but in the quiet I could hear the rattle at the back of his throat. 'So that,' he said, 'is why I don't like camping.'

'And why,' I added softly, 'you became the consummate actor.' I took his hands and kissed the tips of his fingers. His eyes were nearly black with pain, and I could see him trembling just the slightest bit, the one thing he could not control.

My cheek was pressed against his damp chest. I understood what he needed. I had been there, after all. I wanted to speak but I was careful not to show pity, so I chose the words that could either close the subject or offer Alex a lifeline. 'I don't know how you did it,' I whispered.

Alex kissed the top of my head, gentle, tender. *He doesn't want to talk about it anymore*, I realized, and as if the unspoken sentence had decreed it, the tension drained out of Alex's shoulders. I wondered whether he would bring up a different topic of conversation, like maybe the wedding, or simply pull me close for comfort and try to sleep.

Alex's voice cut through my thoughts. 'How I did it was easy,' he said softly. His hands ran over my shoulders to my collarbones, the touch of a lover, as if he had no idea that his words and his actions stood at odds. 'I used to stay up all night thinking of my goddamn father,' Alex said. 'Of my hands around his throat, squeezing out the life.'

For the second time that night, Alex had fallen into a deep sleep, but this time he was having nightmares. He lashed out, striking me across the stomach and waking me. He was speaking in French, but so lightly that even if I had understood the language I wouldn't have known what he was saying. I sat up and brushed his hair back from his temples, feeling the fever that flooded his skin.

'Alex,' I whispered, thinking it was best to shake him into consciousness. 'Alex.'

He sat up and rolled over, pinning me to the ground with his body before I could take a breath. He was staring through me, his eyes pale and shining. One arm was braced across my shoulders, keeping me still, and the other pressed my neck down to the ground, fingers gripping at my jaw.

I tried to speak but Alex's palm pressed against my windpipe. Panicking, I thrashed and kicked my feet. *He doesn't know what he's doing. He doesn't know who I am.*

His fingers tightened and my eyes teared. Flailing with my legs, I managed to bring my knee up to his groin. Alex howled in pain and rolled away from me, leaving me flat on my back to let the world swim dizzily into place, to suck bright white air into my lungs.

Alex sat up, holding his hand against his genitals. I tried to speak, but nothing came out of my mouth, and instead I rubbed my hand up and down my throat. I tried not to think about what Alex would have done if I hadn't freed my legs.

'What's the matter,' he said, still a little dazed.

I dragged myself up to my elbows. 'You had a nightmare,' I rasped. I swallowed past the pain.

Maybe it was the light that hit me when I half sat, but Alex suddenly seemed to come to his senses. He reached one finger to the curve of my neck, touching the five red marks that by tomorrow would be bruises. 'Oh God,' he said, pulling me into his arms. 'Oh, Cassie, my God.'

That's when I started to cry. 'You didn't mean to do it,' I sobbed, and I felt Alex shake his head. 'You didn't know it was me.'

Alex held me away from him so that I could see his face, cut with the pattern of shame. 'I'm so sorry,' he said. Without another word, he pushed himself up and walked to the opposite edge of the campfire, lying down on his side, facing away.

I watched him, and letting only seconds go by, I picked up the blanket and stretched out beside him. Whether or not he realized it, he needed me. The very worst thing for him would be to sleep alone.

'No,' Alex said. He turned to me, revealing even more fear and rage in his eyes than when he'd been gripping my throat, but I realized that this time it was directed at himself. 'What if I do it again?'

'You won't,' I said, and I believed my words.

Alex rolled over and kissed me, touching the marks on my jaw and throat as if this time his fingers could erase the ache. He stared at me until he took the absolution offered in my eyes. 'Cassandra Barrett,' he said softly, 'you are one of a kind.'

My wedding gown came from the Bianchi factory in Boston; my silk slippers were sent from the bridal district of New York City;

fresh white roses and stephanotis had been flown in from France
for my bouquet. The crates and cartons traveled Africa by train,
then Land Rover, accompanied by a small, dark seamstress who
asked to be called Mistress Szabo, and who was responsible for
the last-minute alterations that would make the ensemble seem
as if it had been spun only for me. She knelt at my feet while I
fingered the pattern of seed pearls at my waist and watched Jennifer
run down a wedding checklist for the thirtieth time that morning.

'Miss Barrett,' the seamstress snapped. 'You will not fidget.'

I stood at attention, which was very easy to do in the stiff
white satin and mounds of petticoats. I wondered how everything could possibly stay pristine white on the jeep ride from the
lodge to the small wooden chapel. I wondered how I'd keep from
ripping off my veil and letting it fly into the wind; kicking free
my shoes and hiking up my heavy skirts to run through the hot,
familiar sand.

'There,' Mistress Szabo pronounced. She pulled herself to her
feet, her knees creaking, and clasped her hands in front of her.
'Sì, bella,' she murmured. She wove her way to the narrow bed
and whisked Jennifer toward the door. 'Come, come,' she said.
'The bride needs a minute to herself.'

Jennifer checked her watch. 'We're ahead of schedule,' she said.
'You can have five.'

I didn't really want to be alone, but I didn't want to be with
them, either. I stood in front of the cheval mirror with a crack
down the middle, seeing my face split into halves that did not
quite line up.

With the exception of Alex's engagement ring, I wasn't wearing
any jewelry. But my throat was ringed with the proof of Alex's
nightmare, a necklace of amethyst bruises. I had borrowed
pancake from the makeup trailer and applied it before Mistress
Szabo arrived, but that didn't keep me from knowing what was
underneath.

I closed my eyes and made myself think of Connor. There had

been a time, not too long ago, when I believed that he would have been the one I married, if he had still been alive. And if he'd been here – even if he hadn't turned out to be the groom – he would have told me to make Alex wait. To take a little more time to come to a decision.

But I didn't want a little more time. I wanted Alex.

At that realization, I understood why, lately, I hadn't been dreaming of Connor as much; why it had been getting more and more difficult to picture his face. He was leaving me. I had made a decision; Connor had accepted it. He would no longer play devil's advocate; he would no longer intrude on a good night's sleep; he would no longer be the one taking care of me.

I sat on the edge of the bed, wiping under my eyes to catch the mascara and trying to even my breath. I felt the same ache in my chest that I'd felt years ago when Connor had died by degrees in my arms. For a moment I remembered us the way we had been, sitting side by side beneath a summer sunset, building our childhood with bone-clean Popsicle sticks and hot whispered dreams. And then I let him go.

'Stop.'

I could barely hear my own voice, but the chauffeur of the limousine – God only knew where Alex had found one in Tanzania – immediately screeched the brakes. Before he could turn around and inquire what I needed, I had opened the door and started running.

I figured someone would come after me. And would have caught me, too, because I couldn't really gain speed in a twenty-pound gown, a corset laced tight around my waist. I slowed only once to kick off the low-heeled slippers, thinking that I could run faster barefoot.

My veil streamed out behind me in a misty fog and sweat started to run down my neck and the sides of the dress, but no one was following. When I realized that, I slowed down, half hopping, pressing my hand to the stitch in my side.

I couldn't go through with this wedding. Our relationship, our attraction, had not been crafted in the real world. I was supposed to believe that a few magical weeks under the African sun would erase the differences between our lifestyles, that I could come home and slip into Alex's glittering Hollywood whirl without missing a beat.

All I had ever wanted was an affiliation with a university, a professorship, and a stunning piece of research. I had never even pictured someone like Alex, so how could I fit him into my plans? I sat down in the tall grass in the middle of nowhere, my skirts making a cloud around me.

It might have been hours; the only way I had to measure time was by the fact that I'd lost my veil and that my pancake makeup had pooled in a brown edge around the sweetheart neckline of the wedding gown, no doubt revealing my bruises. Alex's footsteps whispered through the tall grass, and he crouched down beside me. 'Hi,' he said, picking a blade and setting it between his teeth.

I could not look at him. 'Hi,' I said. He grasped my chin and pulled my head up until I saw him, breathtaking in his black tails and snowy shirt.

'Jitters?' he asked.

I shrugged. 'You could say that.'

His eyes flickered to my throat. Guilty, I reached for his hand. 'Alex,' I said, taking a deep breath, 'maybe this isn't the best idea.'

'You're absolutely right.'

Stunned, I blinked at him, wondering if he'd bolted from his own limousine and, purely by chance, had wound up at the same spot on the plain that I had. He squinted into the sun. 'I shouldn't have planned such a *fais-dodo*. A big shindig. It would have been better to do it quietly, just you and me, without everyone around.' He turned to me. 'I guess I figured this was the kind of wedding every woman wanted. I just temporarily forgot that you aren't every woman.'

'I was thinking more along the lines of canceling it entirely.' There, it was out in the open. I hunched forward, waiting for Alex to yell or jump to his feet, to contradict me.

'Why?' he asked softly, and it was my undoing.

I knew he was thinking of what had happened the night we went camping, but that was only part of it – I certainly didn't blame him; it was more a matter of my being in the wrong place at the wrong time. The problems ran deeper than that. I hadn't known he was racked by nightmares. I hadn't known how much he'd been forced to survive on his own. I sensed that the Alex Rivers I knew was just the very tip of the iceberg, that strange currents and dark passions were somewhere underneath the surface.

'I don't know anything about you,' I said. 'What if the Alex who saves me half his breakfast and plays Marco Polo in the pond behind the lodge is just another character you're playing?' The unspoken sentence hung between us: *What if the real Alex is the person I saw the other night?*

Alex looked away. 'I think the line is: For better or for worse.' He stood up and turned his back to me. 'I told you before I wasn't acting out my attraction to you, Cassie,' he said. 'And I suppose that you'll just have to believe me. As for the rest, well, like anyone else, I'm a lot of different people rolled up into one.' He faced me, pulling me upright. 'Some better than others, I'm afraid.'

I glanced down at my beautiful wedding gown, the one for which Alex had sent halfway around the world. Its lace hem was dragging on one side and a string of beads had popped from the bodice to trail over the skirt. Across the back were stripes of red earth, contrasting with the satin like blood. I pictured Alex slipping into character under the milky eye of a camera; Alex playing stickball in the puddles behind the lodge with round-bellied native children; Alex leaning toward me in the night, branding me with his own terror. 'Who *are* you?' I said.

He gave me a smile that slipped under my defenses, an amulet

I could carry with me for the rest of the day. 'I'm the man,' Alex said, 'who's been waiting for you all his life.'

He held out his arm for me, and without hesitation I walked toward him. We were late to our own wedding. With every step back to the waiting limousine, my misgivings faded. All I could think was that I loved Alex. I loved him so much it hurt.

Chapter Fourteen

Alex tried to time his arrivals at LAX so that they fell in the thin hours of the night, two or three a.m., when only the die-hard reporters hounded the gate and the baggage claim area. The day we were to leave Kenya, where we'd flown for a honeymoon, Alex woke me by laying his palm against my cheek. 'Cassie, *chère*,' he said, kissing me into consciousness. 'Cassie.'

I sat up, noticing the neatly stacked piles of clothing, the precise line organization of Alex's shoes and toiletries, all waiting at attention to be transferred into a suitcase. Never in my life had I packed as well as Alex could, and this sort of surprised me, because I had figured there were three or four servants at his beck and call who'd do his packing for him. I rubbed my hand over my eyes. 'Is it time to go?' I asked.

'In a minute.' He stared out the window at the fading moon, which outlined the Ngong hills in silver. 'I have to tell you something,' Alex said.

My whole body stiffened. This was what I had been waiting for, wasn't it? The punch line, the realization that I had been living some kind of lie. *Surprise*, he was going to say, *those vows were a farce. The priest who performed the ceremony was an actor*. I looked away, not willing to let Alex know I had been expecting his words all along.

'No matter what, when we get back I want you to understand something.' He took my hand and pressed it against his chest, where his heart beat strong and slow. '*This* is me. I may say things and act different from any way you've ever seen me act before, but that's because I have to be what people expect me to be. It's not real.' He gently touched his lips to mine. 'This is real.'

Stunned, I couldn't say anything at first. Alex's eyes turned the color of rain. His mouth tightened, so slightly that someone who did not know him as well as I did might never have noticed. Under my palm, his heart began to race.

He was scared. He thought that I'd come home, see him for what he really was, and leave. He had no intention of letting me go; he was simply afraid that I'd *want* to.

But then Alex couldn't know that the last time I had been in LA, the days had run together, one indistinguishable from another. He couldn't know that my skin seemed to hum when he touched me; that I had never thought I was beautiful until I saw myself through his eyes. He didn't know, as I did, that I was the anti- dote to his pain; that he soothed me like a healer's balm. I smiled and offered the comfort I had believed I would be needing. 'You'll see,' I said. 'Everything's going to be fine.'

Alex tucked me under his arm, and I turned my face in to his chest, but even closing my eyes couldn't block out the sight of over sixty people jostling each other at the airport security gate to touch Alex's sleeve and to scream questions and snap photo- graphs of the newly married couple. I breathed deeply, smelling the soap from the inn in Kenya and the warm spice that came from Alex's skin, and when I dug my fingers into his side he hugged me a little tighter. 'Ten more minutes,' he whispered, brushing his lips over the top of my head. 'Ten more minutes and I'll have you safe in a car.'

I took a deep breath and straightened, intending to at least act the way I thought Alex Rivers's wife should act: cool and un- flappable, not some wilting flower. But by turning out of Alex's shielding arm, I was giving the reporters their first full glimpse of my face. Bulbs exploded until all I could see were spots, dancing across my black field of vision, and Alex had to stop or risk my falling down.

'When did you get married, Alex?' 'What's she got that no one else has?' 'Does she know about you and Marti LeDoux?'

I blinked. 'Marti LeDoux?' I murmured, smiling.

Alex groaned. 'Don't even ask,' he said.

My eyesight came back into focus just in time to see one reporter straining at the velvet rope that held him back. He pointed to my stomach. 'Should we be expecting a little Rivers in the near future?'

Alex moved so fast that even the cameras couldn't catch him lunging at the reporter and grabbing hold of his shirt collar. I stretched out my hand toward Alex, trying to give the reporter the benefit of the doubt for what might have been a completely innocuous question. But before I could say anything to Alex, a mountain of flesh pushed past me, trailing a cloud of heavy floral perfume and a riot of teased red hair. The woman pulled Alex away from the reporter and anchored him to her side with her arm around his waist, then came to stand beside me and put her arm around me as well. 'Play nice with the other boys, Alex,' she murmured, 'or you won't be playing at all.'

Alex's eyes burned at her, but he managed to smile for the curious crowd. 'I thought you were going to send out a press release, Michaela,' he said through clenched teeth. 'Not invitations.'

The woman rolled her eyes. 'Is it my fault you're a bigger draw than God?' She winked at me. 'Since Alex doesn't seem to be doing the honors, I'm Michaela Snow. I handle Alex's public relations. Though from what you've seen, you probably know that Alex does not relate very well to the public.' She turned her attention back to Alex. 'And for your information, I *did* send out your release – but you've got to admit that America's most sought-after bachelor marrying an anthropologist, of all things, is bound to stir up some interest. The tabloids have been having a field day

with you – John's got them in the car in case you want a laugh.'
She looked at me. 'According to the *Star*, you are a Martian queen
who's zapped Alex with an extraterrestrial love warp.' She pushed
Alex a few feet away. 'Go on,' she said. 'The sooner you do it, the
sooner it's over.'

I watched Alex walk toward the reporters and the cameras,
and heard the whir of tape being set into motion in anticipation
of a Big Announcement. Michaela put her arm around my shoulders. 'You'll get used to it,' she said.

I doubted it. I didn't understand why these people had gotten
up in the middle of the night to take notes and ask questions
about something that wasn't any of their business. I suddenly
wished I were back in my dusty office at UCLA, where I could
sit for days without a student interrupting or a phone ringing,
and where I was just one of many. I was shocked at the idea that
just by association with Alex, I would have to travel back roads,
wear dark glasses, and let someone else fill my prescriptions. I
could have Alex for the rest of my life, but my life wouldn't be
the way it had been, and that was the price I was going to pay.

Alex was making love to the cameras. He looked just the way
he looked when we were in bed; he turned the same sloe-eyed
gaze and lazy smile on the black lenses and shutters that faced
him. 'Hottest damn place I've ever been,' Alex was saying, in
response to a question about Tanzania. He glanced at me, letting
his stare run the entire length of my body until I blushed. 'Of
course, some days were hotter than others.'

'Let us meet her, Alex,' someone called. And another voice:
'Are you legally married?'

Alex laughed, starting to walk toward me. 'Well, the ceremony
wasn't conducted by a Zulu chief, if that's what you mean. You're
going to have to take my word on this, since the marriage certifi-
cate's already been forwarded to my lawyer for safekeeping.' He
took my hand and gave a quick squeeze. 'May I introduce my
wife, Cassandra Barrett Rivers.'

The cameras flashed, but this time I was ready for them. I smiled, not quite knowing what constituted etiquette at a three a.m. makeshift press conference. Questions started rolling toward me, the words tangling up with each other: 'How did you meet?' 'Were you a fan of his?' 'Is he a good lover?'

Alex lowered his head to mine. 'I'm going to kiss you now,' he said. 'Turn your head to the right.'

Startled, wondering why he was giving me directions for something that up to this point had been natural for us, I stared at him. 'Why?' I said.

Alex smiled, pretending to nuzzle my ear. 'Because that way I'm up-camera,' he said. 'The PR's more important for me than for you.'

He turned me so that the cameras had the best view of our profiles, his hands locked on my upper arms. 'This is your last photo opportunity,' he said to the crowd. 'You forget I'm still on my honeymoon.' He bent toward me, and I watched his lips silently form two words before touching mine. *Be brave.*

I closed my eyes and pretended not to hear the clapping, instead letting my arms creep up around Alex's neck and holding him tight against me. When he broke away from me, I blinked, wondering when he had lifted me off the ground, when his leg had slipped between mine.

'Beautiful,' he whispered, pulling me away from the reporters. 'Hepburn couldn't have done it better.'

Speechless, I turned from him. Did he think I was acting?

Michaela rattled off a list of things that apparently needed Alex's attention and couldn't wait even until morning. I moved woodenly at Alex's side, carrying my big striped bag in front of me like a shield.

The reporters picked up their shoulder bags and their coats, dragging along cameramen and photographers in their wake. It seemed to me that the entire airport had cleared out now that Alex had given the word to leave. We moved through the quiet halls behind Michaela, toward an exit, to the car that would take me to a home I had never seen.

It was only because Michaela was twice as wide as most people that I didn't immediately notice the figure directly in our path. Ophelia stood perfectly straight, unwilling to give an inch, her eyes locked not on me but on the celebrity at my side.

I had not called to tell her I was getting married, because I felt guilty about having a ceremony that she would not be able to attend. So I had wired her after the wedding, apologizing for having to tell her after the fact. As I scribbled out the note for the Western Union man, I had imagined her eyes going wide, her lips breaking into the perfect curve of a smile. I had wanted to tell her that I'd worn her black dress the first night I had dinner with Alex; that he'd removed the lacy bra she'd loaned me. Instead I'd settled for the ambiguous: HAVE MARRIED ALEX RIVERS STOP HOME NOVEMBER 14 STOP BE HAPPY FOR ME.

I had expected Ophelia to live up to the stories I'd told Alex about her and do something outrageous when she first met him. Knowing her, I thought she might wrap her arms and legs around him and kiss him senseless, figuring it would be her only chance. She might beg him to get her a meeting with his agent at CAA, or grovel until he gave her a bit part in one of his movies. When it came to things like that, I had told Alex, Ophelia had no shame.

But Ophelia stood very quietly, not even saying hello to me. She stared at Alex, not with the pure hero worship I'd expected but as if she was sizing him up. My face flamed with pride – here was the first person to question if Alex Rivers was good enough for *me*, instead of the other way around.

I broke away from Alex and ran to Ophelia, hugging her tightly. 'I am so glad to see you,' I said, grasping her hands. Ophelia, struck dumb, was still staring at Alex. I smiled – one day, when she knew Alex as my husband and not as a celebrity, we'd look back on this and laugh.

But as she continued to stand there, silent, I realized there was some current running between Alex and Ophelia that charged the air around me and made me afraid to move. In the ten years I'd known Ophelia, I had never seen her like this. I searched for a hint of the woman who'd lost her job as an office temp by stripping off her blouse and xeroxing her breasts on a co-worker's dare; the woman who had painted a bikini on her body with ketchup and worn it to a casting call in hopes of shocking a director into a role in a Hunt's commercial. The Ophelia I'd lived with did not know the meaning of the word 'sedate', had never been cowed by anyone in her life.

Ophelia dragged her eyes to my neck, and I knew what was keeping her quiet. Underneath the carefully painted base makeup she'd seen what none of the reporters had – the fading sallow fingers that still ringed my throat. Unwilling for her to get the wrong idea, I pulled Alex closer. 'This is Alex Rivers,' I said softly. 'Alex, Ophelia Fox, my roommate.'

Alex turned the full force of his smile on Ophelia. 'Former roommate,' he clarified, holding out his hand to shake.

Ophelia coolly pressed her palm against his and then turned to me, whispering so that only I could hear. 'Not if I have anything to say about it,' she murmured.

She didn't mention the bruises. She didn't need to. The truth was that she'd been harboring doubts before our plane even landed, and she had her case prepared. Her argument was simple: Ophelia thought Alex was setting me up for some kind of terrible fall, or why else would he have insisted on marrying me so quickly in the middle of nowhere, instead of having a big Hollywood wedding everyone would remember for years? 'And,' she hissed as we left Alex and John at the baggage claim area, 'I saw that kiss for the cameras. He *upstaged* you, Cassie. Everyone knows the woman gets to face the cameras.'

I laughed then. Of all the people watching, Ophelia was probably the only one who had noticed. 'What about all those stars who run off to Vegas?' I pointed out. 'God, look at how many reporters showed up at three in the morning just to see what I looked like – can you imagine trying to have a private little wedding here?'

Ophelia jabbed her finger at my chest. 'My point exactly,' she said, leaving me to figure out the faulty logic. Exasperated, she rolled her eyes. 'It *shouldn't* have been a private little wedding,' she said. 'It should have been a media blitz. Every woman in this country wants to know who Alex Rivers married. So why does he hold a ceremony in the fucking Amazon and then sneak into the airport in the middle of the night like he doesn't want anyone to see you?'

'Maybe because he loves me?' I countered. 'The last thing on earth I would have wanted was a huge wedding on a studio's back lot.'

Ophelia shook her head. 'But that's not the way it's done, not in Hollywood. There's something wrong here.' She glanced up at me from beneath lowered lashes, and suddenly I understood just what Ophelia felt was wrong: In the natural order of the movie industry, Alex Rivers should have been matched with a woman who was stunning and ostentatious and larger than life; a woman who would never have agreed to a quiet ceremony; a woman who understood intuitively that a kiss was also a photo opportunity. Alex Rivers should have married someone like Ophelia herself.

I had never had anything Ophelia wanted before. When we went out, she had been the one to turn heads, the one to make people whisper behind their hands. If anything, I had been the foil to her beauty.

But as we waited for Alex and John to bring out the baggage, I could see Ophelia's eyes darting around to the few other cars and limos, hoping to spot someone who recognized a celebrity's chauffeured car and who, by association, was watching her. It was probably the first time she hadn't been the center of attention when she was out with me, and the bottom line was that now, she never *would* be.

I had misread Ophelia's reaction to Alex. She was measuring him up, yes, and the traces of bruises on my neck had thrown her off, but her original objection to him had been his choice of mates. Ophelia didn't intentionally mean to slight me – she hadn't thought that far into it. She just could not understand why someone who had his pick of brightly colored macaws would choose, instead, a simple wren.

My hands clenched at my sides. It seemed my whole world had been reversed. Ophelia, whom I'd considered my best friend, was jealously carping about my marriage. Alex, whom I'd expected to be a shallow, conceited megalomaniac, had protected me, bared his secrets, and stitched himself so neatly into the weave of my heart that letting him go would mean unraveling myself.

As if my thoughts had evoked him, he stepped into the rosy outside light with John, each of them carrying a suitcase. Immediately Alex scanned the limousine island. His eyes reached mine, and the muscles at his shoulders seemed to relax. He had been looking for me.

I kept my eyes on Alex while I answered Ophelia. 'This isn't wrong,' I said quietly. 'And he's not what you're expecting.' I glanced back at her to gauge her reaction. 'We have a lot in common,' I added, but that's all I would say, because I wouldn't break Alex's trust.

'I hope so,' Ophelia said. She stretched out her hand to brush the vanishing spots on my neck that she knew I could not discuss. 'Because you've just moved into a whole different world, and he's the only person you know there.'

Alex's house in Bel-Air sprawled over twelve gated acres and looked exactly like the plantations I'd sketched in my mind when my mother used to tell me about her childhood in the South. It was nearly five in the morning when we arrived, and I stirred from

Alex's shoulder as the car made its way down the long gravel driveway, wishing that my mother had seen where I ended up.

It was not the type of house most actors kept in LA. Modesty had replaced the grandeur of the Golden Age of Hollywood, simply because it bought the celebrities a measure of solitude. But Alex, who had grown up in a trailer park, would want something like this. My throat tightened as I realized that Alex, who so valued his privacy, was willing to trade it all for the opulence he'd missed as a child. I wondered briefly if it worked for him; if cultivating this image for the public erased the memories.

Although it was early, there was a steady hum of activity around the house. A gardener was clipping at a hedge that ran the length of the left side of the house, and a thin stream of smoke arched from one of the small white buildings out back. 'What do you think?' Alex said.

I drew in my breath. 'It's magnificent,' I said. I had never seen a residence like this in my life; and I realized that I would do everything in my power to keep Alex from seeing the tiny apartment I'd lived in with Ophelia, simply so I wouldn't feel embarrassed.

Alex helped me out of the car. 'I'll give you the grand tour later,' he said. 'I imagine you'd like nothing better now than a soft mattress.'

I grinned at the very thought of it: Alex and I tangled under the sheets in a bed that was wider than just one of us. I followed him up the marble steps, smiling as John held the door open for us. 'Here you go, Mrs Rivers,' he said, and I blushed.

Alex brushed past John and propelled me up a glorious, winding staircase that could have been a set for *Gone With the Wind*. 'I'll introduce you to everyone else later,' he said. 'They're dying to meet you.'

What, I thought, *have they been told?* But before I could say anything, Alex opened the door to an oval sitting room that smelled of fresh wind and lemons. He crossed the room and closed a large bay window, letting lace curtains flutter to rest. 'This is the bedroom,' he said.

I looked around. 'Don't you have a bed?'

Alex laughed, pointing out a door that I hadn't noticed, blended between the blue and white stripes of the wallpaper. 'Through there.'

It was the largest bed I had ever seen, stepped onto a miniature platform and pillowed by a big down comforter. I sat on the edge of it, testing, and then I opened up the bag I'd been carrying since we first left Kenya and took out the things I always carried with me on planes: my toothbrush, my toiletry kit, another T-shirt. Wrapped inside the T-shirt was the bottle of snow Alex had brought me in Tanzania, something I didn't want to risk being broken in the baggage compartment. I set it on the maple dresser beside Alex's brush and a tall pile of photocopied screenplays.

Alex wrapped his arms around me from behind and pulled my shirt over my head. 'Welcome home,' he said.

I turned in his embrace. 'Thanks.' I let him unzip my linen trousers and pull off my shoes, tuck me under the covers. I pressed my arms down into the forgiving comforter, waiting for Alex to come to bed.

He turned and started out the door to the sitting room, and I bolted upright. 'Where are you going?' I said, my voice jumping at the ends in panic.

Alex smiled. 'I don't think I can go back to sleep,' he said. 'I'm just going to get some work done downstairs. I'll be here when you get up.'

I thought of how I wanted him to stay with me, to make this unfamiliar room a comfortable place. I ran my hands below the sheets to the spot where he should have been. I imagined the late-morning sun in Kenya, and the way we could remain in bed for hours there without the real world creeping through the thin crack beneath the door. But what was I supposed to say to Alex? *I'm afraid of being alone in this house. I don't know anyone here. I need to see you by my side, so that I understand where I fit in.* Or the deeper truth: *I don't recognize myself. I don't even recognize you.*

The door shut quietly behind Alex, leaving me lost. I told myself to stop acting like a fool, and I fixed my gaze on the jar of snow on the dresser, the only thing in this house so far that I could say was mine. The sun spilled through the French doors of the bedroom like a spreading fire, an accusation. *So,* I thought, *this is how it begins.*

Chapter Fifteen

'Finland.'

'Denmark.'

Alex skimmed his fingers over my ribs. 'You already used Denmark.'

I caught his hands and pressed them against me. 'Dominican Republic, then.'

Alex shook his head. 'I already said that. You might as well admit it, you've lost. There are only two countries beginning with D.'

I raised my eyebrows. 'Is that true?' I asked. We had been playing Geography on a lazy Thursday afternoon, and just for the challenge, we had limited ourselves to naming countries. 'Prove it.'

Alex laughed. 'Gladly. But you get the map.'

I pretended to move, but Alex kept his arm around me, indicating he wasn't about to let me go. He was lying on a hunter-green striped chaise, and I was between his legs, propped against his chest. I stared at the sun as it brightened the edges of a cloud it was hiding behind. 'Do you memorize atlases in your spare time?' I teased, already knowing the answer: Alex had learned geography as a child, self-taught, by speaking the exotic names of places he'd rather have been.

Alex kissed the top of my head, and as if the events were connected, the sun stepped out from its shade. 'I'm a man of rare talents and sensibilities,' he said dryly, and I wondered if he knew how true that really was.

You see, in spite of what I've already told you about our arrival in LA, all my misgivings about Alex had faded. In the week we'd been home, he hadn't gone back to work right away, leaving me to fend for myself. Instead, we had skinny-dipped in the pool, played tag in the lush boxwood hedge maze, and danced bare-foot, without music, on the veranda outside the bedroom. After dinner, Alex dismissed the staff and he made love to me in a different room each night: on the mahogany desk in the library, the Persian rug in the parlor, the white wicker rocker on the screened-in back porch. *This way*, he said, *you won't be able to go anywhere without thinking of me*. In return, I took him to UCLA, to my office, and showed him my work-in-progress at the lab, a reconstructed Australopithecene femur. I introduced him to Archibald Custer, and Alex indicated he might be inclined to give the department a sizable donation if they *upgraded* their tenured teaching faculty. This suggestion – which we hadn't discussed – made me uncomfortable. I was offered an associate professorship and a fine pick of January courses, which I never would have accepted if Alex hadn't asked me to, as a favor. *You've changed my life*, he'd said. *Let me change yours*.

Alex spent so much time at my side – introducing me to his agent, his employees, his friends – that at one point I asked if I was going to have to support us. Not that that was a real problem. Ophelia had been right – Alex made between four and six million dollars per film, and most of the money was rolled into his own production company, Pontchartrain Productions, for tax purposes. He paid himself a salary, but there was so much left over that even the third of his income that was spread out to various char-ities topped seven figures every year.

I was rich. Back in Tanzania, Alex had refused my offer of a prenuptial agreement, saying that he meant this marriage to be for life. I now owned half of a ranch in Colorado; half of a Monet, a Kandinsky, and two van Goghs; half of a hand-carved cherry dining room set that seated thirty and cost more than my undergraduate education. But even the most beautiful furniture in the world couldn't keep me from missing my old red leather wing chair, the first piece I'd bought in California; or from picturing the Salvation Army bureau Ophelia had bought me for Christmas one year, and then painted with peace symbols and daisy chains. My old furniture was worth nothing, did not fit in this house; but when the Goodwill trucks came to pick it up, I cried.

Yet I loved being with Alex so much that for the first time in years I wasn't looking forward to the upcoming term at UCLA; I saw it instead as something that was going to take me away from him. Still, this kind of life took a little getting used to. I had come to expect the reverent whisper of Elizabeth, the maid, as I walked down the hall to find Alex in the morning; I had become accustomed to writing down that I needed avocados and Neutrogena soap from the market and just leaving the list with Alex's secretary. When a hack reporter snuck onto the grounds and I opened the bathroom curtains to find a camera lens staring back at me, I didn't even scream. I calmly told Alex, as if it were something I faced daily, and watched while he called the police.

But we didn't go out. Alex said it was for my own good, that we should let the novelty of the marriage die down a little before facing the public again. He told me, smiling, that he wanted me all to himself. But the more time I spent in my gilded cage, the more I thought of Ophelia's words at the airport. And I knew that no matter how much of a fairy tale I was living now, I wouldn't really be happy until I could build a bridge from the life I had lived in Westwood to this new one in Bel-Air.

Alex had dipped his toe into the edge of the pool and was trying to write my name in script. 'C,' he said. 'A-S-S . . .' He frowned and looked up at me. 'How come you don't like Cassandra?'

I shrugged. 'I never said I didn't like it,' I clarified. 'It's what my mother tried to call me until my father convinced her it was far too much name for a little girl. And then in seventh grade we did this Greek mythology unit, and my teacher made me look up my name.' I recited the facts to Alex as I had that day in front of the class: Cassandra was the beautiful daughter of King Priam and Hecuba. She was given the power of prophecy by Apollo, but when he fell in love with her and she didn't return his attentions, he cursed her so that no one would believe what she foresaw, even though it was the truth.

At twelve, I had liked the fact that Cassandra was beautiful enough to make Apollo fall in love with her, but the way she was forced to live out her life had turned me cold. Stripped of her credibility, she'd become a slave, and then was murdered. 'After we did that unit,' I said, 'I told all the teachers I wanted to be called Cassie, and everyone else just followed.'

Alex lifted me up and twisted me so that we were lying face-to-face. 'Lucky for you, Cassandra,' he murmured, 'that you tend to return my attentions.'

His breath settled into the curve of my neck, and I slid my hands under the band of his bathing suit, shaping myself to his heat. Alex gripped the back of my head and pulled me closer, shifting me off balance until we rolled as a tangled unit off the chaise and onto the grass beside the pool.

'Well,' a voice said. 'And here I thought *I'd* come at an inopportune time.'

I pushed away from Alex and brushed the hair out of my face, straightening to see Ophelia, her arm held by John in a death grip. Her hair was a flyaway mess, her shorts had been torn across her bottom, and every few seconds she tugged her shoulder away from John as if she found him completely distasteful.

John looked at me, and then slid his gaze toward Alex. 'She told Juarez at the gate that she was a friend of Mrs Rivers, but she wouldn't let us call up to the house, so we sent her away. And then she's picked up on the monitor climbing over the east fence.'

'Speaking of which,' Ophelia said to Alex, 'I'll send you the bill for these shorts.' She turned to me. 'And shame on you for not giving me the password of the day.'

'Ophelia,' I said, shaking my head. 'Why didn't you just give your name at the front gate?'

All the fight and bluster drained out of Ophelia, puddling in front of her feet. 'I wanted to surprise you,' she said miserably. 'If I'd let them call you and tell you I was coming, it wouldn't have been a surprise.'

I raised my eyebrows. She was the last person I'd have expected to crawl over the fence of the house. For the past week, I'd been trying to get Ophelia to make the tiniest concessions toward accepting my new life. I knew that in some ways, Alex and Ophelia were too much alike to become friends. Their careers moved in similar self-serving circles; they measured their success by the number of people who recognized them; they both needed me. I knew that deep down Ophelia believed that Alex was taking me away, but I also knew I could change that. Instead of looking at Alex as a threat, I was determined to make her see him as an asset – as a sort of big brother in the business. I told her this repeatedly over the phone. And of course, I wanted Alex to like Ophelia too. She was my best friend – my only friend, really.

Alex had wrapped a towel around his waist to conceal what we hadn't been able to finish, but he easily dismissed John and brought a chair over for Ophelia, entertaining her so smoothly I could almost believe he routinely expected to find women falling over his fences. 'It's my fault,' he said easily. 'I keep forgetting to give the names of Cassie's friends to the guard so they won't be hassled.'

My eyes widened; we had never discussed this. I watched him smile at Ophelia, then watched the last of her edges soften, and I realized that Alex had charm honed to an art. 'Oh!' Ophelia drew in her breath, and then opened up a floral-print canvas tote that was discolored and wet at the bottom. She fished out a long red gift bag and handed it to me. Inside, broken pieces jangled;

I peeked to see shards of green glass and to smell the sweet curl of champagne. 'It hit the ground before I did when I climbed the fence,' she said apologetically. 'It was a house-warming gift.'

I poked a finger through the remains. 'Well, thanks,' I said. 'But Alex has lived here for a while anyway.'

Ophelia grinned. 'It was more to warm the household to the idea of *me*,' she said. 'I've been an asshole. I was hoping we could just start over.' She glanced at Alex, who was sitting next to me on the chaise, absorbing the conversation as it unfolded. 'It's just that when you've known Cassie for as long as I have, and she says she's brought something back from Tanzania, you'd think she means yellow fever, not a *husband*. She's taken more time ordering a drink at a bar than she did hooking up with you. Although,' she conceded, 'when she does get around to making a decision, she has a knack of choosing the very best.'

Alex looked at her for a long moment, one actor assessing the skills of another, and then he slowly nodded his head. 'Well,' he said, 'she *did* pick you as a roommate.'

Ophelia swung her hair over her shoulder and offered a smile. I looked at her, and then back to Alex, and I was reminded of the way I had felt when I first moved to LA: that the people here were part of a tremendous movie set, all healthy and tanned and disproportionately beautiful. 'I *am* sorry about the champagne,' Ophelia said.

'I'm sorry about your *shorts*.' I twisted around so that I could better see the jagged rip along the seat.

Ophelia laughed. 'Actually,' she said, 'they're yours. You left them behind.' Impulsively she leaned across the foot of space that separated us and threw her arms around my neck. 'You'll forgive me, won't you, Cass?' she whispered.

I smiled against her cheek. 'For Alex, yes. For the shorts, never.'

'You know I wouldn't do this for anyone but you.'

At the sound of Alex's voice I looked up from the mirror where

I was putting on my makeup. He was knotting his tie in preparation for a night out on the town that he hadn't wanted in the first place. Ophelia had begged to make amends by taking us out to dinner at Nicky Blair's, which she said she'd pay for if Alex used his clout to make the reservation on short notice. Alex had graciously agreed, but when we were alone in the room I could hear his objections cutting through the tension: *We should just have dinner here. Let the novelty of the marriage die down. We can do this some other time.*

'It won't be that bad,' I said lightly. 'It'll be over before you know it.' I put down the mascara wand and walked into the bedroom in my underwear and slip, coming to stand in front of Alex. I unknotted his tie and redid it, straightening the half-Windsor and then smoothing down the tails. I leaned up to kiss his cheek. 'Thank you,' I said.

Alex's hands ran up and down my arms. 'Oh, it won't be as bad as I'm expecting,' he said. 'That's my trick. If I imagine the absolute worst, I can't help but be pleasantly surprised.' He walked to my closet and picked out one of the outfits that had magically appeared within days of my arrival in LA, a slinky red dress like nothing I'd ever owned before. In fact, most of my clothing was like nothing I'd ever owned before. But Alex knew more about these things – where I would be going and what I would need – so I simply deferred to his judgment.

'It's a Thursday night,' he rationalized, watching me step into the dress and then coming around to zip the back for me. 'So no one from the industry will be around. There aren't any premieres going on, and the reporters should be calling it a day.' He spun me around by my shoulders and smiled down at me. 'All in all, if we're lucky, it'll be dead tonight.'

I almost said what sprang to mind: *Ophelia will be so upset.* She was down the hall in a guest suite, borrowing one of my new dresses and a pair of shoes. When Alex had made the reservation at Nicky Blair's, a swank celebrity hangout, Ophelia couldn't sit still in her chair. It was nice to see her thinking of Alex as an ally instead of an enemy, but I wondered if she'd been swayed to apologize because she really missed me, or because she'd recognized the connections Alex could offer her.

I shook the thought away. Of course she'd come for me; she didn't even *know* Alex yet. And we'd had a terrific afternoon. I'd shown her around the house, laughing at her comments about bathtubs big enough to hold a cast party and whether or not Elizabeth sold Alex's dirty sheets to the die-hard fans clustered at the gate. A little after four we had raided the refrigerator and carried a bag of chocolate chips and some leftover sesame chicken into the maze, where we'd lain on our backs and let the sun slanting through the hedge speckle our stomachs and our thighs. And just like when I had lived in Westwood, we talked about sex – except this time, I wasn't the one simply listening.

It had never been easy for me to talk about that, and Ophelia would have laughed me off if I'd said what I really wanted to. So instead I told her about the exotic places we'd done it: the excavation pit in Tanzania, the last pew of the Catholic church in Kenya, the laundry room closet while Elizabeth was just outside folding clothes. I told her how beautiful Alex's body was, how many times we came together at night.

I did not tell her that he was so gentle he sometimes made me cry. I did not tell her that afterward, he would hold me so tightly the breath was driven from my lungs, as if he were afraid I'd disappear. I did not tell her that every now and then, as he prayed to me with his hands and his heart and his mouth, I felt as cherished and as blessed as a saint.

I did not tell Ophelia these things, but that didn't keep her from seeing them in me. 'Jesus,' she had said, shaking her head. 'You're honest-to-God in love.' I had nodded; I didn't think there were words, really, to explain the connections and dependency Alex and I had between us. Ophelia had smiled. 'No communicable diseases, four times a night, and he hasn't cheated on you yet. As far as I can tell, the man has only one flaw.'

I had leaned up on my elbow. 'And that is?'

'He picked you instead of me.'

Alex's voice startled me back to the present. He had gone to get Ophelia, and now the two of them stood at the threshold of the door, watching me. Ophelia was wearing a dress of mine that I hadn't even seen in the closet yet, something green that swirled around her and caught the flashes in her eyes. Her feet were practically dancing in anticipation of a night out at an exclusive restaurant. As she held on to Alex's arm, they looked every inch the couple.

Ophelia's glance swept me from head to toe. 'My God,' she said, 'you look beautiful.'

I twisted my hands in front of me; I did not yet know what to do with these kinds of compliments. 'So do you,' I said.

Ophelia smirked and turned toward Alex. 'Which one of us?'

I laughed. 'Both of you,' I said.

John was waiting for us at the front door, and he offered Ophelia his arm down the stairs as if he hadn't been the one to apprehend her for trespassing hours before. He opened the rear door of the Range Rover and handed Ophelia inside, then helped me up. 'Tell me,' Ophelia murmured, 'does he take you to the bathroom if you have to go?'

Alex hopped up beside us. 'Well, ladies,' he said, 'I hope you've already had something to eat.'

I glanced at Ophelia, but she just raised her eyebrows. 'I thought we were going out to dinner,' I said.

'We are,' Alex agreed. 'But that doesn't mean you'll have a chance to eat anything.' He turned to Ophelia, as if to warn her about what she'd gotten herself into. 'Unfortunately, you've invited me, and when I'm at a table dinner tends to be less a meal than an event.'

Ophelia tipped up her chin and gave Alex a dazzling grin. 'That,' she said, 'is exactly what I'm counting on.'

*   *   *

To Alex's surprise and pleasure, he made it through his appetizer before someone came by to congratulate him on our marriage. 'Thanks, Pete,' he said. 'Let me introduce you to Cassie, my wife' – he laid a hand on my shoulder here – 'and her friend, Ophelia Fox. Ophelia's breaking into the business.' Alex paused for a beat. 'And Pete is one of the honchos at Touchstone.'

Under the table I squeezed Alex's leg, letting him know how much it meant to me that he'd go out of his way to help Ophelia after all she'd done. He leaned toward me and kissed my neck. 'Don't start what you can't finish in public,' he whispered.

Ophelia kept up a running monologue on which celebrities had entered the restaurant and who had ordered what for dessert. 'I'll tell you,' she mused. 'If I'm going to get discovered, I ought to just glue myself to a chair here and let everyone come and go.'

Alex ate the three shrimp I had left on my plate. 'Not to burst your bubble,' he said, 'but this is about the quietest I've ever seen Nicky Blair's.' As if this were his fault, he smiled apologetically at Ophelia. 'We'll come back here some other time,' he promised.

Every time Ophelia steered the conversation to Hollywood politics or pointed out another studio executive, Alex worked the thread of the discussion back to me. He mentioned how impressed he'd been with my technical knowledge on the set, to which Ophelia just raised an eyebrow and asked, 'Technical knowledge about *what*, exactly?' He told Ophelia I'd been made an associate professor, something that I'd told her three days before but that she apparently hadn't heard. Now, she jumped out of her chair and threw her arms around my neck, calling to a waiter for a second bottle of champagne.

Maybe it was the genuine interest she showed in my promotion; maybe it was simply that dinner had turned out to be much less of a media blitz than Alex had anticipated. But to my relief, by the time the meal was over, Alex and Ophelia were trading the latest Quayle jokes, slapping each other on the back, doing impressions of legendary executive assholes in the movie industry.

Alex insisted on paying the bill, which I had known all along he would do, and which – I think – Ophelia knew all along too. She stood up and braced her hand on the back of her chair. 'Whew,' she said. 'That second bottle goes straight to the head.'

It wasn't a surprise to me that Ophelia was tipsy – I had barely had two glasses of the Cristal, and Alex had drunk only water. Alex slipped an arm around her waist to support her, and then smiled at me and wove his fingers through mine.

When he pushed out the front door, his arm was around one stunning woman, and he was pulling me slightly behind him. Which was why, for a second, I didn't notice the gaggle of photographers, the bright black spots the flashbulbs left behind.

'God *damn*,' Alex muttered, snapping my arm close to his side so that I was forced into the light, unable to shrink away as my natural instinct had been. He dropped his hand from Ophelia's waist, but his image had already been captured on film, his arm tight around a woman who was not his wife.

'This is *just* the kind of crap I didn't want,' he said to no one in particular. I knew what he was thinking, what every gossip column in the country would have to say about this little ménage à trois. I knew what this could do to his polished, pristine image.

THE HONEYMOON'S OVER. ALEX RIVERS'S SECRET LOVE LIFE. TWO FOR THE PRICE OF ONE. Headlines crowded my mind, and I pressed my fingers against my eyes, trying to block out the flashes from the cameras and the fact that my name was going to be dragged through the mud only three weeks after my wedding. I could feel Alex's arm tense beneath my fingers, and I stroked his wrist. *It was only an accident*, I wanted to say. *Nobody could have seen this coming.*

Belatedly I remembered Ophelia, who a minute ago had been too woozy to stand by herself. I looked down at the floor, half expecting her to be passed out, but she was at Alex's side, tall and straight and smiling beautifully, clutching his arm even as he tried to throw her off.

And that's how I knew she had planned the whole thing.

I had forgiven Ophelia the time she wore my pearls to a premiere and lost them in the back seat of a director's limo. I had forgiven her when she left me stranded at the dentist after a root canal because of a casting call for a part she didn't even get. I had forgiven her for using the rent money to enroll in a transcendental yoga class for stress management, for telling me I wasn't trendy enough to come club hopping with some of her actor friends, for forgetting my birthday almost every year we'd lived together. But as I watched Alex seething, shielding me with one arm from an inevitable accusation, I knew that I would never forgive her for this.

Alex murmured something about finding John and the car, and as he moved away I grabbed Ophelia from behind, spinning her around. Even as she turned, she was watching the reporters who were still tracking Alex, her photo opportunity. 'How *could* you?' I said.

Ophelia lifted her eyebrows. 'How could I what?'

I narrowed my eyes. In the ten years I had known Ophelia, I had always been her fall guy, and I had never once complained. But that was before she set out to intentionally hurt me, to hurt my husband. 'You told them we were coming here. You set Alex up.'

Ophelia's mouth tightened. 'Isn't that what you've been telling me to do, Cassie?'

Her words stopped my flood of anger. *Yes, but*, I wanted to say, *you weren't supposed to go about it that way. You weren't supposed to trick him. You weren't supposed to use me*. 'He was starting to like you,' I said quietly.

Ophelia rolled her eyes. 'If the positions were reversed, he would have done exactly the same thing. He probably *has*.'

'No,' I said firmly. 'He has not.'

I turned my head to see Alex storming back. He grabbed my wrist, and without sparing Ophelia even a look, pulled me away from the restaurant.

I let Alex open my car door, and then I leaned my head back, watching the stars wink while he settled down beside me and told John we were ready. 'Well,' he said carefully, 'by tomorrow morning I will have been branded as a two-timing son of a bitch, and the more careful bloodhounds will notice the perversity of me screwing my wife's best friend.' He stared out the window, away from me. 'You realize that from the camera angle, you probably won't be in the picture. Your hand maybe, but that will be airbrushed out. Of course, as planned, your friend Ophelia will feature prominently, with my arm around her waist.'

I touched his leg lightly. 'I'm sorry, Alex,' I said. 'I didn't know she was going to do anything. Ophelia's not usually like that.'

'You're nearly as good an actress as she is,' Alex said. 'I can almost believe you.' He turned to me, his eyes dark. 'I'm only going to tell you this once,' he said, 'so please keep it in mind. I don't like being paraded around like a circus animal. It's bad enough that I have to think twice before I walk outside in the middle of the day, that just because I'm good at what I do I have to live in a fishbowl. But I won't be used, Cassie, not even by you.'

This whole fiasco was indirectly my fault, and because of that, I let him take his anger out on me. 'I understand,' I whispered, and I focused on the shadows of the rolling night.

It was well after three in the morning when I woke up and realized Alex hadn't come to bed. We had come home, and after saying goodnight to John, Alex had walked into the library, shutting the door behind him and making it perfectly clear he didn't want me around. I had walked up the stairs and into the bedroom, letting the carpet sink under my feet. I stripped to my skin, still hoping. I lay in bed and told myself we were bound to have an argument at some point. I fell asleep imagining his hands running down my sides.

When his half of the bed was still empty in the middle of the night, I began to panic. I pulled a thin white silk wrapper from the closet, something that had been in Alex's bedroom before I even arrived. I didn't think he would have driven away without telling me; I didn't want to believe he was with somebody else. Tiptoeing down the hall, I opened the doors to the guest suites, breathing a sigh of relief when each bed was smooth and made.

He wasn't in the library either, or the kitchen, or the study. Hesitant, I opened the heavy front door of the house, leaving it ajar in case it would lock behind me, and I made my way down the marble steps.

The grounds were well lit for the sake of the hidden security cameras, so it was no trouble to find the path that wound behind the house, between the outbuildings, toward the boxwood maze. I was halfway to the gardens when I heard the rhythmic splashing from the pool.

Over the pungent strains of chlorine, I could smell the bourbon, and I did not know if it was because Alex had drunk an exorbitant amount, or because I was naturally attuned to the scent by the memory of my mother. The sweet, strong odor hit me right behind the eyes, just like it used to, and took me back twenty years.

Once, when I was thirteen and I had come to hate the smell of bourbon that seemed to be steeped into the wallpaper of our house and funneled through its air vents, I had emptied every last bottle down the sink. My mother, when she found out, went into a rage. She tore at my shirt, ripping it across the sleeve, and backhanded me across the face before she broke down in my arms, crying like a child. *If you loved me*, she said, *you wouldn't do this to me*. And because I did not know the opposite was true, I swore I wouldn't do it again. I sat at the kitchen table watching her drink a tiny bottle of Cointreau she kept for cooking. As her hands stopped shaking she glanced up at me, smiling, as if to say, *You see?* And for the first time I noticed how very much I was growing up to look like her.

Now a bottle of bourbon lay on its side, dripping into a puddle that ran into the shallow end of the pool. Alex held a second bottle by the neck. He was sitting on the smooth stone bench that lined one underwater side of the pool, and when he saw me step into the spotlight he toasted me. 'You want a drink, *chère*?' he drawled, and when I shook my head he laughed. 'C'mon now, *pichouette*. You an' I know it's in the blood.'

I stood up as straight as I could. 'Come to bed, Alex,' I said, trying to keep the shiver out of my voice.

'I don't think so,' he said. 'I got some swimming to do yet.'

He stood up, and he was completely naked. Under the pale blue glow of the outside lights, he could have been a Greek god. Every muscle in his chest was neatly sculpted, and water dripped down between his legs and over his thighs to create the illusion that he'd been carved of fluid marble. He held his arms away from his body, palms up. 'You like what you see, *chère*?' he said. 'Everyone else seems to.'

He stepped out of the pool, stalking me. My breath caught as he suddenly stood inches away, soaking the hem of the white gown. He hauled me up against him, wrapping one arm around my waist and gripping my chin with his other hand. He was holding my jaw so tight that the skin stretched, beginning to sting.

His eyes had gone nearly black and I couldn't move my mouth enough to speak and it was getting harder and harder to breathe. He was twice as big as me, and drunk, and I couldn't be sure he knew exactly who I was. A cold curl of fear unraveled at the base of my stomach, and that was when I felt Alex start to shake.

It wasn't just the chill of night on his wet body; it was something that came from the marrow of his bones. It worked its way upward from his knees to his hips to his arms, and I knew he couldn't control it, because suddenly he seemed as terrified as I was. He locked his eyes onto mine, as if I would know what to do.

Without thinking, I wedged my hands between us to the tie

of my robe and pulled it free. I pressed myself against Alex, my skin heating his, selflessly absorbing his cold until my body was racked by shudders, while Alex's became calm and warm.

He let go of my jaw, and I rubbed my face from side to side against his chest, feeling the blood rush to my cheeks. When he pulled away from me, his eyes were silver and shot with awareness. Sighing, I relaxed. I knew this stage.

Alex let me take the bottle of bourbon from his fist, and he didn't say a thing as I poured it over the grass near our feet. He watched it steam up and hiss, and then he took the empty glass from my hand and stared at it as if he had no idea how it had ever gotten there.

It was so easy to see him as a little boy when his defenses came tumbling down. I thought of the childhood friends he'd told me about, conjured from books and drawn in the richest colors, taking him on adventures that made him forget where he was. I pictured him hauling up traps of crawfish his father was too drunk to retrieve; wearing a white shirt two sizes too small to an uncle's funeral because his mother hadn't bothered to replace the one he'd outgrown. I gently pulled him down to the green striped chaise we'd been sitting on earlier that afternoon, and I brushed the wet spikes of his hair away from his eyes. He swayed forward a little, unconsciously craving a gesture that should have come years before.

'You know, I never had an in-between,' Alex said. 'My own *maman* and papa didn't give a damn about me, and I went straight from that life to people who pick through my trash, trying to figure out what I eat for breakfast.' He pulled me onto his lap, burying his face in my hair. 'You know what I'd like?' he murmured. 'I'd like to go meet the guy who tailors my suits, instead of having him come here. And I'd like to buy you daisies from a street vendor who hasn't seen my last three films. I'd like to go out to dinner and have your goddamn friend tip off the press and have them say, "Alex *who?*"'

He lifted his hand to cover my breast, and it rested in his palm like a simple, solid truth. 'I used to lie in my bed at night as a kid and wish that someone cared if I woke up the next morning, and not just so there'd be someone to kick around.' He kissed the crown of my head and tucked me closer to his chest, as if he could protect me from his own past. 'Be careful what you wish for, Cassie,' he said softly. 'It might come true.'

Chapter Sixteen

'I brought this for you.'

Alex's voice came from behind me, and without meaning to, my fingers gripped the armrests of the white wicker chair. I did not turn around, staring instead over the balcony of the upper veranda, counting the steps it took for Alex to walk from the door of the bedroom to me.

He set the tea down beside me, centered on a simple saucer with the milk already poured in, which told me that Alex had gone to the trouble of preparing it himself, rather than asking the cook to do it. In the distance, I could hear the sounds of late-afternoon traffic and crying gulls, as if this day had been just like any other.

Alex knelt in front of me and rested his folded arms on my knees. I stared at him as if I was in shock, which I suppose I was. My mind registered the flawless symmetry of his features as if seeing them for the very first time. 'Cassie,' he whispered, 'I'm sorry.'

I nodded at him. I believed him; I *had* to.

'It's not going to ever happen again,' he said. He laid his head in my lap and of their own volition my hands began to stroke his hair, his ear, the line of his jaw that I knew so well.

'I know,' I said. But even as the words came I saw behind my closed eyes the image of those midwestern storms that rip up the world as you know it, and leave, like a sacrifice, a rainbow to make you forget what has come before.

*   *   *

'What's important to remember about the nature of bone,' I told the sea of faces in the lecture hall, 'is that it's not the way we always imagine it to be.' I stepped from behind the podium, coming to stand at a little demonstration table I'd set up before my field anthropology class. We were nearly two months into the course, and I was working hard to give the students the background they'd need for the site excavation we'd do later in the semester. 'When we dig up a bone, we assume it is something solid and static, when in fact it used to be every bit as alive as the other tissues of the body.'

I listened to the scratch of pens on lined notebooks as I counted off the properties of bone in a living organism. 'It can grow, it can be stricken by disease, it can heal itself. And it adapts to the needs of the individual.' I lifted up two femurs from the display table. 'For example, bones become stronger when necessary. This femur came from a thirteen-year-old girl. Compare its width to that of the other bone, which belonged to an Olympic weightlifter.'

I liked giving this lecture. Part of it was the sensationalism of the displays, part of it was breaking down most of the preconceptions the students had about bone in general. 'Bone isn't made of inorganic matter, either, like chalk. It's an organic network of fibers and cells that happen to contain inorganic matter, like calcium phosphate. It's the combination of the two that gives bone its resilience and also its hardness.'

From the corner of my eye, I noticed Archibald Custer leaning against the doorframe. Last year, he had said to me that I treated science like a National Enquirer story. And I had argued, no pun intended, that a dissertation on the nature of bone was too dry to keep kids awake for an hour, much less get them interested in anthropology. Since Alex's grant, Custer hadn't had the guts to criticize my teaching methods, or to move me to a different course. I could probably have lectured naked without there being any backlash.

My eyes roved the back of the classroom, just below Custer's tightly crossed arms. A kid wearing headphones, two girls whispering to each other, and Alex.

Sometimes he came to watch me teach; he said it amazed him how much I knew. He always slipped in after the class started, to keep from drawing attention away from my words; he usually wore sunglasses, as if they were something to hide behind. Most of the students knew I was married to him — I think some of them took the class just to find out what I was like, or in hopes of seeing Alex.

I grinned right at him, and he took off his sunglasses and gave me a wink. When Alex came, I was at my very best. I suppose, in a way, I was acting for him. 'Now, you can see just how much of a bone is organic if you soak it for a while in an acid. This will remove the salts, leaving the organic matter behind in the shape it was before it was placed in the acid. But,' I said, drawing the fibula from a glass tray where it had been soaking, 'once you remove the salts, it's completely pliable.' I picked up each end of the long bone, letting it sag a bit in the middle before I tied it into a loose knot.

'Holy shit,' whispered a freshman in the front row.

I smiled at him. 'My thoughts exactly,' I said.

Glancing at my watch, I stepped back behind the podium and began to shuffle together my notes. 'Don't forget the quiz next Thursday.'

Custer had left, and the students began to stream down the aisles of the hall. Usually after this lecture, a group would cluster around the display table, touching the jellied bone, untying it, running their fingers over the edges. In the past I had answered their questions and let them stay as long as they liked. After all, anthropology was a hands-on discipline.

But this year, in spite of the rapt attention the class had given me and the fact that my lesson hadn't changed a bit, nobody seemed interested. Quietly, I began to straighten up the table, packing away the exhibit bones in layers of soft cotton wool. I wondered if I was losing my touch.

I looked up, remembering that Alex was probably waiting, and saw a knot of students milling around him in the aisle, offering up their anthropology notebooks for autographs.

The blood drained from my face. Wait, I wanted to say, they belong to me. *But the words were stuck in my throat, and even as I let the first wave of anger flood past I realized that I had nothing to be jealous of at all. Alex hadn't deliberately gathered them near, and even if he hadn't been in the classroom, there was no guarantee that any of the students would have come forward to look at my display.*

He pushed past the students and stood with his hands in his pockets, looking over the table and the bones lying neatly in transport crates. 'Don't some of the salts seep out into the soil when a bone gets fossilized?' Alex said loudly.

I laughed; in spite of his apparent undivided interest, I knew exactly what he was doing. 'Sure,' I said.

'So how come you never dig up anything as limp as that?' He pointed to the bone, still knotted, swimming in its acid solution. Two students wandered back down the aisle of the lecture hall, coming to stand on either side of Alex and touching the display femurs in the spots where his fingers had brushed them seconds before. Several other kids joined the group.

'First of all, it's going to take centuries to happen. But even when the calcium content is reduced, it's not quite as drastic, so the bones usually retain their shape. Of course, every once in a while the climate and the soil are right' – I rummaged through a half-packed carton – 'and you get something like this.' I held up an Iron Age jawbone that had been excavated from an Irish peat bog, which was twisted neatly in the shape of a cruller. 'The way other bones were lying on this one was what caused it to take this shape.'

For a while, then, the soft pads of a dozen hands ran over the bone samples I'd brought, and above the heads of the students I caught Alex's eye. He really did know how to ask the right questions. In fact, if he hadn't been such a good actor, he would have made an excellent anthropologist. He walked behind the table and slipped his arm around my waist. As if the students had been cued, they glanced up and dribbled out of the classroom, chattering.

'Happy anniversary,' Alex said, kissing me lightly.

I kept my eyes open. Around us, the dust motes danced in the light that spilled through the windows. 'Happy anniversary,' I said. I stepped out of the circle of his arms and carefully rewrapped the samples the kids had been examining. 'Just let me clean this up and we can get out of here.'

He caught me by the shoulders and pulled me between his legs. 'I want to do an experiment,' he said. 'Are you game?'

I nodded, already seeing his head bend down to kiss me again. His lips moved against mine, making me whisper with him, and he deepened the kiss, cradling my head, keeping me from pulling away.

By the time he lifted his head, I was lying across him, not entirely sure of where I was. 'Just as I thought,' he murmured. 'I wanted to see if bones could go all soft without the acid.'

I smiled into the warmth of his chest. 'Absolutely,' I said.

It had been one moment, one mistake, and as Alex said, it would not happen again. I whispered those words over and over, thinking that these things happened to other people, the ones you heard about on the news, but certainly not to Alex and me.

'Cassie?'

At the sound of Ophelia's voice, I grabbed the afghan that was draped over the other wicker rocking chair and wrapped it around my shoulders. I was not cold, but it would keep her from seeing what had happened.

After that disastrous night out at Nicky Blair's over a year earlier, Ophelia and I had slowly regained ground with each other. I needed her; except for Alex, I didn't really have anyone to talk to. I don't know that she ever said she was sorry, but then again, I stopped apologizing for marrying Alex, and I let her know that my loyalties were with him. As long as they didn't cross paths when Ophelia came to visit, things were usually all right. In fact, our relationship assumed its usual course: Ophelia would come over and talk about herself, and since my life meant discussing Alex, I would sit quietly and simply listen.

Ophelia's head peeked out from the French doors that led into the bedroom. '*There* you are,' she said. 'And here I was beginning to think you'd made some move without telling John first.'

I tried to smile at her. 'This isn't a very good time,' I hedged.

Ophelia waved the idea away. 'I know, I know. The illustrious Riverses have a premiere to attend tonight. I wanted to know if I could borrow your red evening gown.'

I wrinkled my forehead; I couldn't even remember *owning* a red evening gown, but then Ophelia had a better idea of the inventory of my closets. 'What for?'

'I'm singing at a blues club tonight.' Ophelia leaned against the supporting balustrade of the veranda, slinking her arm up over her head in the fashion of a vamp.

'You can't sing,' I pointed out.

Ophelia shrugged. 'Yeah, but the owners don't know that yet and won't find out until I'm already on stage. And you never know who's going to be in the audience, the way I figure it.' She smiled. 'Besides, they paid me up front.'

I couldn't help but laugh; Ophelia was truly the best medicine. 'How in God's name did you convince them you could sing the blues?'

Ophelia started back toward the bedroom, ostensibly to rummage for the evening gown. 'I lied,' she called out.

I pulled the blanket closer around my shoulders, drawing my secret to myself. 'How can you just do that?' I said. 'I mean, don't you ever get your stories crossed?'

Ophelia waltzed onto the veranda with the dress draped over her shoulder. 'Your problem is that you've been too honest for too long. Once you start doing it,' she said easily, 'lying is simpler than breathing.' She held the dress up under her chin and pirouetted for me.

'Billie Holiday would be jealous,' I said. I shifted in the rocker, wincing as my side pressed against the arm of the chair.

Ophelia glanced down at me, and her eyes clouded. 'You're not getting sick, are you?' She tugged at the corner of the blanket. 'I mean, are you cold?'

I let her press her palm against my forehead as I had taught her to do years before, and I pulled the afghan tight around my shoulders. I hated Alex for making me do this. 'As a matter of fact,' I said, 'I may be coming down with something.'

After spending a full year with Alex, I came to see that I had really married many different men – Alex being the stand-in when no one else was around. He couldn't really leave his work at the office, so every character he played made its way into my bed, or sat across from me at the breakfast table. I'll say this – it certainly added variety to our relationship. During the quick eight weeks he'd been shooting Speed, *an action film about a pilot, he'd been cocky and quick and bursting with energy. When he did a summer run as Romeo for a professional theater group, he had come to me at night with all the passion of a young boy in love with being in love.*

I hadn't liked the character of his pilot, but he had been tolerable. And Romeo made me a little edgy, more prone to check in the mirror for new lines and to wonder how I could get so tired in the course of a normal day while Alex seemed to keep going forever. But now that Alex was doing Antony and Cleopatra, *I had come up against the first character I wanted nowhere near me. On my desk calendar at the university, I kept count of how many more days were left of production, how many more days I had to wait before Alex became just Alex again.*

In many ways, playing Antony wasn't much of a stretch for Alex, which is what I think made the role so attractive to him in the first place. Antony was driven by power and ambition, a man who had chosen a queen; a man who, in Shakespeare's words, could 'stand up peerless'. But Antony was also obsessive, judgmental, and paranoid. It was his fixation with Cleopatra that created a chink in his armor – jealousy – which made it that much easier for his enemies to bring them down. Convince Antony that Cleopatra has betrayed him for Caesar, and his world will come crumbling.

Of course, it is also a good star-crossed-love story: When Antony is wrongly convinced that Cleopatra has sided with Caesar, he accuses her, and out of fear for her life, she sends word that she's already killed herself. When the messenger tells Antony she died whispering his name, he is guilt-stricken and runs himself through with his sword, only to die in the arms of a very much alive Cleopatra. Cleopatra, then, rather than bow to Caesar, does truly kill herself with a poisonous asp. It is a story of misunderstandings and of lies that backfire; of a pair of lovers who can only be happy in a world where there is no one else to tempt their faulty judgment.

I was not ready to find an asp, but I understood Cleopatra's claim about Antony being a madman. Sometimes where we were alone, Alex spoke in Shakespearean accent. He would ignore me for hours at a time and then suddenly pull me into the bedroom, where he'd touch me with a need that bordered on violence. It got to the point where Alex would come through the front door and I would wait quietly, not even saying hello, until I could anticipate whether this time he'd invite me out to a moonlight dinner, or scream at me for moving a memo he'd scribbled to a spot where it wouldn't blow away.

He was driving the Range Rover himself tonight, and I was sitting in the front seat – a spot I hadn't occupied in the entire year we'd been married. John had remained at the house to help tape the plate windows and tie down tarps over the shrubs in anticipation of the battering rains that were sweeping up the California coast. Alex glanced at the clock on the dashboard, and then at the clouds roiling in the sky. 'It'll be close,' he said.

We were going to sandbag the beach at the Malibu apartment, and I knew it was the last thing in the world Alex wanted to be doing. That week, Brianne Nolan – Cleopatra – had backed out of her contract under the pretense of exhaustion. But two days later Herb Silver told Alex he'd overheard at a power lunch that Nolan had wanted out of the production because playing second fiddle to Alex wasn't as professionally lucrative as another deal that had just fallen into her agent's lap. I had found Alex in his study at three in the morning, punching buttons on a calculator in an effort to see how much money had been wasted, how much time had been lost.

The production company was going to sue her for breach of contract, and Alex had been in meetings with lawyers for most of the day. As soon as he'd walked through the door he'd told me to find rain slickers and meet him in the garage. It was not just a matter of beach erosion, but of damage that might be done to the apartment.

'Do you think we'll be able to get back to Bel-Air tonight?' I asked quietly, testing the waters.

Alex didn't even glance at me, but a muscle jumped along his jaw. 'How the hell should I know?' he said.

The beach at the Colony was a mob of celebrities in yellow Helly-Hansen coats, reduced to ordinary physical labor by the cruelty of nature. Alex waved to a producer who lived several buildings down from ours and then handed me two rolls of masking tape he'd stuffed into his pocket. 'Start on the inside,' he ordered. 'Then meet me out here.'

I let myself into the apartment and called out to Mrs Alvarez, who was upstairs in the kitchen organizing a parade of hurricane lamps and candles and prepared foods on the table.

'Oh, Mrs Rivers,' the housekeeper said, tumbling down the stairs in a burst of energy. 'They say this storm is going to leave the coast a national disaster.' She wrung her hands in the white apron at her lap.

I frowned. 'Maybe you'd better come back to the house with us tonight,' I suggested. I didn't like the idea of a fifty-five-year-old woman all alone during a major coastal storm.

'No, no,' she argued. 'If Mr Rivers says it's okay, my Luis is coming to pick me up and take me to his place.'

'Of course it's okay,' I said. 'You get out of here as soon as you can.'

As I raced upstairs to tape the tremendous glass walls that faced the ocean, the rain began. Instead of coming down gradually, it hit in a torrent. I stood with my hands pressed against the window and watched Alex working below, hauling sacks and stacking them with a rhythm born of natural grace.

Mrs Alvarez left with her son just as we finished doing everything we could inside. Tugging on my slicker, I stepped through the sliding doors I had criss-crossed with tape and ran across the beach to Alex. Without speaking, I dragged a heavy sack of sand toward the barricade he had begun. My muscles strained with the effort, and sweat ran down the back of my neck under the pulled hood of my coat. I stacked the bags as high as I could, one placed neatly on top of the other, a series of pillars.

The rain began to shriek around us, blowing wet sand from the edge of the ocean into our eyes and making the tide surge up to our hips. Overhead, in the condo next door to ours, I heard the shatter of glass.

I was looking up, trying to note which window had broken and why, when Alex grabbed me by the shoulders. He shook me so hard my neck snapped back. 'Jesus!' he screamed, his voice nearly lost in the wind. 'Can't you do anything right?' He kicked at the piles of sandbags I'd meticulously made, and when they didn't topple he threw his weight into them, knocking them over into the raging surf. 'Not like these,' he bellowed. 'Like mine.' He pointed to the barrier he'd crafted, a neat overlay like an interlocking wall of bricks. Roughly, he pushed me aside and began to add onto his wall with the drenched sacks of sand he'd knocked down from my piles.

I shielded my eyes and looked to the left and the right, wondering if my neighbors had heard or seen Alex yelling at me. I stared for a moment at my hour's worth of work, now draining in a heap at the edge of the ocean.

It was my fault; I hadn't been thinking. A strong gust would easily tear down standing piles, but a staggered wall like Alex's could withstand much more abuse. Soundlessly I stepped up beside Alex, carefully mirroring his movements and his placement and even his stride so that he would find nothing lacking in me. I ignored the sharp ache in my shoulder and the knot in my back, determined, this time, to do it right.

Alex stepped onto the veranda, watching Ophelia check me for a fever. 'Cool as a cucumber,' she said, but she was staring at

Alex. She set her hands on her hips. 'Cassie isn't feeling great,' she said. 'Maybe you should leave her home tonight.'

Alex smirked. 'And take you instead?'

Ophelia flushed and looked away. She squeezed my shoulder, a goodbye. 'I was just going,' she said, and she deliberately pushed past Alex on her way out.

I watched her go, pretending to see her long after her shape had disappeared through the gauzy curtains of the bedroom. I stared at the patterns in the lace. I didn't want to look at Alex.

'Did you tell her?'

'What do you think?' I turned my face to him, noticing the lines of pain that shattered the clear gray of his eyes, and I knew I couldn't hurt him any more than he hurt himself. I swallowed and glanced away.

Suddenly Alex had me cradled in his arms, the blanket falling away to reveal the red marks on my arm and the swelling near my ribs. He carried me into the bedroom and stretched me gently on the bed, so carefully I did not even stir the comforter. He unbuttoned my blouse.

He brushed his lips over each spot, each ache, taking the pain and leaving behind a salve of tears. I held his head against my chest, thinking that this tenderness hurt even more. 'Shh,' I said, stroking his forehead. 'It's all right.'

What struck me first about the hand was that the bones stretched out toward me, as if they meant to pull me back if I happened to have any intention of walking away. I took out a small brush and began to clear away the twigs and loose fragments of dirt, revealing a nearly intact wrist, and five metatarsals still curled around a stone tool. I ran my fingers over the fragments, the tiny chisel, and then I smiled. Maybe it wouldn't have pulled me back. Maybe it would have attacked me.

The hand was set in sedimentary rock as high as my shoulder, and it was noticeable enough for me to wonder how it had managed to remain undiscovered all these years. The site wasn't a new one in Tanzania; for decades, it had been combed by anthropologists.

I was dizzy. I knew instinctively that this was Something Big, even before sending samples for dating. My pulse began to race as I realized that this discovery would prove that hominids had the mental capacity to create their own tools, rather than just using those naturally shaped by water or fossilization. I would go home a hero. I would tell Archibald Custer to go fuck himself. I would be as famous as Alex.

I was dying to tell him. Since the base camp didn't have a phone, I would drive into town tonight and call home. I had not liked the idea of being away from him for a full month, but I was doing my field study during intercession at the university, and Alex was filming twelve hours a day anyway. I spoke to him on Sundays and Wednesdays, sitting on the dirt floor of the all-purpose store in town. I'd tuck the receiver into my ear and scratch his name in the red earth with a twig; store up the sound of his voice so that I could draw it out late at night and pretend that he was lying beside me.

I squinted into the hot midday sun, touching the striated gray areas to the left of the hand. In the distance I could hear the ting of picks and the sound of laughter tripping on the wind. There were several graduate students working with me, one of whom had found a mandible the other day, but there had been no other startling discoveries. I smiled and stepped around the corner of the cliff, where I could be seen by them. 'Wally,' I called. 'Bring a tarp.'

The rest of the day was spent in painstaking excavation, because it was so rare to find something as fragile as a fossilized hand that risking even the tiniest digit of a finger would be unthinkable. I worked with two of my students, one helping me do the removal and the cleaning, one labeling the bones with India ink for later reconstruction. Another student was sent into town to wire UCLA of our preliminary findings and to bring a packed sample to the general post office to be sent out for dating. Dinner, a celebration, consisted of Chef Boyardee spaghetti and three bottles of local wine.

I watched the students build up the campfire and weave scenarios in which I became the most highly touted guru in physical anthropology and they became my disciples. When one of their ploys involved burying Professor Custer alive so that some poor graduate student could dig him up millennia from now, I laughed with them, but mostly I watched the flames leap in time to the blood inside me. I came alive on excavation. It wasn't just the discovery of the hand, although that had my senses singing. It was the joy of looking for the unknown, like you were onto a buried treasure, or sifting through the Christmas presents to find the one you'd been hoping for. When Alex's movie had come out, the one we'd met on, that was the strongest personality trait his character had shown. I could remember watching the dailies, and telling Alex how impressed I was, and Alex saying that he had taken that from me.

It took the operator ten minutes to get a line to the States, and even then I only had a marginal chance of catching Alex at the house. When he answered himself, his voice groggy with sleep, I realized that it must be the middle of the night. 'Guess what?' I said, listening to my own voice in a tinny echo at the edges of the line.

'Cassie? Is everything all right?'

I could almost see him sitting up, switching on the light. 'I found something. I found a hand, and a tool.' Without letting him interrupt to ask questions, I launched into a monologue about the odds of a discovery like this, and what it was going to mean to my career. 'It's like an Oscar, for you,' I said. 'This is going to put me over the top.'

When Alex didn't say anything at first, I thought maybe I had lost the connection and had been too busy talking to hear. 'Alex?'

'I'm here.' The resignation and the stillness in his voice made my breath catch. Maybe he was worried that this was going to take me away from him even more. Maybe he thought I would actually put my career first, instead of him. Which was an entirely ridiculous idea, and if anyone should understand that, it was Alex. They were on equal footing in my life. I needed them both; I couldn't live without both.

Belatedly I remembered Antony and Cleopatra. The film seemed to be cursed. Although they'd replaced Brianne Nolan with another *actress, last Sunday Alex had mentioned something about the director walking out because of a dispute with the cinematographer. Closing my eyes against my stupidity and my insensitivity, I gripped the receiver of the phone. I swallowed, putting as much brightness into my voice as I could. 'Here I am rambling on and on,' I said, 'and I haven't even asked about the movie.'*

There was a beat of silence. 'It's very late,' Alex said. 'I'd better go.'

When he hung up, I listened to the dead line until the Tanzanian operator got back on and asked in her musical voice if I wished to place another call. Then I drove back to the base camp and walked into one of the work tents, turning on the overhead light so that it bathed the table in a soft yellow glow. My hands were lead-clumsy as I touched the thin bone chips that were going to change my life. I lined them up by number, this half of the hand that had been excavated, and tried not to wonder why Alex had not even said 'Congratulations.'

Three days later I had received wires from Archibald Custer and from two museums expressing interest, but I had not heard from my husband. The hand lay in all its glory, itemized and recorded for posterity, reconstructed on a bed of coarse black cotton. We had been taking the obligatory photographs, the ones we could send out before the actual bones went around for exhibit. I stood with my hands braced on the edge of the table, sweat running down my back. Wally, a graduate student who was writing his thesis under my tutelage, was packing up the Leica and its lenses. 'So what do you think, Professor Barrett?' he said, grinning. 'We gonna be mobbed at the airport?'

We were not scheduled to leave Tanzania for another two weeks, and I knew that Wally was joking, since the anthropological community was too small to generate more than an occasional article in the Wall Street Journal. *Unbidden, a memory of my first return to LAX with Alex came to mind. I imagined that kind of media circus for a dusty, tired scientist holding a crate full of bones. 'Somehow,' I replied, 'I doubt it.'*

Wally stood up, brushing the red earth from his shorts. 'I'm going to bring this back to Susie before she pitches another fit,' he said, and he moved to the front flap door of the tent. He lifted it partway, then let it fall as if he'd seen a mirage he couldn't quite face. He blinked, and pulled aside the canvas again.

In the middle of the base camp was a pickup truck, and Koji, one of our native scouts, was unloading boxes stamped with the seal of *Les Deux Magots*, the Parisian restaurant. My little group of assistants stood in awe, watching crates of lobsters and fresh fruits and wheels of Brie being gently lowered to the ground. I had seen the likes of this only once before. Wally stepped into the sunshine, leaving me an unobstructed view. 'Now I know,' he murmured, 'there is a God.'

'"God" is a bit much,' a voice said. 'But I'll settle for sainthood.'

I whirled around at Alex's first words. He stood a few feet behind me, having entered through the rear flap of the tent. His hands moved restlessly at his sides, and I realized that he was more nervous than he wanted me to see.

'I thought, What do I bring a woman who's about to change the course of human evolution? And flowers just didn't seem to cut it. But I remembered from the last time I was in Tanzania that the local cuisine leaves a little to be desired—'

'Oh, Alex,' I cried, and I threw myself into his arms. His hands roamed over my back, relearning my body. I breathed in the familiar smell of his skin and smoothed the wrinkles of his traveling clothes. 'I thought you were mad at me,' I said.

'Mad at myself,' Alex admitted. 'Until I realized I had deliberately acted like an asshole just so that we could kiss and make up.'

I held his face in my hands. I was filled to bursting now that he was standing in front of me, wondering how I hadn't noticed how very empty I had been. 'I forgive you,' I said.

'I haven't apologized yet.'

I rested my forehead against his chin. 'I don't care.'

He gently tipped my face up toward his. Outside, I could hear the splintering of a crate being split open, and the delighted cries of the graduate students ripping out its contents. 'If this is truly like winning an

Academy Award,' Alex said, 'then I'm more proud of you than you can possibly imagine.'

I leaned against him, thinking that the praise I had received from Archibald Custer and all the accolades the hand would bring me paled in comparison to Alex's words. His was the only opinion that mattered.

We had a sumptuous meal that night, even if the smoky flavor the campfire gave the veal piccata was a little unorthodox. Alex talked easily with my assistants, making them laugh with stories about the mistakes he'd made playing an anthropologist on film until I came along to correct him. When the five kids took a few bottles of Bordeaux and suggested moving the party to the raw ground near the excavation site, Alex declined their offer. He picked up the last bottle of wine and then held out his hand to help me up, as if by prearrangement.

He tied the flaps of my tent shut, and I stood with my back to him, glancing at my comb and my toothbrush and tube of Crest beside the chipped washbasin. I frowned; there was something I had to tell Alex that I couldn't seem to remember. His hands came to rest on the sides of my waist. 'What is it with you and me and tents and Tanzania?' he said.

It was impossible not to think of the first night we had made love – not with the fire dancing orange on the canvas, and the low wind moaning through the hills, and the heavy, sable folds of an African night pressing us even closer.

We came together the same way the rains come to Central Africa: quickly, without warning, bringing a fury so intense that for the days it lasts you stare out the window and wonder if the world has ever been any other way. When it was over we lay in each other's arms, half dressed and drenched in sweat, fingers restlessly moving over bare skin just to keep the connection.

We drank the Bordeaux straight from the bottle, watching the silhouette of the fire with a lazy contentment born of knowing there would be a slower, sweeter next time. I absently traced my fingers along Alex's wrist. 'It means a lot to me,' I said. 'Your coming here.'

Alex kissed my ear. 'What makes you think I did it for you?' he said. 'Three weeks of abstinence is hell.'

I smiled and closed my eyes, and then I stiffened and bolted upright. *Abstinence.* Suddenly I remembered what I had forgotten to tell Alex.

When I had unpacked in Tanzania, I realized I had left my birth control pills at home. At first I'd considered having a prescription filled here, if they even had that at the local pharmacy; then I'd realized that if I was half a world away from Alex there was little chance of my getting pregnant. But now Alex was here, and we had slept together, and there were no guarantees.

'Just out of curiosity,' I said, turning around to face him, 'how do you feel about fatherhood?'

Alex's eyes darkened and something in them closed off from me. 'What the hell are you trying to tell me?' he said, biting off each word.

I put my hand on his shoulder, realizing this sounded much worse than it actually was. 'I left my Pill at home. So I haven't been taking anything for a few weeks.' I smiled at him. 'I'm sure nothing at all's happened,' I said. 'I'm sure I'll be fine.'

'Cassie,' Alex said slowly, 'I do not plan on having children.'

I don't know why we hadn't discussed this before; I had assumed that he'd want to wait awhile, but that eventually he'd want a family. 'Never?' I said, slightly shocked.

'Never.' Alex ran a hand over his face. 'I have no intention of being like my own mother and father.'

I relaxed; I knew Alex, and there was no chance of that happening. 'My parents weren't exactly Ozzie and Harriet either,' I said, 'but that wouldn't keep me from having kids of my own.'

I closed my eyes, picturing a beautiful little boy running across the lawns at the house, his feet picked up by the sheer joy of the wind. I imagined him here in Tanzania, digging at my side with a plastic shovel and bucket. I knew, given time, I could bring Alex around.

He pulled me down into his arms, taking my silence for rebellion. 'Besides,' he pointed out, 'how are you going to become the next Margaret Mead if you're about to give birth? You can't take your hand on a lecture circuit if you're barefoot and pregnant.'

I questioned the validity of that, but in some ways Alex was right.

Maybe soon, but now was not the time. I rolled over and faced him on the narrow cot. 'So which one of us is going to sleep on the floor?'

Alex laughed. 'Chère,' he said, 'you ever hear of Russian roulette?'

When I got back to the States, I went on a series of lectures at several universities, discussing the implications of the hand and tool on the evolution of the human mind. I did not like being away from Alex for so long, but he was busy filming Antony and Cleopatra. It did not matter if I was in Boston or Chicago or Baltimore. Alex was working twenty-hour days, so even if I'd been in LA, I wouldn't have been able to spend time with him.

Alex's voice rolled down the stairs from the bedroom. 'Sometimes we see a cloud that's dragonish, a vapor sometimes like a bear or lion, a towered citadel, a pendant rock, a forked mountain, or blue promontory with trees upon it, that nod unto the world and mock our eyes with air.'

I sighed with relief as the taxi driver set my bag inside the front door. I hadn't kept him up waiting; he was doing what he usually did the night before filming a critical scene – rehearsing. I knew that I'd find him stalking the sitting area of the bedroom, wearing a ratty Tulane T-shirt and his boxer shorts, and I smiled at the comfort of the familiar.

My plane had been delayed from Chicago because of thunderstorms, and at around nine o'clock I called to tell Alex that I didn't know if I'd even make it into LA tonight. 'Just go to sleep,' I said. 'If I come home, I'll get a cab and let myself in.' I knew that he had a draining day tomorrow, filming the scene where Antony realizes Cleopatra's betrayal and then learns of her apparent suicide. Plus, there had been more trouble with the film. Initial rushes used as teasers for movie previews had had a negative audience reaction. Alex had told me over the phone. 'They laughed,' he had said, shocked. 'They watched me running myself through the gut with a sword and they laughed.'

I wished I had been here to help him with his retakes and to offer the bright side to all the bad press the movie was getting in entertainment shows and gossip columns. Even in Chicago, there had been a *short item in the* Tribune *saying that Antony and Cleopatra was rumored to become one of Hollywood's most expensive flops. When I'd read it over a room service breakfast at the hotel, I'd had to fight the urge to call Alex right away. I knew that in a week this first rush of publicity would be over. Better to soothe Alex face-to-face, I thought, than to spill words over a cold, crackling telephone line.*

Besides, I had something that was going to completely take his mind off the movie. I couldn't be entirely sure yet, since I hadn't had time to go to a doctor, and I was only a week late. But still, I had a hunch. I had considered this over and over on the flight home, realizing that Alex was going to have a fit when I told him about the baby, but I'd worked out a dozen scenarios in my mind. In one, he just stood speechless. In another, I said that the best-laid plans don't always work the way you want. In a third, I patiently reminded him that he'd been the one who wanted to play with fire. All the scenes ended the same way, with us curled up together in the window seat, Alex's hand pressed against my stomach, as if he could help me to carry our child.

I stared at my suitcase, deciding to leave it right there in the parlor, because after all I wasn't supposed to be lifting heavy things. With every step, I heard Alex testing another line, sometimes repeating it with the emphasis on different words: I made these wars for Egypt . . . She has robbed me of my sword.

I smiled, thinking of Antony's crisis of masculinity, and then of the news I had for Alex. Drawing in a deep breath, I stepped across the threshold of the bedroom suite. 'Hi,' I said.

Alex turned to me, his eyes black with anger. 'She has robbed me,' he said more slowly, 'of my sword.' He took two steps toward me, coming to stand perfectly still only inches away. 'Well,' he demanded, 'I suppose you're going to try to explain.'

My mouth dropped open and my arms ached, waiting for a homecoming that did not materialize. 'I told you I'd be late,' I said. 'I called you as soon as I knew.' Carefully edging past Alex, I slipped my coat onto a chair. 'I thought you'd be happy that I made it home tonight.'

Alex spun me around by the shoulder. 'Your plane wasn't late,' he said. 'I called the airport.'

'Of course It was,' I snapped. 'Whoever you talked to read the computer wrong. Why in God's name would I lie to you?'

Alex's mouth tightened. 'You tell me.'

I rubbed my temples, wondering what kind of stress Alex had to be under to dream up whatever wild schemes were running through his head. 'I can't believe you checked up on me,' I said.

The corner of Alex's mouth tipped up. 'Well,' he said, 'I don't trust you.'

The flat truth of his statement cut through my anger; the strain of a whole week of appearances caught up with me. My eyes filled with tears. This was not the evening I had planned; there would be no late-night snack in bed, no simple touches, no stunned wonder at the life we had created. I stared at Alex and wondered what had happened to the man I knew.

As soon as the first tears ran down my cheeks, Alex started to smile. He grabbed my shoulders hard. 'Which one is it, pichouette?' he said, his voice spilling like silk. 'Did you come from some other man's bed? Someone you picked up in Chicago? Or were you just wandering the streets, holding on to your little week of glory, in case failure is catching?'

I heard in his words how much he hated himself, and even as I was shaking my head I reached toward him, offering me, the only thing I had. Alex caught both of my wrists in one hand and punched me in the side, his chest heaving with the effort. I did not move; I did not even let myself breathe. I simply couldn't believe I was watching this happen, feeling it happen to me. No, I thought, but there weren't any words.

When he pushed me away from him I hit the edge of a bookshelf, and as I fell to the ground a rain of hardcovers and glass paperweights followed. I scooted backward, trying to get away, but when he kicked me I took the blow in my abdomen, and then rolled to my other side. I covered my face and I tried to make myself as small as possible — so small that Alex would not see me, so small that I could forget myself.

I knew that it was over only because I heard the sound of Alex's crying over the throb of my body. He touched my shoulder, and God help me, I turned toward him, burying my face against his chest and heaving with sobs, seeking comfort from the person who had caused the pain. He rocked me back and forth in his lap; he whispered that he was sorry.

When there was nothing left inside me Alex stood up and went into the bathroom. He came back with a washcloth and wiped my face, my nose, my throat. He tucked me under the covers and sat on the edge of the bed. When he thought I was asleep he spoke again. 'I didn't mean to,' he murmured, and his raw voice cracked in the middle. He started to cry again; then he walked into the sitting room and put his fist through a wall.

When the bleeding started last night, I told myself that it was just my period, and I squeezed my eyes shut and whispered the sentence like a prayer until I believed it was true. And it might have been: I knew nothing about miscarriage, but I wasn't in much pain – although that could have been because I had simply gone numb.

I allowed myself to think of what might have been a baby only once, when it wasn't even light outside this morning. I decided not to tell Alex. There was no need; he felt awful enough. When he woke up, he lifted the sheets and looked at the swelling marks on my arms and the purple bruise on my stomach. 'Don't,' I told him softly, touching his cheek, and I watched him leave for the studio under the burden of his own guilt.

But now he was home again, and we were supposed to go out to a premiere. I turned to Alex, lying on the bed beside me where he had fallen asleep after Ophelia left, his arm possessively draped over my waist. Very gently I lifted his hand, slipping out from underneath him, and I walked into the adjoining sitting room.

I had cleaned up the books and the paperweights this morning, but I could still see them splayed across the hardwood floor.

Mindlessly I sat down on a love seat and picked up the television remote control, switching on the power. On the screen were two misshapen animals, a cartoon. One was beating the other over the head with an anvil. The second one smiled, and then his body shattered and fell away, leaving only a skeleton.

So, I thought, *it is like this everywhere.*

Alex came out a few minutes later and sat down beside me. He kissed me so sweetly that I pictured my heart like that cartoon animal, falling away to leave an aching core. 'Will you go with me?' he asked.

I nodded; I would walk across hot coals and breathe fire if Alex wanted me to. I would give up my soul. I loved him.

It's hard for you to understand, but I knew it wouldn't happen a second time, because I realized that I was partially at fault. It was my job to keep Alex happy; that was what my vows had amounted to over a year ago. But I had done something wrong, something that upset the balance and pushed him over the edge. I would find out what that was, so he would never feel that way again, so it would never come to this.

Alex pulled me into the bedroom and helped me into a skintight black dress that was cut out at the shoulders but covered virtually every other part of my body from my neck to my ankles. 'You look beautiful,' he said, leading me to a mirror.

I stared at my bare feet, my twitching hands, and at Alex's eyes, which still looked so wounded. You could not see the bruises on me at all. 'Yes,' I said. 'This is fine.'

We arrived at the premiere with twenty other chauffeured cars, and we waited in turn to pull up to the spot where everyone was getting out. Fans and paparazzi had formed two lines leading to the door of the theater, and a couple of reporters were positioned right at the curb, so that their voice-overs could catch the moment the celebrities stepped from their cars.

It was nothing new; Alex and I had been to many premieres in the past year. He stepped out of the car first, tall and striking in a crisp white shirt and tie. He waved to the crowd, and the sun caught his wedding band, shooting off a bright ray that temporarily blinded me. Then he gently helped me out of the back seat, anchoring his arm around my side, careful to let his hand rest lower on my hip than usual, where it wouldn't hurt.

It was common procedure to stand there for a moment like a reigning king and queen, so that people could take their pictures and cheer and get a good long look. The entertainment reporter beside me was practically yelling over the crowd that was roaring Alex's name. 'Here's Alex Rivers and his wife, Cassandra. Rumor has it that *Antony and Cleopatra*, Alex Rivers's new film, is in dire straits,' she said. 'But as you can see, his fans have no doubt that whatever problems the production's run into, Alex will find a way to iron them out.' She threw a meaningful glance back over her shoulder, meant to be caught by the camera. 'It seems,' she said, 'that everything Alex Rivers touches turns to gold.'

Alex guided me forward, his hand light and gentle on my back. I took one last look at that reporter, and then I threw back my head and laughed.

Chapter Seventeen

I heard his footsteps coming up the stairs of the apartment, and now fully awake, I jumped up from the bed where I had been taking a nap. With my heart lodged at the base of my throat I smoothed the comforter, erasing the pressed image of my body so that he would never know.

It was April, and I was on sabbatical from UCLA, but Alex didn't like the idea of my having nothing to do. He'd told me that more than once, sometimes teasing, sometimes so seriously that I would *look* for things to do to keep busy: dipping already clean crystal chandeliers, taking an aerobics class I hated, redecorating the apartment, which had been beautifully furnished to begin with. The truth was that the past year had been draining, between making full professor at the university and balancing those commitments with scattered lectures about the hand, which was currently on display at a museum in London. This month I had simply been looking forward to resting.

But I didn't want to upset Alex, either.

I stood up and ran my hand over my hair, making sure that none of it had slipped out of its barrette while I was asleep. My pulse began to race and I counted off the seconds until Alex would throw open the door. Frantically I looked around for something that would make me look like I had been working, finally seizing a pad and a pencil. I sat down at the escritoire and mapped the first thing that came to mind: a linear tree of man's evolution.

One minute passed; two. I pushed back the chair and willed

myself to cross the room and open the door. My face was flushed by the time I twisted the doorknob, and I flinched a little, not knowing what to expect on the other side.

There were curtains, fluttering in the waves of heat. Mrs Alvarez had opened the windows before she left to go to Trancas Market. But it was dead silent in the house, which meant she hadn't come back yet.

I walked down the stairs and opened the front door, peeking my head outside. I called out, waiting for an answer, and I checked the bathrooms and the study and the porch before I realized that I was nervous over nothing. I had only imagined the footsteps. Alex had not come home at all.

You know, for six months after that first time, Alex was the model husband. He never failed to ask me what was going on at the university; he built me my own laboratory on the grounds of the house as a birthday present; he commissioned an artist to paint my likeness and he hung it in his study across from his desk, where he said he could always keep his eyes on me. When I gave lectures about my hand, he attended and clapped more loudly than anyone else; for a few months, he even hired a completely unnecessary secretary to record my speaking engagements and to organize the tear sheets about my discovery into some sort of scrapbook. At night he touched me reverently, and he held me very close when he slept, as if he still thought I might run away.

If anything, it brought us closer. I know you don't understand, and I can't explain any better than this: I loved Alex so much that it was easier to let him hurt me than to watch him hurt himself. Physical pain was nothing compared to seeing the look that shuttered Alex's eyes when he couldn't live up to his own expectations.

I was not afraid of Alex, because I understood him. I tried to keep everything steady and smooth at home, as if that might give him a baseline from which to work. Sometimes that backfired –

it gave him an excuse to explode. When I moved a pile of scripts so that his desk could be dusted, he yelled at me for over an hour. But he didn't touch me, not in anger, not for a while.

He was filming *Insufficient Grounds* – a movie I knew nothing about because I hadn't had time to read the script – the second time it happened. We had been staying at the apartment because I was having the walls repapered, and it was easier to just sleep there than to make the trip to supervise every morning. Alex came home around dinnertime, when Mrs Alvarez had already laid out the meal and gone to her son's for the weekend.

I was standing in front of the table when I heard John drive up outside. Checking last-minute details, I stretched my hand out toward Alex's place setting and realigned the knife, fork, and spoon, so that the edges all were level.

'Hi,' Alex said, coming up behind me to slip his arms around my waist. He smelled of the cold cream used to take off makeup at the end of the day. He was still wearing his sunglasses. 'What's for dinner?'

I turned in his arms. 'What did you want?'

Alex smiled. 'You have to *ask*?' He lazily started unbuttoning my shirt. 'Aren't you hot?'

'No,' I laughed. 'I'm *hungry*.' I lifted the cover from a serving platter, letting the smell of fresh-steamed snow peas and kung pao chicken tantalize Alex. 'Why don't you get undressed?'

Alex started downstairs toward the bedroom and I spooned rice and chicken and vegetables onto our plates. I sat patiently with my napkin in my lap until Alex returned, now wearing shorts and a pale blue pocket T-shirt that took on the color of his eyes. 'You seen my sneakers, *pichouette*?' he asked.

I furrowed my brow, trying to remember where they were. At some point over the course of the day, I had noticed them, tangled with the brushes and tubs and paste of the wallpapers.

'Oh!' I exclaimed, remembering. 'They're on the porch.'

The porch at the apartment was really a lanai that overlooked the beach-level deck. We kept our plants out there, and a very ugly cigar store Indian statue that Alex could not remember acquiring. Alex walked to the sliding doors and stepped outside, locating his sneakers and slipping them on his feet.

Immediately he shook them off again, cursing a violent streak in French. He lifted one to his nose and grimaced, hurled it as far as he could into the living room. It hit the new white silk wallpaper, leaving a dark muddy patch.

Very deliberately, Alex closed the sliding door and then walked around the apartment, shutting the windows I had opened to let in the ocean breeze. When he had sealed us off from everyone outside, he started to speak. 'Some goddamned cat peed in them,' he said. 'What I want to know is what they were doing out there in the first place.'

I put down my fork on the edge of the plate, careful not to make the slightest noise. 'You left them out there?' I suggested.

'You were here all fucking day!' Alex yelled. 'It never crossed your mind to bring them inside?'

I didn't understand why this was a crisis. I knew that Alex had another pair of sneakers, older ones, downstairs in his closet. At the house there were at least three more pairs. Unsure of what exactly he wanted to hear, I stared down at my plate, at the cooling chicken.

Alex grabbed my chin and forced it up. '*Look* at me when I'm talking to you,' he said. Then he grasped my shoulders and shoved me sideways, toppling the chair so that I lay sprawled half beneath it.

I closed my eyes and curled up, waiting for what was going to happen, but instead I heard the key turning in the front door. 'Where are you going?' I whispered, so quietly that I didn't think Alex would hear me.

'For a run,' he said tersely.

I struggled to a sitting position. 'You don't have your shoes,' I said.

'I'd noticed,' Alex said, and he slammed the door shut behind him.

I sat for a few moments with my knees huddled to my chest, and then I stood up and began to clear away the plates. I left Alex's in the microwave, but I scraped mine into the trash. Then I walked around opening the windows that Alex had closed. I listened to the drifting sounds of dogs barking at the incoming tide, of a volleyball game in progress. I waited to hear Alex running back to me. I convinced myself that nothing had happened, so that when he returned, there would be nothing to forgive.

Herb Silver handed me a second glass of champagne. He stood with me in a corner of the crowded lobby, popping little rolled pigs-in-blankets into his mouth. 'You know,' he said, 'Alex gets these just for me. Because he knows I won't eat those fancy schmancy oysters and puffy things.'

'Quiches,' I said.

'Whatever.' He slung a beefy arm around my shoulders. 'Take deep breaths, hon. He'll be back soon.'

I smiled apologetically, wishing I weren't so obvious. I enjoyed Herb's company, and I appreciated Alex's making sure I was being taken care of, but I would much rather have been with Alex himself. And I would have been, if we were attending a premiere of anything that wasn't his own film. Tonight, though, he had obligations and interviews to complete; people he needed to talk to about the financing of his next picture. I would only get in the way. Craning my neck, I tried to catch a glimpse of him through the milling throng of well-wishers.

Alex was nowhere to be found. Resigned, I turned to Herb. He was actually here with Ophelia, not because he was her agent but because he wasn't about to turn down the pleasure of escorting a pretty woman to a media event. I had asked him as a personal favor, just as I had asked Alex if he could wrangle an invitation for her. I noticed her across the room, wearing one of my dresses, talking to an actor on the verge of breaking into the big time.

'Ophelia looks like she's having fun,' I said, picking up the thread of the conversation.

Herb shrugged. 'Ophelia could have fun at a funeral if it was packed with industry people.' His face blanched, as if he just realized that he'd insulted my friend. 'I don't mean anything by that, *bubbelah*,' he said. 'It's just that Ophelia is nothing like you.'

I smiled at him. 'Oh?' I asked. 'And what exactly am I like?'

Herb grinned, showing the gold fillings in his back teeth. 'You? You're good for my Alex.'

The lights blinked, and the guests began to shuffle into the theater. Critics flipped open their memo pads and uncapped their pens. Herb glanced around anxiously, waiting for Alex to claim me before he went inside.

'Go ahead,' I urged him. 'I'm perfectly capable of taking care of myself.'

'Ach,' Herb said. 'I already know the story. What's a minute or two at the beginning?' He crossed his arms and leaned back against the wall.

My eyes scanned the stream of people, wondering if Alex had forgotten me. 'I don't even know what it's about,' I confessed. 'I was too busy to read the script this time.'

Herb raised his eyebrows. 'Let's just say it's a departure for Alex. I doubt you've seen him like this.' Herb started to grin. 'Speak of the devil,' he said.

Alex wound my arm through his. 'Sorry,' he said. 'Even movie stars have to take a leak every now and then.' He thanked Herb for taking me under his wing, and then walked me into the darkening theater.

I leaned toward Alex as the credits began to roll on the screen. 'Herb says I won't even recognize you.'

Alex sucked in his breath, caught my hand in his. 'Cassie,' he said softly, 'promise me you'll remember that I'm acting.'

He knotted his fingers with mine and squeezed, settling our hands on the armrest between us. He would not let go.

The thing that made this film different from the others Alex had done was that here he was a villain. His other characters had had flaws of some kind, but not enough to be cast into such black relief. It took me very little time to realize what *Insufficient Grounds* was about.

Alex was playing a man who beat his wife.

I did not realize how tightly I was gripping Alex's fingers, or that I felt so dizzy that if I had stood and run out of the theater like I wanted to, I would have collapsed. I watched the very first scene unfold in a pristine bathroom, where the counters were spotless and white and the towels were neatly folded over their racks. Alex pulled back the shower curtain to reveal the hot- and cold-water faucets, one of which was not set at a ninety-degree angle to the ceiling. Alex dragged a woman who was not me into the bathroom, forced her to see her mistake, and threw her on the tile floor.

I was watching the story of my life.

But on movie sets they had stunt doubles; they taught the actors to choreograph false punches. I tried to remind myself that the actress had not been hurt at all.

Then I turned toward Alex, who was looking at me and not at the film. His eyes reflected back the characters that were going through our motions on the screen. *Promise me you'll remember that I'm acting.* 'Why?' I asked, but Alex only bent his head toward mine and whispered he was sorry.

After the movie was publicly released and Alex was given glowing reviews for accepting a role that altered his image as a character actor, we went to the ranch in Colorado. Of Alex's three residences, it was my favorite. Sprawled across three hundred acres of lush fields, it was bordered by the blue swells of the Rockies. It was cut into ribbons by a clear, winding stream so cold that it numbed your ankles. I knew the facts about the elevation in Colorado, but as soon as I stepped through the gates of the ranch, I found it much easier to breathe.

Even the stables and the main house were built along different lines from the LA residences. They were Spanish style, stucco sand red tile roofs, geraniums tumbling over the edges of hand-fashioned window boxes. The skeleton staff that took care of the horses and the ranch when Alex was in California seemed to hide in the folds of the hills when we came to stay, making me feel that only Alex and I had access to this little sliver of heaven.

The first few times we'd been to the ranch, Alex had taught me how to ride. It was something he'd learned years ago for *Desperado*. I was good at it, and I liked it.

Alex had bought me a mare named Annie, who was ten years old but acted like a skittish filly. Two out of three times when I mounted her, she'd try to buck me off. Still, she was nothing compared to the horses Alex preferred. There seemed to be a new one every time, just green-broke, and half the thrill for Alex was keeping himself in the saddle.

'Race you,' I said, watching Alex pull back on the reins to keep Kongo stepping lightly. I danced Annie around in a tight circle. 'Or are you afraid you aren't going to be able to control him?'

I was teasing Alex; I knew that if he felt confident enough to set himself in the saddle, he'd manage to bend the horse to his will. But Kongo was a monstrous stallion, eighteen hands and black as pitch, and he showed no inclination to do anything Alex wanted. 'I think you ought to give me a handicap,' Alex said, grinning, and as if he understood English, Kongo turned and started trotting in the wrong direction.

'Not on your life,' I said, and I dug my heels into Annie's flanks, flying through the gate toward the valley where the stream took three hairpin turns to a little grove shaded by aspen trees, whose silver leaves tinkled on the wind like the bells of a tambourine.

Alex made it to the grove a full four lengths ahead of me, and then broke down to a trot, circling to cool off his horse. He slid off Kongo's back and tied him to a low branch of a tree, then helped me off Annie. He lowered me slowly down the length of his body, and I wrapped my arms around his neck and kissed him. 'What I like about you,' he murmured, smiling, 'is that you're not a sore loser.'

We let the horses graze and sat at the edge of the stream, dangling our bare feet in the frigid water. I stretched back, leaning my head in Alex's lap.

I woke up when my skull thumped against the stones at the edge of the water. Alex had vaulted onto Kongo's back. 'Annie just tore loose,' he said. 'I'm going after her.'

I knew that Alex would be able to overtake Annie. I wondered how she had gotten free. It was possible that she'd chewed through her reins; with her temperament that wasn't out of character. But it was just as possible that I'd done a shoddy job of tying her up, and that when Alex came back, there would be hell to pay.

By the time I saw Alex thundering toward me, I was standing very still. He stopped the horses three feet away, panting, not looking at me. Then he dismounted and knotted Annie's reins and Kongo's around the trunk of a different tree.

He hadn't said a word during this entire prelude, and I knew that he was taking his time before he dealt with me. He turned around, but I couldn't read his expression. When he took a step closer, I instinctively backed away.

Alex's eyes opened wider. Then he held out his hand, the way you would to a dog that is unsure of your scent. He waited until I placed my palm against his, and then he jerked me into his arms. 'Jesus,' he said, smoothing my hair. 'You're shaking.' He stroked the side of my neck. 'Even if I hadn't caught her, she would have made her way back to the stables. You had nothing to worry about.' But I couldn't stop shivering, and after a moment he gently pushed me away, still holding my arms. 'My God,' he said slowly. 'You're afraid of me.'

I lifted up my chin and shook my head, but I was trembling, which ruined the effect. Alex sank to the ground and bowed his head. I sat down beside him, miserable that I had ruined what had been a perfect afternoon. I realized that it was up to me to bring us back to center, so I took a deep breath. I stood up and waded into the stream again, bending at the waist and reaching my fingers into the water. 'Rumor has it,' I said, 'there are trout in this stream.'

Alex's head lifted, and he smiled at me gratefully, running his eyes appreciatively from my hair to my bottom to my bare feet. 'Yes,' he said, 'I've heard that.'

'And rumor has it,' I continued, 'that you can catch a fish with your bare hands.' As I spoke, a skinny spotted trout slipped between my palms, making me gasp and splash backward.

Alex came to his feet, stepping into the water behind me. 'Assuming you wanted to learn,' he said, fitting his thighs to the backs of mine, 'the first thing you'd do is stop moving around so damn much.' He bent over me, so close that his lips brushed my ear. His arms pressed the length of mine, down into the water, where my hands rested in his. 'The next thing you'd. do is stay perfectly still. Don't even breathe – a trout'll run away if it even *thinks* that you're here. And now you close your eyes.'

I turned in his arms. 'You do?'

'That way you can just feel the fish.'

I obediently closed my eyes, letting the cool air fill my lungs, enjoying the sensation of Alex's body cradling mine at so many different points.

When the trout slid over the palm of my hand, a quick silver tickle, Alex's fingers tightened. He jerked back our arms and the fish slapped against my chest, thrashing in the hollow between my breasts. Together we fell backward onto the banks of the stream, laughing.

We stared at each other, inches apart, Alex's hands still holding mine. Where his wrists pressed against me I could feel his pulse, a simple steady match to my own. We did not try to extricate ourselves from the knot made by our bodies, not even when Alex reached over to set the trout into the stream again. Together we watched it navigate a rocky shore, disappearing as quickly as a doubt.

What I remember about this particular fight was not what had caused it or even how Alex came after me. I just know that it happened in the big bedroom at the house, and that one of us hit the dresser during the struggle. So the image that stayed with me was not the heat of Alex's words or the sting of his palm across my shoulder; it was the moment that the jar of snow Alex had brought me in Tanzania rolled from the dresser and shattered on the smooth wooden floor.

It was an accident that could have happened long before if a maid had been clumsy or if I had turned around too fast when getting dressed. But it hadn't. For two and a half years, the little glass jar had stood, tightly capped, between my hairbrush and Alex's, as if it were the link that held them together.

Alex stood over me, breathing heavily, watching the water spread across the floor. I sluggishly wondered if it would leave a stain, and I found myself hoping it would, just so there would be something left.

Instead of apologizing or gathering me to him, Alex knelt down and began to pick up the larger fragments of glass. One of them cut his thumb, and I watched with fascination as his blood swirled in the puddle of water.

I think that was the thing that put me over the edge. 'If you touch me like that again,' I said softly, staring at the water, 'I'll leave.'

Alex did not stop what he was doing. He picked up those pieces as if he truly thought he'd be able to put them back together. 'That,' he said quietly, 'would kill me.'

I took my purse and a jacket and walked down the stairs,

shaking my head when John asked if I needed a ride. I wandered down the streets of the neighborhood, gulping in the stale, processed air.

When I came to St Sebastian's – yes, our church – the first thought I had was that I could seek refuge. I could hide inside and never come out again. Maybe if I sat long enough in the cool, dark pews, tracing the shadows cast by stained glass, the world would go back to the way it had been.

I wanted desperately to be a Catholic, or any denomination, really – but I could not honestly say I believed in anything. I had my doubts about a merciful God. I closed my eyes, and instead of praying to Jesus, I prayed to Connor. 'I wish you were here,' I whispered. 'You don't know how much I need you.'

I sat on the pew until the unforgiving wood cut into the backs of my thighs, and by that time the only light in the little church came from the glowing white candles that sat on a table toward the rear. I stood up, dizzy, and understood that I still believed in one other thing. I believed in Alex and me. In spite of this cycle, I believed in us, together.

I slipped out the heavy door of the church and hailed a taxi to take me home. When I touched the front door, it swung open. The parlor was pitch dark. Alex was sitting on the bottom stair, cradling his head in his hands.

I realized two things that night: that Alex thought I'd left for good, and that no matter what I had said in the heat of the moment, it had only been an empty threat. From the very second I'd walked out that door, I'd simply been making my way back.

Chapter Eighteen

Piled beside me was a stack of slush screenplays. It wasn't my responsibility, but I liked reading through them. I'd close my eyes and try to imagine Alex moving through the written direction, Alex speaking the words on the page. Most screenplays I put aside after the first couple of pages, but the ones that looked more promising I passed on.

I was in Alex's office on the Warner Brothers lot. On days when I was not teaching or not in the mood to do research, I'd curl up on the overstuffed sofa, waiting for him to finish whatever it was he was doing that day, so that we could go home together. Today Alex was in the sound studio, dubbing his latest film. It would be several hours before he came for me. Sighing, I picked up the script on the top of the pile and started to read.

Two hours later I threw down the screenplay and raced across the main thoroughfare of the Warner Brothers lot. I had a vague idea of where the sound mixing was done, but I barged into three different rooms before I found the one where Alex was working. He was bent over an electronic board with a technician, and when he saw me he pulled the headphones from his ears.

I ignored the tight set of his mouth at the interruption, the look that promised I'd be lectured later. 'You have to come with me,' I said, in a tone that brooked no argument. 'I have a movie for you.'

The very first image in *The Story of His Life* was of a man watching his father die. In a hospital room twisted with tubes and wires and beeping machines, he leaned toward the paper-thin cheek and whispered, 'I love you.'

The screenplay was about a father and son who have never communicated, because that was their personal definition of what it meant to be a man. Having lost touch with his father, who has always been overbearing and critical, the son comes home when his mother is killed in a car accident. He is now a well-traveled photojournalist; his father is what he has always been, a simple, uneducated Iowa corn farmer. The son sees immediately how little he has in common with his father, how old his father has become, how difficult it is to live in the same house when the woman who served as a buffer between them is gone.

For complicated reasons, the son begins to do a photo exposé of his father versus the government, objectively portraying him as an independent farmer victimized by price ceilings and no longer able to survive on his crops. Flashbacks show the events that built up the wall between the father and son; the rest of the film follows the gradual tearing down of that wall, as the son lays down his camera and works at his father's side in the fields, beginning to understand him firsthand, not just as an observer.

The climax of the screenplay involves a stunning scene between father and son. The son, who has repeatedly reached out to his father, has still been kept at arm's length; in fact, the only times they've seemed to connect are when they move side by side through the rows of corn. Rebuffed by his father's criticism of what he's grown up to be, he finally explodes. He yells that he's given the old man every chance to see him for what he really is; that any other father would be proud of how far his son has come; that he'd never have had to run halfway around the world to find his place if he'd been accepted in his own home. The father shakes his head and walks away. When the old man isn't standing before him, the son notices the view – a sweep of land that his family owns. And he realizes that when he was little, he'd stand there and see the rolling green of the fields only for their boundaries, only for what lay on the other side.

But he also realizes that the reason his father hurt him as a child was because it was easier for him to let his son view him as a strict, demanding tyrant, instead of seeing him for what he really was – a farmer who'd never made anything of himself. Even being cast as a bastard was better, in his mind, than being seen as a failure.

There is a quiet reconciliation in the film that takes place at the harvest without any words, because in the past words have only driven them apart. And then at the end of the screenplay, the son publishes the photo-essay, which he spreads over his father's hospital bed: emotional images not of a victim or a failure, but of a hero. The direction calls for a fade to white, and then comes a final scene in which the father, decades younger, lifts a smiling infant in his arms. We have come back to the beginning. 'I love you,' he says, and the screenplay ends.

I knew when I read the screenplay that Alex had to do it. I also knew that I was playing with fire. To act the role of the son would mean bringing even more anger to the surface. To work through the confrontational scenes would mean facing his own rage. And Alex would leave the set and come home and ease the new, raw pain by hitting me.

But I knew that he never meant to hurt me. And I knew that it all pointed back to the part of Alex that still believed he wasn't good enough. If Alex was forced to look at that side of himself, maybe it would be exorcised forever.

I thought he was going to kill me. He was standing over me in the bathroom, kicking me again and again, his face shaking with fury. He pulled me up by my hair, and as I wondered what else he could possibly do, he threw me back against the toilet and stalked away.

Trembling, I stood up and splashed water over my face. This

time he had backhanded me across the mouth, which was surprising – bruises were hardest to hide on my face, and he didn't usually lose control enough to strike me there. I pressed a wad of toilet paper against the blood at the corner of my lips and tried to recognize the woman who looked back at me from the mirror.

I didn't know where Alex was going and I didn't particularly care. I had been expecting this. Alex had finished reading *The Story of His Life* today, and I knew he'd feel this way afterward. It was the first step he'd have to take to healing; the second step would be his commitment to making the film.

I pulled on a nightgown and slipped between the covers, turning away from Alex's side of the bed. A while later he came soundlessly into the room and began to strip off his clothes. He got into bed, pulled me into his arms, and looked out the window at the same stars I was trying to put into patterns.

'I didn't go to my father's funeral,' Alex said, and I started a little at the timbre of his voice. True, there was no one else in the house at this time of night, but some things were better whispered. 'My *maman* called me up and told me he was a sorry son of a bitch but that it would be the Christian thing to do.'

I closed my eyes, picturing in my mind that scene from the screenplay that you are left with, of a father lifting his son into the air. I pictured Alex sitting beside his father's hospital bed. I saw the cameras rolling as he got his second chance.

'Course, I figured since he was the devil himself, Christian charity didn't quite apply to him. I've never even seen his goddamn grave.' Alex's hands ran up and down my ribs, over places he had hurt hours before. 'I'm going to direct it and co-produce,' he said quietly. 'This time around, I want to be the one in control.'

Jack Green sat next to me while a male stand-in his approximate size had cameras and lights arranged around him. He was a veteran actor who'd done everything from comedy in Marilyn Monroe

vehicles to the dramatic portrayal of an alcoholic that had won
him an Oscar in 1963. But he could also whistle 'The Battle Hymn
of the Republic' through his armpit and shuffle a deck of cards
with more finesse than a Vegas dealer, and he knew how to shoot
the heads off the cattails that grew in the tall Iowa grass. Next to
Alex, he was my favorite person on the set.

He was playing the role of the father, largely due to Alex's
persuasion, since Jack hadn't made a film since 1975. At first, it
had been fun to watch the people scurrying around on the set,
unsure whether they should kowtow first to Jack, the legend, or
to Alex, the god. And no one could be sure how Jack would take
to direction from Alex. But after seeing the first batch of dailies,
Jack had stood up and turned to Alex. 'Kid,' he had said, offering
his hand, 'by the time you get to my age, you may just be as
good as me.'

Now Jack raised his eyebrows, asking me if I wanted another
card. We were playing blackjack, and he was the house. 'Hit me,'
I said, tapping the top of the book we were using as a lap table.

Jack overturned the ten of diamonds and grinned. 'Blackjack,'
he said. He shook his head appreciatively. 'Cassie, you got more
luck than a three-titted whore.'

I laughed and jumped off Alex's chair. 'Don't you need to get
ready or something?'

Jack lifted his head and scanned the flurry of activity. 'Well,'
he said, 'I suppose I could try to earn my keep.' He smiled and
tossed me his script, which to my knowledge he hadn't cracked
since he'd stepped on the set ten weeks ago, although he'd yet
to miss a line. He moved off toward Alex, who was gesturing to
the director of photography.

I hadn't talked to Alex all day, although that wasn't unusual.
During the weeks he'd been filming *The Story of His Life* in Iowa,
Alex had been busier than I'd ever seen him. There was always
a line of crew people waiting to ask his technical opinion about
something; there were reporters trying to get advance press

interviews; there were backers to meet with about financing. In a way, Alex thrived on the stress. His career was on the line: not only was he attempting a film in which he wouldn't be seen as a traditional romantic lead, he was directing for the first time. But all the pressure seemed to take his mind off the fact that the movie he was making and the emotions he was calling forth in front of a camera were hitting very close to home.

Alex had insisted on filming the confrontational scene between the father and son last. He'd allowed two days of filming for it, today being the first, because he wanted to catch the scene during the gloaming, when the hills and the cornfields in the distance were purpled by the sun. I watched a makeup artist step up to Jack and dampen his back with artificial sweat, ring his neck with something that looked like dirt. He looked up from her ministrations and gave me a wink.

'It's a good thing he's forty years older than you are,' Alex said from behind me, 'or I'd be jealous as hell.'

I pinned a smile on my face and turned around, not quite knowing what I would see when I met Alex's eyes. I think I was more nervous about this particular scene than he was. After all, I had just as much resting on it as he did. If it was a success, it was going to make this film a masterpiece for Alex. But it was also going to change my life.

I wrapped my arms around his neck and kissed him lightly. 'Are you ready?' I asked.

Alex stared at me for a moment, and I could see all of my fears mirrored back at me. 'Are *you*?' he said gently.

When the assistant director called for silence, and the sound tape was up to speed, I drew in my breath. Alex and Jack stood in the middle of the field leased from a local farmer. They were backed by a transplanted row of corn that was much higher than it should have been for this time of year, but that was the way the prop department had turned the reality of April into the illusion of September. The first assistant director called for action, and I watched as a mask neatly dropped over Alex's features, turning him into someone who was only vaguely familiar.

The wind whipped across the tall grass as if it had been cued, and Jack turned his back on Alex and leaned on a shovel. I watched Alex's face mottle with anger, and heard him choke on his rage until he had to speak or be suffocated. 'Turn around, goddamn you,' he yelled, laying one hand on Jack's shoulder.

As it had been rehearsed, Jack slowly pivoted toward Alex. I leaned forward, waiting for Alex's next line, but nothing came. The color drained out of Alex, and he whispered 'Cut,' and I knew that in Jack's face he had seen his own father.

The crew relaxed, rewinding and repositioning while Alex shrugged and apologized to Jack. I inched closer to the scene of the action, until I was standing next to the cameraman.

When the film began rolling again, the sun had dropped, cradled by the sky before night fell. It made a beautiful picture: the vivid resentment written across Alex's face, and Jack silhouetted by the fading light, looking more like a memory than a man.

'You tell me what I'm supposed to do,' Alex shouted, and then suddenly his voice cracked, making him sound like the teenager berated by his father in the flashbacks already filmed. During the rehearsal, Alex had had his character yell through this entire scene, hoping to provoke his father. But now his voice softened until it was a whisper. 'For years I figured, the bigger the better. I kept saying this was going to be the one time you noticed.' Alex's voice broke. 'I wasn't even doing it for me, after a while. I was doing it for *you*. But you don't give an inch, do you, Pa? What did you want from me?' Alex swallowed. 'Just who the hell do you think you *are*?'

Alex reached out and grabbed Jack, another move that hadn't been rehearsed. I sucked in my breath, seeing Alex's tears, noticing the way his fingers flexed on Jack's shoulders. You couldn't be entirely sure if Alex was planning to throw Jack to the ground, or if he was clinging to him for support.

And Jack, just as surprised by Alex's action, simply stared into his face, seeming to challenge him for a second. But then he stepped out of Alex's reach. 'Nobody,' he said, his scripted answer, and he turned and walked out of the range of the camera.

I ducked out of the way as the high boom the camera was mounted on swept suddenly to the left to catch Alex in profile. He stared out at the fields of corn, seeing, I knew, a muddy bayou with clinging vines, a trap of crawfish on the porch of a rotting restaurant, his father's chiseled face – a more dissolute double of his own – the image he'd fought and, ironically, had still grown into.

The sun slid behind the fence that at this point seemed to be supporting Alex. He closed his eyes; he bowed his head. The cameras kept whirring because no one had the presence of mind to call for a stop to the action.

Finally Jack Green stepped forward. 'Cut, goddammit,' he yelled. After a second of silence, the crew burst into applause, realizing they had just seen something very rare and fine. 'You better wrap that one,' Jack called to Alex, 'because I don't get any better.'

A few people laughed, but Alex didn't even seem to hear. He moved straight from the fence through the filling darkness, pushing past people who stood in his way. He walked right into my arms, and with everyone watching, he told me that he loved me.

In February, Alex and I sat in bed at the apartment, watching on television as the president of AMPAS and last year's Best Supporting Actress read off the nominees for the five major categories of the 1993 Academy Awards. It was just before six in the morning, since everything had to be done on Eastern Standard Time. Alex pretended he didn't much care one way or the other, but beneath the sheets, his feet were cold and restless.

Alex was nominated for Best Actor and Best Director. Jack Green was nominated for Best Supporting Actor. *The Story of His*

Life was up for Best Picture; overall it had garnered eleven nominations in different categories.

Alex shook his head, smiling from ear to ear. 'I do not believe this,' he said. 'I absolutely do not believe this.' He rolled toward the nightstand and disconnected the telephone.

'What's that for?' I asked.

'Herb's going to call, and Michaela, and God knows who else has the number here. Jesus, I'll be swamped till I go to Scotland.' He was going to start shooting *Macbeth* in a couple of weeks. He rolled back to face me, his eyes shining. 'Tell me I'm not dreaming.'

I reached out to him. 'Here,' I said. 'I'll pinch you.'

Alex laughed and pressed me back against the bed. 'I can think of better ways,' he said.

Before we'd even had breakfast, Alex had been scheduled to do a Barbara Walters pre-Oscar broadcast interview. John came by to tell us that a throng of fans and reporters had set up camp outside the gate of the house. And that afternoon, when I went to the OB/GYN to confirm my twelve-week pregnancy, the doctor congratulated me, and said Alex would be hard-pressed to decide which of the day's announcements was more exciting.

I waited two weeks to tell Alex about the baby, planning to mention it the night before Barbara Walters was scheduled to interview us from the living room of the house. I hadn't told him right away, because I didn't want to steal his thunder. And it really did take two weeks for the obligatory interviews and fanfare to die down. I told myself that these were the reasons I had kept the news to myself; that it had nothing to do with the fact that tomorrow he could tell the world and give Barbara Walters the scoop of a lifetime.

We hadn't been trying, but I apparently fell into that two percent of women on the Pill for whom accidents happen. It never occurred to me that Alex might feel the same way about having children as he had three years earlier. As far as I could tell, he had laid the ghost of his father to rest in the past, where it belonged.

In the ten months since *The Story of His Life* had wrapped, he hadn't lost control. He'd finished a starring role in a light romantic comedy without incident. And even during these past two weeks when tension was building all around him, he'd shown no inclination to strike out at me. It had been so long that it was difficult for me to remember that it had ever happened.

I was nervous about telling Alex we were going to have a baby, so I took the coward's way out and decided to let something else do the speaking for me.

I asked John to take me to Rodeo Drive, even though I never shopped there. He dropped me off a few blocks from my intended destination. I put on my sunglasses and walked to a narrow store called Waddle-potamus, filled with dangling mobiles and Steiff bears. I picked out a stretchy cotton playsuit so tiny I couldn't believe anything alive would ever fit into it. It was embroidered with a dinosaur, and I pictured telling Alex that I had tried to find something appliquéd with the image of *Homo erectus* but I hadn't had much luck.

I was so excited by the time I got back to the house that I fairly flew up the stairs. I threw open the door of the sitting room and came face-to-face with Alex. 'You're late,' he said tightly.

I beamed at him. 'You're early.' I thrust the box behind my back, hoping he hadn't noticed it.

A muscle jumped at the edge of Alex's jaw. 'You said you'd be here when I got home. You didn't tell anyone you were going out.'

I shrugged. 'I told John,' I said. 'I had an errand to run.'

Alex hit me so swiftly across the chest I didn't have time to see it coming. Stunned, I looked up at him from the floor where I had fallen, crushing the box, its festival of ribbons.

I did something I hadn't done in the three years this had been happening: I cried. I couldn't help it; I had believed that we'd started over, and now Alex, who had never disappointed me, had taken us back to the way it was before.

When he started to kick at me I rolled away from him, feeling his shoe strike me in the back, the kidneys, and the ribs. I crossed my arms protectively over my stomach, and when Alex came to his senses and knelt down beside me I would not look at him. I rubbed my palms over this life I was holding like a good-luck charm. I listened to his whispered pleas, his apologies, and I thought, *I hope this baby hates you*.

Barbara Walters was much prettier in person than she was on the air, and she moved through our house with the self-assurance of a general, strategically moving furniture and flowers to make room for lights and cameras. She was planning to interview Alex for about an hour, and then she wanted me to step in so that she could ask me questions as well. In the meantime, I sat very straight next to the segment producer, trying to ignore the pain in my back and my side.

When the camera began to film, it was focused directly on her as she gave her prewritten rundown of Alex's career, beginning with *Desperado* and ending with the ongoing production of *Macbeth*. 'Alex Rivers,' she said smoothly, 'has shown himself to be more than just another pretty face. From his very first feature film, and in nearly every movie thereafter, he has shied away from traditional romantic leads to play, instead, flawed and frightened men. It has set him apart from other talented actors, as has his unheard-of near sweep of the Oscar nominations with his first attempt at direction, *The Story of His Life*. I spoke with Alex at his Bel-Air home.'

At that line, the cameras swung to include Alex in the shot. 'Many people use your name to define the word "star". What would you say characterizes a star?'

Alex leaned back against the sofa. He crossed one leg lazily over the other. 'Charm,' he said. He grinned. 'And whether or not you can get a table at the studio commissary.' He shifted slightly. 'But I'd rather be thought of as an actor than a star,' he said slowly.

'Can't you be both?' Barbara pressed.

Alex tilted his head. 'Sure,' he said. 'But one is a serious vocation, and one is smoke and mirrors, and it's hard to be considered a dedicated professional when you're labeled a "star". I never asked for all the trappings. I just happen to like doing what I do.'

'But unlike many actors, you weren't a struggling waiter for ten years before you broke into the business.'

Alex smiled. 'Two years. And I was a bartender, not a waiter. I can still mix a hell of a Long Island Iced Tea. But no, I got very lucky. I happened to be in the right place at the right time.' He glanced at me. 'Actually, that's sort of been the story of my life.'

Barbara smiled at the neat segue. 'Let's talk about that – *The Story of His Life*. How autobiographical is that?'

For the slightest moment, Alex looked unnerved. 'Well,' he said slowly, 'I had a father, but the similarity ends there.' I glanced away, staring out the window at the storm that was gathering. We were going to tape this outside by the pool, but the weather had been too risky. Somewhere in the back of my mind I was aware of Alex feeding Barbara Walters the lines he'd fed me in Tanzania about his childhood before he told me the truth. I blinked at a streak of lightning, and I thought of how very tired I was.

'Some critics say that you've pushed past being a sex symbol and that you use your looks to get to the chinks in the armor, so to speak – to expose what lies beneath a character.' Barbara leaned forward. 'What sort of chinks are there in your own armor?'

A smile slipped sideways over Alex's face, the same smile that was going to make a million women catch their breath when they watched on Oscar night and that, even now, had my heart racing. 'What makes you think I have any?' he said.

Barbara laughed and said it might be the perfect time to

introduce me, Cassandra Barrett Rivers, Alex's wife of three years. She waited for me to settle myself on the couch beside Alex as I had been directed to do, and then let the cameras start up again. 'You two have certainly been spared a great deal of the negative publicity that usually strikes couples in Hollywood.' She turned to Alex. 'Is that, again, a matter of being in the right place at the right time?'

I sat as quiet as a stone, smiling up at Alex like an idiot. 'It's more a matter of not being in the wrong place at the wrong time,' he said. 'But then again, we're a pretty ordinary couple. We stay home a lot. I guess we don't really give people much to talk about.'

'You think viewers out there believe that you two eat crackers in bed and watch cartoons on Saturday mornings and jog on the beach?'

Alex and I looked at each other and laughed. 'Yeah,' he said. 'Except Cassie doesn't jog.'

'You're an anthropologist,' Barbara said to me, swiftly turning the conversation. I nodded. 'What attracted you to a celebrity as "big" as Alex Rivers?'

'I wasn't attracted to him,' I said flatly. 'The first time I met him I intentionally poured a drink in his lap.' I told the story of my arrival on the movie set in Tanzania, and while Alex squirmed uncomfortably in his seat, most of the crew Barbara had brought with her started laughing. When filming picked up again, I leaned imperceptibly closer toward Alex, a show of support. 'I suppose I don't see him as a lot of other women do,' I said carefully. 'He's not a celebrity to me; he never really has been. It wouldn't have mattered if he sold used cars or worked in a coal mine. He's someone I happen to love.'

Barbara turned to Alex. 'Why Cassie? Out of all the women in the world, why her and only her?'

Alex pulled me closer, and my eyes glazed a little as my sore side touched him. 'She was made for me,' he said simply. 'That's the only way I can explain it.'

Outside, there was a roll of thunder. 'One last question,' Barbara said, 'and it's for Cassie. Tell us what America doesn't know about Alex Rivers that you think they ought to know.'

Shocked, I stared at her, my mouth slightly ajar. The air in the room became heavier, and the rain hit like a fall of stones against the French doors. I could feel Alex's fingers digging into my shoulder, and with every breath there was a quick ache under my ribs. *Well, Barbara*, I could say, *for one thing, he hits me. And his father was terribly abusive. And he's going to have a baby, but he doesn't even know that yet because I'm too afraid of his reaction to tell him the truth.*

I forced myself to relax in Alex's grasp. 'Nothing,' I said, my voice just over a whisper. 'Nothing you would ever believe.'

Chapter Nineteen

I used to think my suicide note would have read, *You won*. Not that it had been a game – but at the very worst times, I knew that Alex could always act better than I could; that when I cracked under the pressure and told someone the truth he would still be able to save face. And in Los Angeles, a city he commanded, who would people believe?

But the real reason I could never tell anyone the truth about our marriage had less to do with my fear of not being believed than with Alex himself. I just didn't want to hurt him. When I pictured him, it wasn't standing with his fists above me. I saw him slow-dancing with me on the veranda, latching the clasp on an emerald necklace he'd just brought me, moving inside me with a striking sense of wonder. This, to me, was Alex. This was the man I still wanted to spend my life with.

I never would have left him if there weren't somebody else involved. But I forced myself to set an ultimatum in my mind. *One more time*, I thought, *one more threat to this life inside me, and I will go*. I tried not to think of it as leaving Alex; I imagined it instead as saving my child. I didn't let myself think about it any more than that, because so much of me was hoping that it wouldn't happen.

But then Alex had heard, the day he left for Scotland, about being placed second on the Barbara Walters broadcast, instead of third. And he was superstitiously sure that it was a forecast of what was to come at the Academy Awards in March. He wouldn't win his Oscars; he would be a failure. He had told me these things, and then he had lashed out.

Well, you know the rest. I must have passed out from the head wound sometime after I left the house, because I knew enough to leave. I met you purely by accident at St Sebastian's cemetery and you took care of me until Alex came charging in from Scotland and took me home.

So I had come full circle: in late February, several days after you'd turned me over to Alex at the police station, I was standing in my bedroom closet getting ready to pack so I could return to Scotland with Alex. Then I found the box with the extra pregnancy test. And I tried to make myself believe that I would be taking a piece of Alex with me when I ran away again.

An hour after I'd left the house I was well out of Bel-Air, but I had nowhere to go. The banks were closed and I had less than twenty dollars in my wallet. I didn't think of you, not right away. Again I considered running to Ophelia; and again I couldn't, because it was where Alex would expect me to go.

I didn't feel comfortable enough to turn to a colleague from UCLA, and I couldn't hide in my office, since that would be the second place Alex would check. And then I remembered what you said to me Wednesday morning, and the way you looked at me after Alex's fight at Le Dôme. I knew you would take me in; I knew it maybe even before I left the house, so I waited at the corner for a bus that would take me toward Reseda.

Your home could fit into a corner of ours, and the trees on your front lawn are all in varying stages of death, but I have never seen any place so inviting. A warm yellow light floods the front porch, and when I step under its glow I feel protected, not on display.

You open the door before I have a chance to knock. You don't seem surprised to see me; it is as if you have been waiting all along. You pull me into the tiny entry hall and close the door behind me. It seems perfectly natural that you haven't spoken a word when you begin to run your hands gently over my back, my ribs, my hips, hesitating at the spots where I have been bruised. You sense the places through the cotton of my shirt, as if you are feeling for the change of temperature that comes with pain.

And Will, when you are finished, you look at me. Your eyes are as dark as Alex's during a rage. I stare back at you, not knowing how or where I am supposed to begin.

I don't have to. You put your arms around me, giving me the simple beat of your heart to measure time. I keep my hands balled at my sides, stiff in another man's embrace. 'Cassie,' you whisper into my hair, 'I believe you.' Outside, an owl sobs. I close my eyes, lean into your faith, and I let myself go.

1993

A long time ago, when the world had just begun, six young women lived in a village set beside a huge boulder. As was their custom, one day while their husbands were out hunting, they went out to dig for herbs. Some time passed, each of the women rooting with her digging stick, and then one of the wives found something new to eat.

'Come and try this,' she told her friends. 'This plant tastes delicious!'

Within minutes, the six women were all eating sweet onions. They were so tasty that they ate until the sun set. One of the wives looked at the dark sky. 'We'd better get home to cook dinner for our husbands,' she pointed out, and they all left.

When the husbands came home that night they were exhausted but happy, since they had each killed a cougar. 'What smells so awful?' one man asked as he stood in the doorway of his lodge.

'Maybe it is some food that has spoiled,' another husband suggested. But when they leaned over to kiss their wives hello, they realized where the odor was coming from.

'We found something new to eat,' the wives said, bubbling with excitement. They held out the onions. 'Here, try them.'

'They smell terrible,' the husbands said. 'We won't eat them. And you're not going to stay in the same lodge as us, not smelling like that. You'll have to sleep outside tonight.' So the wives gathered their things and slept beneath the stars.

When the husbands left to go hunting the next day, the wives returned to the spot where they had dug up the wild onions. They knew their husbands didn't like the smell, but the onions were so delicious that the wives could not help but eat them. They filled their bellies and stretched out on the soft red earth.

The husbands came home that night, gruff and irritable. They had not caught any cougars. 'We smelled like your onions,' they accused, 'so the animals ran away. It is all your fault.'

The wives didn't believe them. They slept outside a second night, and a third, until a week had passed. The wives kept eating the onions that were so delicious, and the men could not catch any cougars. Frustrated, the men yelled at their wives, 'Get away from us! We can't stand your onion smell.'

'Well, we can't get any sleep outside,' the wives countered.

The seventh day, the wives took their woven ropes with them when they went to dig the onions. One wife carried along her baby daughter. They scaled the large rock beside their village and turned their faces to the sinking crimson sun.

'Let's leave our husbands,' one wife suggested. 'I don't want to live with mine anymore.' The wives all agreed.

The oldest wife stood on the boulder and chanted a magical word. She tossed her rope into the sky, and it hooked over a cloud so that the ends hung down. The other wives tied their own ropes to the one that was swinging and then they stood on the frayed edges of the ropes. Slowly they began to rise, swaying around like starlings. They moved in circles, passing each other, reaching higher and higher.

The other villagers saw the wives ascending in the sky. 'Come back!' the People called as the women floated over the camp. But the wives and the little girl kept going.

When the husbands returned that night, they were hungry and lonely. They wished they had not driven their wives away. One of them got the idea to go after the women, using the same kind of magic they had. They ran to their lodges and brought their own ropes, and soon they too were rising in the night.

The wives glanced down and saw the husbands coming after them. 'Should we wait for them?' one woman asked calmly.

The others shouted and shook their heads. 'No! They told us to leave. We won't let them catch us.' They danced and swung on their ropes. 'We will be happier in the sky.'

When the husbands were close enough to hear, the wives shouted for them to stop, and the men stayed right where they were, a little behind their wives.

So the women who loved onions stayed in Sky Country. They are still there, seven stars that we call the Pleiades. The faintest of all is the little girl. And the husbands, who will not go home until their wives do, remain a short distance away, six stars in the constellation Taurus. You can find them shining up at their wives, wishing maybe that things had turned out a different way.

— Monache Indian legend

Chapter Twenty

In the dark, beneath a pouch blessed with good medicine, Cassie told Will the story of her life. She talked the whole night. At times Will only watched her; at times he held her while she cried. And when her voice fell quiet, Will sighed and leaned back against his nearly new couch, painfully aware of the awkward and suffocating silence. Cassie sat now with her head bowed, her hands clasped between her knees.

Will could not have said how, but he'd known Cassie was going to show up on his doorstep. He'd known before she flattened her shirt against her stomach that she was pregnant. He'd known that it was up to him to spirit her away. What he could not understand was how, even now, she could worry about hurting Alex.

'I just have to leave for a little while,' she said abruptly, startling Will. She nodded slightly, as if she was still trying to convince herself. 'It's the end of February now, and I'll have the baby in August.'

'I could be wrong,' Will said carefully, his first words in hours, 'but I don't think Alex will just sit around for six months, waiting.'

Cassie turned her face up to his. 'Whose side are you on?' she asked.

The problem was that Alex Rivers had the money and resources to find her anywhere. 'What I need,' Cassie mused, 'is a place where he'd never even think to look.'

And that was when Will understood why the spirits had brought Cassie to him at St Sebastian's, a week ago. He pictured the tar paper shacks that served as houses in Pine Ridge, the willow skeletons of sweat lodges that dotted the plains like the carcasses of mythical beasts. Like everyone else, the government had basically forgotten about the Sioux; most Americans didn't know living conditions like theirs still existed. For all intents and purposes, the reservation could have been on a different planet.

Will listened to the fragile hitch of Cassie's breathing and turned her hand over in his, palm up, as if he could read her future. 'I think,' he said quietly, 'I have just the spot you're looking for.'

So after being in Los Angeles for all of two weeks, Will Flying Horse boarded a plane and headed to the place he hated more than anywhere else in the world.

When he arrived in Denver to make the connecting flight, his throat tightened up and his head spun. He was imagining, already, the red dust of the Pine Ridge Reservation; the vacant-eyed Lakota, who waited for their own lives to speed by them. He stared out the scratched window of the plane, knowing it would be at least an hour, but still expecting to see the sharp, rocky needles of the Black Hills. He pictured them ripping through the belly of the little plane, scattering gray and wine-red luggage.

Beside him, Cassie was asleep. He wanted to wake her up, just to remind himself why exactly he had come full circle when he'd been running in such a fixed line. But she'd had so little rest the night before that the skin beneath her eyes was blue-bruised. He envied her – not her exhaustion, and certainly not her life, but her ability to look at this trip as a fresh start instead of a foot-dragging trudge backward.

He would get her set with his grandparents, but that was where his obligation ended. He'd go back to LA and pick up where he'd left off: days filled with traffic detail and speeding violations, and stifling, quiet nights. He could make detective in another year, and if he got out more with the guys, he could find some leggy young thing to stretch across the other half of his bed.

The truth was that he did not understand his newly adopted city. He couldn't remember the LAPD's special rules about arresting politicians or celebrities. He didn't know what to say in bars when flawless women told him they read crystals, or were on the water diet. His breath caught every time he merged on the freeway and saw a rolling carpet of cars, more people concentrated in one steel knot than in the entire town where he'd grown up. But regardless of what he cared to admit to himself, this is what he would tell the Lakota people he saw during the weekend: *Life's great out there; I'm on the fast track; I wouldn't trade it for the world*.

In her sleep, Cassie's head lolled to the right, coming to rest on his shoulder. She restlessly crossed her arms over her abdomen, protecting her child.

Now, *that* was something Will could understand. Not the ego-serving me-first attitude of Los Angeles, but the concept of extended family. Hell, his own parents had died, but there had always been people to look after him, even if it meant giving up something in their own lives.

Will breathed in the honey of Cassie's hair, shocked by the smell of his own shampoo. He rested his cheek against the curls, calmed by the awesome responsibility of being her deliverance.

During the eighty-one years he had been alive, Cyrus Flying Horse had made and put up fence posts, taken care of cattle, dug potatoes, ridden broncos for prize money. He had been a rodeo clown, he had repaired roads, he had exterminated rattlesnakes. Up until three years ago he had been working at a factory that manufactured fishing hooks, but now he just fashioned hooks for the hell of it; he was technically retired, which as far as he could tell only meant there was never enough to make ends meet. And this was even with Dorothea working three days a week in town at the cafeteria. She brought home minimum wages, a perfume mixed of grease and labor, and the leftover fish sticks and meatball subs. But Cyrus worried more about filling up his day with activity than about a lack of money. He had relatives, and that was the Lakota way – you took care of your own, even if you barely had a pot to piss in.

He sat on a stump outside his government-built house, the wood having softened to his bottom after all this time. The snow was melting; it was still cold, but nice enough for you to forget winter if you stayed long enough in the sun. Today, he was doing a crossword puzzle. It was not exactly a mental challenge; he'd gotten it from Arthur Two Birds, who had erased all his pencil answers, so even when Cyrus got stuck he could take out his bifocals and peek at the shadows of the words that wouldn't come.

His face was lined, like the craggy landscape of the Badlands, the otherworldly patches of the Black Hills where, as a child, he had believed evil spirits lived. Of course, he knew now that evil did not seat itself in rocks. Instead it seeped into people, becoming as distinctive a part of them as their scent or their fingerprints. Had he not seen it in the glittering blue eyes of the *wasicun* clerk at the BIA? In the tired mouth of the banker who had repossessed the first truck he'd ever bought? In the dazed, drunken glow of the traveling salesman whose careening car had killed his only son a hundred years ago?

Cyrus sighed and bent his head to the frayed paper. Some of the clues were beyond him: *Marla's man* had filled in as *Trump*, which Cyrus had always believed was an ace; and apparently *Bert's buddy* was *Ernie*. He was especially pleased when he'd get an answer without having to check Arthur's work. *'Outcry of the greedy,'* he read aloud, tapping the pencil to his temple. He hunched closer to his lap, carefully forming the letters in the four little boxes. M-I-N-E.

'He can really dish it out,' Cyrus said, turning the phrase over and over, giving emphasis to different words in hopes that the answer would come in a flash.

'Chef,' said a voice behind him; then a light laugh. He hadn't even seen Dorothea approaching, but he nodded and filled in

what now was crystal clear. He rolled the pencil into the cross-word puzzle and stood up, stamping slush from his boots. He followed his wife into their one-room house.

Dorothea shrugged off her parka and began to unpack containers of coleslaw and turkey loaf, the blue plate special of the day. Her hands fluttered nervously over the plastic tablecloth like two scattering birds. Finally, she sat down and turned bright black eyes to her husband. 'Today,' she told him. 'Úyelo. He is coming.'

Cyrus looked at the plump curve of her hips, the heavy braid of white hair that quivered down her wide back. She had always been in touch with the spirits. He sank heavily into a chair across from Dorothea, pretending to be annoyed with her mystical hints. This was a game they played, one that had been going on for sixty years. He stabbed at the turkey loaf with his fork. 'You're crazy, woman,' he said gruffly, when what he really meant was, *You are my life.* 'How can you know this?' he said. *You can still amaze me.*

Dorothea made a noncommittal sound. Then she turned her head and sniffed, as if the answers came to her on a Chinook wind. She swung her gaze to him, level and dark, and she pointed a bent, knotted finger. 'You watch,' she said, the trace of a smile peeking out from behind her warning. She reached across the table and grasped Cyrus's hand with a strength and a conviction that speeded his pulse. He looked up at her. *I love you*, she was saying, clear in this space between them where there were no words. *Walk beside me forever.*

Alex made two phone calls. The first was to Herb Silver, ordering him to postpone the production of *Macbeth* indefinitely; to ware-house all the scenery and props in Scotland and send everyone else home until Alex sent further instructions. The second was to Michaela, telling her to anticipate the publicity such an abrupt change in schedule was going to cause. 'I don't care what you leak to the press,' Alex said wearily. 'Make up some excuse that doesn't sound like I'm covering for a stay at the Betty Ford Clinic.'

'What's really going on, Alex?' Michaela demanded, but Alex couldn't speak past the closing of his throat. He hung up on her before he was forced to recount what had happened.

Cassie had left him. Again.

Except this time it was different. There hadn't even been a fight, a catalyst. She had just taken off as if it had been premeditated.

Alex stretched back on the bed and touched the pile of clothes she had been packing for Scotland, clothes that wouldn't make a hell of a lot of difference now. Goddammit, last week had been perfect. He had been keeping himself in check, refusing to let it start all over. And it had been working: when he laid his hands on Cassie he'd been gentle and tender and everything she deserved. He had watched Cassie, in return, giving him tiny pieces of herself – a kiss here, a question there, a memory. Alex had been gathering these tokens like wildflowers, waiting for the moment when he would have all of her, a lush bouquet that bloomed in his presence.

He had given her back her past, with a few details missing that she'd obviously figured out herself. He never meant to hurt Cassie, God, not Cassie, and every time he struck her he swore that it wouldn't happen again. He wasn't just saying that; he really did mean it. If he could have found a way to turn the red rage into himself instead of toward her, he would have done it in a heartbeat.

Alex rolled to a sitting position and looked out at the rainy morning. He'd spent most of last night with John, scouring the neighborhoods surrounding Bel-Air. John had even checked the police station, discreetly. None of the airlines or bus depots had had a passenger with her name, married or maiden. Finally, Alex had given up. He'd gone to sit in the bedroom, not sleeping, just waiting for her to come back to him.

She had to come back. If the press found out that Cassie had left him, or even that she was missing, all kinds of rumors were going to fly – about infidelities, divorce, maybe even the sorry truth. Whatever form it took, the publicity generated would decimate his chances for the Oscars. He had always been able to count on his sterling reputation.

Alex ran his hand over his stubbled jaw. She had to come back. He couldn't live without her. Cassie was the only person in his entire life who had reached into him and pulled out the fine, glowing soul and said over and over, *Yes, you are good*. He remembered that once in the redwood forests they had seen two separate giant sequoias that had twined around each other, leaning into the same sun, until they had grafted themselves together into a single tree. He would not admit this to anyone but himself, but Cassie was, simply, the point at which Alexander Riveaux ended and Alex Rivers began.

At exactly nine o'clock, a maintenance man unlocked Cassie's office door at UCLA for Alex. 'Thanks,' he said, staring at the man, unsure of whether or not he was supposed to tip him. Alex closed the door, checking the leather swivel chair for Cassie's imprint, searching out clues that would suggest she'd recently been there.

He was sifting through the research on her desk when the door swung open. 'Good morning,' a gravelly voice intoned, and Alex glanced up to see Archibald Custer bearing down on him, his hand held to the voice microphone at his throat. 'Oh.' He let his eyes sweep the room, searching for Cassie. 'I was told your wife had been ill. When I saw the light on, I thought . . . well, I was just looking for her.'

'She isn't here,' Alex said, gesturing. 'You probably noticed.'

Archibald Custer stared at him strangely. 'But *you* are,' he said.

Alex glanced down at his fingers, clutching a manila file marked *Personal and Confidential*. His thoughts tumbled over each other: Cassie was not here. Cassie had not told Custer her whereabouts, or he wouldn't be looking for her also. 'She asked me to send her some things,' Alex said, pretending to be completely surprised when Custer raised his eyebrows at this mention of Cassie being somewhere other than LA. 'Ah . . . she must not have had a chance to phone you yet. Her father's been hospitalized, in Maine, and she was called in to look after him.' He glanced at his watch, an easy prop. 'I'm sure she'll be getting in touch with you in no time. Family emergencies, you understand.' He tapped the file on the edge of the desk. 'Is there something I can ask her for you? Or send to her with all this?'

Custer flapped about for a moment, taking in the carelessly tossed files and the clutter that defined the little office. Satisfied that she had indeed left last-minute, he shook his head. 'We'll get someone from the department to cover for her until the situation sorts itself out,' he said graciously. 'Tell her not to worry about it.'

'No,' Alex said. 'I'm sure she won't.' He watched Custer leave, and then sank down into the chair behind the desk. Christ, he was *helping* Cassie. He had just smoothed one of the snags in her escape. He stared blankly at the manila folder, at the rough black-and-white photos scattered across the desk's surface. Skulls, and a pelvis, and a series of bones that might have been fingers once. Nothing out of the ordinary for Cassie. She'd been studying things like this since before he'd even known her.

He was up and through the door before he could map out where he was going. Turning through the winding campus roads of UCLA, he made his way to the highway, to Westwood. He remembered which apartment was Ophelia's only because of a stooped palm tree in front of it that Cassie said had always reminded her of an old man.

Alex rammed his fist against the door. 'Goddammit, open up, Ophelia. I know she's in there.' He took a deep breath, ready to break down the door with his shoulder, the way his stunt doubles had done in the past.

Ophelia cracked the door, a sliver of darkness. Her cigarette smoke rushed out through the narrow opening. 'Jesus Christ,' she muttered. 'Looks like I've been granted a fucking audience.'

She unlatched the chain and pulled the door open, standing in front of Alex in a peach chiffon robe that was virtually transparent. Underneath she wore nothing; Alex dispassionately noticed that the shadow between her legs did not match the hair on her head. She blew a ring of smoke into Alex's eyes. 'To what do I owe the honor?' she said, pinching the bridge of her nose.

'I've come for Cassie,' Alex said, already pushing past Ophelia into the tiny living room of the apartment.

He felt hands picking at the back of his shirt, ineffectual, like the feet of tiny wrens. 'Well, you might want to start by looking in a place where she *is*,' Ophelia said. 'I haven't even talked to her since that day at the apartment. I thought she'd be in Scotland with *you*.'

Alex peeked behind the floor-length hanging curtains, peered into closets. 'You're a shitty liar, Ophelia. Just tell me where she's hiding.' He barreled into the kitchen, checking the pantry and the floor-level cabinets, knocking over a half-finished bottle of cabernet.

When he turned back to Ophelia, her eyes were so wide Alex could see a ring of white going all the way around her irises. Good, he had her terrified. He grabbed her by the shoulders, shaking her hard. 'Did you put her up last night? Did she tell you where she was headed?'

Ophelia let out a little cry, and at that the bedroom door creaked open. Alex released her abruptly, running around the corner and slamming into a man in a flowered silk robe, still groggy from sleep.

'Alex, Yuri. Yuri, Alex.' Ophelia ground out her cigarette against the half of an orange fermenting on the kitchen counter. 'See, Alex? I *haven't* been hosting Cassie. I was otherwise occupied.'

Alex didn't even bother to glance at her. 'Get out,' he murmured to Yuri.

A dawn of recognition flashed across Yuri's eyes. 'Hey,' he said. 'Aren't you—'

'Out,' Alex yelled. He propelled Yuri to the door and locked him on the other side of it, still wearing Ophelia's robe.

Ophelia threw herself at Alex, yelling and scratching. 'How *dare* you,' she screeched. 'You walk right into my apartment like you own the fucking world and—'

'Ophelia,' Alex said softly, his voice breaking, 'I can't find her. I looked everywhere. I can't find Cassie.'

Ophelia absently rubbed her hand over her black cast, watching Alex Rivers sink onto her stained couch. Her mind raced through possibilities and places that she was certain Alex had already tried. What would make Cassie leave in such a goddamn hurry? If it was Alex, didn't Cassie know that she would have done anything to help?

Ophelia stiffened her spine and walked toward Alex until she was standing directly in front of him. 'What have you done to her?' she said, her voice tight and cold.

Alex buried his face in his hands. 'God,' he said. 'I don't know.'

It was a two-hour ride from the Rapid City airport to Pine Ridge, and as Cassie bounced up and down in the rental truck she noticed two things: that the land stretched unmarked so far it could have been a sea, and that the deeper they drove into this swirling red earth, the more uptight Will became.

There was a policeman at the border of the reservation, someone who gave Will a high five and let his eyes slide down Cassie in the passenger seat. '*Hau, kóla!*' he said. He began speaking in a language Cassie did not understand. To her surprise, Will whipped off his sunglasses and started to talk to the policeman in the same dialect, then pulled the car onto a grass trail.

'What did he say?' Cassie asked.

'He said hi,' Will muttered. 'In Lakota.'

'Lakota?'

'The language of the People.'

Cassie brushed a flyaway strand of hair away from her mouth. 'Is your Sioux name *Kóla*?'

Will couldn't help himself; he laughed. 'No,' he said. 'It means "friend".'

Cassie relaxed in her seat. If they were back on the reservation and Will had already seen someone he knew well, it was a good omen. 'So he's a friend of yours,' she said, making conversation.

'No,' Will said. 'He's not.' He ran his hands over the steering wheel, telling himself Cassie had no right to demand explanations about his life and yet knowing that she wouldn't shut up until he told her more. 'He's tribal police. We were in the same grade together in school. Once, he got three kids to hold me down and he took dog shit and smeared it all over my face.' Horrified, Cassie stared at him. 'Said it would take some of the white out from my skin,' Will said.

'Kids are cruel,' Cassie murmured, feeling she should say something.

Will snorted. 'So are Indians.'

Cassie turned her face to the windshield, wondering how Will even knew where to drive. There were no roads, only dirt paths worn through the snow, or little runners like the kind left by cross-country skis. From time to time, Will would take a left or a right. His eyes never flickered from the expanse in front of them. 'You know,' Cassie said haltingly, 'you might try giving it a chance, instead of telling yourself how much you hate it.'

Will slammed on the brakes until the truck skidded to a stop. Cassie felt herself being strained against the seat belt, then falling back. Instinctively, her hands went to her abdomen. Will stared at her, incredulous, and then with a look of utter disgust he turned away and started to drive again.

It sobered her. After all, Will – who did not really know her

– was going out of his way to give her shelter. She had no right to pry into his life, much less criticize the way he lived it. 'I'm sorry,' Cassie said.

Will didn't answer, but he gave a terse nod. A few moments later, the empty plain gave way to a little cluster of hovels, some substantial log cabins and others fashioned out of plasterboard and tar paper. Three children were running through the snow in sneakers and short-sleeved shirts, switching at each other with pine branches. 'These are your nearest neighbors,' Will said, slowing the truck and pointing to the individual houses. 'Charlie and Linda Laughing Dog, Bernie Collier, Rydell and Marjorie Two Fists. Abel Soap lives over the hill there, in that bus.'

Cassie tried to keep the nervous laughter from bubbling up past her throat. A day ago she'd bathed in a green marble tub with gold-plated fixtures. She'd walked on carpets softer than a breath and had wrapped herself in a dressing gown of violet Chinese silk. She had been a little uncomfortable with the scope of Alex's luxury, but this was the other extreme. She was in the middle of nowhere, hidden among people who did not know about running water, who lived in broken-down school buses. She dug her nails into her palms to keep from grabbing at Will's coat and begging him to take her home.

Cassie bit her lip and glanced at Will again, now aware of the pain that he carried, the heavy failure that pulled down the corners of his mouth. What could it feel like to finally leave here only to be dragged back weeks later by someone else's sorry circumstances? When Cassie reached across the seat and squeezed his hand, Will returned the gesture, but not before she noticed the surprise in his eyes.

He pulled the truck into the front yard of a small cement-block house. Immediately, a black mutt that was tied to a fence post began to wail. Will jumped out of the driver's seat and knelt in front of the dog. 'Hey, Wheezer,' he said. The dog wiggled its back end so hard it fell over sideways. 'You miss me?'

Cassie sat for a second in the cab of the truck, collecting her breath and her thoughts. When she stepped outside, she sank knee-deep into the snow. She shuffled her way to Will and the dog. 'Is there always this much snow?'

Will jumped at the sound of her voice, as if he'd forgotten she was there. 'Actually,' he said, swinging toward her, 'a lot of it's melted. Most winters the drifts are bigger than you.'

Wheezer jumped up and put his paws on Will's chest. His ears flattened; he began to whine. Will looked over the dog's head to the front door of the cabin, which was slowly swinging open.

Cassie watched a man step onto the front porch. He was as tall as Will, but his skin seemed to hang loosely on his frame. His face was the color of walnuts and was riddled by so many wrinkles it nearly appeared smooth again. He came down the steps and stood in front of Will, murmured something in Lakota and embraced him.

Cassie shifted nervously, knocking her feet against each other to clear off some of the snow. Wheezer nuzzled her hand, looking for food. 'Sorry,' she whispered. 'I don't have anything.'

At the soft syllables, Will and his grandfather looked up. But before Will could introduce her, a woman appeared at the doorway. She had a long white braid pulled over one shoulder; her eyes burned with the fire of stoked coals. Her fisted hands were planted on her hips, ready for a confrontation, and when she spoke in her low-pitched voice, her words were in perfect English. 'So,' she said to Will, although her eyes never moved from Cassie. Her glance went from Cassie's hair down to her snow-soaked knees, and then snapped up again, clearly finding her lacking. 'You come back from the big city, and *this* is what you bring us?'

Cyrus and Dorothea Flying Horse's house was one of about a thousand subsidized by the government for Sioux senior citizens.

They'd moved into it only ten years before; Will had done much of his growing up in a log cabin like the ones they had passed on the drive through the reservation. But the government houses were considered plush by Lakota standards. They had running water and electricity, and a toilet that worked some of the time. With the exception of the narrow bathroom at one end of the house, the rest of the building was a single room.

The kitchen area, where Cassie was sitting, was very clean and seemed to have been fashioned out of scrap Formica from the 1950s. The countertops were avocado green with little gold flecks, the table that jutted out from one wall was a fake pink marble. There was one hanging row of unpainted cabinets, missing their doors, but most of the cans and glass jars were stacked below the sink and counter on shelves made of boards and cinder block. There was a refrigerator – the really old kind with a big fan on the top – that gasped and shuddered every few seconds.

The rest of the house consisted of the large living area and the 'bedroom', shut off from the rest of the space by a calico curtain. A mismatched sofa and armchair sat on a rust-colored throw rug. On one corner of the couch was a ball of yarn speared with knitting needles, on the other end a leather purse intricately half sewed with blue beads. A large wooden spool, the kind used for electrical wire by contractors, was now a coffee table, and it was piled high with magazines dated three or four years back.

Cassie hadn't seen the bedroom, where Will had gone to talk to his grandparents in private. She heard them whispering, hissing really, but it didn't make much difference, since they were speaking Lakota. She rapped her fingers on the Formica table and counted to ten. She rubbed her knuckles over the slight swell of her belly. *You know*, she silently said, *I'm doing this for you*.

Will came out from behind the curtain first, his face set. Then came his grandmother, her arms crossed over her chest, and finally his grandfather. It had been more difficult than he'd imagined, since Cyrus and Dorothea had never heard of Alex Rivers, so they couldn't possibly understand why Will had had to bring Cassie all the way to Pine Ridge. He had told his grandparents everything, including the physical abuse and Cassie's pregnancy, but they stood before her now, looking at her as if she were some kind of scarlet woman who'd brought this on herself.

'Cassie Barrett,' Will said, intentionally leaving off her married name, 'these are my grandparents, Cyrus and Dorothea Flying Horse. They'd be happy to have you stay here until the baby comes.'

Cassie couldn't help the flush that ran up her stomach and breasts and flooded her face. She told herself it wasn't shame, it was relief. 'Thank you,' she said quietly, holding out her hand. 'You don't know what this means to me.'

Neither Cyrus nor Dorothea took Cassie's hand. She waited a moment, then wiped it on her coat and let it twitch at her side.

Will stepped closer to her and leaned toward her ear. 'I'm going to make up some story to leave you here alone with them,' he murmured. 'Trust me; it's just a matter of them getting to know you.' He squeezed Cassie's shoulder and turned back to his grandparents. Dorothea had already moved off to the kitchen to begin rinsing plates. 'I'm going over to Abel Soap's to see if he's still breathing,' Will said easily. 'He owes me fifty bucks.'

He loped toward the door, where Wheezer was already waiting. 'Remember,' he warned his grandparents. 'English. You promised.'

The door sealed shut behind Will with an indrawn breath, and Cassie stared at it for several seconds. Over the running water, Cassie could hear Dorothea muttering in Lakota. Occasionally she'd glance over her shoulder, as if to see if Cassie had left yet. Obviously the old woman spoke English; she should at least be giving Cassie a fair chance. Straightening, Cassie turned to Cyrus. 'Can you tell me what she's saying?' she asked.

Cyrus shrugged and walked toward the couch. 'She wishes Will had taken you with him.'

For a few minutes Cassie stood in the center of the living room, wavering between having a good cry or just walking out that front door and continuing until she got back to Rapid City. Cyrus settled onto the middle cushion of the couch, which heaved under his light frame, and picked up the knitting. He looped the yarn around his fingers and clicked the needles faster and faster until they chattered like teeth. Dorothea finished washing the dishes and started to sweep the spotless kitchen floor.

In fact, neither of Will's grandparents showed the slightest inclination toward making Cassie more comfortable, or talking sociably to her, and neither seemed to think this behavior was unaccountably rude. Cassie vaguely remembered a colleague who had done his dissertation on what he referred to as tipi etiquette: how the Plains Indians of the nineteenth century had lived. She could recall something about women on one side and men on the other, about warriors eating before anyone else, about the impoliteness of walking between a person and the central fire. Cassie didn't know if these customs still held, but she felt there was a set of rules that she hadn't been told, rules she would have to divine herself.

She began by straightening up the magazines. Cyrus looked over his needles once, grunted, and kept on knitting. When Cassie had made two neat stacks, she stood up and walked into the kitchen area. She rummaged through the shelves until she found a stack of white dishcloths, and she wet one with soapy water and began to scrub down the front of the refrigerator.

Dorothea didn't look up at Cassie, didn't even acknowledge that Cassie was less than three feet away. 'You know,' Cassie said, her voice too loud and bright for the tiny house, 'I have a friend at UCLA who specializes in Native American anthropology.' She didn't add that the man was a cultural anthropologist, so she'd barely spoken to him in three years. Instead, she racked her brain trying to remember his course syllabus and her own graduate work.

'The truth is,' Cassie continued, 'I don't know anything about Indians. I don't know what Will told you, but my specialty dates back before that.' She rinsed her dishcloth in the sink. 'Except for weapons,' she said. 'I'm pretty good with weapons. I did my dissertation on violence, on whether it was learned or innate—' Cassie stopped, thinking of the irony of that, given what her marriage had come to. When nobody responded, she kept speaking. 'Let's see . . . I can remember a New Mexico group called the Clovis culture that invented a stone spearhead that could be lashed to an arrow, which obviously made it easier to kill mammoth . . .' Cassie's voice trailed off, thinking of this group of nomads forty thousand years ago slaughtering a huge, shuddering beast; and then Cyrus's own grandfather, who might have hunted the buffalo in much the same way just a hundred and fifty years earlier. She stopped herself from continuing, realizing she sounded as if she was giving a lecture. Over her head, Cyrus and Dorothea exchanged a look: *Is she always like this?*

'Well,' Cassie said more quietly. 'You probably already know this.' She shook her head, calling herself a fool for coming on like a locomotive when she should have been creeping along quietly.

Dorothea came over to her and wrung the dripping dishcloth, draping it over the sink and gesturing with her hands so Cassie understood this was the way she liked it to be. Dorothea glanced around the gleaming kitchen, nodding, and then pulled on her parka. She crossed in front of Cassie, grasping Cassie's chin with strong fingers and turning her face up. In Lakota, she said something, a strange collection of clicks and syllables that Cassie thought softer than a lullaby.

After Dorothea walked out the door, Cyrus stood by the window, watching her go back to work for the afternoon shift. He knew what Cassie was about to ask. 'She says you should remember something while you are with the People,' he translated. 'What you consider these specimens of history are still our great-great-grandfathers.'

He did not turn from the window, but he held up his hand, beckoning Cassie. She stood and walked over to Cyrus, and he settled his arm around her shoulders in a gesture that was not an embrace but more of a prodding. His long, straight fingers rested on her collarbone. Cassie gazed at the vast landscape with Cyrus, knowing he did not notice the oceans of snow, the corpses of abandoned trucks, and the tattered tarpaulins blowing off a neighbor's hut. Instead he saw the place where his ancestors' footsteps lay beneath his own, the place that – because of this – he would call home.

Will sat up from the pile of blankets he was using as a bed and stared at Cassie, asleep on the pull-out couch. When he lived with his grandparents it had been his bed, and he watched her body press into the hollows in the mattress he himself had made.

He was drenched with sweat; he had been dreaming of her. Crazy as it sounded, she had been a Kit Fox, a member of one of the ancient warrior societies. Every Sioux boy had grown up hearing of the Kit Foxes and the Strong Hearts, wishing that the People were still at war with the Chippewa so they too could count coup and prove their bravery. The Kit Foxes had been the most dramatic. They had worn red sashes they would peg to the ground, meaning they'd fight on that spot until they won, they were killed, or they were released by a friend. Will could remember how he'd played at this behind the school during recess; how once he'd filched his grandmother's shawl to use as a sash and had been grounded for a month.

In the dream, Cassie's belly was swollen with her child, and she wore the sash high, just below her breasts. From a distance Will saw her stake herself to the soft earth and begin to sing.

> I am a fox.
> I am supposed to die.
> If there is anything difficult
> If there is anything dangerous
> That is mine to do.

Out of nowhere, Alex Rivers appeared, circling around her, coming closer and closer. He cuffed Cassie across the side of the head, and from where he stood Will shouted out to warn her, but she did not move. She stood her ground, even when the blows brought tears to her eyes.

Will dreamed that he screamed at the top of his lungs and started moving, racing toward the spot where Cassie was. Without losing speed, he reached down and pulled up her stake, wrapping his arm around her hips and forcing her to run just as fast as he was.

He woke up panting, angry and somewhat amazed that Cassie lay three feet away from him, curling and uncurling her fingers in her sleep. He moved quietly, in rhythm with the sounds of his grandfather's breathing coming from behind the bedroom curtain, and sat on the edge of the mattress.

Cassie was awake before his entire weight had eased down. Will put a finger to her lips, and then pointed in the direction of the curtain. 'I'm leaving tomorrow,' he whispered.

Cassie struggled to a sitting position, but Will held his hand on her shoulder, pressing her back. 'Why?'

'Because I have a job in LA. Because I hate it here.' Will smirked. 'Take your pick.'

She had to know it was going to come to this; he'd as much as said it straight out. But to his horror, Cassie gulped back a sob. 'You can't leave me here alone,' she whispered, knowing full well that he could and he would.

When she turned away from him, he stroked his hand over her brow, feeling guilty. Cassie was small and plain, the girl next door; he'd seen a hundred women prettier than she was. He wondered what it was about this woman that could rob his mind of set intentions, that could trap a movie star into marriage.

Will stared at the back of Cassie's head, forcing himself to remember the way he'd kept his thumb over his grade school report cards when he carried them home, because the students were listed not only by surname but also by the percentage of Indian blood in their veins. He tried to think of the winter he and his grandparents had lived on beef jerky and canned squash because the government rationing program had gotten screwed up. *Yes*, he thought, *I need the distance*. But even as Will thought this he lay down beside Cassie until her quivering back was pressed tight against his chest. He did not move against her, not wanting to make this into something it wasn't. Instead he listened to her heart, and to his grandparents' soft snores, twisted around each other. He gently covered Cassie's stomach with his hand. 'You won't be alone,' he said.

Chapter Twenty-One

During March, while the snow at Pine Ridge melted to little patches and drifts caught between the cottonwood trees, Cassie grew accustomed to the reservation. Because it was her safe haven, she did not see it for what it was – a place with more murders per capita than anywhere else in the United States, a people bled dry by poverty and indifference. Instead she chose to notice how beautiful the nut-brown Sioux babies were, how the mud puddles reflected her growing form, how the sun became tangled in the branches of trees, and how the quiet had a noise all its own.

'You coming or not, *wasicun winyan*?'

Dorothea's voice startled Cassie from her position at the window. She still did not feel comfortable with Dorothea, but she wanted to get out of the house. 'I'd love to,' she said, pulling her coat on and struggling with the tight buttons at the stomach. Dorothea was off from the cafeteria today, and because the ground had thawed considerably, she was going to replenish her store of roots and herbs.

In the weeks that Cassie had been staying with the Flying Horses, she had come closer to understanding them. And although Cyrus and Dorothea weren't actually friendly, they didn't cut her down, either; in fact, they went out of their way to make introductions when townspeople eyed her curiously. Cassie was beginning to see that things were different here – that a man might wear the same shirt five days in a row because it was his only one; that a mother was more likely to feed a child HoHos and orange soda than fresh grains and milk. She had altered her concept of time – set hours for breakfast and lunch and sleeping – to Indian time, which meant you ate when you were hungry and you rested when you had the need. And she was growing accustomed to the Lakota scarcity of words. She realized now that unlike whites, who chattered to fill up the spaces in conversations, the Lakota simply believed it was perfectly all right to say nothing. So Cassie moved through the woods in companionable quiet beside Dorothea, listening to the wind and the dry grass crunching beneath her feet.

'*Wanláka he*? Do you see that?' Dorothea called. She was pointing to a familiar tree, still bare.

'Cedar?' Cassie said, feeling she was being tested.

Dorothea nodded, impressed. 'It's too early now, but we boil the fruit and leaves and drink the remedy to cure coughs.'

For the next hour and a half, Cassie listened to Dorothea describe an ancient art of healing. Some of the items were still sleeping through the winter: cattail's down, which was used like gauze; sweet flag for fever and toothache; slippery elm as a laxative; wild verbena for stomachache. Dorothea brushed off the roots of the false red mallow, which would become a salve for sunburns and open wounds. She picked wolfberry, because it soothed Cyrus's tired eyes.

When she sank back against the trunk of a cottonwood, oblivious to the wet earth seeping through her polyester pants, Cassie did the same. 'I didn't know you were a medicine woman,' Cassie said.

Dorothea shook her head. 'I'm not,' she said. 'I just know some things.' She shrugged. 'Besides, there is a great deal I cannot do anything about. That's what a medicine man is for. We have Joseph Stands in Sun – Cyrus introduced you to him in town last week. There are some sicknesses that live here' – she pointed to her heart – 'and there are some sicknesses that you can't heal.'

'You mean something like cancer,' Cassie said.

'*Hiyá*,' Dorothea replied, scowling. 'That's just something evil in the body. Marjorie Two Fists went into Rapid City and had the cancer cut out of her breast, and she's been fine for years. I'm talking about something evil. In the *ton*. The soul.' She stared fixedly at Cassie. 'The People believe that a baby is born either good or bad. And that is that. You can make changes up until the time of birth, but afterward it can't be helped. And a bad baby will grow up into a bad man.'

Dorothea's eyes bored into Cassie, and she turned away. In a society where someone else's children were a gift that could grace your own household, how could Dorothea fathom a father who demeaned his son? A mother who forgot he existed? Cassie wanted to tell Dorothea that her husband hadn't been born bad; that he had simply been convinced of it so many times he began to act the part.

A cold wind settled over the thicket, taking away Cassie's thoughts. She looked at Dorothea's bulging apron. 'You and Joseph Stands in Sun must take a lot of business away from the town doctor,' she said.

Dorothea picked at a twig, splitting the bark to reveal a tiny green bud. 'Sometimes it is easier for people to come to me than to make the trip all the way to the doctor; some people don't trust the doctor.'

'Why?'

Dorothea puffed out her cheeks. 'Because we have always had medicine men, I guess, but we haven't always had *wasicuŋ* doctors.'

'*Wasicuŋ*. What does that mean?' Cassie said quickly, recognizing the Lakota word. 'It sounds like what you call me. What everyone calls me.'

Dorothea looked surprised, as if an idiot would have picked this up before. 'It means "white",' she said.

Cassie turned the word over in her mouth, testing its dips and chirps, like a mourning dove's call. 'It's pretty.'

Dorothea pulled herself to her feet and looked down at Cassie. With typical Sioux bluntness, she said, 'It comes from three Lakota words, the ones that translate to "fat, greedy person".'

Cassie slogged quietly through the mud, forcing herself to stay silent. Nobody had asked her here, nobody had to like her. For her whole life, she'd been playing roles where she tried to please and inevitably failed, simply because of who she was: a helpless child, Alex's wife, a white woman. She wondered if, as Dorothea said, this was something she'd been born to, something defective in her spirit.

She almost walked directly into Dorothea because she didn't notice that the old woman had stopped moving. 'You know,' Dorothea said easily, 'when I was a child, I had seven sisters. We lived a little closer to Pine Ridge town. Of course, my parents did not have money for enough food or clothing, much less toys, so all we got to play with were old buttons and Salvation Army teddy bears at Christmas, and things we could make ourselves. My oldest sister taught us how to make gourd dolls out of the squash that grew wild, and rags we could find in trash barrels. We'd wrap the rags around the bulb of the squash like a kerchief, and knot the fabric into arms and legs.

'They were something, those dolls. And what I remember was that each year while my sisters were trying to find a smooth green squash without bumps on its face, I would look for the parti-colored ones, the ones that streaked yellow and green, half and half.' Dorothea suddenly grasped Cassie's hand, and Cassie was amazed at the power in her thin brown fingers. 'Hybrids are strong, you know. They last longer. And in their own way, they are beautiful, Cassie, *han*?'

The women walked carefully, both unwilling to break this gossamer thread that Dorothea had netted between them by speaking, for the first time, Cassie's given name.

As Alex Rivers knotted his black bow tie, he thought about Macbeth, the character he'd shelved for a month before resuming production last week. He was starting to understand the makings of the character, much more so than he had when he'd first undertaken the film. There was a terror to Macbeth's marriage – a realization that the woman standing before him was not the same woman he'd married; that she had a capacity for acting a way he'd never believed possible.

His personal situation was clearly different, but still familiar. Certainly mistakes had been made, but he'd never figured it would come to this. When he'd come into the house and found Cassie missing, he had been tempted to check the rooms twice, the closets and the attic. It was hard to accept that she had actually gone. It happened to other people, especially in Hollywood, where weddings were more a confection of publicity than a wellspring of love. But it had never been like that between him and Cassie. He hadn't believed Cassie could walk out that door, mostly because he couldn't admit to himself that maybe he needed her more than she needed him.

Alex dragged a comb through his hair and straightened his wingtip collar. In five minutes he'd leave for Melanie Grayson's place. She was his Lady Macbeth; they'd go together to the Dorothy Chandler Pavilion where the Academy Awards ceremony was held. He stared into the mirror, not quite able to place the face that he saw. He knew that the greatest acting job of his life would not be the one for which he might receive an Oscar, but rather the one he would give tonight when in front of thousands he'd have to pretend that he gave a damn whether he won or not.

Herb was waiting downstairs with a white Mercedes limousine. 'I tell you, tonight I got heartburn,' he said. He grinned at Alex. 'You talk to Cassie?'

'Just got off the phone,' he lied. 'She wishes me luck.'

'Agh, luck,' Herb said. 'You're a shoo-in. It's a shame she couldn't make it out here, even for the night. But I know what it's like in those touch-and-go situations, you don't want to leave them alone for a minute.'

Alex nodded. 'She says maybe if I win, her father will make a dramatic recovery.'

'From your lips to God's ears,' Herb murmured, and then he pushed Alex toward the door. 'Let's get Melanie, and then we schmooze.'

Alex didn't even get out of the limousine when they pulled into Melanie's driveway; he figured this was far from a date, and he wasn't planning on giving the wrong impression. He let Herb escort her from the door to the back seat of the car, where Alex had already poured her a glass of champagne. 'You look lovely,' Alex said, knowing it was expected.

Melanie smoothed down the white satin skirt that clung to her like a snake's skin. 'This old thing?' she said, smirking. They all knew she'd spent an exorbitant amount of money on the ostentatious dress, and that she'd tried to bill it to the *Macbeth* production. She pointed out that she never would have had to be so careful about her appearance if she hadn't been seated beside Alex, on whom the cameras would focus at least three times that night.

He stared out the window as the traffic began to grind to a halt several blocks in front of the building. Cassie would never have worn a dress like that. She would have had something original, of course, but simple and beautiful. Just like her.

He found himself getting angrier and angrier at Melanie as the car crept along. Her thigh was pressed too closely to his; her hair was the wrong color; her perfume wasn't Cassie's. 'You nervous?' she purred, rubbing his forearm.

Alex didn't answer. He stared down at her hand on the sleeve of his coat as if it were a tarantula.

'Kids, kids,' Herb bellowed from the seat facing them. 'Let's kiss and make up,' he said. 'Remember, this is good publicity.'

Alex knew that Herb was right; rumors were flying about the former shutdown in production of *Macbeth*, so many that Alex was beginning to remember the hell he'd gone through with *Antony and Cleopatra*. Maybe he was just doomed when it came to Shakespeare.

'Yeah, Alex,' Melanie breathed, inches away from his face. 'Let's kiss and make up.'

Alex twirled his wedding ring around his finger, a habit he'd taken to lately, as if it were a necessary reminder. *If you win*, he warned himself, *no matter what, do not jump up and embrace her.*

Herb patted Melanie's knee. 'Leave him alone,' he sighed. 'He's brooding.'

'I know,' Melanie said huskily. 'That's what we all love about him.'

Alex ignored their senseless patter until their limousine was next in line. 'Ready for the vultures, darling?' Melanie asked, snapping closed her compact.

Alex stepped into the afternoon sunshine first, squinting and holding his hand up in a half-wave, half-sunshield. He reached into the bowels of the limousine to help Melanie out, watching her turn on a smile with the wattage of a nighttime beacon at a maximum-security prison. She lightly placed her hand on his arm, and at his low growl, removed it.

There were too many shouts and catcalls to hear the reporters or to notice the flashbulbs and the rolling tape. He walked beside Melanie, nodding and grinning, trying for a facial expression that said he was not too sure of himself, but still confident about his chances.

The man walking in front of him was a producer over at FOX, and although Alex could not remember his name, his stooped gait and liver-spotted hairline were familiar. He and his wife were tiny and hunched over, and Alex wondered if that was the burden of age or simply of a long Hollywood marriage. They meandered down the red carpeting so slowly that several times Alex was forced to stop with Melanie and simply stand, smiling like an idiot. The man turned and noticed for the first time that Alex was behind him. He stopped dead in his tracks, holding out a hand. Alex shook it. 'Golf balls,' the man said.

'Excuse me?'

'Golf balls. When I saw your movie, I had golf balls in my throat. That's how much it moved me.' He reached up and squeezed Alex's shoulder. 'The best of the best tonight, eh?'

Alex had heard that kind of comment before about *Life*. Everyone had an estranged father or sister or friend, and Alex's role had encouraged them to make their peace. Alex Rivers, king of mending fences. Sultan of reconciliation. With the ultimate skeleton in his closet: a wife he had driven away.

As he waited on the red carpeting he heard the word 'sweep', and he knew that people were talking about the potential for *The Story of His Life* to walk away with an Oscar for each of its eleven nominations, including the golden trio of Best Actor, Best Director, and Best Picture. *Sweep. Sweep. Sweep.* The syllable fell onto his ears over and over, lulling Alex into a daydream of what this could have been like, how it would have felt to have Cassie standing close to him, what the reporters would have said when he pulled her into his arms and swept her down the aisle in a Cinderella waltz, as if nothing this night could matter more than her.

They had been staying in the same one-room house for three days now, so it was ridiculous to call it a date, but Cassie still felt self-conscious about wearing an old shirt of Cyrus's and a pair of Dorothea's chartreuse elastic-waist polyester pants. Will knocked on the front door as if he weren't temporarily living there. When Cassie opened the door, his gaze took in her neatly braided hair, her oversize clothes. 'Well,' Will said. 'Aren't you pretty as a picture.'

'Give me a break,' Cassie said, bursting into laughter. 'I have no waist and I've never put anything this color on my body before.'

It was the first time Will had come back to Pine Ridge since leaving her a month ago. He'd told his supervisors there had been a death in the family, which bought him a week of bereavement leave. He wanted to believe that nothing short of a funeral would induce him to return to Pine Ridge, but in truth, he only wanted to take Cassie to the Oscars. The nearest TV was twenty miles away in a bar, and he knew that she'd never have gone herself.

'So,' she said, pulling herself up into Will's rented truck. 'What am I missing in Los Angeles?'

Will shrugged. 'You know. A lot of smog, some torrential rains, Hollywood hype.' He glanced at her quickly, hoping she understood he did not mean to include her in the last of that list. In fact, he had been listening closely to those ridiculous entertainment reports, but nothing had been said about the disappearance of Cassie Rivers.

The building was unnamed and unmarked, because everyone knew where and what it was. It was fairly full since it was the closest place off the dry reservation where you could get a drink, and Will hoped that wouldn't be a problem. He had not told Cassie, but it was known that knifings and rapes were frighteningly common in the parking lot, that the police stayed away instead of asking questions. Behind the scarred bar hung an old, faded sign, *Lel Lakota Kin Iyokipisni*, 'No Sioux Allowed.' It was sliced through the middle by a tomahawk that was wedged into the rafter behind it.

Cassie was the only white person in the bar, and one of a handful of women. She fluttered nervously behind Will, trying to ignore the stares thrown her way like challenges. She followed him to a corner table where there was an unobstructed view of the television. Her chair was pressed beside the jukebox, and while Loretta Lynn warbled, Cassie held her hands to the lit-up selection box, seeing her fingertips glow pink with the light.

'They're watching *hockey*,' Cassie said. It had never occurred to her that anything other than the Academy Awards would be the selection of choice. True perhaps in LA, but not in Pine Ridge, where the nearest movie theater was an hour away.

Will stared blankly at the fuzzy screen, watching the puck zip across the grayish ice. 'Leave it to me,' he said. He stood up and lifted one leg over the back of his chair, like a dismounting cowboy. Walking up to the bar, he leaned his elbows on the sticky wooden counter. '*Hau, kóla*,' he said, trying to catch the bartender's attention.

The man was very fat and wore his hair in two long black braids wrapped with shoelaces at the ends. He was drying a shot glass. 'What can I do you?' he said dispassionately.

'I need a Rolling Rock and a glass of water,' Will said. 'And the lady would like to switch the channel.'

'Fuck that,' the bartender said, uncapping a cold bottle on the edge of the bar. 'Three bucks.'

Will had been expecting this. He handed the bartender a fifty-dollar bill straight from his pay envelope, the likes of which he would have been willing to bet the man had never seen before in his life. 'You put on ABC by nine o'clock,' Will said, 'you get to keep the goddamn change.'

When he handed Cassie her water, she was sitting on the edge of her seat. 'Will they watch it?' she asked, her voice thin and breathless.

'No problem,' Will said. He tipped the neck of his beer to Cassie's glass in a toast, thinking that, miraculously, this hellhole corner of South Dakota agreed with her. 'Rumor has it you've become some Big Indian,' he said.

Cassie flushed. 'Thanks,' she said.

Will laughed. 'To a lot of Lakota, that's an insult worthy of a fist-fight,' he said. 'It wasn't meant as a compliment.'

Rolling the glass between her palms, Cassie glared up at Will. 'At least I'm trying to fit in,' she said pointedly.

Like you never did. The gibe hung in the air in front of them, and although Will had believed that the thick skin he'd cultivated could protect him, he was shocked to see how much the things

Cassie hadn't said could still hurt. His grandfather was half in love with her; his grandmother couldn't stop talking about her. It stung to know that someone with no Sioux blood running through her veins could carve a niche for herself when he'd never even gained a toehold.

Narrowing his eyes, Will did what had come naturally during all the years he'd lived second-class in Pine Ridge: he struck back. He nodded slowly, as if he'd been considering Cassie's daily routine for quite some time. 'You've got the elders wishing all *wasicun* were like you. Tagging along with Cyrus; asking the medicine man about berries and roots. Quite the little squaw.'

Cassie lifted her chin, unwilling to defend her actions to the very person who'd brought her there. 'What am I supposed to do all day? Lie on the couch and watch my waist disappear? Besides, it's like Girl Scouts – surviving in the forest overnight and all that. It's good to know. Suppose I got stuck in the woods and twisted my ankle—'

'Suppose there were woods in LA, and that all the twenty-four-hour pharmacies were closed?' Will snorted and took a long pull of his beer, finishing it. 'You *are* planning on going back, aren't you?'

Cassie's face closed in on itself, and for an awful moment Will thought she was going to cry. Out of nowhere, he remembered being in second grade, when a new kid had entered the school. Horace was only one-quarter Indian, and Will had made friends with him, figuring that he owed it to someone who took him out of the scapegoat position. It worked: the same bullies who'd stepped on his sandwiches at lunch and broken his pencils were now asking him to pitch their baseball games and inviting him over on weekends. Will could remember the warm feeling that grew from his stomach when he understood he was being accepted, and before he knew it he was acting like them. He didn't even realize it until one day after school he hid behind a copse of trees, waiting for Horace to round the bend, and with all the other kids he threw stones and twigs until Horace ran.

But not before Will had seen his face. He was looking straight at Will, at nobody else, like he was plainly saying, *Not you too.*

Will shook his head to clear it, unsure what that had to do with Cassie, except for the horrible feeling that had seized him when he realized just how much he'd hurt someone who'd done absolutely nothing to him. 'Hey,' he said, trying to lighten the mood. He nodded in the direction of the television. 'You're going to miss your show.'

As he had asked, the bartender had switched the channel fifteen minutes before the broadcast of the Academy Awards. Will didn't have a clue what was on beforehand; he figured it was some stupid sitcom. But looming over his head was Alex Rivers's face, and sitting beside him on a couch was Cassie herself.

'The Barbara Walters interview,' Cassie murmured. She was holding her cocktail napkin so tight her knuckles blanched and the wet paper ripped down the middle. Then she started to laugh hysterically. 'He was supposed to be on second. Not last. Second.'

A thousand things were cutting through her mind: What if he'd known he was scheduled third all along? Would they never have had that argument? Would she not have had to run away at all? She stared at the familiar curtains of her living room, at the storm whipping through the azalea bushes outside. She took in the bouquet of lilies that some set dresser on Barbara Walters's crew had placed on the coffee table where there was usually a big book of *New Yorker* magazine covers.

But most of all she looked at Alex, who was sitting right next to this shadow of herself, looking fresh and clean shaven and just as he did every morning when he came out of the bathroom and took her breath away. On the television, his hands strummed restlessly over her shoulder. He was telling the world that Alex Rivers and his wife watched Saturday morning cartoons in bed.

Oh God, Alex. Cassie fought back the urge to let the tears well into her eyes, to stand up and touch her fingers to the TV set as if she could stroke warm flesh. Until she saw him again, she had not realized what she had been missing.

Then she heard her own voice. Cassie blinked, forcing herself to turn from Alex's reactions to her own mouth forming the words. She shifted uncomfortably in her chair, thinking how odd her voice sounded, not like hers at all. 'I expected him to be a hotshot celebrity pushing around his weight to show who was in control,' Cassie heard herself say, 'and I'm sorry to say that at first, he didn't disappoint me.' She saw Alex's eyes flash at the turn of her sentence, which really did make him sound like a fool. Even though it had happened weeks ago, Cassie flinched. She wondered if the rest of the world could see that quick anger just below the surface; if they noticed that she leaned a little to the left, away from her injured side; if they recognized the ghost of a bruise beneath the gauzy sleeve of her blouse.

They cut most of the interview when Cassie talked. In fact, Barbara Walters ended with Happily Ever After, asking Alex, 'Why Cassie?' And Alex stared right at the camera and said, 'She was made for me.' Cut, clip in the quick kiss he'd given her at the end of the interview, which some editor had frozen so that Alex's lips were fused to hers eternally even as Barbara Walters started her wrap-up to the commercial.

Will glanced at Cassie. She was staring at the Pampers ad as if she did not understand the mechanics of how Alex had disappeared from the screen and was still wondering how to get him to come back.

He stood up and walked to the bar, ordering another beer. 'And chips or something,' Will added. 'It's going to be a hell of a long night.'

'I can't believe he brought someone else.'

Cassie had been saying that since the montage at the beginning of the Academy Awards, where Melanie something or other had stepped out of the same limousine as Alex. She had drunk her second glass of water in its entirety before Alex had even made it through the doors of the Dorothy Chandler Pavilion. 'That bitch,' she whispered, all the while tracking Alex, only Alex.

It looked promising: in the first major award of the evening, Jack Green had won Best Supporting Actor, and had metaphorically toasted Alex with a wave of his little gold statuette. From there on, for two and a half hours, the name of the film would come up every now and then – cinematography, editing, sound mixing. Will had lost count of the number of Oscars actually won about an hour ago, when he'd finished his sixth and final beer. He didn't know how Cassie was still sitting up, much less staying awake.

He put his head down on the table in front of her. 'Wake me in the last fifteen minutes if he wins anything big,' Will said.

Cassie nodded, swallowed. She ran her finger through the salt at the bottom of the peanut bowl. 'You know why they're called Oscars?' she said some time later, to no one in particular. 'A secretary who worked at the Academy of Motion Picture Arts and Sciences said it reminded her of her uncle Oscar. Isn't that the stupidest thing . . . that you've ever heard?'

Because he heard the hitch in her voice, Will squinted open one eye. Tears were running down Cassie's cheeks; for all her ramrod-straight posture she was falling apart. He pushed his chair around the sawdusted floor until it touched the side of Cassie's, and he pulled her into his arms. 'It's okay,' he said, wondering how long he'd been asleep, if Alex had already lost, if he'd just missed it.

'It's not okay,' Cassie said against Will's shoulder. 'It's never been okay. I ought to be sitting in the second row there. I ought to be the one whose face comes into the viewfinder every time the camera runs across his row.'

'Look at the bright side,' Will said. 'You'd probably be fast asleep by now.'

'But I'd be fast asleep *there*,' Cassie said. 'It's the most important night of his life and I'm a thousand miles away.'

But you're not, Will wanted to say. *You're here with me*. He looked
at her so intently that she stopped crying and simply stared back.

And then they announced the nominations for Best Actor.

As easily as she would step out of the front seat of a car, Cassie
disengaged herself from Will. She shrugged off his arm and leaned
her elbows on the table, inches closer to her husband. When the
television replayed a short scene from *The Story of His Life*, Alex's
reflection shimmered in a pool of condensation caught on the
table between Cassie's flattened palms.

And the Oscar for Best Actor goes to . . .

Cassie stopped breathing. The televised light bathed her face,
making its planes and angles shine.

Alex Rivers.

Cassie's eyes gleamed, and with a palpable hunger she watched
Alex walk up the aisle to the podium to accept the little statue.
Will wondered if she realized that she was reaching toward the
television with her right hand, as if she'd be able to touch him.

He didn't give a damn about Alex Rivers's Oscar, but he could
not tear his gaze from Cassie. He'd thought she looked good when
he first brought the truck around at his grandparents', but before
his eyes she had turned into a creature of grace and glow. When
Alex was on that screen, she came alive.

Will had never been so angry in his life.

Four weeks ago when Cassie had shown up on his doorstep,
he had seen the evidence of the illustrious Alex Rivers's rage; he
had understood the burden she'd been left with. But until now,
Will had had no idea just how much of Cassie herself Alex had
taken away.

Alex's golden hair was brighter than the Oscar, and Cassie
watched his hands flex around the statuette's body. He was looking
right at her. 'I'd like to thank Herb Silver, and Warner Brothers,
and Jack Green and . . .' Cassie tuned out his actual words,

watching instead the lines of his mouth, pink and sculpted, and imagining it coming over hers. 'But this award is for my wife, Cassie, who found me the script and convinced me that it was something the public would want to see, as well as something I needed to do. She's with her father tonight because he's ill, and when I spoke to her a few hours ago, she was upset that she couldn't make it back here. Well, I was a little nervous, so I didn't get to say everything I needed to before I hung up the phone. What I wanted to tell her is this: *You could be halfway around the world, Cassie, and you'd still be with me.*' He cleared his vision, now looking at the sea of faces staring up at him. 'Thank you,' he said, and all too quickly, he was gone.

Cassie watched him accept his two other Oscars. It was clearly Alex's night, and yet he never failed to mention her. The second time, he told the world he loved her. The third time, he whispered, 'Hurry home,' so softly Cassie wondered if anyone else watching had even heard.

When Will pulled her up and propelled her out the door of the bar, she tried to picture what her night might have otherwise been like. She would have worn a froth of a gown – Alex would have seen to that – and every time his name was called he would have turned to her and lifted her out of her seat in his embrace. She could feel his strong arm, the itch of his tuxedo jacket under her fingertips, as she moved through Spago and The Gate with him, circulating the post-Oscar parties. She would hold two statues, still warm from where Alex's hands had wrung their naked necks. Then she would go home and drop the awards onto the carpet and Alex would pour himself into her, hot, frantic, the very essence of success.

But instead Cassie walked into the cold March night, dizzied by the rash display of stars, and remembered her life for what she'd made of it.

Will watched her mouth turn down at the corners. She'd been moping through the whole broadcast, in spite of the fact that slick Alex had told the twenty million people watching that his entire life revolved around his wife. Hell, he'd even admitted she was out of town, although he'd candy-coated the circumstances. He was no fool, he knew she'd be watching. Will would have peevishly said the whole speech was calculated, if he hadn't noticed with his own eyes that Alex had managed to put into words the exact way Cassie had been staring at that television screen.

Alex probably did love her, for whatever that was worth, and Cassie seemed to believe it carried considerable value. But Will thought it might kill him to actually see them together again. She'd probably cling to Alex as if her knees didn't work and Alex would look at her like, well, like Will had been looking at her all night.

'That was something,' Will said noncommittally, unlocking the passenger door of the truck.

'Mmm,' Cassie said. She looked miserable.

'Your husband just cleaned out the Oscars,' Will muttered. 'It would make sense for you to show a little emotion.' He grabbed Cassie's shoulders, shaking her lightly. 'He misses you. He's crazy about you. What the *hell* is your problem?'

Cassie shrugged, a delicate tremor that worked its way under Will's palms. 'I guess I still wish I had been there,' she admitted.

Will exploded. 'Four weeks ago you couldn't think of anything but getting away. You showed me the places where he'd kicked you in the ribs and hit you across the neck. Or have you forgotten about that side of your charming husband, just like he probably was hoping you would when you watched tonight, so you'd come crawling back?' He glared at Cassie, who was standing mute, her mouth slightly parted. 'Believe me,' he said, 'I know better than anyone. You can't have the best of both worlds.'

She stared at him as if she'd never seen him before, and tried to take a step back. But Will would not let go of her. He wanted her to realize that he was right. He wanted Cassie to be able to slice away all the pretty packaging Alex had handed her tonight across the airwaves and see him for what he really was. He wanted her to look at him – Will – the way she had looked at Alex.

Will tightened his grip on Cassie's shoulders and pressed his lips against hers. Frustrated, his mouth ground into hers, his tongue forcing his way until, with the gentleness of a saint, she yielded under his touch. Her arms crept around his waist slowly, a white flag, a selfless surrender that ripped at the edges of his conscience.

He stepped away abruptly, angry at himself for his lack of control, angry at Cassie for simply being in the wrong place at the wrong time. Another man's wife. Pregnant. Stomping to his side of the truck, he swung himself into the cab and turned over the ignition. He flicked on the headlights, spotlighting Cassie. She was frozen in the moment. Her hand was pressed to her mouth; her wedding ring gleamed like a prophecy. From this distance, Will could not be sure if she was wiping away the taste of him, or trying to hold it in.

Alex Rivers – the most sought-after actor/director in Hollywood at the moment, which was a little after four a.m. – sat in the dark in his Bel-Air study. He eyed the three gold statuettes he'd lined up in front of himself like decoys at a shooting gallery. What a night it had been. What a hell of a night.

He had never wished more fervently that he was drunk, but no matter how much champagne he'd consumed in honor of himself that evening, oblivion wasn't coming. He had left the last party a little over an hour ago. When he'd walked out, Melanie was going to snort coke in the bathroom with a costume designer, and Herb was negotiating Alex's rapidly rising salary with a huddle of producers. The snafus plaguing *Macbeth* were suddenly forgotten by the industry; Alex was a golden boy once again. When he paused at the threshold of the door, everyone was saying his name, but nobody even noticed he'd left.

He wondered if Cassie had been watching tonight, then lashed out at himself for even wondering.

This was *his* night. For Christ's sake, how long had he been working toward this? How long had he been in the process of proving himself? He ran his hands over the bald heads of the statues, amazed at the way they seemed to retain the warmth of human touch.

He picked up his first Oscar, weighing it in his palm as he would a baseball. Then his fingers closed around it. 'This is for you, *maman*,' he said, and he hurled it across the study with such force that it cut the wallpaper and dented the Sheetrock with its impact.

He picked up the second one, the one for his father, and threw it in the same direction, grunting with satisfaction as his fingers released the smooth metal.

His lips stretched in the imitation of a smile as he walked toward the third Oscar. Save the best for last. He gripped the narrow body, thinking of his dear, devoted wife, and he stretched back his arm.

He couldn't do it. With a strange keening sound at the back of his throat, Alex fell heavily into the desk chair. He ran his fingers over the statuette as if in apology, as if he were feeling the soft curve of Cassie's neck and the blunted edges of her hair. He pressed the heels of his hands against his eyes when they started to sting; he lowered his head to the desk.

Best Picture, Best Actor, Best Director, Worst Husband. Alex had seen the parallel before where art imitated life, but never had it rocked him to the soul. His acceptance speeches tonight had been carefully written, plotted word by word to catch Cassie, wherever she was, and reel her back to him. He was only beginning to see how much he had really meant the things he said.

He could wake up tomorrow with a hundred movie offers and a going salary of twenty million per film, but it wouldn't be enough. It would never be enough. He would trade it all and live in a cardboard box on the beach if he could rip out of himself the part of him that caused her pain.

In the shifting shadows of his study, Alex Rivers whispered aloud the secret that none of the glittering people still partying on Sunset Boulevard knew: He was a nobody.

Unless. Until.

She made him whole.

When the private line of the telephone rang beside his head, he knew he had conjured her. He picked up the receiver and waited to hear Cassie's voice.

There was no way Alex could know the trouble Cassie had gone to to find a phone. It had meant sneaking past Will, who was pretending to be asleep on the floor but had let her go without a word. It meant taking Will's truck, without permission, to the Catholic church and waking the priest and hoping her white skin could convince him of a fabricated emergency. It meant waiting through several false starts with her heart at the back of her throat until a South Dakota operator finally reached Bel-Air.

'Alex,' she whispered. Her word was an embrace. 'Congratulations.'

It had been so long, and he was so shocked that his televised speech had actually brought her to him, that Alex could not speak at all for a moment. Then he hunched his shoulders forward, as if he could cradle Cassie's voice with his own physical presence. 'Where are you?' he asked.

She had been expecting this. She didn't want to divulge anything; she only wanted to hear Alex. 'I won't tell you,' Cassie said. 'I can't. But I'm all right. And I'm very proud of you.'

Alex realized he was drinking in her voice, storing it inside himself to play again and again. 'When are you coming back? What made you leave?' He reined in his emotions. 'I could find you, you know,' he said carefully. 'If I wanted to, I could.'

Cassie took a deep breath. 'You could,' she said with a practiced bravado, 'but you won't.' She waited for him to contradict her, and when he didn't she told him what he already knew. 'I won't come back because *you* want me to, Alex. I'll only come back because *I* want to.'

It was a lie; if he'd broken down and begged her she would have taken the next plane to LA. She was bluffing, and maybe Alex knew it too, but he also knew how much was at stake. Cassie had never hidden from him before, after all. And if ensuring a happy ending meant playing by her rules, he would do whatever she asked.

So he swallowed his pride, his fear, and his failure. 'Are you really all right?' he asked softly.

Cassie curled the phone cord around her wrist like a bracelet. 'I'm okay,' she said. She glanced up to see the priest's silhouette at the rectory door. 'I have to go now.'

Alex panicked, gripping the phone more tightly. 'You'll call back?' he pressed. 'Soon?'

Cassie considered this. 'I'll call back,' she conceded, thinking about the baby and what Alex had a right to know. 'I'll call when I want you to come for me.'

She wanted him to come. She wanted him. 'Are we talking days? Weeks?' Alex asked. He let a grin dance under his words. 'Because after tonight, my schedule's a nightmare.'

Cassie smiled. 'I'm sure you can prioritize,' she said. She hesitated before giving Alex a gift to keep through the months that would stretch out ahead. 'I miss you,' she whispered, no longer smiling. 'I miss you so much.' And she put down the phone before he could hear her fall apart.

Alex stared at his Oscars. The proofs of his success lay toppled on the floor, scarring the wood when they had landed. The last statuette stood beside the telephone. Cassie had severed the connection; all that remained was a dull dial tone. Alex did not notice when he began to cry. For an hour, he held the receiver like an amulet, even when the tuneless voice of an operator told him over and over to hang up and try again.

Chapter Twenty-Two

Cyrus had repeated the third grade for eight years, not because of his limited intelligence but because in the 1920s, the reservation's school didn't go any higher. He had a rudimentary knowledge of reading and writing, but math other than addition and subtraction was beyond him and his spelling was phonetic. His specialty was history – not the white man's history, as he told Cassie, that the missionary teachers had tried to cram down their throats with their textbooks, but the way it really was.

Because Dorothea spent so much time at the cafeteria, Cassie was left alone with Cyrus quite often. She had a feeling he liked having the company; he'd put away his knitting and sometimes he whittled when they walked together, but mostly he just made conversation. He told her stories that had been passed down to him from his own father – Indian myths, boyhood tales about Crazy Horse, near-eyewitness accounts of the Battle of Little Bighorn and the tragedy at Wounded Knee.

Yesterday, Cassie had asked Cyrus to take her to *Paha Sapa*, the Black Hills. She knew that fossils had been found nearby, and that there had been controversies about removing them from the sacred lands of the reservation. It wasn't that she was planning to start a huge excavation, which the tribal council would certainly veto, but she was itching to at least find the clues that would lead her to believe there was something below the surface – the pitted rock, the overgrown vegetation. She felt compelled to take advantage of living among the Sioux, scant miles from their ancient burial grounds. For years, her colleagues had been trying to get access to places like this, and had repeatedly been refused.

Today she had borrowed Abel Soap's army-issue jeep and packed a picnic lunch. Just in case, she told herself, she'd tossed in a pick and a spade that Abel had offered her from his junk shed. Cyrus had swung himself into the jeep like a man much younger. 'You know,' he said, 'Sioux kids believe that the bogeyman lives in the Badlands.'

Cassie had smiled. 'I'll take my chances.'

But several hours later, with the strange smooth rock-scape spread in front of them, it was easy to see why impressionable kids would believe such a thing. Unlike the peaks and turrets of most of the Black Hills, the Badlands were flat and low, like a hollow of gigantic boulders that over time had melted into each other. The wind moaned through the sparse pine trees that lined the upper ridge, and swept into the knotty valley like a whirlpool.

'You going down there?' Cyrus asked, coming to stand beside Cassie on the ledge.

Cassie glanced at him. 'Why? Are you coming?'

'Hell, no,' Cyrus said. 'I can think of better places to die.'

A chill ran down her spine at his words. 'What do you mean by that?' she asked, but Cyrus had walked to the back of the jeep and could not hear her.

He returned with her pick and her shovel, and held them out. 'You want these?'

Cassie nodded and tucked them into the belt she'd borrowed from Cyrus. She'd taken to wearing other people's clothing since hers no longer fit. She watched Cyrus pull a piece of cold meatloaf out of the hamper and sit cross-legged on the ledge in front of her. Gingerly she reached over the edge with her foot, gripping a rock and feeling for a toehold as she began her descent into the valley. She ran her hands over the stone walls, supple as marble and veined with lichen.

'Should have brought a Ghost Dance shirt,' Cyrus called from somewhere above her. 'That way the bad spirits can't get you.'

'That's a good idea,' Cassie said, panting, not having the slightest idea what he was talking about. 'And after I find one, I can make a fortune selling them to the doomsday preachers on the Avenue of the Stars.' She slipped her foot down another notch in the natural ladder, nearly twisting her ankle on the rounded surface of the boulders that made up the valley floor.

'Don't laugh,' Cyrus said. 'There really were shirts that the People believed kept you invincible. My great-grandfather had one. They were sort of a fad in the 1880s, part of a new dance that was supposed to bring back the dead warriors and the buffalo, a whole new world without the white man.' Cyrus stood up and leaned over the lip of the valley. 'You gonna eat the meatloaf?' he yelled.

'No,' Cassie said. She shaded her hand with her eyes. He was twenty feet above her, looking down, as if his interest could guarantee her safety. 'You go ahead.'

'Well, anyway, my great-grandfather brought the Ghost Dance from a Paiute medicine man back to the Sioux. And he had this shirt with him, painted with the sun, the moon, the stars, and magpies. Dorothea has it packed away somewhere. As long as you were wearing that shirt, no harm could come to you.'

'Like a rabbit's foot,' Cassie said, digging with her pick at a little notch in the rock. Even if she did find something, she thought to herself, it would probably be a mastodon, not an ancient human.

'Yeah,' Cyrus said, 'except it didn't work like it was supposed to. The white army thought if it was such big medicine, the Sioux had to be planning some kind of attack against them. So they told the People they couldn't do the Ghost Dance.'

Cassie felt the sun heat the crown of her head, and she was reminded of her first days in Tanzania with Alex, when she had believed that nothing could go wrong; that truly, they were invincible. Who was she to judge a Ghost Dance shirt? Love, at least at the beginning, could be just as powerful a charm.

'You know of Sitting Bull?' Cyrus said. 'That's how he died. He was living the old ways, ghost-dancing at Standing Rock, and the government agents got the tribal police to arrest him for it. His own *people*.' He shook his head. 'When he fought back, they started to shoot. Sitting Bull was killed, and most of the Sioux with him were too.'

Cassie turned her face up when Cyrus started to laugh; it was the last sound she'd expected to hear on the heels of his story. Her pick was suspended midswing. 'Now, picture this,' Cyrus said. 'Everyone's looking around, trying to make sense of what's happened, and suddenly a horse shows up and starts weaving around in a circle.'

'Sitting Bull's?' Cassie asked, transfixed.

Cyrus nodded. 'Before he came to the reservation, Sitting Bull traveled with Buffalo Bill Cody's Wild West show, and this circus pony had been a parting gift. So when the shots that killed Sitting Bull rang out, this horse comes out of nowhere and goes into his routine. Seems that was the way they had started the show.'

Cassie's hand had dropped to her side. She found herself listening only to Cyrus, to his story and to the cry of a hawk somewhere in the distance. She slowly stuck her pick inside the belt loop, beginning the ascent out of the bleached valley.

Up top, she sank down beside Cyrus, rubbing her arms, trying to remember even one anecdote her mother might have told her that hinted she came from stronger stock than her own parents. But all she could recall were stories of a southern graciousness that Cassie later learned did not exist, and the wheeze of her mother's slurred voice falling off in midsentence. 'Your grandfather told you this?' Cassie asked.

Cyrus nodded proudly. 'Like I've told Will. And you.'

Cassie winced at a stitch in her side. Her body was not what it used to be. This child was already making demands. She smiled past the pain and hauled herself to her feet. 'We can go now.'

Cyrus peered at her carefully. 'Did you find anything?' he said, surveying her empty pockets, the untouched spade.

In the past, for Cassie, anthropology had meant physically taking something away, but now the thought of chipping at the Black Hills made her feel a little sick. She was starting to wonder if the excavation of a culture had to involve laying open the earth. She imagined Cyrus's great-grandfather spinning in his Ghost Dance shirt; Sitting Bull bleeding on the cold ground while only a circus pony pranced in his honor; Will perched on a pine-board floor learning his history through his grandfather's voice. There was some phrase the Sioux used as a sort of benediction when they ended a ritual. Dorothea tossed it out the way she herself would casually say 'God bless you' to sneeze. Cassie frowned, furrowing her brow, until the words came to her: *Mitakuye oyasín.* 'All my relatives.'

Cassie closed her eyes and pulled tight the edges of Cyrus's tales; she pictured again that dancing horse. 'Yes,' she said. 'I found exactly what I came for.'

Alex thought the man resembled a ferret. He had shiny little brown eyes and a pointed nose that looked pert on Cassie but rodentlike on Ben Barrett. He was telling the *Hard Copy* reporter that he had never even had a common cold, much less been on his deathbed in some Augusta hospital like *that liar Alex Rivers* was saying.

'And what's more,' Ben Barrett, his father-in-law, sputtered, 'I haven't heard from my little girl at all this year.' Something had been edited here, so that when the camera cut back to Ben he was bleary-eyed. He nodded his head. 'He's covering something up, ayuh.'

Alex took a deep breath and settled himself as deeply as possible into Michaela's office couch. Several feet in front of him Herb paced back and forth, riffling through every tabloid on the supermarket stand, all of which had different suggestions for what had happened to Cassie, ranging from kidnapping to murder at Alex's hand.

It wouldn't have been a big deal – Alex had won slander suits before – but Cassie *had* been gone for two months, and this was her own father. The more the rumors flew, the more the magazines questioned Alex's calm and Alex's silence. One of the tabloids had even gotten a statement from the latest private investigator Alex had hired – something noncommittal, but Alex had fired him immediately for talking.

Cassie had called him that one time, but Alex hadn't told anyone. It had taken the edge off his fear for her safety, yet it had not altered his plan of action. He still had detectives digging for information. Cassie had said she would call again, and maybe she would, but if in the meantime Alex discovered her whereabouts, he'd be on his way. After all, if she had the right to leave, he had just as valid a right to convince her to come back.

Michaela was the one who had initially spread the excuse of Cassie being with her sick father, and at the time, under the pressure of the Oscars, it had seemed like a good story. After the first couple of detectives couldn't turn up any clue to Cassie's whereabouts, Alex had even started to believe his own lie.

The videotape of the *Hard Copy* show fizzled to a series of black and white stripes, and Michaela heaved herself out of her chair and shut off the VCR. 'Well,' she said. 'The proverbial shit has hit the fan.'

Alex rubbed his finger along his upper lip, trying not to feel as if he was on trial. Herb leaned toward him, so close that when he yelled Alex could see the spittle catch at the ends of his mustache. 'Do you know what this could do to you?'

'Herb,' Alex said calmly, 'I just won three Oscars. People aren't going to forget that so fast.'

Herb glared at Alex, shaking his head. 'What they remember is the bad, the sensational. Like whether the Best Actor cut his wife up into little pieces and buried her in the basement.'

Alex stiffened. 'Give me a break,' he said. But his mind was already racing. Herb and Michaela would stand beside him, but they would demand the truth. They would want to know why they had been kept in the dark.

He was going to have to give a flawless performance in front of the two people he'd trusted enough to see him with his guard down.

Michaela settled into the wing chair across from him as if she had all the time in the world. Overhead, the ceiling fan whistled. 'Okay,' she said, drumming her fingers on her stomach. 'What the fuck is going on?'

Alex lowered his eyes, unwilling to give them the whole truth, but using instead the shock value of the statement they would never expect to hear. 'Cassie left me,' he murmured, and he let the ache he kept tight under wrap work its way to the surface all over again.

The bent-willow frames of the sweat lodge reminded Cassie of a woolly mammoth. There was something about the curved bars of wood that made them look like ribs, as if a creature had sloughed its way to the middle of the plain to die. She sat down on the cold ground, opened the notebook she'd bought a month before, and pulled a pencil stub from her coat pocket. Flipping to a blank page, she surveyed the sketches she'd done to pass the time when she had first arrived: skull dimensions, 3-D images of the hand, a multilayered mock-up of an Australopithecine man she wanted to use as a handout in one of her courses. But in the weeks she'd spent on the reservation, her drawings had changed. She wasn't sketching skeletal figures from her research anymore. Here was a picture she'd done of Dorothea, asleep in the rocker; and one of a buffalo herd that she'd re-created from Cyrus's stories; and another, a memory left from a dream in which she'd seen the face of her baby.

Maybe it was the stripped-down atmosphere of Pine Ridge that had changed her sketching style. In LA, there was so much glitter surrounding you that cutting back to the basics was refreshing. But here, where there was little but the Spartan stretch of land and sky, every word you spoke and relationship you wove and picture you drew embellished itself into a thing of substance.

Cassie tucked the pencil behind her ear and critically assessed her mammoth, then glanced at the rough willow frame that had inspired it. How strange it felt to look at things and – instead of reducing them to their skeletal elements, as she'd been trained – to see so much more than what had been laid before her.

She was so engrossed in her mammoth sketch that she did not hear the footsteps behind her. 'If that's a *ta-tánka*,' Cyrus said, 'you've got it all wrong.'

Cassie glanced up at him. 'It's a mammoth,' she explained. 'Not a buffalo.'

Cyrus squinted. 'Mammoth,' he muttered. 'Whatever you say.' He waved his book of crosswords in front of her. 'You gonna give me back my pencil?'

Cassie flushed. 'I didn't mean to steal it. I couldn't find any others.'

Cyrus made an indeterminate noise and held out a hand to Cassie. 'Get up,' he sighed. 'You're going to freeze that baby.'

She waved him away. 'Let me do the tusks. I'm almost finished.' She sketched for a moment. 'There,' Cassie said, tilting her pad up to Cyrus. He looked at a picture of a sweat lodge that had a trunk and tusks growing out of its flap door. 'What do you think?' she asked.

Cyrus rubbed his hand down over his face to hide a smile. 'I think it looks like a sweat lodge,' he said. He reached for Cassie's hand and pulled her to her feet.

'No imagination,' Cassie pronounced.

'It's not that,' Cyrus said. 'How come white people look at a puddle and try to tell us it's the ocean?'

Cassie fell into step beside him. 'Maybe I should watch a sweat,' she suggested, offhand, thinking if she sounded nonchalant Cyrus would be more inclined to agree. Being an anthropologist, she had convinced herself that her interest was purely natural. She would have loved to know what went on inside the frames, which stood as testaments to the young boys who fasted under the tutelage of medicine men in an effort to understand themselves. She had seen the reverence with which Linda Laughing Dog's oldest son had prepared himself for the ritual. He had come back drained and exhausted, but glowing from the inside as if he now knew how to fit together the pieces that made up his life.

If only it could be that easy.

'*Ecún picášni yeló*,' Cyrus said. 'It's impossible.'

'It would be an intriguing piece of research—'

'No,' Cyrus said.

'I could sit—'

'No.'

Cassie tossed him a smile, and for a moment, Cyrus forgot that she saw prehistoric beasts in the frames of sweat lodges, that she was using every trick in the book to be admitted to the inner circle of a Lakota rite of passage. He considered – not for the first time – how odd it was that Cassie, who had carved her place in his family, had come to them through Will, who had always wanted out.

Shaking his head, Cyrus stretched his arms over his head. He laid the book of crosswords on the frame of the sweat lodge and started to walk over the ridge that swelled farther east of the house. '*Léci u wo*,' he said. 'Come here.' When he reached a small copse of trees that rested at the base of a larger hill, he stopped. 'This was where Will built his sweat lodge,' he said.

'*Will*?' Cassie said, surprised. 'I didn't think he'd be into that sort of thing.'

Cyrus shrugged. 'He was young at the time.'

'He never told me,' Cassie said, realizing as the words were spoken that although Will knew the intimate details of her private life, there was a great wealth of information about Will Flying Horse that she did not know. She tried to imagine Will at the same age as Linda Laughing Dog's son, with his thick black hair long down his back and his muscles just starting to take a man's shape. 'Did it work?'

Cyrus nodded. 'Not that he'll ever admit to it,' he said. 'In my grandson's mind, being one of the People is something you can discard, like an old jacket.' He was standing with his face to the wind, and Cassie watched him cup his hands around the air as if he needed to keep it all from rushing by so quickly.

'Is that why he left?'

Cyrus turned to her, his black eyes sharp and measuring. 'Don't you think that's something Will ought to tell you?'

'I think it's something Will would go out of his way *not* to tell me,' she said carefully.

Cyrus nodded, admitting the truth of Cassie's statement. 'You know that Will's mother was *wasicuη wínyan*, like you,' he said. 'You know that Will worked on the tribal police force before he moved.' He took a step forward, willing to tell Cassie his grandson's secrets but unable to look her in the eye while doing it. 'The tribal police are like any other small police force, I guess. They do the usual – breaking up domestic spats, taking home drunks, keeping the kids from drinking beer down at the lake. And they pretty much turn their heads if it makes sense – you know, they don't want to get one of their own in trouble, so they're likely to give a warning instead of a fine.

'Will was a good officer. He'd been working there for five years or so. Everyone liked him, and that kind of thing was important to Will.' Cassie nodded; she understood. 'About five months ago there was a big accident right in Pine Ridge town. Drunk driver. Some guy drove another car off the road, killed a family of four, and then wrapped his own jeep around the telephone pole in front of the general store. Course, he walked out of his car without a scratch.'

Cyrus closed his eyes, remembering the sirens of the beat-up police cars that he'd heard even in his sleep; the dark blood on the front of his grandson's regulation shirt when he'd come home that night. 'A long time ago Will's parents were killed in a car accident by some crazy drunk *wasicun* salesman; that's how come he grew up with us. So I suppose something just snapped in him when he saw that man get out of his car. He walked over and beat him within an inch of his life. Took three other tribal officers to get him away. Will was fired about a week after that.'

Indignant, Cassie turned to Cyrus. 'That's ridiculous. He could have sued them.'

Cyrus shook his head. 'Too many people wanted Will gone. See, the family that was killed belonged to the visiting brother of one of the elementary school teachers. White. And the drunk driver Will nearly murdered was Lakota.' Cyrus whistled through his front teeth. 'A white family getting killed was a tragedy, to be sure, and there was no question in anyone's mind that the drunk driver, red or white or whatever, was going to go to trial. But what Will did – flying off the handle like that – was a mistake. Will didn't seem to have his priorities straight. All of a sudden everyone was remembering that he was *iyeska*, half white, and that seemed to be the half that was in control, since a fullblood Indian would've cut the guy some slack.'

'How could they possibly see that as a racial issue?' Cassie said, folding her arms across her chest. 'What must your neighbors think of me?'

'They like you,' Cyrus said. 'You blend in with the People. Not because you try to, but because you don't try *not* to. Will – well, Will was always building walls, standing a little ways apart.'

Cassie thought about Will in Los Angeles, standing out just as sorely as he had at Pine Ridge. She thought about the beautiful quilled moccasins and the deerskin mural packed in boxes in his Reseda apartment. She thought of him beating a drunk driver until his knuckles were scraped and bruised, until blood covered his uniform, until it became impossible to tell if the man was Lakota or white. She thought of what she might have said to him if she'd known all this earlier: that she now knew, from personal experience, you just couldn't shut your eyes and pretend a part of your life didn't exist.

Mindlessly, Cassie bent down and picked up a branch of a young willow sapling that had broken off during a storm. She flexed the stick in her hands, bending it in half, testing its endurance, considering what Cyrus had told her. And when the willow snapped, tried to its limit, she was not surprised at all.

Will couldn't get away from Alex Rivers. His name was in every newspaper, every magazine, splayed across the racks at the supermarket. He'd seen his picture so many times he was willing to bet he knew Alex's features better than Cassie did. He was even starting to feel sorry for the guy. In the wake of some statement made by Cassie's father, rumors had flown. Cassie had become some kind of Jimmy Hoffa mystery, and Alex was suffering the consequences.

The article he was reading said that the Japanese firms backing *Macbeth* had withdrawn their support, leaving Alex as the sole creditor for a forty-million-dollar flop. Supposedly his Malibu apartment was up for sale. His next two film deals had disintegrated; his silence regarding Cassie's disappearance was universally damning, traced to either his culpability or a sick obsession with his career that obliterated everything else. There was even a nasty hint that the reason an Oscar winner like Alex Rivers had nothing else in the works was because he couldn't keep his head out of the bottle long enough to find a decent script.

Will folded the magazine in half and stuck it behind the sun visor of the squad car. 'How much longer?' he asked, turning to Ramón, still his partner.

Ramón stuffed the rest of his fried egg sandwich in his mouth and checked his watch. 'Ten minutes,' he said. 'Then it's show-time.'

Tonight he'd been assigned to a charity ball. It was given by some organization whose name he'd forgotten, and it sponsored a very worthy cause – some handicapped children's ranch in Southern California. Still, Will couldn't believe this was the way he had to earn a living.

The highlight of the evening involved seven sagging society matrons wearing beaded evening gowns and five-foot-tall floral headdresses concocted by a variety of florists from the Tournament of Roses parade. The women staggered down a runway, smiled in spite of the steel back braces supporting their necks, and supposedly raised a shitload of cash.

Will and Ramón were there to keep a semblance of order.

What was even more shocking was the fact that they were *needed*. Three hours before the shindig even started, some skinny little twit with a nametag that read *Maurice* had accused another florist of stealing his birds-of-paradise. Will had to pry him off the thief's back, after he'd already stomped on a once-white string of lilies.

'Let's go,' Ramón said, pulling himself out of the car.

Will set his cap low over his eyes and walked toward the Beverly Wilshire Hotel. He told himself this was not just a security guard's job. He told himself he'd make detective soon.

Ramón took one side of the runway and Will took the other. There was a dimming of lights, a flurry of thick percussed music, and then the first model appeared.

Her headdress was made of carnations and spelled out the year 1993. You could see how hard it was for her simply to walk. Behind her, on a huge screen, were the gap-toothed grins of bald children on horses; sickly adolescents floating in inner tubes.

A woman, the emcee, sauntered up beside Will, handing him a shopping bag stuffed with tiny wrapped packages. 'Here's your goody bag,' she trilled. She beamed up at the stage. 'I keep hoping that next year I'll be chosen. As a mannequin, you know.' A second model appeared on the runway. She was singing 'Hooray for Hollywood', and the violets growing out of her hair were fashioned into a Panavision camera, with an ivy-woven roll of film sprocketing over her shoulders.

Will thought about Cassie. He wondered if she had gone to functions like this with Alex; if she had felt as out of place as he did. Quietly, under the hum of the music, he unwrapped three of the little presents. A bottle of designer perfume, a pair of aviator sunglasses, edible massage oil.

Across the way, Ramón was clapping to the beat. Will glanced around at the faces bobbing over the satin gowns and the tight-necked tuxedos. They had been pulled and tucked and sculpted and shaped, primped and posed and colored. They were artfully wrapped packages without any of the messy tape showing; they were working unnaturally hard to look natural.

They looked like everyone else in LA.

In that quick clarity which comes once or twice during one's life, Will understood that he was not supposed to be here at all. He remembered his days on the tribal police, where he'd arrested deadbeat husbands and confiscated six-packs from teenagers, all the while thinking there was more to life than that. And maybe there was – but he wasn't any closer to finding it now than he had been in South Dakota.

He was so busy watching the audience that he didn't know what hit him. But the fourth model had caught her heel on a divot in the runway and had inadvertently swung her head, loosening the pins and the glue that secured a fountain of flowers to her scalp. Will was buried in a heap of tea roses and tiger lilies, huge hothouse poppies, stephanotis. He slipped on the shimmering petals and fell backward on the floor.

A crew of doctors who staffed the Southern California ranch rushed up from their table to make sure that he was all right, but not before the model herself, leaning over in mortification, pitched from the high runway on top of Will. She was sprawled across him, a fiftysomething grand dame with tears of failure in her eyes and a dress cut too low.

'Ma'am,' Will said politely, 'are you all right?'

The woman sniffed delicately, and then seemed to notice him. She smiled seductively, stretching the skin of her face-lifted cheeks to its limit. 'Well, hello there,' she said, deliberately slipping her thigh between his legs.

And that was how Will knew he'd be going home.

Three – two – one – white. The film projecting into Alex's private screening room ran through to the end, leaving him to stare at absolutely nothing. He pushed a button on his remote control and sighed as the room sank blessedly into black. Better this way; easier.

He picked up the bottle of J&B sitting next to him and tilted it up, only to remember it was empty. He'd finished it sometime during Act III of *Macbeth*, when he had realized that the critics were right: the movie was horrible. They wouldn't even be able to give away video copies to high school English teachers.

He had wrapped up production several weeks ago; this was the first complete version of the film. And he couldn't blame the problems on the rough editing; he knew he should have cut his losses months before. But in Hollywood, that meant admitting failure, and no producer with an eye on the future could afford the stigma. So he'd plodded through the filming, praying it would turn out better than it had felt scene-by-scene.

It seemed, these days, no one was listening to Alex's prayers.

He rubbed his eyes, which constantly burned. 'Everyone has a flop,' he said out loud, trying the words on for size. He was overdue for one anyway. You couldn't romance success for ten years without also courting disaster.

Of course, not everyone's life fell apart at the same time as his career.

He closed his eyes and rested his head on the back of the chair. He was eight years old again, sitting outside at Deveraux's, waiting for his father to finish his card game. It was oppressively hot, but that was nothing new. All the windows at Beau's were open, and he could hear the clink of beer glasses being set down on the rough wood tables; the slap and giggle of the redheaded waitress when Beau pinched her; the cracking claws of crawfish as people cleaned their plates. A lively zydeco wafted from the inside speakers through the Spanish moss that curled around Alex's head.

'You ain't got nothin' left to bet 'cept your kid,' Alex heard, 'and he ain't worth the shit on your shoes.'

He stood up and climbed the low branches of the tree that stood closest to Deveraux's, wetting his bare feet with the muck of the swamp and stretching across a low-lying limb. His father must have lost again, maybe even used up more than just the money he'd gotten from his haul of crawfish. 'Spot me, Lucien,' his father said. 'I'm good for it.'

From behind his father, he saw Beau shake his head slightly at Lucien, but the big bald man just crossed his arms over his chest and laughed. 'You gonna lose again, *cher*,' he said, 'but don' let it be said I ain't a good sport.' He dug a roll of bills out of his chest pocket and thrust a handful at Alex's father. But before Andrew Riveaux could take the cash, Lucien pulled it just out of reach. 'Wait a minute,' he said. 'Seems to me if I'm gonna pay you, you ought to whore for me.'

With the entire restaurant laughing, Andrew Riveaux stood up and wiggled his ass around the card table. He sashayed and pouted and acted like a floozy until Lucien took pity on him and handed him the money. Alex's face had been pressed against the windowsill the whole time. He felt his gorge rise and even so, he couldn't bring himself to look away.

Alex's eyes snapped open. He stood up and drew wide the curtains, turned on every single light in the little projection room.

Then he picked up the portable phone and dialed directory assistance in Maine. He put through a call to Benjamin Barrett.

'Hello?'

Alex swallowed. 'Mr Barrett?'

'Ayuh?'

'My name is Alex Rivers. Cassie's husband.' There was a long, indrawn breath, and then silence, which Alex decided to use to his advantage. 'I've heard what you've been saying, and I wanted to, well, apologize for using you as an excuse a few months ago.'

'You don't know where my daughter is, do you?'

Brief anger welled up in Alex at this paternalistic display, since in the three years he'd been married to Cassie the man had never visited, never invited them to Maine, never even called to say hello. 'No,' he said, keeping his voice level. 'But I'm trying.' He rubbed his hand down his face. 'You don't know how hard I'm trying.'

'What I don't understand,' Cassie said, staring at the gossip column Will had brought her, 'is why my father would lie and admit he's seen me. I mean, it makes perfect sense for Alex to do it since people are going to ask, but my father has nothing to lose.'

'Except you,' Will pointed out. 'You don't know how ugly that whole thing got; what people were accusing Alex of. Collusion. Murder. Even you – one magazine said you had a European prince as a lover, and you'd run off with him to the jungles of Africa or something.'

Cassie laughed, rubbing her hand over her growing stomach. 'Oh, right.'

Will didn't tell her what he wanted to, which was that she was beautiful, even bloated out of shape with Alex Rivers's child. 'It occurred to me that maybe Alex paid off your father,' he said.

Cassie immediately shook her head. 'He wouldn't do that.' Her face brightened. 'He probably thought I'd hear what the papers were saying about me, and he wouldn't want me to be hurt. He'd tell my father that, and my father would retract whatever he said for my sake.' She beamed at Will. 'You see?'

He didn't see, but he still could not make Cassie understand that. 'The funny thing is that out of all the stories flying around Hollywood about you two, no one's come up with the truth.'

Cassie began to dig a pebble out of the ground. 'That's because no one wants to believe it,' she said.

They were sitting outside the frame of a sweat lodge, inside which a Sioux wedding was taking place. Will had been back for a week now, having broken his lease in LA. He told Cassie he wasn't planning on staying in Pine Ridge, but he wouldn't go back to LA, either. He figured he'd wait until the baby was born, and then when Cassie left, he'd go too.

He only sometimes let himself think that Cassie would come with him.

He'd returned in time to see his old betrayed friend Horace get married. He had long ago made his peace, but it surprised him to find out that Horace had never left the reservation. In fact the woman he was marrying was a fullblood Sioux.

Horace had met Cassie in town at the feed and grain, which he now managed. She had been buying food for Wheezer, and she needed him to carry it out to the truck, where Wheezer was jumping around in the flatbed. 'I know that dog,' Horace had said, and that's how they'd figured out they both knew Will.

Horace and Glenda were sitting inside the sweat lodge with Joseph Stands in Sun, the medicine man. No one else but the best man was around – the guests would come later for the civil ceremony – but Horace had specifically invited Cassie and Will. Will had been asked to keep the hot coals going on the vision hill so the stones would be ready when Joseph passed them inside the canvas flap.

'I think they're coming out,' Cassie whispered. She was trying not to admit it to herself, but she was entranced. This was the closest she'd come to a Lakota ritual. The physical anthropologist in her scorned her interest; the cultural anthropologist she'd buried deep inside her whispered that she should take notes; but the woman in her had only seen two people very much in love enter the sweat lodge to seal their vows.

Will had passed the last four stones to Joseph twenty minutes ago; they had watched the steam hiss out the edges of the seamed canvas. The flap opened, and Joseph stood up, old and bent and utterly naked. He smiled at Will and walked down the path that led to a little stream.

Glenda was next, and then Horace. Neither of them seemed to care that they were wearing nothing except necklaces strung of bright ribbons, each signifying a different issue in marriage – their relationship to each other, to God, to the planet, to children, to society. 'Hey,' Will called, grinning. 'Aren't you going to kiss the bride?'

But Horace just smacked Glenda on the bottom and raced her to the stream. Their ribbons flashed like rainbows over the water.

Beside Will, Cassie sniffled. He turned her chin so that she was facing him. 'You're *crying*?' he said.

Cassie shrugged. 'I can't help it. I cry at everything these days.' She stared into the open flap of the sweat lodge, still pouring steam. 'That's the way a wedding ceremony ought to be done,' she said. 'It's for you and him and nobody else. And there's nothing you can hide.' She struggled to her knees, then rolled to her feet, pressing her hand to the small of her back. 'I would have liked to get married like that,' she said softly.

In the distance, Glenda laughed, her voice wrapped delicately around her new husband's. Will stood up next to Cassie and stared where she stared, trying to see what she was seeing. 'Okay,' he said lightly, 'when?'

Cassie turned to him and smiled. 'Oh, I don't know. Next Tuesday. And then we'll wire the papers so they *really* have some dirt on me.'

Will didn't say anything, not even when Cassie slipped her

hand into his and began to pull him down to the bank of the stream. '*Taŋyaŋ yahí yélo*,' she said haltingly. *I'm glad you came.*

And although he couldn't force the words past his lips, he knew he was too.

To the day, it had been four full months since Cassie had disappeared, three months and six days since she had called. Alex sat on the veranda outside the bedroom, nursing another drink, trying not to feel sorry for himself.

He had a routine by now, one that involved running through a list of memories he had of Cassie so that she'd become almost real: Cassie bent over a moldering bone in the single light of her laboratory; Cassie making fun of a producer's Elvis swagger, or of an actress's habit of cracking her anorexic knuckles; Cassie's hair spilled over her shoulders as his mouth traced a path down her stomach; and yes, the one he forced himself to remember – Cassie curled into herself at his feet, bleeding and beaten and still reaching out to soothe *him*.

He'd made himself a vow. He'd do anything to get her back. He'd go see a shrink. He'd join a therapy group. Hell, he'd even do an exclusive baring his soul to *Entertainment Tonight*. His reputation couldn't become much more shredded than it already had, and any backlash he'd suffer from coming clean still wouldn't compare to the pain Cassie had taken over the years. He told himself this every time he lifted his drink to his lips, but of course, it was an empty toast. The person who most needed to hear it was still gone.

There was a knock at the bedroom door, and Alex growled. He wasn't in the mood for any of the staff. They asked him things he didn't give a flying fuck about anymore, like what he wanted for dinner and whether his appointment with Mr Silver was still standing. 'Get away,' he yelled. 'I'm working.'

'Like hell you are,' came a woman's voice, and then a heavy high-heeled footstep. Alex leaned his head against the back of the wicker chair and closed his eyes, wishing he hadn't recognized the voice. 'In fact, I probably get more work than you do these days.'

Ophelia stepped in front of him, smart in a tailored beige linen suit and a wide hat that was more suited to Ascot than LA. She bent down and pulled the glass out of Alex's hand, ran her fingers over the light growth of beard on his chin. 'You look terrible, Alex,' she said, 'although I imagine these days you don't have many visitors.'

'Ophelia,' Alex sighed, 'what the hell do you want from me?'

Ophelia sank down in front of Alex so that they were exactly at eye level. They stared at each other, neither willing to break away. 'Let's just say it's in our best interests for me to come to bury the hatchet,' she said. 'It's been four months and Cassie still hasn't gotten in touch with me or with you—'

Before he could remember to act, Alex turned his face away.

'Holy shit,' Ophelia said, her mouth dropping open. 'You've heard from her.'

Alex shook his head and began to cover his mistake with a run of words.

'Alex,' Ophelia interrupted, 'give me a break.' She stood up and slapped a pair of white gloves against her thigh. 'I came over here to join forces, but you've already found Cassie.' She peered at him. 'So why aren't you with her?'

'She wouldn't tell me where she was,' Alex admitted. 'Just that she was all right. And that she'll call when she wants to come home.'

'And you've been trying to track her since then?' She cocked her head. 'Of course you have. If you weren't preoccupied with Cassie, you might have actually *noticed* that your entire career is shot to hell.' She laughed; a bright, clarinet sound. 'She really called you. Well. Maybe I wasn't giving credit where credit was due. I may not like you very much, but Cassie seems to. *Still*. So I'm willing to take it on faith that you honestly care about her too.'

Alex lowered his eyes. 'Jesus Christ,' he muttered. 'Make your point.'

Ophelia knelt beside Alex and plucked the glass from his hand. 'My point is this,' she said coolly. 'You don't deserve Cassie, but apparently she hasn't run away for good. And Cassie most certainly doesn't deserve to see you like this when she walks back through the front door.' She emptied the highball onto the wide wooden planks of the veranda and pulled Alex up, dragging him into the bedroom to the mirror that hung over his dresser. She stood behind him while he glanced at his bloodshot eyes and sallow skin, while he breathed in the sour smells of bourbon and self-pity that perfumed his clothes. 'Alex,' Ophelia said, clasping his shoulders and forcing him to stand taller, 'this is your lucky day.'

Will sat in the dark corner of Joseph Stands in Sun's lodge, wondering where an eighty-seven-year-old medicine man could be this late at night. He had been here for over an hour; he wasn't even quite sure why, but he wanted to talk to the old man and he knew it had to be soon.

There were beautiful beaded artifacts hung on the walls, and a long stretch of deerskin with a mural about the slaughter of some Chippewa by a Sioux hunting party. There were bundles of curled dry tobacco and sage tied to the hinges of the door. A star quilt, one Joseph used for healing ceremonies, was draped over an Adirondack rocking chair.

That's where Will was sitting now, holding the Big Twisted Flute that Joseph had carved sometime before Will was even born. It was a knotted tube of cedar, long and thick, painted with the image of a horse. It had the ability to give a young man power over a young woman, and Will remembered Joseph telling him the story of how he had seduced his own wife. 'I dreamed of the music,' Joseph had said, 'that came from her soul. And when she heard it she left her parents' lodge and followed the melody until she realized she was only following me.'

Will ran his fingers over the air holes of the flute, the mouth-piece. He touched it to his lips and blew once, making a sound like an unmilked cow. Then he rocked back and forth, tapping the flute against his wrist, watching the moon slide through the cracks in Joseph's front door.

He recalled a dream that began with thunder. He was in the middle of a storm, the rain lashing his bare shoulders and his back, and he was screaming for the doe to move. He knew that the lightning was coming, that it was going to hit the spot where she stood, but she was perfectly still, as if she didn't even know it was raining. She was the most stunning creature Will had ever seen, with a high curved back and chains of dandelions around her stepped ankles. A road opened up before him; he saw that he could walk to where the doe stood, or move off to the right where there was no rain at all. It was so easy to just turn and leave, and he didn't want to be flooded by the rain.

He started toward the doe. He shouted, pushing her with his fists, and finally she bolted down the other path into the sun. Will tried to follow, but at that moment the lightning that he had known was coming split down his back, searing him with fire and breaking his bones. He fell to the ground, amazed that there could be this much pain in the world, and he knew that he had saved her.

It stopped raining, and he lifted his head – the only part of him he could still move – to find the doe standing over him, nuzzling the palm of his hand. Then the doe was gone and Cassie was there, touching him, healing; and safe, because of him.

Will looked up when the door swung open. Joseph Stands in Sun pulled off his jacket and sat down on the edge of a picnic bench. He waited for Will to say something.

Will shook his head clear. It would mean coming back to Pine Ridge – not just physically, but in his *ton*, his soul. Then again, he realized, he had fit in no better in California than he had among the Sioux; maybe it was his fate to shuttle between the two worlds for the rest of his life, until he found some hybrid oasis like the home his parents had created.

He handed Joseph his Big Twisted Flute. There was only one strain of music that Cassie would hear, because she herself had played it a thousand times. Eyes glowing, Will leaned toward the medicine man, and asked how he could take away her pain.

Chapter Twenty-Three

Marjorie Two Fists looked up from the pair of child-size moccasins she was beading and watched Cassie make another mistake. '*Hiyá*,' she said, pointing. 'If you don't concentrate, you'll have to throw the whole thing out.'

Cassie pushed her needle through the soft leather, knowing she was inept at something these old women could do skillfully, despite their failing eyesight and arthritis. 'I'm sorry,' she murmured.

Rosalynn White Star glanced over her bifocals. 'She's always sorry,' she said.

At that, Dorothea snapped her head up. 'Better sorry than stupid,' she said pointedly to Rosalynn. 'She's got other things to think about.'

Cassie heard Dorothea's words, but she didn't pay them much attention. It was the end of the Cherry Ripening Moon, the month she called July, and her baby was due in a matter of weeks. Her body seemed too heavy to carry, although this was nothing compared to the weight of her mind. With every kick and tumble of the stranger inside her, Cassie was reminded of Alex, of what he still did not know.

She still missed him. In her dreams, she imagined Alex forgiving her, pulling her close to his side. She saw his face in the deposit line at the bank in Rapid City; in a play of light over the Black Hills; reflected in a rain puddle. She tried to think of the things he would say when she showed him his son or daughter, but that meant seeing herself back in Los Angeles, away from these rolling plains, and this Cassie could not picture at all.

It had become more comfortable than home. She couldn't deny that she still loved Alex, always would, but neither could she forget that the five months she'd spent in Pine Ridge, she had been free. She hadn't spent her afternoons guessing Alex's moods and acting accordingly. She hadn't awakened in the middle of the night, terrified she had again done something wrong. She hadn't been beaten, bruised, punched.

Once, when she was in Pine Ridge town, she'd seen an adolescent boy kick a stray dog that had run off with a pack of cigarettes from his back pocket. The dog was old and half blind, probably had mange, but Cassie had run up and thrown herself between the boy and the mongrel. Some people on the street had pointed, laughing at the pregnant lady bent over a mutt, her belly grazing the earth, her voice screaming at the boy who'd done the damage. 'Witkowan,' they had called her. *Crazy woman*.

But for Cassie it had been instinct. She had re-created the reservation as a sort of neutral ground, a place where safety was guaranteed. She wasn't willing to let her image be threatened.

These days Will was never around – Cassie felt she saw him even less now that he'd moved back temporarily to Pine Ridge. He spent a great deal of time with Joseph Stands in Sun, and he wouldn't tell Cassie anything, except that he was finally learning the ways of the People.

Cyrus and Dorothea and everyone else were busy getting ready for the *wacipi*, the big powwow held at the start of August. With some of the other elders, Cyrus went out looking for the forked cottonwood tree that would be used for a pole during the Sun Dance. Dorothea spent all her free time canning blackberry preserves and gentian root tonics, which she planned to trade at the festivities for the intricate shawls and rough woven rugs that others had crafted. When she had finished packing a large carton with her wares, she told Cassie she was going to Marjorie Two

Fists's lodge to do quilling and beading, and asked Cassie to come to take her mind off her troubles.

So Cassie sat for the third afternoon in a row with a group of old women, feeling less and less adequate as she ruined the bead-work on bracelets and jackets and moccasins. Dorothea laid aside the pouch she'd been embroidering and picked up the edge of Rosalynn's quilt. 'This will make a good trade,' she said. 'That's the best part of the weekend.'

'Oh, I don't know,' Marjorie said. 'Even if I'm too old to dance, I like seeing the young ones in their costumes. I like listening to the drums. So loud.'

Dorothea laughed. 'Maybe if Cassie stands close enough to the music the baby will come early.'

It was the last thing Cassie wanted to happen. She didn't know anything about infants; she hadn't considered the actual facts about this one, like diapering and burping and nursing. She was thinking of the baby more as the means to an end, but there was something about that end – the finality of it – that she didn't really want to see.

The door swung open, and there, framed by the light summer rain, was Will. Without realizing what she was doing, Cassie stood up, letting the moccasin she'd been working on fall to the floor so that beads scattered and rolled into the cracks of the smooth pine boards. 'Oh,' she gasped, bending down as best she could to collect what had fallen.

'I know, I know,' Marjorie murmured. 'You're *sorry*.'

'Afternoon, ladies,' Will said, grinning. 'How's it coming?'

Dorothea shrugged. 'It'll be done when it's done,' she said.

Will smiled; that fairly summed up his philosophy of life. He looked at Cassie. 'I thought you might want to take a walk or something.'

Marjorie stood up and took the beads from Cassie's palm. 'That's a great idea,' she said. 'Take her before she destroys anything else.'

Dorothea looked from her grandson to Cassie and then back

again. 'She's in a mood,' Dorothea warned. 'Maybe *you* can snap her out of it.'

That was exactly what Will had planned to do. He imagined Cassie should be in high spirits these days, knowing that soon she'd be a good thirty pounds lighter, but she seemed to slip further and further away by the minute. Almost as if, Will admitted, she was already making the break.

He had one chance, and it was coming. The day of the big powwow, he would make her understand. But in the meantime, it couldn't hurt to try to make her smile. 'What do you say?' he pressed.

Cassie peered over his shoulder at the open doorway. 'It's raining,' she said.

She shifted her weight to her other foot. She had wanted to see Will for days now; she was restless; she should be jumping at the chance to leave this dreary little tea party – what was her problem? 'We'll get wet,' she said. 'We can't go for a walk.'

Will's eyes began to shine. 'Okay,' he said. 'We'll do something else.' Suddenly he was standing in the circle of women, trying awkwardly to fit his arms around Cassie's bulk. He started to hum and whirled Cassie around in an offbeat two-step, crushing moccasins and knitting bags under the heels of his cowboy boots. Rosalynn, delighted, began to sing in a high sweet soprano.

Cassie's face turned bright red. With no sense of balance, she found herself clinging to Will's shoulders for support. She barely saw Marjorie stand up, grinning, to move her chair out of the way as Will steered them toward the open door.

Dorothea, Marjorie, and Rosalynn stood eagerly pressed against the streaked windows, watching the couple and clapping, remembering days long ago when they had whispered beneath a blanket with a lover; or had shaken the package of their future, trying to see inside; had maybe even danced in the rain. Cassie listened to the rich, woven sound of the old women's laughter, a different kind of music entirely, which seemed as fresh as the giggles of young, courted girls.

She stared into Will's eyes as they crossed the threshold into the storm. Splashing through puddles, she could feel herself stepping on his feet, feel the baby in her rolling slow, feel the rain cool against her cheeks. It washed everything away. For a lovely, sodden moment, Cassie truly believed that it could stay like this.

Halfway between Marjorie Two Fists's house and her own home, Dorothea sat down to think about the ways that history repeated itself. It wasn't that she was tired, or that the bag that contained her beadwork had suddenly grown too heavy. It was that all of a sudden the spirit of Anne, her late daughter-in-law, had been walking beside her, and the frost of her breath on Dorothea's neck made it impossible to go any farther.

Zachary, Dorothea's only child, had fallen in love with the white schoolteacher thirty-six years earlier, and although she had never wanted to hurt her own son, Dorothea had done everything in her power to stop the attraction. She had left the appropriate roots and dried flowers under Zachary's mattress; she had prayed to the spirits; she had even consulted Joseph Stands in Sun. But this was meant to be. In fact, the day that Anne left Pine Ridge to distance herself from Zachary, the day that Zachary saddled a horse and rode miles to find her, Dorothea had been standing only yards away, watching the whole thing and shaking her head.

Dorothea would never have admitted it at the time, but Anne became her obsession. When it was clear that Zachary was going to marry her come hell or high water, Dorothea told him not to expect her as a wedding guest. But she made a point of watching the woman who would be her daughter much more closely. She stood outside the classroom of the school where Anne taught and familiarized herself with the lifts and valleys of her voice. She followed her into the general store and kept track of the items Anne bought: talcum powder, ginger drops, blue eyeshadow. She went to the government offices and memorized her credentials, her blood type, her Social Security number.

Three days before the wedding Anne had fallen asleep beneath a cottonwood outside Dorothea's house while waiting for Zachary. Dorothea had silently knelt beside her and touched the incredibly translucent skin of her cheek. Mesmerized, she crouched for nearly ten minutes, committing to mind the map of pale veins that crossed the white line of Anne's throat.

'What are you doing here?' Anne asked in English when she woke up.

'I might ask you the same thing,' Dorothea said, speaking Lakota.

Anne struggled to a sitting position, aware that 'Waiting for Zack' was not the answer to the question Dorothea was really asking. 'I love him just as much as you do,' Anne said quietly.

'That,' Dorothea answered, 'could be the problem.'

She stood, ready to make her way back into her house, but she was stopped by Anne's voice. 'I'd like you to come to the wedding,' Anne called out, in Lakota.

Dorothea immediately switched to English. 'I won't set foot in a white man's church,' she said.

'Still,' Anne said, almost casually, 'I'll see you there.'

Dorothea whirled around. 'And how do you know this?'

Anne smiled. 'Because nothing could keep you away.'

The day of the wedding, Cyrus had begged Dorothea to reconsider, if only for Zack's sake, but Dorothea remained in her housecoat, sitting on the worn brown couch. The minute he left, however, she dressed and walked to the nearest road, hitch-hiking her way into town. She arrived at the church, and true to her word, stayed outside, peeking through a crack in the makeshift wooden walls. The minister was offering his final blessing, after the damage had been done. Muttering to herself, Dorothea watched Zachary's dark hand gently squeeze his new wife's.

When Dorothea looked up, Anne wasn't staring, besotted, at Zack, or even paying attention to the minister. She was half turned to the back of the church, looking right through the crack in the wall at Dorothea. She winked.

Dorothea stumbled backward into the dusty street, and then she let herself laugh. It was the first of many times her daughter-in-law had exceeded her expectations. The first of many times Dorothea had admitted to herself how much she liked Anne, how much respect she had for her, and – now that she was gone – how much she missed her.

'You know that after the accident, Zack let go because of you,' Dorothea said aloud. 'He wouldn't have lived without you.' She knew it would be that way with herself and Cyrus, too – once one of them joined the spirit world, the other would die quickly so they would be together again. It had taken Dorothea years to understand, but now she was a firm believer: love was that way. You could not render it in black and white. It always came down to the strange, blended shades of gray.

Cassie sat beside Cyrus on a low folding beach chair in the shade, waiting for the beginning of the Sun Dance. The four flags at the top of the sacred pole waved in the dry wind: white, yellow, red, and black, like the four races of man. An eagle looped lazily overhead, which sent a cheer up from the observers. 'Good medicine,' Cyrus whispered to Cassie.

It was the final day of the powwow, and Cassie was entranced. She had walked with Dorothea among the heavily laden trading tables, picking out a wide hammered bracelet for herself and a brightly woven swaddling blanket for her unborn child. She had peeked into the canvas tipis set up by the families who lived farther away, amazed at the juxtaposition of eagle-feathered war bonnets and Levi's blue jeans, draped side by side on wire hangers.

Today was the last day of the Sun Dance, the most sacred dance of the festivities, the only one that required months of preparation and training on the part of the participants. Cyrus had not told her much about it, just that it was a ceremony in praise of the sun, a ritual for growth and for renewal. For the past three days, Will had been one of the dancers, much to

Cassie's surprise and delight. She liked seeing him dressed like the others, stamping and whirling around the central pole the way his ancestors had been doing for years. 'I don't know what made you do it,' she had told him after the first day of dancing, 'but you're a wonderful Indian when you try.' And Will had grinned at her, had almost looked proud to see himself through her eyes.

Cassie sat forward as the men filed out of the sacred lodge, led by Joseph Stands in Sun. Like him, they were all wearing long red kilts, their chests striped with blue paint. They wore wreaths on their heads woven of sage, and they carried eagle-bone whistles. Cassie tried to catch Will's eye as he moved past her, to wish him luck or to say break a leg, but he kept his face turned up to the sky.

Joseph Stands in Sun walked up to Will, waiting beneath the forked cottonwood pole. He murmured something in Lakota, and then lifted a bright silver skewer. For a moment he held it up, and Cassie watched the sun reflect off its polished, speared tip. Joseph leaned close to Will, whose back stiffened. It was not until Joseph brandished a second skewer that Cassie realized that the medicine man had pierced the skin of Will's chest, that blood was running down his stomach.

Like the other dancers', Will's two skewers were tied to rawhide thongs that dangled down from the top of the sacred pole. With Joseph leading them, the men began to dance, much as they had the other three days. The drums beat, but no louder than Cassie's pulse. She gripped the armrests of her chair, her face drawn and white.

'You knew,' she whispered to Cyrus, although she did not take her eyes from Will. 'You knew and didn't tell me.'

Will whirled and sang. His entire chest was slick with blood, since every time he twisted he tore the wounds. He pretended to pull away from the skewers, and Cassie stared, horrified, as his skin stretched to its limit.

Cassie grabbed Cyrus's arm. 'Please,' she begged. 'He's hurting himself. You have to do something.'

'I can't do anything,' Cyrus said. 'He has to do this himself.'

Cassie let the tears run down her face and wondered why she had ever encouraged Will to accept the Lakota side of himself. This was barbaric. She pictured him in his neat LAPD uniform, his cap tilted low on his forehead. She saw him standing near her in the emergency room the day he'd found her, his arms crossed with concern. She imagined him dancing with her in the summer rain, her baby kicking between them.

'Why *this* dance?' she whispered brokenly, thinking of the other ceremonies she had seen, ones that hadn't involved self-mutilation. She turned her head, shocked to see the milling crowd with smiles spread across their faces, enjoying the taste of someone else's agony.

'He's not suffering,' Cyrus murmured. 'Not for himself.' He pointed to the dancer beside Will. 'Louis dances the Sun Dance so that his daughter will live, even though her kidneys are dying. Arthur Peel, over to the right, has a brother still missing in action in Vietnam.' He turned to face Cassie. 'The dancers take pain upon themselves,' he said, 'so someone close to them won't have to feel it.'

As the dance drew to a close, Joseph Stands in Sun stepped from the circle. The men began to twist and pull in earnest, straining to free themselves. Cassie stood up, helpless, and felt Dorothea's hand on her calf. 'Don't,' Dorothea said.

Suffering so someone else didn't have to suffer. Sacrificing your body for someone else's well-being. Cassie saw the skewer split another inch of Will's skin, watched the blood run down his chest.

He was looking at her. Cassie dragged her eyes to meet Will's, locked her gaze with his. His image flickered, and she pictured her own body, bleeding and broken at Alex's feet, a venting ground for anger that had no connection to her. Will was only doing for Cassie what she had spent years doing for Alex.

When the skin of Will's chest ripped ragged from the skewers, Cassie cried out. She ran forward and knelt beside him, pressing the wounds on his chest with sage from his wreath and then with the hem of her shirt. His eyes were closed, and his breathing was fast and shallow. 'It still hurts,' she whispered. 'Even when you're doing it for someone else, that doesn't stop your ribs from getting cracked, or your wrist from swelling, or your cuts from bleeding.'

Will opened his eyes. He reached up his hand to wipe the tears from Cassie's cheeks. 'You did this for me,' Cassie said. 'So it would hurt less when I did it for *him*.' Will nodded.

Through her tears, Cassie laughed. 'If I didn't know you better, Will Flying Horse, I'd say you're acting like some Big Indian.'

Will grinned at her weakly. 'Go figure,' he said.

Cassie brushed his hair away from his face. She rubbed her fingers lightly over the gaping edges of Will's wounds. Even Alex, who had offered her the world, had never given her so much.

Two weeks after the Sun Dance, Cassie went into labor. She would have had plenty of time to make the drive into the clinic in town, but she wanted to have the baby somewhere familiar. And so, ten hours later, propped up in the bed where Cyrus, Zachary, and Will had all been born, she was screaming at the top of her lungs.

Dorothea stood at the foot of the bed, measuring Cassie's progress. Will was next to Cassie, suffering her death grip on his hand. 'Less than an hour now,' Dorothea said proudly. 'Baby's crowned.'

'I'm going to go,' Will said, trying to tug free, but Cassie wouldn't let him leave. He had been uncomfortable in the first place, but Cassie had begged. He might still have found the fortitude to refuse if Cassie hadn't been seized by a contraction just then that had nearly doubled her over in his arms.

'Please,' Cassie panted. 'Don't leave me to do this all by myself.' She grabbed handfuls of Will's shirt.

But then she couldn't talk because her belly was knotted up

and this unbelievable pressure was forcing itself down through her lower half. Ridiculous, wasn't it, that she'd run away to save this baby's life, only to die in the end? She took a deep breath and fell back against the pillows again. *I understand you*, she silently told the baby. *I know how hard it is to go from one world into another*.

'Here it comes,' said Dorothea. Cassie could feel the cool pressure of Dorothea's fingertips breaking the seal of flesh around her baby's head. She struggled up, dug her fingernails into Will's hand, and bore down.

Ten minutes later, Cassie felt something long and wet slip between her chafed thighs. Dorothea held up a squalling, stunning bundle. '*Hokšíla luhá!* A boy!' she crowed. 'Big and healthy, even if he is a little pale for my tastes.'

Cassie laughed, reaching out her hands, first noticing the tears in the corners of her own eyes. She jiggled the baby in her arms, trying to get comfortable, not really knowing exactly how that should feel. The baby opened up his mouth and howled.

'It even sounds like you,' Will murmured, and Cassie remembered he was there. His hand stroked the back of her head, lightly, as if he were awestruck and not sure he should be allowed the contact.

'How do you feel?' Will asked.

Cassie glanced up at him, struggling for the right word. 'Full.'

'Well, you look a lot more empty.'

Cassie shook her head. How could she explain it? After all the longing she'd done for Alex, she wasn't alone anymore. This tiny wriggling thing completed her too, in a different sort of way.

A boy. A son. Alex's child. Cassie rummaged through the epithets, trying to find the one that best fit the baby in her arms. He had turned his face toward her breast, as if he already knew what he wanted out of this world.

'You're just like your father,' she whispered, but even as she said the words she realized they weren't true. The face looking up at her was a tiny replica of her own, except for the eyes, which were certainly Alex's. Clear and pale, the silver of a fresh-minted coin.

There was nothing about Alex in the mouth, in the shape of the fingers and feet, in the length of the torso. It was almost as if the lack of contact had diminished Alex's mark on his own infant.

The baby burrowed closer to Cassie, demanding her heat. And she thought about how she was his only means of support – for food and shelter and warmth right now, and later, for love. He would come to her when he drew his first crayon picture, coloring half the kitchen table as well. He'd hold out a scraped elbow and believe a kiss could quit the sting. He'd open his eyes every morning and know, with that sunny childhood certainty, that Cassie would be there.

He needed her, and that, Cassie realized, was the way in which he most resembled Alex.

But this time, being needed wasn't going to be synonymous with being hurt. This was her second lease on life. She and this baby were going to grow up together.

Will touched the baby's hand and watched his fingers close like a summer rose. 'What are you going to call him?'

The answer came to Cassie so quickly she realized that she had simply been carrying it all along. She thought of the very first time she had been loved by someone who wanted nothing in return. Someone who had given her enough hope to believe, years later, that Alex still might change, that there might be someone like Will, that a child might consider her his very world. 'Connor,' she said. 'His name's Connor.'

Within two weeks Cassie was light on her feet, joyous. After carrying around so much extra weight, she could not get used to the spring in her step. But she also knew that part of it came from a decision made only hours after she had given birth to

Connor. She wasn't planning on leaving, not immediately. Maybe three months, maybe six, maybe longer. She told herself she wanted Connor to be strong before making the trip, and none of the Flying Horses challenged her. In fact, Cyrus had given her a traditional cradleboard as a baby gift, and when he passed it across his own bed, he had simply looked her in the eye. 'It will be nice,' he said, 'to take him to next year's powwow.'

She was going to contact Alex as she'd promised; she owed it to him, but she had put it off for a week, and then Will's truck had broken down and she didn't have a way to get into Rapid City. So, blissfully free from her obligations, she sat on the porch with Dorothea, shelling peas for dinner.

Connor was in his cradleboard, swaddled tight, wide awake. Most of the day he slept, so Cassie was surprised – she'd just finished feeding him and he was still alert, his light eyes surveying the landscape.

'Giving up your nap?' she asked. She popped a pea into her mouth.

'You,' Dorothea scolded. 'We won't have enough for tonight.'

Cassie put her bowl to the side and stretched out, lying back against the rough pine boards and staring at the sun. She could not look at it now without thinking of Will, of the puckered pink scars that still frowned across his chest.

Connor started to cry, but before Cassie could even sit up, Dorothea had clapped her hand over the baby's mouth. Startled, Connor widened his eyes and fell quiet.

Dorothea took her hand away and looked up to see Cassie staring at her, furious. 'What the hell do you think you were doing?' Cassie demanded.

It felt strange to be so self-righteous on someone else's behalf, especially when motherhood was such a new thing, like a pretty party dress you could take out of your closet and try on but felt nervous about wearing around all day. 'He was crying,' Dorothea said, as if this explained everything.

'Yes, he was,' Cassie said. 'Babies cry.'

'Not Lakota babies,' Dorothea replied. 'We teach them early.'

Cassie thought of all the archaic family values she'd run across in cultural anthropology, including the Victorian tenet that children should be seen and not heard. She shook her head.

Dorothea looked surprised herself. 'I know it used to be done in the days of the buffalo because if one baby scared a herd away, the whole tribe would go hungry. I don't know why we bother anymore.'

'Well, I'd rather you didn't,' Cassie said stiffly. But she was thinking of all the times she had lain beside Alex in the dark, stifling tears of pain. She remembered hearing the sound of his hand striking her, and her intake of breath, but never hearing a cry. She considered the lesson she'd learned in her marriage: that if you were quiet and blended into the background, you were less likely to make waves.

She glanced at Connor, peaceful, willfully silent. One day, in the long run, it was a skill he might need.

The truth of that nearly broke her.

Cassie sat in the driver's seat of Abel Soap's jeep, bent forward at the waist as if she'd been punched in the gut. She had borrowed the jeep to come to the feed and grain in town, which housed the nearest pay phone. Talking to Dorothea earlier had convinced her she could no longer put off the inevitable. She would call Alex and tell him where she'd been all this time. She would have to trust him with the truth.

The thought made her slightly dizzy. There was no proof Alex had changed during the past six months, no indication he wouldn't lash out at her – and Connor – during a rage. She had left Alex so that her baby wouldn't suffer before it was born. How could she even be considering taking Connor back now?

Her mind raced. She could leave Connor with Dorothea and Cyrus and go back to Alex herself, for a little while, just until she saw that things had changed. If she did it soon, in the first few months, Connor might never know the difference. But she couldn't leave Connor. She'd only too recently discovered him to be able to let go.

She got out of the truck and walked into the store. Horace waved as she struck through the cluttered aisles toward the pay phone. For several moments she held the receiver in her hand, as if it had the same power and irrevocable impact as a loaded gun.

When Alex's voice came over the line, her milk let down. Cassie watched the dark patches spread on her T-shirt and hung up.

A few minutes later, she tried again. 'Hello?' Alex said, irritated.

'It's me,' Cassie whispered.

She could hear the background noise – water, or maybe a stereo – being switched off. '*Cassie*. God. Did you just call?' Alex's voice sounded round, filled to a bursting point with shock and joy and relief and other touches she could not name.

'No,' Cassie lied. This time, she could not let him sense her indecision. 'You're all right?'

'Cassie,' Alex said, 'tell me where you are.' There was a silence. 'Cassie, *please*.'

She ran her fingers over the cold snake of metal that connected the receiver to the pay box. 'I need a promise from you, Alex.'

'Cassie,' Alex said, his voice low and urgent, 'come home. It won't happen again, I swear it. I'll see anyone you ask me to. I'll do anything you want.'

'That's not the promise I need right now,' Cassie said, stunned by the sacrifices he was willing to make to his pride just to have her return. 'I'm going to tell you where I am because I don't want you to worry, but I want to stay here another month. I want you to swear to me that you won't come till then.'

He was thinking of what she could possibly be doing that would require another month away: some underground activity, or a delayed visa, or a calculated goodbye to a lover. But he forced himself to listen. 'I swear,' he said, digging for a pen. 'Where are you?'

'Pine Ridge, South Dakota,' Cassie murmured. 'The Indian reservation.'

'The *what*? Cassie, how—'

'That's it, Alex. I'm going to get off now. I'll call in a month and we'll figure out how and when I'll come back. All right?'

No, she could hear him thinking. *It is not all right. I want you here, now, mine.* But he didn't say anything and she took this as a sign of hope. 'You won't break your promise?' she asked.

She could feel him smile sadly all those miles away. '*Chère*,' he said softly, 'you have my word.'

Chapter Twenty-Four

C assie pressed herself across Connor's fiery, wriggling body, pinning him to the examination table while two white nurses straightened his flailing arms to draw blood. Her head was just below Connor's mouth, and he was screaming convulsively, his chest rising and falling in exaggerated rasps. Before they began, the nurses had asked her if she wanted to leave the room. 'Some parents can't take this,' one said. But Cassie had merely stared at them, incredulous. If she fainted right on top of her baby, so be it. 'I'm all he has,' Cassie said, the best explanation she could offer.

It was killing her. She couldn't stand to see his tiny form shaking with fever; she couldn't listen to cries that – even three weeks after his birth – seemed to come from deep inside of her. Cassie watched the vials of blood flow one after another. 'You're taking too much,' she whispered to nobody. She did not say what she really was thinking: *Take mine instead.*

The clinic doctor in Pine Ridge town had sent them to the hospital in Rapid City. Too young, he had said. Bacterial something or other. Maybe pneumonia. The nurses were asking the lab to do a full blood workup. Then there would be an X ray. They would keep Connor overnight, or as long as it took to bring down his temperature.

Cyrus, who had driven her all the way to Rapid City, was waiting downstairs in the lobby, unwilling to go any farther into the hospital after having watched his son die in it. So when the lab returned the results, she sat in a thin metal bridge chair, alone with Connor, who was connected by wires and tubes to a portable IV machine. He was being given saline solution, with an antibiotic. The doctor had pronounced him dehydrated, and this Cassie knew to be true, since her breasts were aching and had long since leaked through the front of her shirt. Connor had fallen into an unconscious exhaustion a few minutes before, and Cassie found herself wishing she could do the same thing. She thought of all the times she'd offered her body to Alex rather than see him suffer, and shook her head at the fact that this one time, when she so gladly would have taken the pain to spare Connor, she was not given the chance.

The door to the tiny room flung open, and Cassie turned her head with a slow grace born of fatigue to see Will standing at the threshold, his eyes wide and dark, his chest heaving. 'My grandfather called,' he said. 'I came as soon as I could.'

He took in the image of Cassie, straight-backed, feet wrapped around the legs of the frame chair, her arms clutching Connor to her stomach. He saw the little brace on Connor's arm, the point of the needle beneath the white surgical tape where it entered the vein, the fingerprinted smudge of blood on the baby's forearm.

Cassie looked up at him. Will threw his hat onto the linoleum and knelt at her side, turning her face against his neck and sliding his arms beneath hers in an effort to buoy Connor. 'Céye šni yo,' he said. 'Don't cry. It's all right.' He smoothed her hair and felt her tears soaking his collar.

Cassie's fingers gripped and released his light chambray shirt. Will tenderly brushed a kiss over the top of her head, forcing himself not to remember his father lying pale and fading in a hospital bed a few floors above them. He held his fingers to the folds of Connor's neck, seeking the simple pulse, and tried to act the way he thought he should in a situation he knew nothing about.

*   *   *

'Do you trust me?' Will asked for the second time.

Cassie stared at him from the other side of the hospital Isolette, a domed plastic bubble that had sealed her away from her child for the past two days. In spite of the Tylenol and the pediatric ibuprofen and the sponge baths, Connor's fever was still alarmingly high. The doctor had as much as said he didn't know what to do.

Cassie nodded and watched Will's face split into a dazzling smile. He came around to her side of the Isolette and held his hands over the warm plastic dome. From that angle, his stretching fingers blocked Cassie's view of the lines and tubes that were invading her son's body. She stared up at Will as if he'd already worked magic. 'Do whatever you have to,' she said softly. 'Whatever you think will help.'

The doctor was paged to tell Cassie this wasn't a wise idea, but she simply shook her head and leaned back slightly, where Will was standing for support. She watched the interns disconnect the IV from Connor. As she held her child again in her arms, his eyes opened for the first time in forty-eight hours.

'At least take this,' the doctor urged, pressing into Cassie's free hand the tiny dropper of infant Tylenol. Cassie nodded, turned, and with Will, walked out of the hospital that had done nothing at all for her son. She very gently got into Will's pickup truck, careful not to jostle Connor. And as soon as they were on the open highway, she threw the bottle of medicine out the window.

In the middle of the night, in the Flying Horses' living room, they sponged the heat from Connor's little body. Then Cassie pushed aside her nightgown so that the baby could nurse. Will sat across from her, his fingers stroking the hot smooth skin of Connor's bowed calves.

They laid the baby down in the middle of the fold-out bed when he fell into a fitful sleep, and then they sat, cross-legged, on either side of him. Outside, a brisk wind picked up, and a truck roared into the darkness.

'Is everything ready?' Cassie asked.

Will nodded, then rubbed his hand over the back of his neck. 'My grandmother says she's taking care of it.' He started to speak, but hesitated and looked up at Cassie. 'I don't have any right to tell you what to do. I'm not his father. If it doesn't work,' he said, 'I'll never forgive myself.'

He was so intent on his thoughts that he did not notice Cassie getting off the bed, coming to stand behind him. He felt her tentatively touch the back of his head, her fingers thread through his hair. And his back stiffened involuntarily as he realized that *Cassie* was reaching out for *him*.

He did not turn to look at her. 'What are you doing?' he said, angry at the rough edges of his voice.

Almost immediately Cassie lifted her hand away, and Will swung around. She wrapped her arms around herself. 'I – I needed—' Her voice broke, and she lifted her eyes to meet Will's. 'I just wanted someone to hold me,' she said. 'Please.'

The simple fact that Cassie had asked such a favor of him nearly brought Will to his knees, but that soft-spoken 'Please' at the end of her sentence broke him. He stood up and folded her into his arms in one swift motion, pulling her against his hips.

After a few minutes Will stepped back, pushing Cassie against the edge of the bed. He let her stretch out on her side, facing the baby, and then he lay down close behind her. He pillowed her head on his arm and together they watched Connor's measured, ragged breathing. He mindlessly whispered Lakota endearments he knew Cassie could not understand, phrases he thought he had forgotten long ago. He fell asleep mouthing the words 'Waste cilake,' Sioux for 'I love you,' and did not hear the last thing Cassie said before she too drifted off. She had been looking at Connor, at the tipped curve of his nose and the tiny perfection of his fingernails, and feeling behind her the warmth of Will's body, like a safety net. 'No,' she had murmured past the constriction of her throat, 'you're *not* his father.'

Joseph Stands in Sun was lying prone on the sage-strewn floor of Cyrus and Dorothea's living room, wrapped in a star blanket, pretending to be dead. The furniture was sitting in the front yard, so there was plenty of room even outside the string-cordoned sacred square for the onlookers. They sat on the floor, their backs to the four walls. Some of the people Cassie recognized as neighbors. Others were there simply to lend support during this *yuwipi* ceremony, the finding out and curing of ills.

Beside her, Will squeezed her hand. Connor was lying in his cradle-board, no better than he had been when he left the Rapid City hospital. It had been four days now, four days of a spiraling fever and frightening convulsions and endless cries. When Will had driven up to his grandparents' house late last evening, Dorothea was waiting on the porch. She came down to the truck and held out her hands for Connor so that Cassie could step down easily. Clucking her tongue, she shook her head. 'No wonder,' she'd said knowingly. 'This isn't the kind of sickness white medicine can fix.'

Joseph's grandson, who sometimes acted as his singer, was chanting the *yuwipi* songs and beating the ceremonial drum. He stood in front of the makeshift altar, on which sat Joseph's buffalo skull, a red and a black staff, an eagle feather, and a deer tail. There was no light in the room, unless one counted the strips of moon that had made their way inside.

Cassie was dizzy, and she didn't know if it was from simple exhaustion or the overwhelming scent of the sage, which carpeted the floor and was worn in the hair of every onlooker. Will, who had done his best to explain the ceremony to Cassie before it began, had said that sage was the sacred plant of the spirits. Any messages they brought to Joseph, the representative of the 'dead', would be carried along the sage.

In the shifting currents of the night, shadows and sounds filled the living room. The noises were high and strained, inhuman, urgent. 'The spirits are here,' someone said, a voice Cassie had never heard before but that could have been entirely familiar, could even have come from herself. She felt her shoulders pushed out of place by the ringing cry of an eagle, and although she squinted her eyes to see better, she could not tell whose hand had flung a string of stars across the ceiling. She kept one arm linked with Will's, the other wrapped around the frame of Connor's cradleboard, as if she feared that something might steal him away. But she could hear his deep belly giggle, and she turned to see his clear, shining face being brushed by the softest of wings.

When the ceremony was over, the lights were turned on and Joseph Stands in Sun was unwrapped from his star quilt. He shook the sage from the handworked pattern, taking his time to fold the quilt and rearrange the collection on the altar before he came toward Cassie. But instead of speaking to her, he walked to Connor's cradleboard and knelt in front of it. He pressed his hand against the baby's forehead, then reached for Cassie's wrist and urged her to do the same.

Connor was flushed and sweating, but making soft, happy sounds that buffeted through her heart. His fever had broken. Amazed, Cassie turned her face up to Joseph's.

'Úyelo. His father is coming,' Joseph said simply. 'Like you, his body was burning with a fear of the unknown.'

Behind the frayed curtain that separated their bedroom from the rest of the house, Cyrus and Dorothea were still wide awake. They lay on their backs staring at the ceiling, their bony fingers knotted together between them.

'What are you thinking?' Dorothea whispered, careful to keep her voice down so as not to disturb Cassie and Connor and Will, who slept in the living room. She ran her hand up Cyrus's forearm, feeling not the wrinkled skin and sinews of an old man but the thick muscle she remembered from her youth.

'I'm thinking of the first time I touched you,' Cyrus said.

Dorothea flushed and swatted blindly at him, but she was smiling. 'You crazy old fool,' she said.

'I used to stay up at night thinking of ways to get rid of your grandmother,' Cyrus said. 'She went everywhere you went.'

'Well,' Dorothea mused, 'that *did* keep you away.'

Suddenly Cyrus laughed. Dorothea rolled toward him, her hair spreading across his chest, and clapped her hand over his mouth. 'You want to wake them?' she hissed, but Cyrus was still laughing.

'It's just that I remember what the old woman said when I asked her advice on how to get you to pay attention to me.' He propped himself up on one elbow. 'She told me that *her* husband had killed a buffalo in her honor.'

'There weren't any more buffalo in the thirties,' Dorothea whispered, grinning.

Cyrus smiled. 'Your grandmother told me that was my problem, not *hers*.' They both laughed. 'At least she had the good sense to fall asleep long enough for me to kiss you,' Cyrus said. He leaned over Dorothea, smoothing her long white hair back from her forehead, much as he had done the very first time. He leaned forward and touched his lips to hers.

'She wasn't asleep,' Dorothea murmured against his mouth. 'She told me so the next day. She said she was getting tired of you hanging around all the time, so she figured she'd better hurry things along.'

Cyrus's eyes widened. 'I thought she hated me,' he said.

Dorothea laughed. 'That too.'

They both settled down on their backs again, staring up at the ceiling and listening to the symphony of the owls outside. Dorothea's hand crept between them blindly to find Cyrus's, and she threaded her fingers through his. She thought of Cassie lying in the fold-out bed, time ticking before her like a life sentence as she awaited the arrival of her husband. She considered how different the white girl's life might have been if she'd been born a hundred years earlier, like Dorothea's grandmother; if this Alex had courted her under the cover of a buffalo hide blanket; if abuse had been something never even considered, because it went against the grain of the tribe.

Cyrus squeezed her hand just as surely as he'd been reading Dorothea's mind. 'It was easier back then,' he said flatly.

Dorothea rolled toward her husband, burying her face against the hard bones of his shoulder so that he wouldn't know how close she'd come to crying. 'It was,' she whispered.

Dorothea did not say why she stayed home from the cafeteria the next day, but Cassie knew, simply by the way she sat in the rocking chair beside hers on the porch and waited, unmoving, in a silent show of support.

She also knew that the time had come, when just after noon, Dorothea softly whispered, '*Koképe šni yo*' – *Don't be afraid* – and stood up. The wind whipped her skirt around her ankles as she came to stand beside Cassie's chair, but by the time the unfamiliar black Bronco pulled to a stop in the Flying Horses' front yard, she had gone inside.

Cassie knew no one would come out and bother her while she was speaking to Alex. Not Cyrus and Dorothea, who believed this was her business alone, and not Will, who was sitting with Connor. And for right now, anyway, that was the way Cassie wanted it. Her palms were damp and she wiped them on the front of her shift as she stood up and stepped toward the porch railing, trying to hold fast to her fury.

Alex shut off the motor of the Bronco and tugged off his sunglasses. It was Cassie. It was really Cassie. After months of agony, he was ten feet away from his wife.

He stepped out of the car and stared up at her. She seemed to be smaller than he'd remembered. The imagination that had

served him so well as a director began to function double-time:
he pictured the wind blowing her hair around her face, her lips
breaking into a delighted smile, her feet flying over the rough
boards of the steps. He envisioned her soft skin pressed against
the lines of his body; he saw himself carrying her into whoever's
hut this was and stretching her out on the whitest of sheets and
burying himself inside her.

'Alex,' Cassie said. Having been warned by Joseph Stands in
Sun of Alex's preemptive arrival, she'd planned all night to take
him to task. *You lied*, she would accuse. *You gave me your word.*
But it had been so long that she found her anger fading and she
stared at him the way she used to when she first saw the dailies
of his films – awestruck and overwhelmed by his beauty, his very
size.

He stopped in front of the porch, underneath the railing where
she stood, like he was playing Romeo to her Juliet. Then he
reached up, gazing at her hand as if he'd never seen anything
like it, and touched his fingertips to hers.

It was the physical contact, the stepping of the movie idol off
the screen, that jolted Cassie. She jumped back as if she'd received
a shock, and let the tears run down her cheeks. She thought of
Alex wearing his dinner jacket and serving her wine on a Tanzanian
set. She imagined him draping a pillowcase on his head and doing
Lady Macbeth while standing on a coffee table. She considered
Connor, living proof that the sweet ache of coming together could
create something perfect. And she did not remember why she
was supposed to be angry; or why, exactly, she'd left.

Then Alex was standing beside her, wrapping her in his
embrace. 'Don't cry,' he begged. 'Please, Cassie, don't cry.'

'I can't help it,' Cassie said, but she was already wiping at the
tears, ready to do anything she had to to keep that raw, bleak
note out of his voice.

He was running his fingers over her face, remembering the
features. Then he smiled and sat down on the top step of the

porch, pulling her to sit beside him. He wrapped his hand around the nape of her neck and kissed her so gently she felt her resistance shatter like glass. His hands came to rest at familiar spots on the sides of her breasts; the pattern of his breath was an old, slow song. Cassie rested her forehead against his, tamping down the stirring fear which she had begun to associate even with Alex's softest touch, assuring herself that things would be different now.

'I had two more weeks,' she murmured.

Alex squeezed her waist. 'It was harder knowing where you were and not being able to go than not knowing at all.' He kissed her again. 'I thought if I came in person I might be able to argue my case.'

'What if I still decide to stay?' Cassie said.

Alex glanced out at the plain. 'Then I'll develop a taste for South Dakota.'

Cassie shook her head. There was no point arguing over something that had already been done; something she knew, deep down, she had wanted. Besides, she was hardly the person to complain about a breach of trust, when Connor was just on the other side of the door.

'So,' Alex said, smiling. 'What do we do now?'

Cassie smiled back, relieved, more than willing to put off the time for explanations. 'I don't know. You're the one who reads all the good scripts. What happens in the movies?'

Alex scuffed his boot against the step and looked down, but he didn't stop rubbing his thumb over the back of her hand, as if to remind himself that Cassie was indeed flesh and blood. 'Usually the hero and the heroine ride off into the sunset.'

Cassie bit her lower lip, as if she were considering this. 'Then we still have a good seven hours to sit here on the porch,' she said.

Alex's eyes grew dark, lazy. 'We could go *inside*,' he suggested.

Cassie knew exactly what he was thinking, and laughed out loud at the thought of Alex walking into the living room, expecting to make love, only to find Cyrus, Dorothea, Will, and Connor staring him down. 'I don't think you want to do that,' she said. 'It's a little crowded.'

Alex frowned, thinking of the goddamn tabloids that had ripped Cassie apart after she left, linking her with every man from the Shah of Iran to JFK Jr. He told himself she was not living with another guy. She wouldn't have been so relaxed. She wouldn't have kissed him like that. She couldn't have. 'You don't live here alone?' he said carefully, keeping the emotion out of his voice. Cassie shook her head.

'It was a nightmare,' he said. 'A reservation's a big place. I didn't think I was ever going to find you. When I got here yesterday, no one would tell me where you were. They all looked at me and pretended they didn't speak English, or else they told me it was none of my business. What is *with* these people, anyway?'

Cassie just shook her head. Pine Ridge was probably the only place in the world where her own group of supporters was stronger than Alex Rivers's fan club.

'So I finally bribed some teenager by giving him a fifth of vodka, and he gave me directions here.' Alex looked around at the landscape. 'Wherever "here" is, exactly.'

'It's the Flying Horses' house,' Cassie said, but that was all she was willing to offer. She slapped her palms on her thighs and affected a bright smile. 'So,' she said, walking away from Alex. 'What have you been doing since the Academy Awards?'

She turned around for his answer and stumbled against Alex, who was standing several inches too close. 'I don't want to talk about me,' he said softly, gripping her shoulders. 'I know exactly what I've been doing for the last six months – I was trying very hard to kill myself, the slow, poisonous way: letting my career go to hell and drinking myself into a stupor because I didn't have you around.' His hands dropped to his sides and his voice fell so quiet Cassie had to lean forward. 'I don't know what exactly it was that made you go that day,' Alex said, 'but I have a good

idea. And I want you to know that I'll do anything you want –
I'll even sleep in a different bedroom. But God, Cassie, please say
you'll come home.' He looked at her, his lashes dark with tears.
'You're too much a part of me,' he said. 'If you cut yourself free,
pichouette, then I bleed to death.'

Cassie stared at Alex, feeling the balance of the world shift
under her feet. She'd spent three years afraid of the ways Alex
reacted to her; now he was afraid of how she would react to him.
She had bent over backward to make him happy; now he was
offering the same bargain to her: therapy, counseling, even celibacy,
because that was what he thought would please her. Figuratively,
he was on his knees before her – just as she had literally been
countless times in the past.

A beautiful nugget of optimism burst inside her, flowing through
her system until it heated the ends of her fingers. She placed her
hands against Alex's cheek, thinking of all the times she had
pictured this moment: when Alex would begin to keep his promises; when he willingly would start to change their lives; when
he would never risk her again.

Cassie brushed away Alex's tears, humbled by the fact that this
man, who never cried, was doing so for her. It *was* different, this
time. He had seen that she had the power to leave, and because
of that, she was now an equal. He had admitted there was something wrong between them. He was depending on her for help
again, except this time her involvement would not be as a sacrifice, but as a savior.

She smiled at Alex. 'I want to show you what I've been doing
since I left,' she said. Turning on her heel, she pushed open the
door of the little house, ignoring the questioning glances from
Dorothea and Cyrus. She looked at Will, but only because he was
holding the baby. His eyes were dark and hooded, his lips drawn
into a tight line.

Cassie took a deep breath and scooped Connor from Will's
shoulder. She stepped outside and closed the door behind her,

bouncing the baby to keep him happy. Then she held Connor out in her arms, an offering. 'This is Connor,' she said. 'Your son.'

Alex took a step backward. He made no move to touch the baby. 'My *what*?'

Cassie pulled Connor close to her chest. 'Your son,' she said again, wondering what had gone wrong when everything was beginning to seem picture perfect. 'I was pregnant when I left. That last time you – that last time, I realized that I had to keep the baby safe. But I wound up with amnesia, right back where I had started. So I had to run away all over again.' She looked down at the top of Connor's head. 'I never would have left because of you, Alex. I only left because of the baby.'

Alex's jaw tightened, and a muscle jumped along his throat. His senses were reeling, his knees could barely support him. *A son? His?* He pictured, fleetingly, his own father, jeering at him when a low cypress branch knocked him from the pirogue into the deep brown mud of the swamp. He remembered that white smile, the bitter racket of his laugh as he held out his hand to pull Alex back into the boat. He remembered hating that he had to grasp his father's hand, that there had been no other way out.

'Don't think about it, Alex,' Cassie gently warned. 'You aren't like him. I can prove it.'

Alex looked up just as Cassie plunked the squirming infant into his arms. Reflexively he caught Connor under the bottom and around the shoulders, jiggling him up and down to keep him from making any noise. His fingers gradually closed around the baby's skin, stroking. He could smell detergent from the diaper, and powder, and something unnamed that he could only think of as what *pink* would be, if it had a scent. Connor opened his eyes, silver. Completely startled by the mirror image, Alex choked on the burst of a laugh. He wondered if his father, or his mother, or anyone, had ever held him like this. He wondered, if you did it right from day one, whether it could make all the difference in the world.

*   *   *

Alex had wanted to leave right away for Rapid City to catch the next plane to Los Angeles, but Cassie had simply told him that was impossible. 'I have friends here,' she said, 'responsibilities.' She laid her hand on his arm. 'If I can't have two more weeks, give me till the morning.' She saw the flash of disappointment in his eyes when she told him she wouldn't be accompanying him back to his motel, planning instead to spend her last night with the Flying Horses. But true to his new word, Alex simply nodded, kissed her goodbye, and promised to meet her the next morning in front of the grade school.

For a few minutes Cassie had stood with Connor on her shoulder, watching Alex's Bronco disappear in a cloud of red Dakota dust. Then she fixed the happiest smile on her face that she could, and pushed open the door to the house.

Cyrus was knitting again, and Dorothea was chopping a ginger root to use in a stew for dinner. Will was nowhere in sight, which surprised her since the house had only one door and she and Alex had been in front of it the entire time. Dorothea looked up as the door whispered shut. 'So,' she said, 'you go back to the big city with him.'

Cassie tucked Connor into his cradleboard and sank down beside Cyrus on the couch. 'I have to,' she said. 'It wouldn't be fair to him otherwise.'

Dorothea pointed her paring knife at Cassie. 'Seems to me, he hasn't always been fair to you.'

Cassie ignored Dorothea. Tomorrow she would be back in LA. She would go to her office, first thing, and talk to Custer; then she'd visit Ophelia. She'd discreetly call a hotline or a shelter and ask for the names of reputable therapists in the area. She would have to find someone to babysit for Connor . . . Here she broke off her thoughts, laughing. Surely *someone* on Alex's staff would be capable of watching a baby for an hour or two.

But the truth was, she didn't know anyone on Alex's staff as well after three years as she had come to know Dorothea and Cyrus in just six months. And Will, well, she would try to make him understand, but she knew how angry he was going to be. She pictured him leading her around a corral on a six-year-old cousin's pony when she was pregnant, sitting beside her on the couch when her water broke and soaked his jeans, making her laugh with stories about giving Clint Eastwood a ticket for speeding down Hollywood Boulevard. Sometimes, when Connor became very crabby just before dinnertime, Will was the only one who could get him to quiet down. Cassie wondered how she was going to get by without Will, and out of nowhere, his words came into her head: *You can't have the best of both worlds.*

'Where's Will?' she asked.

'Went for a run,' Cyrus said. 'Climbed right out the window because he didn't want to bother you two.'

Cassie flinched. 'If you don't mind watching Connor,' she said to Cyrus, 'I'm going to try to find him.' She had walked with him before and knew all his favorite haunts.

She found Will where the woods opened into a clearing at the edge of a stream. He sat with his knees drawn up to his chest, drawing great gulps of air into his lungs.

'Hi,' Cassie said. She sat down beside him, but he didn't turn to face her, or acknowledge that he'd even heard her say hello. 'Alex is gone,' she said hesitantly, and at that Will's head swung toward her.

'He left for LA?'

Cassie shook her head, embarrassed for deliberately misleading him. 'He went back to Rapid City. He's going to pick us up tomorrow morning in town to go to the airport.'

Will tried to smile, but the light didn't quite reach his eyes. 'So,' he said. 'What time do we meet him?'

Cassie laughed. 'I meant Connor and me. As far as Alex knows, you don't exist.'

Will turned his face toward the water and set his jaw. 'Why

didn't you tell him? Maybe he'd get jealous and go after me. Maybe I could save you a couple of cracked ribs, another fight—'

'Stop,' Cassie said softly, touching Will's arm. 'He's not like that anymore.'

Will snorted. 'Hell, of course he's not. His punching bag has been out of town.'

'He's going to get some help. He admitted something was wrong. All I have to do is find a therapist.'

Will picked at a blade of grass. 'No guarantees,' he said curtly. 'Old dogs, new tricks – you know what they say. What are you going to do when he goes after the baby?'

Will watched her face freeze at the very idea, something he imagined she'd been trying hard not to consider. *Fine*, he thought, watching her work to keep her emotions in check, *let me burst her little bubble*. He wanted to hurt her. He wanted to see her cry just like he was doing on the inside.

'He won't touch Connor,' Cassie said emphatically. 'That would hit too close to home for him.'

'No pun intended,' Will bit out.

Cassie jumped to her feet, showering Will with the pieces of grass she'd been ripping to shreds in her lap. 'What is the matter with you?' she said, her voice thick with tears. 'I thought you were a friend of mine. I thought you would want me to be happy.'

I do, Will thought. *I just want you to be happy with me*. 'Funny,' he said. 'You figured that the only way *I'd* be happy is if I did the things you thought would be best for me.'

Cassie glared at him. 'What do you mean by that?'

'You know. "Don't turn your back on your Sioux blood, Will." Hanging up my goddamn medicine bundle in LA so it stared me in the face every time I passed it by.'

'You pulled it off the wall,' Cassie said. 'How was I supposed to know any better?' She poked at a rock with her toe. 'Besides,' she said smugly, 'I was right. Look at how much you've changed since you've come back to Pine Ridge – it's obvious that the only person who gives a damn about your being half white is you.'

Will pulled himself to his feet, staring right at Cassie. 'What I want to know is how come *I'm* not allowed to turn my back on my history, but you don't have to play by the same rules?'

Cassie took a step backward. 'I don't know what you're talking about.'

Will grabbed her shoulders. 'You do. You know what he's done to you before, you know he's going to do it again.' His mouth twisted. 'I couldn't escape the past, no matter how hard I tried. Neither can Alex, and neither can you.'

Cassie knew the advice she'd given Will served her own situation just as well. There was, really, nothing you could use as a blueprint for your life, except your past. There was no starting over. There was only picking up the pieces someone had left behind.

'That,' Cassie said, her voice breaking, 'is exactly why I have to go back.'

After Cassie spent the early morning saying goodbye to Cyrus and Dorothea, Will drove her and Connor into town to meet Alex. Connor had been fussy in the car, and Cassie handed him to Will, knowing that Alex was watching from across the street and grateful that Connor's cries had offered her an excuse to do so. After all that Will had seflessly given her and Connor, she could not go without letting him hold the baby a last time.

They had come to a fragile peace. Cassie fiddled with the drawer of the glove compartment, pretending to check inside for anything that might be hers. Across the seat, Will was rubbing his hand across Connor's frail back. 'Well,' Cassie said brightly. 'You'll write and tell me where you wind up?'

Will glanced up at her. 'I said I would.'

Cassie nodded. 'Yes, you did.' She reached out her arms, and Will placed the baby in them, their hands brushing each other.

Then she looked out the front window of the pickup, trying to commit to memory the flagpole in front of the school, the hot red dirt caked into the tires of the truck, the tilt of Will's hat on his forehead. 'I'm going to miss this place,' she said.

Will laughed. 'Give yourself ten minutes,' he said. 'It's real easy to forget.'

Cassie looped her hand through the straps of Connor's diaper bag. 'Well then, I'm going to miss you.'

'Now that,' Will said, grinning, 'will take longer than ten minutes.'

Cassie lurched across the seat, throwing her free arm around Will's neck. Will hugged her back, taking away the soft grass scent of her hair, the smooth curve of her bare shoulder, the timbre of her voice. Connor lay pressed between their chests, like the shared heart of Siamese twins.

It was Alex who pulled them apart. Cassie heard his deep voice through her open window, where he'd come to stand. 'Sorry,' he said. 'But I don't want to miss that flight.'

Will released her. He stared at Alex, nodded. He touched the baby's dewy cheek.

'Thank you,' Alex said graciously. He lifted the baby from Cassie's arms through the window, as if he knew that was the sure way she would follow. 'I appreciate your taking care of my family.'

My family. Will narrowed his eyes. He didn't trust himself to say anything.

Alex settled Connor on his shoulder, then looked at Will again. 'I know you,' he said simply.

Will smiled broadly. 'I broke up a fight of yours once. I was with the LAPD.'

'Well,' Cassie said between them, and Will turned to her. Always the peacemaker.

She didn't say anything, but she didn't get out of the truck right away, either. Instead they slipped into that comfortable zone where there didn't have to be words. They caught each other's eyes. *I love you*, Will thought.

I know, Cassie answered. But while he was still savoring that smallest triumph, she slid from the truck and walked right out of his life.

When the Riverses' scheduled plane took off from Rapid City, Will was more drunk than he'd ever been. He planned to be unconscious by the time Cassie landed in LA with her husband and her son.

He cursed himself for ever picking Cassie up from that goddamn cemetery. He cursed himself for quitting the LAPD, where he would have been able to keep an eye on her. The way things stood now, she was dead to him. Or as good as dead.

It was this thought that got his mind turning. There was a common practice among the People, the giveaway, that came on the anniversary of a relative's death. The grieving family showed their respect for the dead person by making gifts and saving up staple foods and offering them as presents to as many people as possible. Will vaguely remembered the year that his own father had died, how his grandparents had saved up to make a good showing that proved how much they had cared for their son.

He remembered that when his father died, Joseph Stands in Sun had told him about ghost owning, the ultimate giveaway ceremony which had transpired in the days of the buffalo. For a family that lost a child, not only would food and skins and utensils be saved up over the year. In addition, the couple would give to other members of the tribe their own horses, their very tipi, even the clothes off their backs, all as a tribute to someone well loved. 'You give till it hurts,' Joseph had said.

Wild-eyed, Will began to rummage through the back of his truck, finding little of value except for an old shotgun and a sheepskin jacket that had belonged to his father. He drove through town like a madman, stopping at Bernie Collier's, a neighbor he had never liked. He banged on the door until it swung open under his pounding.

'Will,' Bernie said carefully, taking in Will's unkempt hair and the untucked edges of his shirt.

'I got something for you, Bernie,' Will said, thrusting the shotgun into his hands. 'No strings attached.'

He turned on his heel before Bernie could call after him, jumped into the truck and sped toward the Laughing Dogs' house.

Linda Laughing Dog frowned when she saw him, and waved her hand in front of her face, trying to ward off the smell of whiskey. 'Come on in, Will,' she said. 'Let me get you some coffee.'

'No coffee,' Will said. 'I'm here to give you something.' He held up the sheepskin jacket. 'Think how many kids will go through the winters in this,' he said. 'It's yours. Do what you want with it.'

Rydell Two Fists adamantly refused to take his truck, and Will sat down on the stump in front of his log cabin and bawled like an infant before he figured out what he could do with the keys. He went around back to the old knotty pine where Rydell and Marjorie kept their mutt tied up, and threaded the key ring through the dog's collar without even waking it.

Giveaway worked; he was coming to see that. He ran through the back woods to Joseph Stands in Sun's lodge, feeling lighter than he had in months. He stripped off his coat as he ran. He left his hat on a clothesline, his boots in front of the cabin of a stranger. He gave his shirt to a little girl who was dragging a bucket of water back up to her parents' home.

By the time he reached Joseph's lodge, he was wearing only his jeans and his underwear, and he was shivering from the cold. He obviously hadn't drunk enough, he thought, if he could still judge the temperature and if he was too embarrassed to knock on the door and give the medicine man the last of his clothes. Instead, he stripped down to his bare skin, folding his jeans and his shorts and leaving them in a neat pile in front of Joseph's door.

He began to run wherever his legs would go. As he stepped on thistles and pinecones his feet began to bleed; still he kept running. He was an animal. He was primitive. He could not think and he could not feel. He came to a high butte that he did not recognize, and there he threw back his head and cried in pain.

He had only one more thing to give away, something that he knew was worthless, but something all the same. Will yelled the words over and over in English and in Lakota, sobbing and scratching at his own skin when he needed to remember how much it hurt to be here when she was gone. 'Imacu yo,' he shouted to the spirits. 'Take me!'

Chapter Twenty-Five

The reporters and photographers waiting at the security check-point at LAX were taking bets. 'I still say he's gotten rid of her,' a man from the *National Enquirer* said. 'As in six feet under.'

The *People* reporter sniffed. 'Then why go to all this trouble to announce their arrival in LA?'

'You ask me,' a cameraman said, 'they're comin' back together, but she ain't gonna look too happy about it. I think he's paid her off. What's a couple million if it puts you at the top of the box office again?'

An NBC entertainment reporter checked her lipstick for smears in the reflective lens of a camera. 'Mark my words,' she said emphatically. 'Alex Rivers is a has-been.' She turned to her colleagues, jostling each other like greyhounds at the gate as the loudspeaker announced the arrival of flight 658 from Denver. 'There's nothing that man can do that will make women drool again. Fact is, no matter what the circumstances were, she left him, which only proves he's not the sex symbol we all thought.'

In the first-class lounge, Cassie finished diapering Connor. Alex sat across from her, one leg casually crossed over the other at the knee. He held a mug of coffee in his hands. 'I'm going to have to learn how to do that,' he said.

Cassie glanced up at him. For the life of her, she couldn't picture Alex's hands doing something as mundane as diapering their son. 'Now *that*,' she said, 'would make a wonderful press conference.'

Shifting, Alex set down the mug. 'You don't mind, do you?'

He was talking about the reporters who were waiting like vultures to be tossed some carrion. Alex had warned her about the tip to the media when they were somewhere over the Rockies. And of course she'd said she understood – if it was indirectly her fault that Alex's popularity was suffering in Hollywood, it was her obligation to bolster his image as much as she could. Still, Cassie couldn't help but remember the first time she'd landed at LAX with Alex, nearly four years earlier, the first time she'd been given a taste of a life devoid of privacy. After so many months at Pine Ridge, it was a difficult adjustment to make.

'I don't mind,' Cassie said softly. She handed the baby to Alex. 'I just wish Connor wasn't being used as a pawn.'

'I won't let the flashbulbs hit his eyes, and I won't let them ask too many questions. I promise.' Alex grinned. 'Think of it as his first screen test.'

The door to the private sitting area flew open, and the huge bulk of Michaela Snow filled the threshold. She gave Alex a brilliant smile and then turned to Cassie, raking her over from head to toe. 'Good to see you again,' she said coolly, and Cassie froze in the motion of putting the diaper wipes back into the carry-on bag.

'Michaela,' she said, tipping up her face with a genuinely warm smile.

Michaela stared at her for a moment, long enough for Cassie to self-consciously consider her own shapeless brown shift and worn tennis shoes – a far cry from the fashion statement expected of Alex Riverss's wife. Michaela turned back to Alex. 'You almost ready?'

Cassie felt a chill make its way down her spine as she realized that Michaela's attitude was a preview of the reception she would receive in Los Angeles, where the majority of people she knew were Alex's friends and colleagues. In their eyes, Cassie had left Alex. In their eyes, she was the one at fault. They did not know the whole story, of course, but that was exactly where Cassie's hands were tied. If she defended her own actions by revealing the fact that Alex had beaten his wife, she would only send his reputation into another uproar. Even if she mentioned it in light of his vow to get professional help, she would still be hurting Alex, and that was the one thing she refused to do again.

She glanced up at Alex, who mistook the look on her face for stage fright and tenderly drew her to her feet. 'Surely the woman who gave birth alone in the middle of nowhere,' he said softly, 'won't be intimidated by a greedy bunch of reporters.'

'I wasn't alone,' Cassie said defensively. She reached for Connor and began to strap him into his cradleboard.

Alex turned to Michaela. 'We'll meet you outside in ten minutes.' As the publicist left, he turned to Cassie. 'Why don't you let me carry that thing,' he said gently, 'and you can hold the baby.'

Cassie's eyes darted to the door Michaela had just exited. She protectively folded her arms over her chest. Was Alex ashamed of her dumpy, functional clothing? Of bringing his child into LA in a Sioux artifact? 'Connor likes the cradleboard,' Cassie said guardedly, clutching at what had become familiar.

'Connor loves his mother,' Alex said. He looked up at Cassie, his eyes pleading the words he hadn't said: *And I want everyone to see him with you*. He waited until Cassie nodded, and then let his breath out in a sigh. He was treading on eggshells, he knew that, but surely Cassie could see the importance of a crowd's first impression.

Alex gathered up the rest of the bags and slung them over his shoulder. He paused at the door of the lounge to turn to Cassie. 'Thank you,' he said softly.

'For what?'

'For what you're about to do for me. For coming back.'

It was the undisguised emotion in his eyes that made Cassie put her fear aside. She took Alex's hand and drew a deep breath.

*   *   *

The rows of black dots swam before her eyes, but even as the throng of reporters continued to flash pictures and roll their videotapes, Cassie kept a smile pinned to her face and her eyes glued to Alex, as if she were falling in love with him all over again.

'I realize,' Alex was saying coldly, 'there's been a lot of conjecture about the disappearance of my wife.' He looped his arm around her waist. 'As you can see, she's quite alive, which rules out one distasteful theory about me. And as you can also see, she's been busy. Our son, Connor, was born on August eighteenth.'

The reporter from the *Enquirer* waved his pen in the air. 'Is he yours?'

Alex's jaw tightened. 'I will not stoop to answer that,' he said.

'Then how come your wife ran away?' asked a *Variety* correspondent.

'She did *not* run away, I *sent* her away. We wanted to have a baby in peace, without the world watching over our shoulders.' Alex's voice dropped dangerously low. 'You people lie in wait like animals and make rumors fester until they take precedence over the truth. Did you ever think about the lives of the people you're ruining? Did you ever think about the kind of damage you're doing when, in order to guarantee privacy, you force someone to take their family away? My career already makes me a public figure. *You* don't have to.' Alex took a step toward the silent group of reporters. 'Before you go pleading the first amendment, think about the rest of us who are pleading the fifth.'

Alex turned to Cassie, who recovered from her shock at the quiet vehemence of his speech to give him a reassuring smile. She slipped her arm around his waist and they made their way down the hall, followed only by the sounds of distant, whirring cameras.

Long after they were out of sight, the reporters stood huddled in a group, stunned and chastised. Instead of smashing cameras and pulling rolls of videotape as some stars were wont to do,

Alex Rivers had managed to shame them subtly and thoroughly. It was obvious that Alex Rivers hadn't done anything to harm his wife. It was just as obvious that she was still crazy about him. And set in front of them was the proof – a beautiful little boy with the legacy of Alex Rivers's silver eyes.

The reporter from NBC gestured to her cameraman and found a quiet place to film her comments. She pulled a compact out of her pocket and smoothed her hair, turning to a UPI representative beside her who was still furiously scribbling down notes. 'I'll be damned,' she said. 'He's turned himself into a hero again. A hundred million people out there are going to see us as the big bad meddling media, while Alex Rivers and his nuclear family come off as crusaders just trying to be normal, everyday people.'

She shook her head, taking small comfort in the fact that *every* network was going to be swallowing some humble pie that day, and raised her hand to signal readiness for the camera. She squared her shoulders. 'Tonight at LAX, celebrity Alex Rivers revealed the answer to the mystery involving his wife's disappearance several months ago. In spite of overwhelming rumors circulated by the media that negatively affected his career in Hollywood, Rivers did not step forward with his wife's whereabouts, which, apparently, he'd known at all times. Cassandra Barrett Rivers returned to LA tonight on her husband's arm, bringing with her Alex Rivers's newborn son.' Here the reporter paused meaningfully. 'It is a sad fact that in today's world a star like Alex Rivers would have to endure a false scandal simply to guarantee his family's privacy,' she said, carefully absolving herself from blame. 'One can only hope that if little Connor Rivers decides to follow in his illustrious father's footsteps, things will be different. This is Marisa Thompson, NBC News.'

Cassie stood in front of the bathroom mirror, running her fingers over the green marble countertop and gold-plated sink fixtures.

She couldn't help wondering what the point of that was. What had seemed luxurious before now seemed simply overdone.

She stepped into the bedroom, turning up the volume of the portable monitor that hooked into Connor's new room. Cassie had been amazed: in the hours since he'd come for her, Alex had had one of the guest bedrooms wallpapered with fat cartoon sheep and tumbling cows, the edging of the sills and doors had been painted bright blue, and sky-colored curtains dotted with clouds fluttered in the windows. Connor was asleep in a whitewashed cradle.

She listened to the even rhythm of her baby's breathing. She shouldn't have been surprised; Alex had always been able to do the impossible.

It was quiet in the house; the staff had retired for the night. There had seemed to be fewer people, and those she'd recognized – like John, and Alex's secretary – were all distantly polite to her, acknowledging her position in the household, but no one was overly friendly. She kept waiting to hear a maid say, 'It's nice to have you back,' or for the chef to touch her arm and tell her he'd missed her, but these things did not happen, and Cassie realized that if she wanted to win everyone over again, the first friend she would have to make was Alex.

She found him downstairs in his study, sitting in the tremendous leather desk chair, his body bent over a list of financial holdings. Spaced across the top of the desk were the three Oscars he'd won when she was in Pine Ridge. She stepped into the room, closing the door behind her.

Alex looked up. 'He's asleep again?'

Cassie nodded. 'For the next couple of hours, anyway.'

She reached across the desk and picked up the Oscar in the corner, smoothing her fingers over the streamlined back and the crossed arms. It was much heavier than she had expected. 'I was so proud of you,' she murmured. 'I wanted to be here.'

'I wanted you to be here too.'

They looked at each other for a long moment, and then Alex's hand covered hers on the Oscar and set it on the desk. He pulled her onto his lap.

Suddenly nervous, she splayed her hand across the sheaf of papers on the desk. 'How much are you worth?' she teased.

Alex looked away. 'Not nearly as much as when you left,' he said. 'You probably noticed we're down to a skeleton staff, and I ought to tell you the apartment's been on the market for a couple of months now. I – I took a big loss producing *Macbeth*.'

Again Cassie felt her stomach cramp at the pain he'd suffered as a result of her disappearance. Trying to smile, she tipped up Alex's chin. 'The good news,' she said, 'is that I've learned a lot about roots and berries. We're in no danger of starving.'

The corners of Alex's mouth turned up. 'I don't think we're quite at the brink of bankruptcy yet,' he said. 'But I would get a kick out of watching you forage your way through Bel-Air.'

Cassie wrapped her arms around Alex's neck and pressed her cheek against his heart. 'I really missed you,' she said. She wished he would put away his files and take her upstairs. She wished at the very least he would kiss her.

'I have a favor to ask of you,' Alex said.

Cassie looked up, and then beamed, realizing he was giving her the choice. Hadn't he said he would sleep in a different bedroom if she wanted? Obviously all he was waiting for was a hint, a clue, a caress.

'I know you're going to want me to see . . . someone. A psychiatrist or something. I was just hoping you wouldn't go mentioning it. You know, to someone like Ophelia, or your cop friend in South Dakota.' He lowered his eyes. 'That's all.'

Cassie felt his words tug at her. Did he really think that after all he'd been willing to do in order to get her back, she might intentionally try to hurt him? 'Alex,' Cassie murmured, 'I never said anything to anyone before. I'm not going to say anything now.' She stroked the back of his neck. 'I have a favor to ask of you too.' Alex swung his head toward her, his eyes glowing. 'I was wondering if we could go to bed,' she said.

Alex's breath drained out in a long sigh. He tucked Cassie's head back against his chest. 'I thought you'd never ask.'

He was as nervous as a teenager. Pacing naked in front of the mirror, he thought about Cassie lying under the covers just a few feet outside the bathroom door. He wondered if her body had changed because she'd had Connor. He wondered what she would be wearing, if anything, and then he thought maybe he should wrap a towel around himself. She might want to talk first. Hell, he didn't even know if it was all right to do this, so soon after the baby.

Placing his hands on either side of the sink, he leaned toward the mirror. 'Get ahold of yourself,' he ordered out loud. He closed his eyes and thought of all the love scenes he'd done over the years, takes and retakes with his hands on the breasts of beautiful women and his mouth roaming over their pancaked skin. He'd been able to act natural in front of an audience of cameramen, directors, gaffers, grips; but with his own wife and no crew in sight, he was terrified of doing something wrong. The truth was, there was no woman who could make him feel like Cassie did. She touched him without ulterior motives; she gave all of herself; she loved him simply because he was him.

He took a deep breath and pulled open the bathroom door. Cassie was sitting propped up in the bed, the sheet drawn to her bare shoulders. The covers moved as she wriggled her toes. 'Oh,' she said, 'I guess you *didn't* fall in.'

Alex laughed and sat on the edge of the bed. 'What did I do to deserve you?'

Cassie gave him a cocky smile. 'You got very, very lucky.' She stretched her hand up to him to pull him closer, and the sheet fell away from her breasts. Alex had only the slightest glimpse of the milky skin, the dark spread nipples, before he crushed her against him.

'God, you feel good,' he whispered against her mouth. He dug his fingers into her hair and kissed her, telling himself to go slowly before it was over too fast. But Cassie's hands came to his waist to unknot the towel and before he could help himself he'd settled between her legs and driven into her, crying out.

He collapsed against her chest, mortified. 'I'm sorry,' he said. 'I feel like I'm fifteen again.'

Cassie stroked his hair. 'It's nice to know you were even more nervous than I was.' She shifted her hips beneath him, and he pulled her onto her side so she wouldn't bear his weight.

He looked down at her body, still lined from her pregnancy and thick at the waist and stomach. 'I'm fat,' she announced.

'You're beautiful,' Alex said. His fingers traced a stretch mark on her hip. 'Is this – okay to do?'

Cassie laughed. 'It's a little late to be asking, don't you think?'

Alex shook his head. 'No, I mean . . . did I hurt you?'

Cassie's eyes met his, and he realized that the phrasing of the sentence went much deeper than he had intended. 'No,' she whispered. 'And you won't.'

She felt Alex moving beside her again and she reached for him, but he gently pinned her arms at the sides of her head. 'No,' he said. 'Let me.'

He began to love her, inch by inch, and this time it burned from behind her skin. When he came into her, Cassie saw for just a moment the skeleton of her life. There was no house, no Oscars, no Connor. There were no old secrets and no residual pain. There was just Alex, and Cassie. She remembered how Alex Rivers had stirred things inside her she'd never known about; how, always, she would love him. And with these beginnings shining so brightly again, it was difficult to imagine that for months she had passed them by without a second glance.

Chapter Twenty-Six

If nothing else, Hollywood had always been fickle, which was why only a few days went by before Alex Rivers was once again the hottest property in town. His Cinderella romance of Cassie had matured – now he was a movie star with family values, someone willing to sacrifice box office success and cancel production if it interfered with the time he needed with his wife. Suddenly, the pariah who had seemingly made a mess of his life was the celebrity whom everyone in America could relate to, a public figure who only wanted to be an ordinary guy.

The house and Alex's production office were flooded with gifts for Connor – baseball mitts and rattles and tiny sweatsuits from fans, sterling spoons and Tiffany place settings from studio executives, who included notes for Alex that said they'd been behind him all along. Screenplays were sent to him by the dozens; Herb Silver called four times a day to offer him packages in which he was being asked to star and direct. Alex took the baby gifts – he liked to watch Cassie opening them – and he skimmed through the scripts, but as for settling another deal, he was planning to wait. He had more important things to do first.

'He smiled,' Alex said one morning, holding Connor up like a loving cup. Cassie grinned and kept walking into the dining room. 'Hang on. I can make him do it again.'

Cassie lifted her eyes toward the ceiling and took a sip of her coffee. 'Maybe you can have him rolling over by the time I get back.'

Alex settled the baby on his shoulder and gave her a jaunty grin. 'Maybe I can,' he said.

He was beginning to think that Cassie had been right. He had wanted to hire a nanny – after all, that's what most couples in his position did when they had a baby – but Cassie wouldn't hear of it. 'I will not have someone spending more time with Connor than me,' she'd said firmly, 'and that's not negotiable.' She had arranged with Archibald Custer to take a yearlong sabbatical. Her heart wasn't in fieldwork, not with Connor to distract her, and anyway, someone else had been teaching her courses. Alex had said she'd be screaming to get out of the house within a week. 'You'll see,' Cassie had said. 'I'll know more about the neighborhood parks than anyone else.'

So far, she had been right. She spent most of her day on the floor of the den with Connor, making faces at him and sticking out her tongue and reading him fairy tales she'd dug up. In fact, the only problem had been that, watching them, Alex had no desire to leave. He'd taken to bringing his scripts home, and reading them in the den where he could watch his wife and his son play.

'What time are you coming home?' Alex said.

Cassie laughed and picked up her jacket. 'Why? So you can have dinner on the table?' She shook her head and kissed him on the cheek. 'You're turning into a house-husband, Alex.'

Alex grinned. 'No one ever told me how much more gratifying a career it was.'

Cassie brushed the top of Connor's head with her lips. 'It also pays less,' she said.

'Have fun with Ophelia,' Alex said.

Cassie groaned. 'She's going to grill me for the next three hours. Do you know she actually asked if being at Pine Ridge was anything like what that white woman went through in *Dances with Wolves*?'

Alex laughed. 'What did you tell her?'

'No buffalo,' Cassie said, 'more snow, and worse clothing.'

She shook her head and walked across the parlor, dodging a maid who was carrying a stack of tablecloths. When she got to the door, she turned around, biting her lip and checking to see that the hall was clear of people. 'You didn't forget about tonight?'

Alex looked up at her the way he often did these days, as if he did not entirely trust himself to believe that she was there, and that if she walked out that door she would actually come through it again only hours later. 'I didn't forget,' he said.

Dr June Pooley was the one therapist Cassie had spoken to who did not insist that the only way a battered wife could change her circumstances was by getting herself out of her husband's physical range. She told Cassie about something called battered women's syndrome, and she said that it was a sickness, like alcoholism. And as with alcoholism, through certain kinds of therapy both abusers and victims could come to understand their problems and the best way to deal with them.

'If you're an alcoholic, you have to understand that you'll never be able to take a drink again. Not to toast your brother's wedding, not to fit in at a business lunch, never. If you're being beaten,' Dr Pooley said, looking at Cassie and then Alex, 'or doing the beating, you have to understand that the impulses that let you get into those situations will have to be channeled elsewhere if you're going to remain together.'

Alex wove his fingers between Cassie's and squeezed her hand.

Dr Pooley took a deep breath. 'You should also understand that the odds are against you. But even if you were to divorce each other, without therapy, it's almost a given that Alex would find a woman with a personality type like Cassie's and take out his rage on her, and that Cassie would search out someone like Alex who would, in turn, abuse her all over again. No matter what happens, you're taking a step in the right direction. The first part of therapy for each of you is going to be to see other people like yourselves, in the same situation you've been in.'

Cassie looked up at Alex, who was staring with calm, clear eyes at the therapist who was going to change their life. He didn't seem nervous at all – not about coming to the quiet oak-paneled office, and now, not even about admitting to a group of un-familiar men that he hit Cassie. Cassie frowned at that, thinking ahead for Alex. She knew about doctor-patient confidentiality, but she wasn't sure if the same would hold true for the members of the support groups. And obviously, that was a requirement for Alex.

'It's clear that you've made a commitment to each other, which I appreciate,' Dr Pooley said. She checked a clipboard, then looked up at Cassie. 'I can put you into a women's group on Wednesday night,' she said. 'And our men's group meets on Sundays.'

'That's not a problem,' Alex said.

'I like her,' Cassie said as they were slipping into bed. 'What did you think?'

Alex yawned and turned off the light. 'She's okay,' he said.

'She didn't do a double take when you walked through the door,' Cassie pointed out. 'She didn't ask you for your autograph.'

Alex nuzzled her shoulder. 'She'll have it dozens of times over,' he said. 'Every time I send her a check.'

In the dark, Cassie turned to Alex and pressed her palms against his chest. 'You don't mind talking about us in front of strangers?'

Alex shook his head and bent his mouth to Cassie's breast. He could taste the faintest traces of milk that his son had left behind, and he suckled gently, loving the idea that she could nourish them both.

'What about what else she said?' Cassie whispered. Alex pulled away from her, hearing the ragged note of fear at the edge of her voice. 'What if we're in the majority and we can't stay together?'

Alex gathered her into his arms and rubbed his hands down her back. 'You have nothing to worry about,' he said simply, 'since I'm never going to let you go.'

Like the other seven women in her therapy group, Cassie was married to a man who was wonderful ninety-five percent of the time. Like the other women, Cassie had spent more time as a child taking care of her parents than they had spent taking care of her, but no one had ever given her any credit for it. And then her husband had come along. He was the first person who made her feel special. He told her he loved her, he wept when he hurt her. He told her she was able to take care of him and soothe his pain as nobody else could.

Like the other seven women, Cassie didn't want Alex to hit her, but she knew he couldn't help it. She believed that in some way, it was her fault for not being able to avoid it. She felt sorry for him. She could convince herself it would never happen again, because she had been fixing problem situations for so much of her life that for her own well-being, she simply had to believe in her ability to set things right.

And oh, there were rewards. Flowers, and tenderness, and smiles meant just for her. When she got it right – when she didn't send him over the edge – her life was better than anyone else's.

But like the other women, Cassie understood that it wasn't normal to freeze up when her husband touched her shoulder, since she didn't know whether to expect a kiss or a kick in the ribs. She understood that it wasn't always her fault. That she didn't have to be unhappy more than she was happy.

Dr Pooley sat right in the circle with the women, many of whom, Cassie was surprised to see, were well dressed and well spoken. Somehow she had expected to be included with the wives of truck drivers, of welfare recipients. For the first few minutes she sat quietly, saying no more than her first name by way of introduction, and stared at the tulip-shaped bruise on the collar-bone of the woman across from her.

The session that night was a story swap. Dr Pooley wanted everyone to think back to the very first time an incident of abuse had occurred. Cassie listened to a lawyer tell of her live-in lover, who had barricaded her in the bathroom for forty-eight hours to keep her from going out with her colleagues. Another woman cried as she described her husband dragging her from a dinner party where he accused her of talking too much to a male neighbor, and then punched her in the mouth until two teeth came out and blood gushed and she couldn't talk anymore at all. Others told of objects being hurled at them, of bones being broken, of fists being slammed through glass windows.

When Cassie was the only one who hadn't spoken, she glanced up shyly at Dr Pooley and started to describe the time she'd come back from her Chicago lecture on the hand. She talked slowly about the plane being late, about Alex's accusations as to where she had been, carefully censoring any information that would point clearly to Alex's career and reveal his identity. She felt lighter with each word she spoke, as if she had been carrying around stones in her heart all these years and was only now able to cast them away. By the time she finished, having talked about the baby that might have been, tears were running down her cheeks and Dr Pooley's arm was around her shoulders.

Shocked at her lack of composure, Cassie sat bolt upright. She hastily wiped her face. 'I have a son now,' she said proudly. 'My husband is wonderful with him.' And then, more softly, absolving Alex: 'That other time, he didn't know.'

As the group broke up, gathering their purses and their fragile understandings to take back to their homes, Cassie lingered behind. She waited until she and Dr Pooley were the only ones in the meeting room, and then she tapped her lightly on the shoulder. 'Thank you,' Cassie said, shrugging a little. 'I'm not quite sure for what, but . . . thank you.'

The psychotherapist smiled. 'It'll get easier each time you come.'

Cassie nodded. 'I think I expected to feel like I was going to have to defend myself. Like no one would understand how I can still love Alex after what he's done. I thought they'd all look at me like I was crazy for sticking around for so long.'

Dr Pooley nodded. 'We've all been there,' she said.

Cassie's eyes widened. 'You too?'

'I was married to a man who beat me for ten years,' she said, 'so I'm the last person who's going to judge you for your decision to stay.' She held the door open so Cassie could walk through.

Cassie continued to stare at the therapist. 'I – I'm sorry. I just never would have guessed.'

'Well, we don't all brand it across our foreheads, do we?' she said gently.

Cassie shook her head. 'But things are better now?' she asked, trying to take as much hope as she could home to Alex.

'Yes,' Dr Pooley said, sighing. She looked at Cassie for a long moment. 'Now that we're divorced.'

Alex was circling his hips, pressing deep inside of her, running his mouth in a hot path down the curve of Cassie's neck, when Connor began to scream through the monitor beside the bed.

Cassie's breasts tingled as her milk let down, and she felt it dripping down both sides of her as Alex rolled off her for the second time that night. He lay on his back, staring up at the ceiling, his jaw clenched. 'For God's sake, Cassie,' Alex bit out. 'Can't you make him shut up?'

But she was already pulling on a peach satin wrapper and making her way toward the door. 'I'll be back in a minute,' she said.

It turned out to be nothing at all, just a pacifier that had become wedged underneath Connor's neck when he shifted. She rubbed his back and watched his sobs soften into hiccups, thinking how absolutely helpless he was.

Tiptoeing out the door, she made her way down the hall to the bedroom again. Alex was still, his back turned away from her side of the bed. When she closed the door behind her, he made no move to face her.

Cassie slipped under the covers and curled her body against Alex's back. 'Where were we?'

'Jesus, Cassie. I can't turn myself on and off like a goddamn faucet. I can't make it through a meal, I can't sleep the entire night, I can't even finish *making love* to you without being interrupted by that kid.'

'That *kid*,' Cassie said, 'is not doing any of this on purpose, Alex. You're not the only parent in the world. Everyone's life changes when they have children.'

'I never asked for him.'

Cassie's hand froze on Alex's hip. 'You don't mean that,' she whispered.

Alex glanced at her over his shoulder. 'If you won't accept a nanny, then you'd better find a night nurse. I'm not putting up with this. Either you hire someone or I move across the hall.' He pulled a pillow over his head.

Cassie thought of something Dr Pooley had mentioned during her group session the previous night, something about the personality traits of the abuser. Husbands don't want their wives to have close friends, she had said. They don't like the thought of someone else making demands on the person whom they see as belonging entirely to them.

At the time, Ophelia had come to mind, and Alex's inability to forgive her for the one and only mistake she'd ever made in connection with him. But now Cassie was starting to see Dr Pooley's statement in a different light. She glanced at Alex's hands, clutching the pillow to his head. He couldn't stand to see someone who needed Cassie as much as he did. Not even his own son.

'Alex,' Cassie whispered. 'I know you're not asleep yet.' She tapped his shoulder and tugged the pillow away from his ear.

Alex groaned and rolled onto his stomach. 'I'll hire someone. I'll start looking tomorrow.'

Alex opened his eyes and propped himself up on his elbows. He smiled hugely at her, and with his hair all mussed he looked like a child. 'You mean that?' Cassie nodded, and swallowed past the lump in her throat. She listened to the background noise of Connor's breathing over the monitor. 'Good,' Alex said, gathering her into his embrace. 'I was beginning to feel neglected.'

His mouth came over hers hungrily, stealing her breath and her reason. 'No,' she whispered, ignorant of the tears balanced at the corners of her eyes. 'Never.'

Dear Cassie,

    I hope you and Connor are doing okay and that you're happy back in LA. Pine Ridge isn't the same without the two of you. In fact I think the only reason I was starting to like it was because it seemed different when you were here. Brighter, I guess. Not so dingy and not so faded.

    I'm writing because I promised to let you know when I got a new job. In another week I'm moving out to Tacoma, WA, and starting with the department there. One of these days, when I get my act together, I may actually stick around long enough somewhere to get promoted.

    If you're not completely shell-shocked by LA, like I was when I first got there, then maybe you even think about us from time to time.

    I miss the baby. I miss you. And, damn, if that isn't the worst kind of hurt.

    Take care, wasicuη winyan.

                                            Will

Alex hung up the telephone and glanced at his watch. He had just made an appointment to meet Phil Kaplan in an hour to finalize a verbal commitment to produce the movie Alex planned to do next. He'd found the script by accident in a slush pile; it was priceless but had serious flaws that he now had an Academy Award-winning screenwriter working on. He was already daydreaming about the scenes, directing them over and over in his mind. He'd scribbled down his first choices for the primary roles, stuffed the list into his pocket to discuss with Phil.

Of course, if he had dinner with Phil, he was going to miss that therapy group for the second week in a row.

Cassie had taken Connor to the beach with Ophelia and a carload of sun-shading umbrellas; she wouldn't have to know right away.

Alex picked up the phone to call Dr Pooley, then put the receiver back in its cradle.

He had promised Cassie.

He could reschedule Phil.

Who, no doubt, would commit himself to somebody else by tomorrow morning.

He told himself he wouldn't even be considering skipping the group meeting if he didn't feel in his gut that this film could be even more successful than *The Story of His Life*. And all the elements had unfortunately happened to fall into place on a Sunday afternoon. He told himself that a year from now, when he swept the Academy Awards again, Cassie wouldn't even remember this.

He picked up the phone again. There was another session next week, and Cassie would understand.

She always did.

The following Wednesday Dr Pooley pulled Cassie aside after the women's group session. 'You should consider asking Alex,' she said carefully, 'if he's really serious about getting some kind of help.'

Cassie stared at the therapist. 'Of course he is,' she hedged, trying to imagine what kind of things Alex could have said at his own group session that would bring a censorious remark from Dr Pooley. When she had asked him about it, he'd said it went fine.

'I know *you* are,' Dr Pooley said. 'But that's not the same thing. I understand missing one session for a business commitment, but two in a row seems a little extreme. If he's going to try to save your marriage with therapy,' she pointed out, 'he ought to start by showing up.'

'He wasn't there last Sunday,' Cassie said slowly, suddenly understanding. She turned the words over in her mind, wondering where Alex had been, why he had lied. Lifting her eyes, she smiled apologetically at Dr Pooley. 'He just closed a very important deal,' she said. 'I'm sure things will be different now.'

'Cassie,' the doctor said gently, 'you don't have to make excuses for his behavior anymore.'

During the long ride home, she didn't bother to make conversation with John like she usually did. She stormed into the house, calling Alex's name so loudly her anger filled the corners of the front parlor.

'In here,' Alex said.

Cassie opened the door to the den, where Alex was sitting on the couch with a newspaper opened over his lap. A bottle of whiskey was wedged between the cushions to his right. 'You're drinking,' she said, snatching the bottle away from him and setting it on the bar across the room. She stood with her arms crossed over her chest, beside the playpen where Connor was gurgling.

Alex smiled lazily. 'Connor had his bottle,' he said. 'I figured I deserved one too.'

'You didn't go to the group session last Sunday,' Cassie said flatly.

'No,' Alex admitted, the word long and drawn. 'I was busy resurrecting my career. My reputation. You know, the one you keep knocking down so easily.' He stood up and thrust the newspaper into her hands. 'Tomorrow's *Informer, pichouette*. Came on the front doorstep in a plain brown envelope. And don't just stop at the headlines. The story's on page three, and it's real good.'

Cassie folded the paper in half, scanning the front page. ALEX RIVERS FOOLED BY WIFE'S HALF-BREED LOVE CHILD. There was a picture taken at the airport of Alex with his arm around her; and another of Cassie with Will, walking into the police station months ago, the day Alex had come to claim her.

'This is ridiculous,' Cassie said, starting to laugh. 'You can't possibly believe this.'

Alex rounded on her so quickly she dropped the paper. 'It doesn't matter what I believe,' he said. 'It matters that everyone's going to see it.'

'It's not like this is *Time* magazine,' Cassie said. 'Anyone who reads this rag knows the stories are trash.' She paused. 'We'll sue them. And we'll put the money into Connor's trust fund.'

Alex took a step closer, grabbing her arm. 'They quoted the letter he wrote you that's upstairs. Said you're going to meet him in Washington.'

For a moment her mind considered the mechanics of how Will's note, carefully tucked into her lingerie drawer, had become public knowledge. Cassie was disappointed that someone on the household staff had sold her secrets, but she was absolutely shocked that Alex had been upset enough to go through her mail. 'You don't really think I'm leaving, do you?'

'No,' he said simply, 'since I'd kill you first.'

Cassie felt the air grow heavy in the room, pressing down on her temples and making her limbs swing slowly. She backed herself against a wall. 'Alex,' she said softly, 'listen to yourself. Look at Connor.' She reached out to touch his arm. 'I love you,' she said. 'I came back with you.'

'Goddammit,' Alex exploded, his eyes darkening. 'This shit is going to follow me forever! I could win every fucking award in the world and they'll still be dragging up dirt from our private lives. Someone is always going to be out there looking more closely at that baby than they ought to. Someone is always going to be calling you a whore behind my back.' He grabbed Cassie by the shoulders and threw her heavily to the floor, then ran his fingers through his hair. 'This never would have happened if you hadn't left,' he said, and even as Cassie rolled away from him she could feel his shoes kicking at her sides and her back, his fists swinging at her shoulders and striking her across the side of the head.

When it stopped and Cassie opened her eyes, she was staring into the mesh of Connor's playpen. The baby was screaming the way every inch of her body was, a red, hollow sound. His face was turned toward Cassie's; toward his father, who was bent over Cassie's side, crying.

When Alex touched her, Cassie pulled herself upright. Blood was running from her right ear and she realized she could not hear out of it. She lifted Connor from his playpen, soothing him, whispering to him the assurances she used to whisper to Alex. She stared at the form of her husband, drunk and keening on the floor, and she began to understand. That for the first time, Alex's anger had not simply been displaced and rerouted toward Cassie – it had been *caused* by her. That the rest of her life would simply be strung loosely between hard knots of fear. That her son would watch Alex hurt her over and over, and without any choice in the matter, might grow up to be just like his father.

That Alex, through no fault of his own, could not keep his promises.

She walked across the room and opened the door of the den, glancing at John, who stared a moment too long at the blood running down the side of her face. She turned Connor's face to her chest so that he would not have to see, but she looked once more at Alex, bent over by his own misery. And in the way the most ordinary things have of rearranging themselves into the unfamiliar, Alex no longer seemed to be suffering. He only seemed pathetic.

*   *   *

She never realized that he knew she was crying. In the past when it had happened, she waited until she assumed Alex was asleep, and then she'd let the tears slide down her cheeks in silence. She never made any noise, but Alex could hear it all the same.

He wanted to touch her, but every time he started to reach across the endless three inches between them he couldn't make himself do it. He was the one who had hurt her in the first place. And if she shrank away from him, because after all, there was always a first time, he thought he would break down.

'Cassie,' he whispered. Shadows crowded the bedroom, listening. 'Say you aren't going to go away again.'

She didn't answer.

Alex swallowed. 'I'll go to Dr Pooley's tomorrow morning. I'll postpone the film. God, you know I'd do anything.'

'I know.'

He turned his head toward her voice, clutching at the two syllables like a lifeline, unable to see Cassie except for the silver map of tears on her skin. 'I can't let you go,' he said, his voice breaking.

Cassie faced him, her eyes glowing like a ghost's. 'No,' she said calmly, 'you can't.'

She slipped her hand into his, linking them together. And only then did Alex let his own tears come again, just as quietly as Cassie's. He told himself that there was solace in knowing he hated himself even more than Cassie could. As penance, he counted his way off to sleep, imagining in flashing succession the ravaged faces of his father, his mother, his wife, and his son – all of the people he'd failed.

This time she did not hold herself back. Even though she knew Alex was awake beside her, she was crying. It was not just a matter of leaving, as Alex thought. It was a matter of freedom. She could leave Alex and never be free; look at what had happened when she went to South Dakota to have Connor. To truly make a break, she was going to have to make Alex suffer as much as she did. He couldn't let her go – he *wouldn't* – unless she did something to make him hate her. So she would have to do what she had scrupulously avoided doing for four years now – become one of the people who had hurt him.

She tried to convince herself that if she really did care about Alex, she'd force the break, since having her as a crutch for his rage was only worse for him in the long run. It wouldn't mean that she didn't need him anymore. And it certainly wouldn't mean she didn't love him. Alex was right when he said they had been made for each other. It just wasn't in a healthy, wholesome way.

She remembered Alex standing on the porch at Pine Ridge, telling her she was a part of him. She remembered him holding his hands over her own as they fished without poles in a frigid Colorado stream. She remembered sitting beside him, watching the pair of lions in the Serengeti. She remembered his taste and his touch and the heaviness of his skin against hers.

She did not understand how she had ever reached this point, where she loved Alex so very much that, literally, it was killing her.

Cassie watched the night take on different and somber shades of black as she ran her options through her mind. She closed her eyes, and to her surprise, saw not Alex but Will, tied to a sacred pole during the Sun Dance. She felt the heat rising from the plain, heard the running of the drums and the eagle-bone whistles. She pictured the moment Will tore himself loose, the rawhide ripping through his skin. It had driven him to his knees, but it had been the only way to break free.

The damage was permanent; there would always be scars. But even the angriest marks faded over time, until it was difficult to see them written on the skin at all, and the only thing that remained was your memory of how painful it had been.

Cassie slipped her hand into Alex's, trying to memorize the temperature of his skin, the smell and the very sense of him lying beside her in the night. These were the things she would let herself keep. She rubbed her thumb over the soft lines of Alex's palm, stroking into his grasp an apology for what she had yet to do, and the gentle broken edges of a goodbye.

Chapter Twenty-Seven

For one awful moment, Cassie looked at the pinched, expectant faces spread before her and she thought, *They won't believe me.* She figured they would just laugh out loud. *Alex Rivers?* they'd say. *You've got to be kidding.* And then they'd snap up their notebooks and rewind their video cameras and leave her standing ashamed and alone.

Swallowing her terror and her pride, she shifted on the metal folding chair the hotel concierge had placed in preparation for the press conference. She smoothed down the pleats of her dark blue skirt. *Look like a schoolgirl*, she had been advised. *Nothing savvy, nothing sexy.* As if she had invited the attention, the abuse.

Beside her on an identical chair, Ophelia was holding the baby. Connor had the hiccups, small ragged sounds that Cassie couldn't help thinking sounded like sobs. She knew that at almost two months of age, he could not understand and he would not remember. Just as she knew that every time he reached for her, she would do a double take, seeing his father's image in his silver eyes.

Clearing her throat, she stood up. Almost immediately the crowd of reporters quieted, snapping to attention like a huddle of storybook soldiers. 'Good morning,' Cassie said, leaning toward the microphone, touching it lightly with her hand.

It let out a shattering scream. Cassie stepped back, startled. 'Excuse me,' she said, a little more softly. 'Thank you for coming.'

She thought how absurd she sounded, as if she'd gathered a

group of friends for a tea party. She considered how much easier
that would have been, rather than this unconditional surrender
to a pride of hungry lions. She had no more illusions; Alex had
taken care of that two nights ago. These people were not her
friends, never had been. They knew of her only through Alex;
they had agreed to come only because they thought she'd say
something about him. Cassie herself was incidental. If the reporters
mentioned her at all after taking away her story, she would be
painted as some kind of pitiable freak, or a moron for being
unable to stand up for herself all these years.

Cassie unfolded the tiny piece of paper she'd read over a
hundred times since breakfast that morning, her prepared press
statement. Ophelia had coached her about making eye contact,
about modulating her voice to a low, even pitch – all tricks of
actors to appear more sympathetic to an audience. But as her
fingers froze at the edges of the frayed sheet, shaking it visibly,
she could not remember at all any of the things she had practiced. Instead she began to read, reciting like a second-grade
schoolchild who was too busy sounding out the unfamiliar words
to give the performance any meaning.

'My name is Cassandra Barrett. Most of you know me as Alex
Rivers's wife. We were married on October 30, 1989, and our
marriage has been the subject of media attention on several occa-
sions, most recently the birth of our son. Yesterday, however, I
filed for divorce from Alex Rivers on the grounds of extreme
cruelty.'

The statement, coming less than a month after the united show
of support Alex and Cassie had given at LAX when they arrived
with Connor, created a current of whispers that volleyed over the
heads of the reporters and wrapped themselves around Cassie's
neck, choking. She gripped her fingers on the edge of the podium,
stumbling over the last sentences on the page. 'After this press
conference, any inquiries can be directed to my lawyer, Carla
Bonanno, or to Mr Rivers himself.' She took a deep breath. 'In

the interests of promoting the truth, though, I'm willing to answer some of your questions now.'

Hands shot up in front of Cassie, blocking her view of the one-eyed cameras. Voices tangled over each other. 'Ms Barrett,' one reporter shouted, 'are you still living with Alex Rivers?'

'No,' Cassie said.

'Has he agreed to the divorce?'

Cassie glanced at her lawyer, sitting off to the left. 'The papers will be served today. I don't expect him to contest it.'

Another reporter pushed himself to the front of the throng, waving a microphone beneath the podium. 'Extreme cruelty isn't common grounds for divorce, Ms Barrett. Are you trumping up your charges to expedite the divorce, so you can get your hands on his money?'

Cassie's eyes widened at the snide tone of the man's voice, at the absolute gall that would let him ask something so personal. For God's sake, this was her *marriage*. This was her *husband*. 'I have no desire to take anything from Alex.' *Except myself*, she thought. 'And I haven't exaggerated the charges.' She lowered her eyes, realizing that she had come to the point of no return. She carefully cleared her face of emotion and lifted her head again, staring at everything and nothing all at once. 'I've been physically abused by Alex Rivers for the past three years.'

I'm sorry, I'm sorry, I'm sorry. The litany ran through her mind, and Cassie wasn't sure if she was crying out to God or to Alex or to herself. She felt her heart pounding so fiercely it seemed to be moving the light fabric of her blouse.

'Can you prove it?'

The question came from a woman, and it was softer than most of the others had been, which was maybe why Cassie did what she decided, in a split second, to do. Keeping her eyes trained on the door at the back of the conference room, she slowly opened the top three buttons of her blouse and pulled aside the collar and her bra strap to reveal an ugly, mottled purple welt.

She untucked the blouse from the waistband of the skirt and lifted it to her midriff, turning slightly so that the swollen, black-and-blue ribs were visible.

The conference room exploded in a riot of white flashes and cacophonous sound. Cassie stood very still, willing herself not to tremble, wishing she were anywhere else but there.

When she woke up the morning after Alex had hit her, his side of the bed was cool and the covers had been pulled smooth. For a second Cassie stared at them, at the neatly aligned pillows. Maybe it had never happened. Maybe Alex had never been there.

She showered, gingerly letting the hot water soothe the sorest places, and then she went in to check on Connor. The night nurse turned him over to Cassie so that she could feed him. Sitting in the large rocking chair, Cassie stared out the window at what promised to be a beautiful California day.

'We're going away again,' she whispered to Connor. Then she stood up and carried him over to his changing table, ripping loose the tape of the disposable diaper and arranging a fresh one under his bottom. She stared at his body – the long, wiry legs; the bubble belly; the pockets of baby fat on his arms that almost looked like a grown man's muscles.

When the nurse returned, Cassie smiled at her. 'I wonder if you could do me a favor,' she asked, instructing her to pack up a full diaper bag with several changes of clothing and sleepwear for Connor. And then, leaving Connor in his bassinet, she made her way downstairs.

She didn't stop in the dining room for coffee; she didn't bother to check the library or study for any signs of Alex. The truth was, it didn't matter. She had made her decision last night.

The plan she'd settled on involved his public image. After all, it was what had prompted the fight last night. And, Cassie had to admit, it was as much a part of his life as she was. Once the golden boy didn't seem so golden anymore, and once he'd ascertained who had thrown the mud in the first place, she would be free. Either Alex would have to admit to her accusations and make himself into a figure of public sympathy by going for help, or he'd have to fight back and discredit her story, slandering her. It didn't really matter which course events took. Either way, the outcome was going to ruin Alex; either way, the outcome was going to kill her.

Because she was forcing Alex to stop loving her, but she couldn't make herself stop loving him.

She opened the front door, walking barefoot down the marble stairs and the winding path that led to the pool and the out-buildings. One day she would show Connor pictures of this castle, and tell him how close he'd come to growing up as Hollywood's crown prince. She walked to the second low white building, the laboratory Alex had built for her after they were married.

It was dark and musty; she had been in here for a few minutes at a time in the weeks she'd been back, but there was too much for Connor to get into and she wouldn't leave him alone during the day at the house. Flicking on the lights, she saw the cavernous space flood with the colors of the past: yellowed bones and shining metallic tables, silver instruments and rich red earth.

She found herself wondering what the landscapes looked like where these bones had been procured. And what the people who were supported by these skeletons did in the course of a day. She realized that for someone to whom cultural anthropology had been anathema, her questions were odd and unfamiliar. In a way, it seemed as though anthropology for Cassie had been an explor-ation in a small, fascinating room, and she had just pulled back a curtain on what she had believed to be a closet, only to find a new room, twice the size of the first.

She would always have her work once she left Alex – it had been there before him and it was as much a part of her as Connor – but her research would never be quite the same. She had seen the possibilities, and after Pine Ridge, she did not think she could continue to look at bare bones in a vacuum. If she had learned nothing else from the Lakota, Cassie now knew that although a person was made of muscle and bone and tissue, she was equally formed by the patterns of her life and the choices she made and the memories she passed on to her children.

Before Cassie had left for Pine Ridge, she had been studying a skull from Peru, sent by a colleague, in which a clear disk of bone had been removed from the vault. The scientist who'd sent it to her wanted her opinion as to the nature of the damage. Was it a man-made trephine hole – bored out during an operation for obtaining an amulet, or for alleviating headaches – or was it due to something natural? Cassie sat down at the examination table, scanning her notes for other explanations. *Made by a pick during excavation. The continual pressure of a sharp object in the grave. Erosion. Congenital deficiency. Syphilitic reaction.*

Cradling her own head in her hands, she wondered what some scientist would think about her skeleton if it was unearthed millions of years from now. Would he run his instruments over her ribs, cracked and scarred and mutilated? Would he attribute the bone damage to careless gravediggers? To erosion? To her husband?

Cassie wrapped the skull in cotton and set it back in its packing crate. She layered it in sawdust and shredded newspaper, touching it with the most exquisite care, as if it still could feel the pain of the damage done. Without printing a formal letter, she folded her observation list. She was not the best person to analyze this; not anymore. So she scribbled a note on the outside about not having the time to study the specimen more, apologizing for the months she'd kept the scientist waiting. Then she stuck the letter in with the skull and closed the crate with a staple gun.

Cassie carried the skull back to the house to leave with the outgoing mail, feeling its weight increase with each heavy step. She wondered why it had taken her this long to see that a skeleton could tell you nothing, but a survivor could show you her life.

*   *   *

'What will you do about your position at UCLA?'

'Will you stay in LA?'

'Do you have any plans from here?'

Cassie blinked at the stream of questions, thinking that even if she had a clear picture of where she was headed, the last thing she would do was leave a well-marked trail for the press to follow.

'I've been on maternity leave from teaching,' she said slowly. 'As for whether or not I'll return to UCLA when that's over, it's a decision I'll have to make down the road.'

A man in an olive trench coat pushed back the hat on his head. 'Will you stay at one of your other residences?'

Cassie shook her head. Even if she had wanted the half of Alex's wealth and property that California law entitled her to, she wouldn't stay anywhere she had been with him. At the ranch, at the apartment, God, probably even in Tanzania, the furnishings and surroundings were marked with the image of the two of them together. She hesitated, then bit her lower lip. 'I have several options,' she lied.

She had taken Connor to Ophelia's. 'Jesus,' Ophelia said when she opened the door. 'What the hell happened to you?'

Cassie hadn't bothered to brush out her hair or put on her makeup. She had grabbed the first clothes she could find that morning, and she looked down at her body to see a purple polo shirt and green-and-white-striped cotton shorts. 'Ophelia,' she said simply, 'I need your help.'

The entire time she was explaining to Ophelia the hidden parts of the last three years with Alex, the half hour she spent showing her the bruises that swelled from the underwire of her bra, Cassie did not cry. With her left foot, she rocked Connor in his infant seat, and she answered Ophelia's questions. In the end, Ophelia had cried for her, and had called up the friend of a friend who had connections to an up-and-coming hotshot divorce attorney. When Cassie tried to refuse, Ophelia had looked at her pointedly.

'You may not want a cent from him,' she said, 'but you've got something Alex wants desperately. His son.'

Ophelia had been the one to go to the five banks where Cassie and Alex had joint accounts, and using Cassie's ATM cards, she systematically withdrew a generous sum of money from each. She bought diapers and baby bottles for Connor, since Cassie had left without enough of these.

While Ophelia was gone, Cassie rocked Connor to sleep and set him on the bed that had been hers four years earlier. Then she went into the living room and pulled down the shades, as if people might already be looking in. She reached for the telephone and dialed the number of the pay phone at the feed and grain in Pine Ridge; the place managed by Horace; the place from which she had called Alex a month and a half before.

'Cassie!' Horace said, and in the background she could hear the shuffles and grunts of elderly Lakota men bent over the barrels of rolled oats. She heard the cries of children running to the counter, asking for the free spiced gumdrops. '*Toníktuka hwo?* How are you doing?'

For the first time since she'd taken a taxi from Alex's house, Cassie let her courage waver. 'I've been better,' she admitted in a small voice.

'Horace,' she said. 'I need a favor.'

Just past four in the afternoon, when Ophelia was out at the park with Connor, the telephone rang. Cassie picked it up with a shaking hand. 'Hello?' she said, a little more loudly than she had intended, wondering what she would do if Alex's voice responded. But then she heard Will, tinny and hesitant over a bad connection, praying her name. She bent over, relief having kicked all the air from her lungs.

'Cassie?' Will repeated.

'I'm here,' she said. She paused, trying to string together her words.

'What did he do?' Will said into the silence. 'I'll kill him.'

'No,' Cassie said calmly. 'You won't.'

In Pine Ridge, with a teenage kid stacking oats to his left, Will banged his fist against the wall. He knew, without being told, that Alex had gone after her again. He understood that the phone number Horace had tracked him down to give him was not Cassie's. He was powerless, a thousand miles away, and he waited to see what, exactly, she wanted from him. He did not let himself hope, and he would not let himself offer, but he knew that if she asked he would come for her and hide her forever.

'I'm getting a divorce,' Cassie said. 'I'm going to hold a press conference.'

Will leaned his forehead against the sharp corner of the pay phone. The Hollywood media would rip her apart on their way to destroying Alex. 'Forget about it,' he heard himself say. 'Come with me to Tacoma.'

'I can't keep running away. And I don't want you to rescue me.' Cassie took a deep breath. 'I think it's high time I rescued myself.'

But even as she said the words, her shoulders began to quiver and her body slid deeper into the cushions of the sofa, as if she could no longer muster the support to keep herself upright.

'Cassie, honey,' Will said gently, 'why did you call me?'

She was shivering so violently she did not think she'd be able to speak. 'Because I'm scared,' she whispered. 'I am so damn scared.'

Will thought about telling her she wasn't alone; about hopping on a plane to LA and driving to wherever she was and kissing her until her body stopped trembling with fear and flowed into his. He wondered how he could be such a fool that he'd trade his heart to a woman who would probably love someone else for the rest of her life.

Instead he forced his voice to be steady and clear. 'Cassie,' he said, 'you got a mirror around there?'

Cassie smiled ruefully. 'Ophelia's got three in the hall alone,' she said.

'Well, get up and stand in front of one.'

Cassie made a face. 'This is stupid,' she said. 'I need more than some dumb dramatic exercise.' But she stood up and walked to the mirror, looking at her swollen eyelids, her bruised jaw.

'Well?'

'I look awful,' Cassie said, rubbing her eyes and her nose. 'What am I supposed to be seeing?'

'The bravest person I've ever met,' Will said.

Cassie pulled the receiver closer to her ear, sinking into his statement like a cat in the sun. She was reminded of how, when she had first married Alex, he would call her at her office and, like teenagers, they'd whisper for hours behind the closed door about their future, their passion, their uncanny luck in finding each other.

Cassie stared at her face in the mirror. 'I've never been to Tacoma,' she said, and with her best attempt at a smile, she tucked Will's words inside her and took from them his strength.

'When did the beatings start?'

'Did you know about this before you got married?'

Cassie let the questions puddle at her feet. She glanced behind her, at Ophelia and Connor, for support.

'Are you in love with him?'

She didn't have to answer; she knew that. But she wanted to. If she was going to make the world see Alex as some kind of monster, it was also up to her to make the world see him as the wonderful, warm, caring man who had made her feel complete.

The best approach, she rationalized, would be to make a joke of the question, as if it had been ridiculous in the first place. 'You can ask that of nearly any woman in this country,' Cassie said lightly. But her voice broke gently over the words. 'Who *isn't* in love with him?'

She looked up, searching the rows of reporters as if she was seeking someone out in particular, and then she saw the man in the back corner. She hadn't noticed him before, but then again she hadn't been looking. He was wearing a wool peacoat with the collar pulled up, something far too warm for the day. His face was buried close to his chest, and his eyes were hidden by aviator sunglasses.

Alex looked directly at Cassie and tugged off his sunglasses. He stuffed them into the breast pocket of the coat. Cassie could not tear her gaze from him. He was not angry. Not the slightest bit. It was as if he understood. She caught her breath, checking again to see what she had missed, what he was trying to tell her.

'One more question,' she whispered, her eyes locked to the spot where Alex stood. *Why this way? Why now? Why us?*

She feebly pointed to a man in the front row of the conference room. 'If you could say anything to him now,' the reporter asked, 'without any fear of retaliation on his part, what would you tell him?'

She thought she saw tears glittering in Alex's eyes, and his hand came up from his side as if he was going to reach out to her. *Don't*, Cassie pleaded silently. *If you do, I might follow.* And just like that, his arm fell loose again, his fingers stroking the rough wool of the coat. 'I'd say what he always said to me,' Cassie whispered to him. 'I never meant to hurt you.'

She closed her eyes to compose herself before she dismissed the media crowd that had gathered at her request. When she opened them again, she was still staring at the spot where seconds ago Alex had been standing, but he was no longer there. She shook her head as if to clear it, and wondered if he had really ever been there at all.

Without another word, she turned away from the podium, carefully tucking the back of her blouse back into her skirt. The reporters continued to take pictures and videos of her leaving the hotel conference room: picking up her baby, slinging the diaper bag over her shoulder, moving forward woodenly.

She made her way through the red velvet lobby with people already beginning to stare. Pushing through the revolving door, she stepped onto the sidewalk, drinking the air with huge, heaving gulps.

I did it, I did it, I did it. The heels of Cassie's shoes tapped this refrain on the concrete as she walked to the end of the block. She moved quickly, as if she were late for an important appointment. Downtown LA was busy at lunchtime. Standing at the corner, Cassie clutched Connor to her chest as they were dodged by businessmen and bicycle messengers and beautiful women carrying shopping bags.

There was nothing specific, really, that made her look up. No noise, no bright light, no inspiration. But at that moment, slicing through the heat and the smog overhead, was a circling eagle. She waited for someone else to point at the sky, to notice, but people only shoved and jostled past, wrapped up in their own lives.

She turned Connor's face, so that he could see it too.

Cassie shielded her eyes from the sun, watching the bird fly east. Long after the eagle had disappeared, she stared at the unbounded sky; and even when the flow of human traffic increased and funneled around her, she did not lose her footing.

Book Club Discussion Questions
for *Picture Perfect*

1)   Cassandra Barrett is a highly educated, successful and independent woman when she meets and falls in love with Alex Rivers. What aspect of her character or her past allows a woman of her stature to endure the abuse she suffers repeatedly at his hands?

2)   Hands figure significantly in *Picture Perfect*. Discuss the symbolism connected to them in this novel.

3)   Why does Connor continue to appear to Cassie in her dreams? What does he represent?

4)   Discuss the symbolic nature of birds in *Picture Perfect*.

5)   What is the significance of Cassie's career in anthropology, particularly physical anthropology?

6)   What attitudes toward the study of anthropology – as well as her own life – does Cassie form after her time spent at Pine Ridge?

7)   What does Will learn about himself and about his life through his friendship with Cassie?

8) When Cassie prepares to reconcile with Alex after the birth of their son, Will says to her, 'You know what he's done to you before, you know he's going to do it again . . . I couldn't escape the past, no matter how hard I tried. Neither can Alex, and neither can you.' (p.395) Do you agree with this statement, that who we are and who we will become are determined by our pasts? Do you think it is possible to change?

9) Do you agree with Cassie that the only way for Alex to let go of her is to let the world know the truth about him?

10) What are your feelings toward Alex at the end of the book? Cassie? Will?

Here's what I know about me as a writer: I would write no matter what – even if there was no one out there to read what I'd written.

But the fact that you are there? That's amazing.

I love to hear from you. If you want to let me know what you thought about the questions I raise in this novel, or find out more about what I'm doing next, here are some easy ways to stay in touch:

- Follow me on twitter @jodipicoult
- Like my Facebook page
  www.facebook.com/JodiPicoultUK
- Visit my website www.jodipicoult.co.uk, and sign up to my newsletter.

Thank you for reading!

The best books live on in your head long after they are finished. As you read, you are turning the pages faster and faster to find out what happens next, only to feel bereft when you reach the end.

If that is how you feel now, you might like to join us at www.hodder.co.uk, or follow us on Twitter @hodderbooks, and be part of our community of people who love the very best of books and reading.

Whether you want to find out more about this book, or a particular author, watch trailers and interviews, have the chance to win early limited editions, or simply browse our expert readers' selection of the very best books, we think you'll find what you're looking for.

And if you don't, that's the place to tell us what's missing.

We love what we do, and we'd love you to be part of it.

www.hodder.co.uk

@hodderbooks

HodderBooks

HodderBooks